DEMON'S ANGEL

COPYRIGHT

Cast of Characters

Colorado Chapter

Officers
Demon – President
Buzzard – Secretary/Treasurer - Old Lady Sindy
Thunder – Sergeant-At-Arms
Mace – Enforcer
Sparky – Road Captain

Patched Members
Hellfire - Old Lady – Moira - Children – Demon, Kennedy, Samuel
Bomber - Old Lady – Jeannie
Cad
Ink
Lizard
Pyro
Paladin - Old Lady Jayden
Rusty

Prospects
Dan
Runt
Wills
Smithy – Failed Prospect

Sweet Butts
Bella
Breezy
Sheila
Titsy
Tulia

Deceased Members
Blackie – Previous President
Furnace – Previous VP
Ingot – Previous Enforcer
Taser

Arizona Chapter

Officers
Drummer – President - Old Lady – Sam - Children – Eli
Wraith – Vice President - Old Lady – Sophie - Children – Olivia
Heart – Secretary - Old Lady – Marcia - Children – Amy, Jacob, Isabel
Dollar – Treasurer
Peg – Sergeant-At-Arms - Old Lady – Darcy - Children – Noah
Blade – Enforcer - Old Lady – Tash
Joker – Road Captain
Mouse – Computer Expert - Old Lady – Marianna

Patched Members
Bullet - Old Lady – Carmen
Hyde
Jekell
Lady
Marvel
Roadrunner
Rock - Old Lady – Becca
Slick - Old Lady – Ella - Children Faith
Shooter
Viper - Old Lady – Sandy

Prospects
Matt
Fergus
Truck

Deceased Members

Adam

Buster

Tongue

SATAN'S DEVILS MC

CHAPTER ONE

Demon

As soon as we're through the door of the tattoo parlour and out in the fresh air, Lizard takes out a cigarette and lights it, taking the opportunity to top off his nicotine levels before we get back on our rides. Moving upwind, I lean back against the brickwork, content to wait patiently for him.

He inhales, then breathes out smoke. "What did you think?"

Taking a moment to give his question some serious consideration, I glance around me. Devil's Ink was one of the first businesses to be opened back in the eighties when the motorcycle club became established in Pueblo, even pre-dating the merger with the Satan's Devils. The building itself has seen better days, and the location, well, life has moved on, leaving the shop behind, with the result that it's no longer getting the foot traffic it once attracted. Lizard, as manager and chief ink-slinger, is on the right track with his proposal to move into a more affluent part of town.

"Tattoos are more popular than ever." He fills the silence, mistakenly believing I'm not seeing things in the same way as him. "It's no longer just bikers and military types. People from all walks of life, a lot of women as well. We need somewhere modern, with more room. Extend our piercing services, too."

His last suggestion, offered with a wink, makes me grin. Yeah, clit and nipple piercings are definitely on the up. Cock piercings, too. Personally, I say fuck that shit. I can satisfy a woman enough without putting my dick out of commission for a few months and taking the risk of having to spend the rest of my life pissing sitting down. But there are a few of the brothers that swear by them.

"If we move, Liz," I speak at last, "I'd definitely like to look at expansion. Get another artist or two. A woman to handle some of the more personal shit."

"You spoil all my fun." But he's said it only because it was expected. Lizard's a good man. His throwaway lines hide a seriousness underneath. Previously a Marine, he earned his handle for his ability to stay so still he fades into the background, then to move and pounce startlingly fast. He gave up objecting to how we often shorten his name to the ill-fitting female form years ago. Whatever his moniker, Liz lives and breathes the club, always putting his brothers' interests way ahead of his own.

It doesn't take long to make up my mind. "Bring it to the table. I'll back you."

His quick up-and-down of his head shows my response hasn't surprised him; it would be hard to find an objection. "Already spoken to Buzzard. He's looking at the financial implications."

I'm not unhappy that Lizard has approached the treasurer before speaking to me. If we couldn't afford the move, it would be a non-starter. "You looked at the projections?"

"Yeah, I reckon we could increase our takings enough to pay for a couple of extra hands. Buzz agrees." For years now, it's just been Liz, another tattooist and a part-time receptionist.

"Should be a formality, then." I watch as Liz makes sure he's locked the door. "You gonna show me this new place now?" My question needs no reply. It's the reason I've come along after all.

Getting on our bikes, we ride the short distance to the new mall in town. It's a mix of large businesses with some artisan shops as well. Lizard is proposing we lease one on the end. It's located close to a hair and makeup salon. Not too near to put more manly types off, but with the right displays in the window, we could attract the feminine trade as well. Liz is already adept at inking unicorns and fairies.

The club's tattooist opens the door with the keys the real estate agent had given him. There's not much to see. The shop's devoid of anything inside, bare walls still smelling of paint, plain concrete on the floor. It's a good size and the rent isn't extortionate; priced to attract new business, not to put it off. Liz starts pointing out where the drywall would go to give privacy for the cubicles, still leaving a good-sized reception area as well. It will be his baby, and I let him rattle on as, excitedly, along with lots of gesticulations, he brings his vision to life already knowing he'll have my vote if Buzzard is indeed on board with the costings.

When he runs out of steam, I slap him on the back. "Good work finding this, Brother," I tell him at last, when he's run out of things to offer to persuade me. "Bring it up in church. We can do the internals ourselves."

Lizard beaming, pleased that my endorsement is one step closer to bringing his project to fruition, we at last exit what, hopefully, will be our new premises, stepping outside into the sunlight. While I glance around, noting that the large parking lot would be good for customers, he bounces the shop keys in his hands.

"Best get these back to the agent."

I nod, distracted. My attention has been caught by a blonde head walking past pushing a stroller. *Is that...?* My eyes crease. *I'm sure it is.*

"Liz, I'll catch up with you later," I toss quickly over my shoulder.

Whether it's who I think or not, I know I'm going to have to make sure. *I didn't know she had a baby. Maybe looking after it for someone else? Fuck. How many years since I last checked up on her?* I wouldn't know if she'd gotten married or not. *If it's her, what's she doing back in Pueblo? And, why didn't I know she was here?*

As Lizard nods and goes off in the other direction, I quicken my step, heading the way the woman had gone. It certainly looks like Violet Palmer, but I need to get closer to make sure. I'm assailed by guilt, remembering the promise I'd made to her brother to look out for her. I'd followed her progress through college from afar, getting information from mutual friends. When she graduated and moved out of state, appearing to be settled, she'd gone out of my mind. It dawns on me I probably haven't spared her a thought for what must be all of three years, if not more.

The blonde-haired woman pauses to look into a shop window. My steps come closer together in an effort to catch up. In profile, she even more resembles the sister of my dead friend. So intent on a display she's examining, she jumps when my shadow falls over her.

"Violet? Is that you?" I say quickly. A large tattooed biker would likely scare a young mother if she's not who I think she is. If I've made a mistake, I'll back off fast.

She swings around. One glance into those vivid blue eyes and I know I have the right woman. I'm perplexed when she looks scared, those brilliant orbs looking right and left as if seeking an escape route. Her reaction is puzzling, I'd have expected a welcome. But then, it has been a few years. *What do I know of her nowadays?* I'm wearing my cut and she might not want to be seen with a biker.

My promise to her brother, however much overlooked, means I don't want to leave without some kind of conversation, at least a belated check-in to make sure she's okay.

"Violet." I repeat her name. "I didn't realise you were back in Pueblo. Why the fuck didn't you let me know you were here?"

A purse of her lips, a little sigh of capitulation as she sees she's not going to be able to evade this confrontation, then words finally leave her mouth. "Dave," she acknowledges, for some reason more than a little reluctantly. "I've been back a year and a half." Her hands gesture meaninglessly. "I didn't know I had to check in with you. Nathan was the only connection we ever had between us."

My fingers pinch the bridge of my nose. For some reason, her statement and the tone in which it's delivered, upsets me, leaving me with the feeling I've let her down.

"It's on me, Vi, I should have made more of an effort to stay in contact. I promised Nathan I'd watch out for you."

She startles, and a frown shapes her features. "Whether you pledged that or not was between you and him, and in the end, you didn't." Pain covers her face for a second, then with another little shake, she shrugs whatever is troubling her off. "There was no need. I've done fine without you, David."

I can't read her. It's as if I've annoyed her. *As if I've failed her.* The thought doesn't sit well with me.

Her hands take the stroller again, and she begins to wheel away what a brief glimpse showed me is a sleeping baby. I don't want to let her go, not until I'm satisfied that all's well in her world, just as I'd have wanted Nathan to do for my own sister.

"Hey, wait up." Again I follow her, and wrap my fingers around the handle of the stroller, halting her progress. Pointing down to the quiet bundle, I pry for information. "You're married?"

"No." She doesn't offer a lie, but the truth without explanation, while looking a combination of cross and apprehensive as her eyes scan our surroundings. Mine do likewise. If there's a security guard or cop in the vicinity, a burly biker in his cut might be questioned as to why he's upsetting a young mother.

Having expected an exuberant welcome, this reaction is not what I predicted from Violet. While I knew what she was doing for the first few years, I hadn't actually seen her in person since the funeral. When I'd approached, I'd anticipated her delight at seeing me again, that her behaviour would have resembled what it would have been all those years ago. Back then, she'd been an annoying kid sister trying to tag along with her older brother and his friend. I'd been the same age as Nathan, Violet ten years younger; the gap large enough to be both frustrating and amusing. The kid had had a crush on me from the time she'd turned a teen, her efforts to flirt at that time irritating. Now it seems such attraction has faded in the intervening years. That should have been comforting, but seeing her today, grown into a beautiful woman, for some reason her lack of interest annoys me.

Wanting to continue the exchange, or at least to leave on better footing, I peer down at the blanket covering the bundle in the stroller. "Boy or girl?"

She replies hesitantly, as though not even wanting to give me that much information. "Boy."

Age? Name? Father? A multitude of questions sit on the tip of my tongue but remain unasked. To let them spill would be more like an interrogation. But I can't let her walk away, not like this. Now I've seen her, it won't be possible to forget her so easily. Not now I've got a sense of unease warning me something isn't right. Quickly I scan my surroundings. There's a coffee shop newly-opened across the way. I point to it. "You got time for a quick coffee, Violet? Or have you got somewhere you need to be?"

She's reluctant, but she could never lie to me or Nathan. Oh, she'd tried, but her tells always gave her away. Her cheeks would redden and her eyes would refuse to meet ours. "Mom said to tell you, you had to take me with you." Yeah, right. The memory makes me smile. She'd tried that one more than once, both her brother and I knowing their mother had issued no such instruction. But often, her pout would sway us, and we'd more often than not let her tag along.

For a second her cheeks flush, then her shoulders slump in defeat, accepting that now I've made contact, she won't easily get rid of me. "Yeah, okay. Just a quick coffee. He'll be waking soon and will need feeding."

I've not been around babies, never seen any in my future, so am relieved the bundle in the stroller remains quiet as we enter the coffee shop and place our orders. I'm not surprised we both order the same. My taste for black with one sugar was honed when I was a teenager, and a copycat child developed a liking for the same. It's odd, but I find I'm pleased. At least in this, she hasn't changed over the years. My lips curve as I recall her grimace when she'd taken that first long-ago sip. But she'd obviously persevered, and now it seems to be habit.

We find a table with space for the stroller. The silence is awkward.

"He's good," I point out, for lack of anything else to say.

From my limited experience, I don't know if it's not unusual that she doesn't at least move the blanket to check he's okay, but then I suppose it's probably as true for babies as it is for dogs: if they're sleeping, you let them lie.

"He has a good set of lungs when he's hungry." Without one glance the baby's way, she picks up her coffee, blowing on it to cool it.

I've leapt to assumptions, I realise. "Is he yours?" I belatedly enquire.

Another unreadable expression, then, slightly fiercely, an odd response. "All mine."

"What's his name?"

She takes so long to answer, I start to think she might have forgotten, or be thinking up a lie. But if that's so, for the life of me I couldn't think of a reason. Eventually, just before I have to prompt her, she quietly replies, "Theo. He's five months, to save you the bother of asking."

I'm curious. There's so much she's not telling me. I take a few swallows to re-caffeinate myself. "The father?"

"Not in the picture." This response comes quickly.

Too quickly? I vacillate between an unexpected elation that she has no man tagging after her, or not the one that's fathered her child at least, and rage that someone impregnated her and presumably left her. A hundred things come into my mind that I want to say.

I settle for a casual, "Want me to kill him?"

A laugh's startled out of her. Another one of those vacant expressions follows her momentary mirth. Then she gives my question the weight it deserves. Absolutely zero. In her world, the citizen world, killing is not the answer. In mine, it often is the quickest way to get a problem under control.

I turn to a safer subject. "You were living in New York, last I heard. Thought you were settled there?"

She sighs. "Dave, I know Nathan asked you to look out for me, but that was when I was still a little girl. He's been gone nine years now."

Her reminder makes me frown. I'm only too well aware of the time that the calendar says has passed, though often it seems just like yesterday. My childhood friend, best friend since kindergarten, had followed his dreams. While I'd gone into the motorcycle club, to eventually rise through the ranks to become president, Nathan had become a Marine. He'd been destined for good things, was going to be in the service for life. It had been all he'd ever wanted. He'd lasted eight years until he'd been taken out by a sniper over in Afghanistan. He'd been twenty-six when he died. His sudden and unexpected death shocks me to this day. His life cut so short, mine left with a fucking giant hole in it. A loss to me, his family and his country, while I, an outlaw biker, still breathed. The universe must have a warped sense of humour.

"I promised Nathan, and I let him down." My lips thin. "I'm sorry, Vi. I should have made more of an effort to stay in contact."

A glance at my face shows there's no point in her again denying it. Instead, she focuses on offering absolution.

"Dave, I'm a grown woman. My life has nothing to do with you." She sips her coffee again. "After Nathan died, I moved on. As you said, I ended up in New York. Okay, so yeah, I was settled and happy. Got my degree and the dream job. Shared an apartment with a girl friend. Then, my roommate found a man and moved out. It became a bit of a struggle, rents being what they are, but I was managing. Meant I couldn't save, though." Her hand smooths back her hair which has dropped over her face. "So when the axe fell and the company had to cut jobs, last in, first out, you know how it goes. Well, I hadn't any funds behind me, couldn't afford to stay in New York, so I came back here."

"You working in Pueblo?"

Her eyes close briefly. "Couldn't find much, took shifts as a barista while I was searching for something where I could use my skills. Then..." Her nod at the stroller tells me all I want to know. "Well, he wasn't in the cards when I first came back."

I do the math. Nine months pregnant, five months born. Fifteen months? She's been here for that long and I hadn't known it?

Sending up a belated apology to Nathan for having neglected her, I continue my inquisition. "You living with your folks?"

A blank look, then a nod, a half-smile. I raise and dip my head in return. At least she's not on her own. Whatever the situation, her parents are decent enough and will look after her. *See, Nathan? I've checked in. She's fine. I won't leave it so long next time. But she's doing okay.*

Both our coffee cups are empty. There's a twitch from under the blanket in the stroller. Violet notices. "I've got to go."

She wastes no time standing. I cover her hand with mine as she goes to manoeuvre the stroller.

"Here, Vi. Take my number. If you need anything, let me know."

Looking more like she wants to refuse, but fast realising it's easier to give in, she takes out her phone, which I notice is a cheap basic model. As I rattle off the digits, she taps them in. There's no offer to give me hers in return, which, after the way this meeting has gone, doesn't surprise nor bother me. I'll get our computer guy, Cad, onto finding out all there is to know about her. Any secrets she's buried, he'll ferret them out.

I stay seated at the table as she disappears into the street. I hadn't offered to escort her to her car, sensing she'd already found my presence too intrusive.

Instead, I take a moment to gather my thoughts.

I'd felt elation when I realised it was her, then sorrow at a reminder I'd been remiss in my duties. Pleasure that I had a chance to belatedly fulfil the promise I'd made to her brother, followed by disappointment when my pleasure hadn't been reciprocated, then puzzlement at her attitude toward her baby and her reticence in providing any information. As my eyes watch her until she disappears from sight, I realise that young Violet has evolved into both a beautiful woman and a mystery to be solved.

CHAPTER TWO

Demon

As prez, I, of course, head for my seat at the head of the table. While doing so, I glance around at all the filled seats, my eyes settling for a moment at the occupant of the chair at the opposite end to myself. He's grinning, looking completely relaxed as he jokes with Rusty. The packet of cigarettes which would normally have been close to hand are nowhere in sight. Hellfire, the man who raised me, and the man who'd sat in the president's seat until only recently, has made many changes in his life. Not least, stepping down from being president of the club.

The changes have been good for both him and my mother.

At first, I'd had doubts he'd be able to make a clean break. But after a couple of months in the top seat, I'm convinced there's no way he'd say he made a mistake. In some ways I'm jealous he's been able to walk away without looking back; only a madman would want to head up this particular asylum.

He catches me staring, raises his chin, and his mouth quirks. Yeah, Hellfire is happy being an ordinary member with no special responsibilities. Unlike myself. I carry everyone's weight on my shoulders. I jerk my head back. *My shoulders are broad, old man. I can take it.* He grins and nods. *Sure you can, son. I have faith in you.*

As I allow the men around me to settle, my gaze stays fixed, watching the man who for thirty-five years I'd thought was my father. I'm still coming to terms with the fact he's my brother instead. My father—his, too—was a rapist.

If it wasn't that Hellfire was such a good man, I would be more disturbed about the bad blood running through my veins. But how could I let it worry me when all my life I've admired the man I still call father? That he'd killed my sperm donor long ago raises nothing other than satisfaction. One less thing I'd have had to deal with myself. Black Plate, Blackie, founder of the club, had met his demise the very night of my conception. A club vote, a patching in, and the new member had dispatched him to meet Satan. He'd rained hellfire down on the rapist, hence picking up his handle. Details I'd discovered only three months back.

Thunder, sitting to my left and looking uncomfortable, catches my eye, an unspoken question in his. I shake my head and receive a quick grimace of disappointment. Since I moved a step up at the table, changing my role from VP to prez, Thunder's combining his sergeant-at-arms duties with those of being my second. He's not held back on letting me know he has no desire to change roles permanently. Problem is, I don't know who else I'd trust to be my VP. Time's coming when we'll need to vote on it, but to date, I haven't come up with anyone who I'd propose.

Since we'd had to dispatch the traitor, Taser, trust has been sorely challenged in the club. None of us had expected a member to turn on his brothers. It's hit us all hard, and the dust has yet to settle. All of us would have trusted Taser with our lives. Ingot, our previous enforcer who Taser had murdered, had paid for that conviction with his.

My reminiscence leads me to consider Skull, also at the opposite end of the table. While we were looking for the man who betrayed the club, circumstantial evidence had pointed to Runt, a prospect. He'd been questioned in the MC way. When all we'd gotten back were denials, the interrogation had become painful. For him, not us. We'd made an innocent man hurt. He'd left the club for a month while he sorted out shit in his head. To our surprise, he'd returned, wanting to be part of a band of brothers that took loyalty so seriously. We'd patched him in and, at his request, changed his handle. Runt came in as a prospect but Skull earned his place around this table. He seemed to appreciate the jokes that he had a hard head.

It had been a bad time, but we're out on the other side. It means, though, I'm short a man wearing the VP patch.

As though he can pluck my thoughts out of my head, Thunder gives me a sharp nod of reassurance. *No rush. Might not want it, but while you need me to step up, I have your back.*

As the brothers settle, it's time to get church underway. I bang the gavel, then point with it. "Buzzard?"

"Yeah." The treasurer kicks off with his usual run through of the health of our various businesses. All's looking good.

When he passes the ball to Paladin, I'm pleased to see the member who transferred from the Tucson chapter not much more than three months back handles himself well giving an update on our fledgling security business.

"Another contract?"

"Only a small one," Paladin notes. "But it's all about getting our foot in the door at this stage."

"Any bread's welcomed," Pyro observes.

"Looking to reinvest," Buzzard nods toward Lizard. "Brother here is proposing a new location for the tattoo parlour and expanding business."

I'm not unhappy Buzz brought that up rather than myself. It's not news for anyone, but it is the first time it's been discussed as a proposition rather than a vague idea. It's kicked around for a while, but finally Liz gets the vote he wants, and it's full steam ahead. Rusty and Ink, both handy with a hammer, offer to get on with the drywalling as soon as the contract is signed.

A list is compiled of everything we need, such as looking for additional skilled employees and getting advertising underway to let old and new customers know where we're relocating to. Once we've gotten all that sorted, time's ticked on, and no one has an appetite for much more talk. I sense brothers are getting uneasy, their minds now on alcohol and pussy instead of business.

No point keeping asses in seats without good reason. I bang the gavel, bring the meeting to a close, and am not surprised when I find Hellfire lingering.

"What's on your mind, Demon?"

I half laugh. "That easy to read, Hell?"

The man I still regard as my father laughs. "Only ever since you were a babe in arms. Never could get anything past me."

As it's the truth, I don't deny it. For a long time I'd thought he had supernatural powers at reading minds, until I realised it was all part of being a dad.

"Well, *Brother*," I say with a grin, emphasising the word for two reasons, one to show he's no longer at the head of the table, and the second to acknowledge the true relationship between us, only recently acknowledged. "You're correct, of course."

I wave him out the door.

He gets my meaning, and heads for the bar. Dan, one of our prospects, has a whisky for Hell and a beer for me ready as we approach. Instead of slinging it back in one gulp, then asking for another, Hell sips his drink slowly. Another change, and all to the good. The old man's certainly regained that sparkle in his eyes, his new relaxed lifestyle taking years off him.

As we take our drinks to an empty table, my eyes catch Lizard already with his hand caressing Breezy's bare tits. Christ, that man doesn't waste time before snagging a sweet butt. Not that I blame him; I'll be looking for one later myself.

At last, I turn my attention to Hell. "You'll never guess who I bumped into earlier."

Obviously, he can't. He raises an eyebrow.

Alternating between speaking and drinking my beer, I enlighten him, and relate my encounter with Violet.

"Fuck, Brother. That was a bad business." A shadow comes over Hell's face as he refers to the day we'd received the news Nathan had been killed. Growing up, if I wasn't at Nathan's house, he'd been at mine. We'd been as thick as thieves from the age of four. Hell used to joke he had a third son. It had taken a long time for his loss to sink in, even longer to start to deal with it.

"Fuckin' shocked us all," I affirm. "Fuckin' shame the good die young."

"While the bad go on living." He raises his glass like a salute, then draws a hand over his face. "Got some grey hairs from some of the things you two got up to." His reminder brings a grin to my face. Yeah, Nate and I had gotten up to some shit in our day. "You remember his grandfather's World War II grenade?"

Do I! "Lucky we didn't blow ourselves up."

Hell's shaking his head. "His dad never should have left it lying around. But trying to get the gunpowder out with a hammer?" He barks a laugh. "You should have kids, Demon. Would like to see you handle that shit."

"Good reason I don't and have no inclination to," I reply shortly. "And please, I get the 'kids' talk from Mom often enough."

"Mo just wants to see you settled."

Why settle? I have a club full of whores and hangarounds for when I have an itch to scratch. Why tie myself down when there's no need to? Which reminds me. My eyes again scan the room, seeing Tulia is on her own. I hold up a finger toward her, giving her the signal that she's to wait for me to finish my conversation with Hellfire and not go with anyone else in the meantime. One of the perks of being the prez.

"So," Hellfire draws back my attention. "You're worried about Nathan's sister?"

Trust him to get to the heart of the matter. "I am." I frown.

Worried? Concerned? Feeling guilty I'd been out of touch for so long? Intrigued by the beautiful woman she's grown into? "Not sure I can put my finger on it, but something's not right." An image of her comes into my head. While I'd been checking her out, I hadn't missed the shadows in her eyes. The lines on my forehead deepen.

"You said she seemed down. Post-partum depression?"

"That could be the name for it, but shit if I know." Something he'd probably have more knowledge of. He'd been right by Mo's side while she birthed and raised three kids. Myself, my half-brother and half-sister are all fully-grown now, but I suspect there are things you don't forget. "I don't know, Hell. But I have this nagging feeling that I owe it to Nathan to look out for her."

"Could be you want to know for yourself, too," he observes, sagely.

"Nah," I shut him down fast. "Sure, she's an attractive bitch, but she's Nathan's little sister, for fuck's sake. And a woman like that, alone with a kid in tow, would be looking for a meal ticket."

"Looking for a life-partner," he corrects. He and Mo have been married thirty-six years. A few ups and downs along the way, but they're pretty well matched. Neither tries to hide that they think I should be looking to settle down. He stares at me. "She used to follow you around like a lovesick puppy. She still carryin' a torch for you?"

It's so far from the truth, I laugh. "Not so you'd notice."

"Kid used to think the sun shone out of your ass."

"Not anymore." I recall the dismissive way she'd treated me.

"So, you don't want her, she's not going to give you more than the time of day, but you want to make sure she's not needin' anything because you feel you owe it to Nathan."

"'Bout sums it up." One thing's for certain; my old man's not stupid.

"You're the prez now," he reminds me. "Put a prospect on her. No one gonna question you." He nods toward the bar. "Dan's pretty good."

He's right. Dan is. He's got the knack of fading into the background. When he isn't wearing his cut, of course.

"At least he might find out shit to settle your mind on how she's doing. You could have come across her on a bad day. Havin' a kid isn't easy. 'Specially if she's on her own. Could just have had a sleepless night."

He's right. There could be any number of reasons why Violet didn't resemble the girl I used to know. A few minutes later, when Hell rises to go home to Moira, my mind is a lot lighter. I hadn't liked the idea I'd let Nathan down, that something was going on with his sister that I should have, but hadn't been able to prevent, as I hadn't fucking given her a thought in years. Hell's suggestion of siccing a prospect on her is a good one. At least this way, I could respect her wishes not to interfere but satisfy myself she was happy enough. If something needs fixing, armed with the knowledge of what, I could step up and help.

Not wasting a moment, I give Dan instructions and a description, together with what information I know, such as her family's old address on the assumption that's where they still live. I'm finally free to make my way over to Tulia.

"Prez," she breathes at my approach, her eyes shining with anticipation.

"Doll, you intend on fuckin' the man or the title?" I smirk.

"Does it matter?"

Her husky voice goes straight to my groin. My eyes feast on the tits which are only just hidden beneath her cropped top, and catch the sparkle from Liz's handiwork, her belly-button jewel. Her crotch will be wet and easily accessible under her very short skirt. The fresh scent of shampoo and shower gel are all I can smell, letting me know mine will be the first cock inside her tonight. I don't care how many come after, but I prefer to be the one filling her cunt first.

Or, rather, the condom. Don't want to take any chances.

My hands find her shoulders, turn her around, then walk her across the room and into the prez's, my, office. I admit to there still being a sense of satisfaction being able to bend a slut over the big desk and fuck her there. The girls find it novel, too. The last prez had never made himself available; Hellfire has always been faithful to Moira.

Without pausing more than to raise her skirt to her waist, confirming my suspicions she's foregone panties tonight, and sliding a condom over my cock, I place my hands either side her head, raising it a fraction so she's looking straight at the large Satan's Devils flag hanging on the wall behind the desk, depicting the Grim Reaper and three little demons.

"Watch the devil and feel the demon," I rasp softly into her ear. Now I've positioned her where I want her, her shiver of excitement confirms that my blatant display of power has aroused her. I'm not surprised to find her cunt dripping.

"Demon," she pleads, "fuck me."

Never let it be said I make a woman ask twice. I slam into her again and again until I feel her clench around me. Still holding myself back, I pull out when she's finished her orgasm, lifting her up, seating her, then pushing her back until she's lying flat on the desk, and hammer into her again. I take my time, drawing two more orgasms out of her before finally letting go myself.

My cock's been well worked, my self-imposed discipline having heightened my arousal. When I eventually allow my balls to draw up and release my cum up through my cock and out to flood the condom, I see stars. And a face. Violet's.

What the fuck?

CHAPTER THREE

Demon

There is nothing about Tulia that reminds me of Violet. The sweet butt is auburn with freckles and grey-green eyes; Nathan's baby sister is blonde, her skin fair and like porcelain, her eyes a startling blue. Tulia is slim, Violet curvy, with hips a man could hang onto while fucking. *This is Vi I'm thinking about, Nathan's sister.* Not a random woman who might be up for a good time. My outrageous carnal thoughts are disrespecting both her and my friend's memory.

So disgusted with myself for conjuring up Violet's image at such an inappropriate time, I'm determined to stop thinking about her and our out-of-the-blue meeting. Making a conscious effort, I force her right to the back of my mind.

In that, I'm mostly successful. By Friday, I've barely thought of her once, even forgetting that I'd given Dan the instruction to watch her until I needed to remind the prospect to restock the bar, only to find he wasn't around.

Fuck this. How can I leave the club short-handed just to appease my sense of guilt and what had been my failing? I'd neglected to keep tabs on a woman I'd promised to watch over, and that wasn't down to the MC. I shouldn't use up resources for personal shit. Anyway, Hell was probably right: I'd misread the situation, there was nothing wrong, she'd just worn the harassed look of a woman tired from caring for a young baby.

Or, maybe, she'd taken one look at me and decided she didn't like the adult I'd become. Could have found the young man she'd lusted after as a teenager had turned into someone who no longer interested her. It may be I had brought sad memories of her brother to the fore, making coping with Nathan's loss harder, with me in her face as a reminder. There must be a hundred good reasons why Violet hadn't leapt at the chance to rekindle our friendship.

I'd given her my number. She hasn't called.

I should just drop it. Let her get on with her life and do the same with mine. Her behaviour was probably nothing more than the normal tiredness of a new mother with a young son. My desire to watch over her is an invasion of her privacy. Never mind that I want to know more about the woman she's become, she's not for the likes of me, and I should just leave her alone. I debate calling Dan back immediately, but can make do without him a while longer. The task I need him for isn't urgent.

I'll leave him where he is for now, and then get an update from him when he reappears. If he's seen nothing untoward in the last couple of days, I'll relieve him of his babysitting duties. I'll have done all I can to make sure Nathan's sister is okay and my mind can rest easy. And if her sweet, innocent look is fuel to my mind when I'm taking myself in hand in the shower, well, that's my problem, not hers. No one will ever know except me and my conscience.

Returning to my office, I settle down to what I should be thinking about, rather than a little blonde pixie. It's not long before I have another insight into why Hellfire had no problem giving up the chair. There's more paperwork to running an MC than anyone would ever realise. We own businesses, we pay taxes. I'm in the middle of laboriously going through the figures Buzzard has prepared, settling in for a long afternoon, when my phone rings.

Swearing at the interruption, I press accept. "You got Demon."

"Prez." It's Dan. His tone immediately has me on high alert.

"Speak to me."

"Prez, it's that girl you wanted me to watch."

A growling sound in my throat warns him to get to the point.

"She's in Canon City. I followed her here. Wills was just about to take over from me, so when she was obviously on the move, I decided I'd like to know where she was going so I tagged along. Thank fuck I did. It means there's two of us. Well, look, I don't know how you want us to handle this shit."

"What the fuck are you talking about, Dan? She doing some shopping? What do you mean, you don't know what to do?"

"She's not shopping, Prez. She left her house with a suitcase. Put it in the car. Thought you'd want to know where she's going, if she was going to stay with a friend or something."

Okay, I'm following so far. Haven't heard anything worth the emergency call. Again my growl rumbles down the line to encourage him get on with it. I may change my mind about patching him in if he keeps fucking around.

"She brought the baby with her. We followed them. Prez..." There's a pause, then he gives me the punchline. "She's left the baby in the middle of a shopping centre."

It takes a moment for his wording to sink in. "Left the baby?"

"She wheeled up the stroller. Didn't look at the kid, didn't say goodbye. Just exchanged a couple of words with a woman, then walked off leaving the baby and didn't look back. Something's off, Prez."

There's probably nothing strange. If I didn't have so much respect for Dan, I'd have dismissed it as someone babysitting while Violet can look around the stores. But I do. Despite my earlier thought out of sheer frustration, Dan has proved he can think on his feet. If he reads there's something wrong with the situation, there probably is. Or there could be an innocent reason.

"Prospect, tell me what you saw. The woman she left him with, she look like a friend?"

"Nah. That's what's got me, Prez. I considered friend, relative, sitter. What I'm seeing doesn't match up. That's why I'm following her now. Wills is trailing Violet. The bitch with the baby, well, she's heading straight out of the mall. I'd place money this is no babysitting gig. They exchanged maybe two words. I'd say she's passed the baby on to a stranger. You may think this is fanciful, Prez, but the way Violet walked off?"

Another pause while I chomp at the bit waiting for what I doubt I want to hear. In that he doesn't disappoint. "She doesn't expect to see her baby again."

Jesus! My hand thumps down on the desk. *I knew something was wrong. Fuck knows if I inherited Hell's sixth sense or something.* I hadn't expected this, though. Violet's given her baby away? There must be some explanation.

Thoughts run through my head fast.

She's living with her parents. How can she return to them without the baby in tow? *She had a suitcase.* Was she not planning on coming back to Pueblo?

Is Dan right? Does a stranger have her baby? Whatever problems she has, surely the girl I knew would never give up her child. Not in suspicious circumstances like she has, pass her baby over in a mall and walk off? Thank fuck I had Dan on her, who knows what might have happened to little Theo if I hadn't.

Dan might be wrong.

"Prospect, are you certain this isn't right?"

"Sure as I can be, Prez. There was something about her expression when she left the kid. She'd walked past me, her eyes... Her eyes looked dead."

My gut tells me he's right to be concerned. "Prospect. Can you stop the woman? Question her."

"Kid got a dad?"

"Not that I know of," I admit.

"Okay. I'll do it now. Call you in a minute."

He breaks the connection. I sit staring at the phone, willing him to ring back and tell me he was mistaken; there's nothing wrong at all. I rap my fingers against the desk, then do it again. The waiting is driving me crazy, all concentration to resume my attack on the mountain of paperwork gone.

The phone rings.

"She's given the kid up for a private adoption."

"What the fuck? You gotta stop her." This is not right. *Private adoption?* What checks has Violet made? Bad things can happen to kids palmed off onto a stranger. Anyone can pretend to be someone else nowadays. Adoption can mean a kid disappears, and not always with the right people.

"I told her I was the kid's father. Woman didn't want to draw attention or make a fuss. She wasn't happy, but walked off and left him with me. She's gone."

The woman walked off? Believed Dan's crazy story without evidence? Hell, he's done right getting the kid away from her. Dan will deserve his fucking patch for pulling this off. Now my concern is getting Theo safe. "What transport have you got, Prospect?"

"Wills and I came in the truck."

I think fast. "You bring the kid back to the compound. Any news on Violet?"

"Wills is following her. She's heading for the parking lot. You want him to bring her back, too?"

I do, and tell him so. She's got a fuckload of questions to answer.

"I'll call him. Wills can drive her back in her car and we'll get his bike later." Dan's voice is cold. "What kind of woman fuckin' gives a baby up, Prez?"

I have no fucking idea. One thing I do know, unless it turns out there's a fucking good reason, she's not getting him back. I grow cold at the thought of how easily Dan got him away from the person taking him. If it had been legit, the woman would have put up a fight.

I end the call. Canon City's about forty-five minutes from here. In three-quarters of an hour I'll have a woman, who I'm fast starting to despise, in the compound, along with an innocent kid who it seems she intended to dump. All my promises to Nathan have flown out the window. What did either of us know about Violet? She was sixteen when Nathan died; in the years since she must have hardened and become a bitch. I recall the way she all but ignored her child when I'd met her a couple of days back; I shouldn't have dismissed those warnings. It's clear now: she wasn't simply pleased he was asleep, she'd wanted nothing to do with him.

Thoughts tumble through my head. My mom was raped. My brother stepped up, married her, and brought me up as his own. No suggestion of abandoning me to an unknown fate. Violet? Christ, she dumps her kid, seeming not to care what the fuck will become of him. *She hadn't looked back.*

Calm, Demon. Calm. Mo's situation is probably very different. Violet's got no man to support her. Maybe the kid's dad died and she can't cope. Much as I don't know the woman Violet's grown into, I don't know her circumstances, or what could have driven her to do something so drastic. *Or perhaps she's just taking an easy way out.*

Her kid is Nathan's nephew. My promise to look after his sister must extend to her child.

That day when I met her? I should have acted on what I felt wasn't right. At least I've got a chance to step up now. She can't look after him? Then there's a right way of going about it, and what Violet's done today is definitely wrong.

Forty minutes now. I've got to make plans for the baby when he arrives. Someone will have to watch over him. The sweet butts? Hell, no. They wouldn't have a clue what to do with a kid. Mo? Nah, not fair. She and Hellfire have paid their dues and are now getting their life back on track. They don't need to have a little one in tow.

I open my office door and bellow, "Pal?"

"Prez?"

When he's close enough for me to use a more normal voice, I ask, "Jayden around?"

"Yeah, she's with Jeannie in the kitchen. Whadya need, Prez?"

"She helped with the kids in Tucson, didn't she? Wants to work with kids?"

Pal looks surprised at the topic, but responds, "Yeah, she's planning on being a nanny."

"She know babies?" I ask hopefully.

"Prez," Pal smirks, "you know what the Tucson chapter's like. Can't move for falling over the little rugrats. Yeah, Jay's great with babies."

Thank fuck. "Got a job for you and her, Pal." I fill him in, my voice loud with anger.

Childcare arrangements have been a snap to set up. Now my biggest problem is what to do about her. The bitch who appears to have left her child. Her five-month-old, helpless baby, unable to fend for himself.

My gut clenches at the thought of what could have happened to him had I not put Dan on her. He'd have disappeared, taken off by God knows who and fuck knows where while she'd have gone off in the other direction with her suitcase in hand, and no one would have been any the wiser.

"Calm down, Demon." My father uses a parental tone he's perfected over the years. It never fails to get my attention, and doesn't do so now.

Having told Pal, and not too discreetly, word has gone around the clubhouse, sort of like Chinese whispers. Brothers might accuse women of gossiping, but in truth they're as bad as, if not worse than, any of the bitches. The words 'woman' and 'abandoned baby', and that both being brought back are as much as any of them know. If I was in a better mood, I'd probably be amused at the two-and-two's they were putting together.

Hell, though. He knows Violet. After I've given him more

details, he exchanges them for advice. "Son, don't leap before you know what's going on. Even if she did leave the baby, there could be reasons. Post-partum depression, like I suggested. Don't jump down her throat until you know what you're dealing with."

"Fuckin' depression doesn't make you abandon a kid, Hell." I glare, my eyes half on him, and half on the clock where the minutes are ticking by far too fast.

"You think that? You don't know the half of it, boy," he yells, a bit like he'd done when I was a boy.

"Well?" I challenge. "Even a depressed woman would want her kid cared for. Dropped him off at a hospital or something. Not in the middle of a shopping mall with someone it appeared she didn't even know."

Hell looks like I've gone crazy. "And if she just couldn't cope? It might have been planned for good reason. Babies can drive you up the wall. Screaming for nothing and no way to pacify them. It could have been to give her a temporary break, just a few hours of peace."

"She had a suitcase with her," I remind him, grimly. "She had no intention of going back."

Hell stares at me; he's not backing down. "All I'm asking is that you give her a chance to explain. Don't immediately leap to the conclusion that she's a bad mother."

His reasonable tone is annoying me. Sure, I've painted her black as hell, but I can't get my head around anyone leaving their kid like that. "You didn't see her that day, Hell. I did. She didn't want the kid; that was obvious." As I go back over that morning, it's becoming clearer to me by the minute.

He sighs. "So what are you intending to do, Demon?"

This is the bit I haven't quite worked out. I'm left with ten minutes now. "Make damn sure she can't hurt that kid again. Jay and Pal will be looking after him for now. See what's happened to the father. Whoever he is, I doubt he'd be very happy his son was abandoned. Who knows, he could have been taken by a pedo."

"You're jumping to conclusions, son. You don't know that the father even knows he's a dad."

"'Bout time he found out then, and took over."

All I know is I'm determined, unless Violet comes up with a good fucking explanation for her behaviour, she's not going to have responsibility for him again. In my world you step up, not down.

It's Hell's turn to bang his fist on the desk. With twenty years of practice, he's got the art down better than I. Papers leap and shift, I jump.

"Give her a fuckin' chance, Demon. Listen." He shakes his head. "You've been brought up to make decisions for the club. Sure, you stepped into that chair before it was time, but one thing you need to learn right now—you're the fuckin' prez. You decide what needs to be done. But this club ain't one man. That's why we vote. No one man has all the answers, and no good prez jumps into a course of action without knowing the facts first."

"Facts are clear though, aren't they? That kid's at risk."

"And if there isn't a father in the picture? You intending on putting him in the system?"

"Kid's got grandparents, hasn't he?"

"Facts, Demon. Not suppositions. Facts. The things you don't have at the moment."

He's got a point. "Mo didn't give me up. Neither did you."

Hell sighs deeply, then rubs at his temples. "I had an inkling that might be at the bottom of the way you're reacting. Mo had me. I wanted Mo. Wanted you, too, from the moment I knew about you growing inside her. You were loved, Demon, from the fuckin' start. But if Mo had been on her own?"

Yeah. I look down at my hands. My mom would have tried to get an abortion if Hell hadn't been in the picture, and I wouldn't have been here at all. At seventeen, with no job, parents who would have disowned her, she wouldn't have had much choice.

"Sometimes it's too much for a woman alone. Maybe a helping hand is what she needs. Not fire and brimstone."

My mouth quirks slightly. "Or Hellfire and Demon."

He closes his eyes briefly and nods. "I've got your back. Which is why I'm pushing you now. Thing is, I happen to agree with you. But I'm just saying you need to hear her out, okay? Listen, then decide what you need to do."

The clock ticks mercilessly on. Talking to the man I still view as my father, his years giving weight to his words and experience, has at last calmed my temper some. While I have little doubt in my mind that Violet has proved herself to be an unfit mother, I at least have relented to the extent I will talk to her, see what her side of the story is, before making any decision that affects a child's life.

Maybe if it hadn't been for my background, the event of my conception coinciding with my rapist father being dispatched to meet Satan, I might have been inclined to turn everything over to the authorities from the beginning. Two things stop me. I'm the president of the Colorado chapter of the Satan's Devils; we have no time for the citizen world. The other? Nathan, on his first tour overseas, had entrusted the care of his little sister to me. I'd clearly let both him and her down by assuming all was rosy in her world.

If she wanted to give up her kid, then that's what I'd help her to do. But I'd do it my way and according to my rules.

As a baby's high-pitched cry reaches us, Hellfire and I stand at the same time. He holds the door open. By the time I've stepped out, the baby is already being held in Jay's clearly capable hands, and a pacifier placed in his mouth. Almost on Dan's heels are Breezy and Tulia, who are coming in carrying bags. Immediately, equipment I've never seen before in my life is being placed upon the bar. Jay, baby competently snuggled in one arm, is examining what's emerging from the bags as if ticking off a mental list. Stepping closer I see bottles, formula, and something which apparently is called a steriliser. Not that I could recognise it; I just read the label.

While I was debating with Hell, Jay's obviously got down to the practicalities and has had the club girls go out to get what she knows she needs. I exchange a rueful grin with Hell, then chuckle as I see what the club girls are wearing, wondering what the kids' store thought of that pair turning up, dressed more for twirling around a stripper pole than for taking care of a baby.

I then catch Liz's eyes widening as he quickly turns away, seeing Breezy and Tulia fawning a little too much over the kid. Hmm. Think there'll be more than one man doubling up on condoms tonight.

Violet will be here any minute. I want to keep her off-balance, at least until I know what's going on. "Jay?" As she turns, I point to the kitchen. "Can you take the baby out of sight?"

"Sure, Demon." With a nod, asking no questions, she does. We'd all had our doubts about her at first, mainly down to her tender age of seventeen. But we have none now. She's turning out to have the makings of a great old lady.

CHAPTER FOUR

Demon

"Let me go! What are you doing? Who are you? Where have you brought me?" Violet's shrill voice echoes around the clubroom which has gone silent as Wills brings her through the doorway. All eyes are on the woman who, as everyone knows, abandoned her baby.

I signal Dan. He nods. He goes over and takes her from the other prospect, leaving Wills free to come to me.

His face is grim. "She's not once mentioned the baby. Not one fuckin' word."

"Did you ask her anything about him?"

"Thought you'd want to do that yourself. I, er, I had to restrain her, Prez. She was trying to jump out of the car."

He's right. I do want it to be me who asks her. I nod at his other comment too. I'd have been more surprised had she gone with someone she didn't know calmly. I dismiss him. Our exchange has only taken a second, yet seems to have confirmed my worst suspicions. I gather the resolve to go over to her, this woman who no longer deserves to have a special place in my heart by virtue of being Nathan's sister. She's now the woman who I believe has let his memory down. I wait a moment before approaching, analysing the glances being thrown her way. Some are scornful, some curious, some outright disgusted. Then I look over to see she's managed to get free, turning and attempting to get out the door, only to be secured in the prospect's strong, unyielding arms. Her hands, I notice, are zip-tied, and even across the distance between us, I see angry red welts have already appeared from her struggles.

Her pains are nothing to what her abandoned baby could face in his future, or, as far as she knows, could be suffering even now. Feeling no sympathy, I step forward, at last bringing myself into her line of sight.

She immediately stills. Her eyes widen in shock, then relief. "Oh, thank God! Dave!"

Her heartfelt cry makes me realise Wills, not knowing our relationship, probably didn't see fit to enlighten her as to where she was being taken, or to whom. She may not have even realised she was in the company of a biker. The prospect, quite rightly, would not have been wearing his cut in a cage. But in light of her crime, the thought that for all she knew she was being kidnapped doesn't worry me at all. One thought of her baby and what his future might have held has turned my heart to stone. Even if he had been cared for, it wouldn't have been by his mother.

"Untie her hands, Prospect."

"Dave!" As soon as she's free, she throws herself at me. I stand, arms at my sides. After a second, I put my hands on her biceps and hold her at arm's length. Her face, which had brightened at seeing what she believed was a friendly face, slowly pales. "Dave?" This time, my name is a question.

"We need to talk."

I turn. I hope she'll follow. If she doesn't, one of the brothers will show her the way. Catching a view in the mirror above the bar, I see it's Thunder and Mace who are encouraging her along. I lead her down the basement steps, unlocking the door at the bottom and stepping back to allow her to precede me inside.

She falters when her eyes fall on the workbenches scattered

around, various tools laid out on their surfaces. Most belong to Mace, our enforcer. There's a solitary chair in the middle of the room. As we were not expecting visitors, the customary plastic sheet is missing from beneath it. Whatever, it's an unwelcoming space, and elicits my name from her lips again.

"Dave?" Her voice shakes.

"Sit." My hand, firm but not ungentle, pushes her into the room. Even through the light touch, I can feel her trembling.

She moves, but remains standing, her hands rubbing one wrist then the other. "Dave? I don't understand..."

"Demon," I correct her. "My name's Demon."

Her eyes, looking behind me, catch those of my father, who's followed us down. They widen in recognition. "Mr Black? Please, why am I here?"

With a quick shake of his head he corrects her, "Hellfire." His tone is devoid of emotion. Of course, when she was hanging around with Nathan and myself, she only knew him by his government name.

"I'm Mace." He may have politely introduced himself, but there's nothing welcoming about the expression on the enforcer's face. He turns to me. "You want me go make her sit?"

I shrug. "Up to you." My indifference seems to unnerve her. Behind me, Thunder chooses not to introduce himself. Her eyes flick to him warily before coming back. As I watch her I can't help but take in she's become a beautiful woman.

It won't be the first time what's on the outside covers a rotten core.

"Dave." A look at my set features makes her correct herself. "Demon. Look, let me go. I don't know why you've brought me here, but I'd like to leave. You and I have nothing to say to each other."

She's standing in the middle of the room. I distance myself further, moving to a workbench and leaning against it, my arms folded. "Where's Theo?" I ask, lazily, as if I really couldn't give a damn. As I expect she doesn't.

A quick flash of emotion crosses her face, which is rapidly squashed. "Safe," she replies quickly, her gaze looking from one to the other of us, as if trying to work out what we know.

"You sure about that?" I ask, keeping my incredulity hidden.

A pause, then a firm reply, "Yes."

My fingers clench into fists, and I don't miss the warning shake of Hellfire's head. Mace and Thunder, even though they'd not been party to our discussion and know little more than she'd abandoned the baby, look like they are feeling about the same as I. Momentarily I loosen my hands before my fingers find my palms again, a sign that I'm taking the lead.

"You think that giving a baby to a stranger in a shopping mall is a good way to keep him safe?" I ask, almost holding my breath. This is her chance to deny it. Her chance to tell me it was only for a few moments, then she would be going back. That the woman she'd handed him to was a friend.

Her shoulders slump. A small sob, which I don't believe for one moment, comes out of her mouth, then she admits it when she offers by way of explanation, "He'll be safer with a stranger than with me."

As I'm at a complete loss for words, Hellfire steps in to fill the void, his voice patient, kind. Fatherly. "You thought you couldn't look after him? Were a danger to him perhaps?"

"No, no. I've never hurt him. Never." Her voice, quiet until now, becomes forceful. "I just couldn't protect him if I kept him with me."

Hell sends me another look and moves closer to her. "This isn't what I remember you being like as a little girl, Violet. You were the one who came running that time your brother found an injured critter and you thought he was just going to leave it in the barn. I remember driving you and the boys to the animal sanctuary, as you wanted to make sure it was healed and given a home. You were five years old, and I remember it clearly. That girl would never leave a baby alone." He pauses. I recall the story. Hell, I lived it. I'd been there. But twenty years is a long time.

Who can measure an adult by what they were like as a child? "Violet, have you been unwell since Theo was born? It affects many mothers. You shouldn't be ashamed if you need help. It's there if you want to reach out and take it."

As Violet turns her blue eyes on him, I see from my position that the light has gone out of them. The prospect had been right. They look dead. "I'm in my right mind, Mr... er, Hellfire. I knew what I was doing, and why I was doing it. I had no choice. It was all I could do. I did the right thing."

I can stay silent no longer. Stepping up, I push Hell out of the way and get right up into her face.

"In what universe is abandoning a kid the right thing to do? Tell me that, Violet. What can ever make that right? What do you know of the woman you handed him to? How can giving him to a stranger keep him safe? What the fuck were you thinkin'? What fuckin' planet are you on, woman?"

Her eyes go wide, her cheeks two patches of red. Her mouth opens, then shuts. I wait for a justification that there's no way I'll be able to accept. After a moment, I see her hands curl into fists, see her start shaking, but this time, it's with anger, not fear. When I'm that close, I feel spittle land on my face, as she shouts, "On the planet where I was fuckin' raped."

I can't. I just can't.

As I stand gaping, Hellfire and Mace grab hold of my arms and back me out of the room. I make no resistance, words flying around my head. Images slamming into me.

"You got him?"

"Yeah, Mace. You go keep an eye on the girl. I'll talk to him, okay?" My father's reassuring voice gives the enforcer his instructions while I seem unable to react to anything.

I'm pliant as Hell leads me up the stairs and into my office. Knowing exactly where I keep it—in the same place as he used to—he takes down the whisky and fills two glasses, then pushes one across to me.

"Drink."

My hand cradles the glass, but I make no move to lift it. I stare into the smoky depths for a moment before raising my eyes.

"She was raped, Hell. Nathan told me to look after her. She was fucking raped."

That's the first thing I need to get my head around, that I let her down. But the next? Christ, I can't see my way to be easy with what's spinning in my brain.

I spit it out, "She hates the child as it was a result of a rape."

"Not the words that she used." Hell gazes intently at my face.

"She said he wasn't safe with her."

Hell nods, having to admit, "She implied that."

"Why did she fuckin' have it, Hell? If she was going to have so little regard for it? Or, if she's a fuckin' pro-lifer, why not put it up for adoption before it was born? Why the fuck keep it until it's five months old, then pass it off under dubious circumstances to someone in a fuckin' mall? How the fuck can a woman do that?"

"Jeez, Demon. Ask something hard, will ya?" Hell shakes his head. "I don't know. Maybe he started looking like the man who assaulted her, maybe she's seeing things in him now that weren't there when he was born."

"Did Mom?" My teeth are gritted as the words come out. "Do I look like him, Hell?" Three months. That's all the time I've had to get around how I was brought into existence. Seems it hasn't been long enough.

He laughs scornfully. "What d'you think? You look like me. I look like him, which means you resemble him too. We're brothers, Demon. You know this."

I know that. Yeah. My head sinks into my hands. Twelve weeks or so ago I found out Hell wasn't my father. Now Violet's brought feelings to the fore I never knew I had. My initial reaction had been overwhelming thankfulness that Hell and Mo had brought me up never letting me think for a moment I was anything other than their child. Even when my half-sister and half-brother came along, I was treated no different. I'd never have been told had I not stumbled on the truth by accident. Hell and Mo were going to take that secret to the grave.

What would have happened had Hellfire not stepped up and led everyone to believe I was their son? Alone, would Mo have gone through with that abortion? Or, would she have birthed me and had me adopted, or, as I grew to resemble the man who abused her, could she have acted the same way as Violet? Abandoned me to an unknown fate?

"One thing I'm certain of, is that we don't know the whole story."

"You think?" I know that. I'm also not certain I want to know what happened to her. Despite having promised her brother I'd keep an eye on her, I all but forgot her existence. If I'd been there for her, acted in a brotherly role, would I had been able to stop it happening in the first place? Or been there to support her, so her only option wasn't leaving the baby the way she had, but to go down the proper route to have him adopted?

Pushing aside my untouched whisky, abruptly I stand.

Hell does, too, his arm held out to stop me crossing to the door. "You're not going back down there. Not until you calm down."

"Not going to ask her any more questions, Hell. I don't want to hear answers that might make me want to kill her. No, I'm going to visit her parents."

I need to let her talk, listen to her. But I want facts from another's mouth first. I don't trust a woman who passes off a child in the way she has. Yeah, I've got questions for her loving mother and father. At the very least I'd like to ask where they thought their daughter and grandchild had been headed today. If, as Hell obviously still suspects, she's having a hard time coping as a single mom, why didn't they get her the help she so clearly needed?

Hell sighs tiredly. "I'm coming along. Don't want you to go

off half-cocked. You have got the Black temper." So has he. He's had longer to learn to control it.

I look at him wryly. He knows me too well.

It's doesn't take long to get to our destination; certainly not enough time for the ride to clear my head. The Palmers live on the edge of Pueblo in a decent enough ranch-style house on the edge of the desert. Returning today for the first time since Nathan's death reminds me of when I knew this place as well as my own home. The old ramshackle buildings Nathan and I used to play in look even more run-down now. When was I last here? The day of Nathan's funeral, that's when. I now feel guilty for that. My own pain being so great, I couldn't deal with anyone else's. And Bill and Delilah, Nathan and Violet's parents, had each other to help them grieve. I'd leaned on my club brothers and relied on keeping track of Violet through mutual friends.

The driveway is potholed, our bikes bumping even though we try to avoid the worst of the holes. When we eventually pull up and turn off our engines, the noise echoes around, mingling with the only other sound, birdsong. But from inside the house comes the hum of someone vacuuming.

I take the lead as we walk to the door. In days long past I'd have gone around the back and let myself in, but such familiarity is long in my rearview. Instead I press my finger to the doorbell and hold it until the sound of the housework ceases. Footsteps, then the door is opened.

The person who answers is younger than I expected; not much, but she can't be more than forty or so. A relative? Maybe.

"Can I help you?" She's holding the door only open a crack, her eyebrows knitted together in confusion.

"Is Bill or Delilah here?" Hell's the one to ask, his rich baritone even and non-threatening.

"Bill? Oh my gosh, no. Were you a friend of his? Oh, I'm so sorry. If you don't know... Oh my gosh. How can I tell you?" The confusion has gone, to be replaced by sadness instead.

"If we don't know... what?" Hell asks, but her reaction has given me a good idea what we're going to hear.

"Bill died. It was a sudden heart attack, let's see, that was eighteen months ago. Right as rain one moment, dead the next. Mind you, if you ask me, his heart wasn't in living since the death of his son..."

It seems like she's going to continue. Rapidly I've worked it through and remembered that timing fits with when Violet said she'd come home. To live with her mother? Maybe. "Mrs Palmer? Is she in?"

The woman's eyes narrow. "You really don't have any idea, do you?"

Holding out my hands in supplication, I realise I'll get more information if I offer some up myself. "My name's Dave," I tell her, "This is my father, Carter Black," introducing Hell. "I used to spend half my life here with Nathan before he joined up. I sort of lost touch with the Palmers when Nathan was killed."

"You're David?" She beams. "In her more lucid moments, Delly used to talk about you and Nathan all the time." Her eyes squint. "Yeah, I can see the resemblance now. She had all these photographs. Used to show them to me. I'm the caregiver, you see; I've been helping out a couple of times a week." She steps back and opens the door wide. "You better come in. There's a lot you don't know, and it's not to be discussed on a doorstep."

Within moments we're seated on a sofa but have declined any refreshment. The woman, still nameless, doesn't waste time bringing us up to date. "Delly was going downhill long before Bill died. It was a blessing in a way, some days she hardly knew he was gone. She'd talk about him and Nathan, and you, David, as if you were all going to walk in the door. Other times, well, she'd be near-catatonic. When Violet came home for the funeral, she knew she had to stay. She wanted to be here for Delly's more lucid moments, which we already knew would become fewer and fewer."

"Violet had a baby..."

"Oh, yes. You know that?" Her lips purse, she looks either like she didn't approve, or she knows the whole story which, as yet, I don't. "Delly was quite good with the baby. Whatever she did was out of the goodness of her heart. But she'd get muddled you see. Once she ran a bath of nearly scalding water. Violet had thought Theo was asleep, so she'd gone to lay down for a nap herself. She heard screaming, ran in to find Delly putting him in the tub, already had his toes in the water." Her eyes squeeze tight at the painful memory. "Took him to the hospital, he was fine. Fully recovered, but Vi? Vi near lost it. A second or two later..."

She's shaking her head, her tight expression telling the story of what might have happened.

"Violet a good mother?" Hell asks.

"The best." A vehement nod as emphasis.

So that might explain the reason for Violet leaving. Theo was in danger from her mother. Hang on, no, that doesn't clarify it. What I've heard just raises more questions. "Miss, Mrs...?"

"Hounslow. Vicky Hounslow."

"Ms Hounslow. Is that why Violet left?"

"Oh, goodness, no. After the bath incident Violet made sure Delly wasn't around Theo unsupervised. Delly was deteriorating fast, going further and further downhill. It soon became that she didn't recognise anyone and was becoming a danger to herself, as well as anyone else. In the past few weeks she got violent. I came in more often, but even with the two of us, she became harder to control. She wasn't Delly, wasn't Violet's mom anymore. Just the shell. Violet couldn't cope, not with a baby as well. It wasn't an easy decision, but one that had to be made. Delly needed to be somewhere where she couldn't hurt herself or others. She's moved into a home. Unfortunately," she breaks off and waves her hand around, "this house has to be sold to pay for it. I'm only here to do a final clean-up. You're lucky you came today. Violet left, she's got friends Theo and she can stay with until she could get herself sorted." She sobs, then adds, "I wish it could have been different, but this is best all around."

Hell's eyes are upon me. He might know me well, but I can read him too. He doesn't need words to let me know how much all this is for any woman to bear.

A child born out of violence, a woman quite possibly having problems having so recently given birth, and a mother who she can't rely on and who doesn't even recognise her. On top of that, having to sell her family home.

The reasons for Violet's possible derangement render me speechless.

It's Hell who bids Vicky farewell, and who herds me out of there. Violet would have been mad with grief and not thinking straight. I was right to come here. Although the answers weren't what I'd expected, I'm enlightened as to Violet's mental state and the reason behind it. I'm surprised she's coping at all.

Before we start the bikes, I hear the sound of the hoover start up again and take a moment to look around the place that held so many happy childhood memories. I wouldn't have wanted to hang around to see it being sold to strangers either. I don't blame Violet for leaving when she did. But I do blame her for thinking she couldn't look after Theo.

Why hadn't she asked anyone for help? I might only have met her, but I'd been struck by the compassionate woman we've just been speaking too. I'm certain, if Vicky had known what she had planned, she would have stepped in and stopped her, and found some way to help.

Of course, I'm also guilty. Nathan would have expected the other person she'd have turned to would have been me.

CHAPTER FIVE

Violet

I should be scared, but the luxury of worrying about myself was something I'd given up a long time ago. First Dad's sudden death, then having to deal with Mom and her rapidly-escalating deterioration. Then Theo. The fact I've been brought God knows where, am being held in something that resembles a torture chamber with two scary, non-talkative men glaring at me, barely registers. All my thoughts are on my son. My head is whirling. I walk across to the chair and this time, sit down.

Theo. The baby I love more than myself. What happens to me, I no longer care. I could die happy as long as I know that he's safe, and no one will ever find him. I can't allow myself to harbour thoughts that the way I went about it is wrong, Have to let myself believe in the inherent good in this world, and that even now he's with a family who will care for him and love him. I did what I could.

I'd had barely any warning. No time to make official arrangements for his care. I wasn't even able to do it legally; that would have left a paper trail. My leaving him with the woman at the mall had been an act of desperation. I'd had no choice, and no chance to reconsider. A check of her references, arrangements made, then the handoff. I'll go crazy if I let myself think for a moment it was the wrong thing to do.

There had been no one on my side. No one I could trust. I still have Dave, no, *Demon's* number that he gave me the other day, but what do I know of the man he's grown into? After Nathan's funeral, he hadn't come to my parents' house again. I'd seen him briefly a few times in the distance when I was in my late teens, but never close enough even to say hello to.

Demon. Yes, his new name suits him. He'd always had these remarkable dark eyes flecked with gold which seemed to glow when he'd gotten excited or angry. The main differences since I last saw him are how long he's grown his hair, that he's become even more muscular, and his hardened expression that I don't recall ever seeing before.

I'd seen the patch saying 'President' on his leather vest, and I doubt you get a higher rank than that in a motorcycle club. I'd known he'd joined, that his father had been president before him. But I'd never been exposed to the club or had any reason to think of Dave as a biker. When Nathan was home on leave, they were just two normal friends. Hellfire had never been anything other than Mr Black to me; he was my brother's friend's father, not a criminal. It wasn't until later, when I was older, that I'd heard rumours of the sort of things they were into. Drug running and guns.

Nathan had still been friends with Dave, and I'd often wondered why. My brother had stood for law, democracy and the right to freedom. He didn't join up to escape or get thrills; he'd really believed in what he was fighting for. Was going to be a career soldier, and I used to imagine him becoming a general one day. All that ended with the sniper's bullet. Yeah, I couldn't reconcile what I knew of my brother and the man whose friendship he'd made sure to maintain every time he came home on leave.

Now I'm in Demon's hands, and I neither know nor care what he's going to do with me. What I can't understand is why he's so upset about Theo? Why he's so angry with me? Why had I blurted out that my son was the result of me being raped? And why had Demon walked out before I could explain the danger Theo was in?

Will Demon be returning? I frown as I stare down at my fingernails, bitten so short they're barely there at all. If he does, will I want to tell him anything? Surely, he won't turn me into the authorities for abandoning my baby? That can't mean anything to him, can it?

You're Nathan's sister.

Is that it? Does he think he's responsible for me, as he was my brother's best friend? Huh! If so, where was he when I buried my father? Where was he when my mother scalded, and could have killed, her grandchild? Where was he when I wept through the night when she first hadn't recognised me? Where was he when I mopped up the blood when she hit me across the nose?

There's no clock down here, and I refuse to ask—Mace, wasn't it?—how much time has passed. I refuse to try and get information; it really doesn't matter to me. For the first time in months, I've no invalid or child to look after. No pregnant body to care for. Nothing else to think about except how much I miss my baby. Theo's gone now, I'll never see him again.

My plan had been to leave Theo and then kill myself. The world wouldn't miss me, and it would mean Theo would be safe forever. I'd left no clue, nothing for anyone to follow. The assumption, hopefully, would be he'd disappeared with me. Demon has to let me go, then I'll put my original plan into play. Soon I'll be breathing no longer and won't have to think anymore. I don't even have a plan how to do it, but know it needs to be done.

If Theo's father finds me, he'll try to make me talk. I don't like to think of the methods he'd use to force me to give my son up.

But I've nothing to tell. I don't know where Theo is. That's the bargain I'd made. No information given in either direction.

If I'm going to die, I'd rather do it painlessly.

Seeing Demon the other morning had brought back happier memories. Oh, I know I used to annoy him and Nathan; I'd been so irritating, telling them Mom had said they had to let me play with them. That squirrel Hellfire had mentioned? That was one of those times. I shouldn't even have been there. The memory brings a fleeting smile to my face.

I'd looked up to my big brother, but even more, had revered his handsome friend. I'd even boasted at school he was my boyfriend, back when I'd been five and him fifteen. It wasn't until I reached puberty that I knew what it was to wish that could be reality. Oh, how I plagued him when Nathan was at home on leave. I'd been sixteen the year we lost my brother. My cheeks redden as my thoughts make me blush. Demon was twenty-six, and embarrassed when I'd dressed up when he'd come over, at my early attempts to put on makeup, and oh, my vain endeavours to flirt. Looking back now, I can see how I'd made him uncomfortable. Back then, my only desire had been to steal a kiss.

I hadn't been successful.

I'd left, gone to college, after that moved to New York. Lost my virginity to someone with long, almost-black hair and dark eyes, and looking back, every boyfriend thereafter was a Demon stand-in. Would I have been able to handle the real thing? Hell, no. As today has shown, he might be an attractive package, but what's inside is rotten to the core. I hadn't missed the inherent violence that he seemed to only just be holding back.

This Demon no longer attracts me. If I cared enough, I'd be scared.

Theo. No. Don't go there. Don't think about him anymore. A silent prayer for his safety, that will have to be enough. Jeez! Suddenly it hits me. I'd been so deep in my misery, I hadn't asked the obvious. *How does Demon know what I'd done? How does he know I handed Theo over?* For a second, I worry he might have upset all my plans. But it's me he brought here, not Theo. *Please, let Theo be gone, where neither I nor anyone else will ever be able to find him.*

A sob starts to rise; I push it back down. To keep my mind occupied, words come out of my mouth. "Aren't you bored?"

My sudden question takes Mace by surprise, and he needs a moment to answer. His eyes flick first to the other man, then back to me. "Bored? No."

"You're not curious, either?"

"Nah. What reasons you had for what you did are between you and Demon. No concern of mine."

"No thoughts? You're not going to berate me?"

His head tilts as he thinks about it. "I reckon you're going to get what you deserve."

Maybe I won't need to kill myself. Maybe Demon will do it for me. Do I want to know? While I'm wondering what question to formulate next, Mace turns his back. *Conversation over.*

His companion? One look shows it's not worth wasting my words.

I swear this building's making noises, subtle creaks and groans, but otherwise, down here, no sound reaches us. If half the rumours about the Satan's Devils are true and my suspicions correct about what the basement is used for, I expect it will be soundproofed. Time's dragging. Whatever will happen, I just want to get it over with. I'm starting to wonder whether it's possible to die just from the pain I'm feeling inside. All my life's been about loss, my brother, father, and then my mom's living death. Theo was mine, a life dependent on me. A living, breathing creature who carried part of my soul as well as my blood. As he grew I knew I'd see Nathan in him, Dad as well, even my mother. Wrapped in an exterior that would be unique to him too. I'd never blame him for his existence; both he and I were innocent in that. His start to life never for one minute made me love him less.

The door opening makes me jump. I didn't even hear footsteps.

Demon enters alone, pulling the door shut behind him. "You can leave us, Mace, Thunder."

I watch, wondering whether they can sense the danger in the air, the threat that violence may well be done. Would they be worried about leaving me alone with Demon? But if either of the two men have such concerns, they don't show them. Mace leads the way to the closed door and opens it again.

In the brief moment the heavy wood is held open, sounds reach us from up above. Music playing, voices talking. Laughter, and the unexpected wail of a hungry baby. A cry I know well, and which has its normal affect, amplified as it's been so long since I last fed him. My breasts swell, my nipples leak, and the front of my shirt dampens.

I stand so fast the chair topples over. "Theo. How? Why? What?" Then realising the questions don't matter, torn between being beyond grateful I've been given another chance and the hopelessness that my hurriedly thought out and executed plan had failed, I'm rushing toward the door, but come up against an immovable force.

"Where do you think you're going?"

"To feed Theo. He's hungry. He needs me."

"Fuckin' shame you didn't think about that earlier."

I slap at him; he takes hold of my wrists. I kick at his legs, it's like kicking tree trunks. It's only when I raise my knee that he moves back, somehow swings me around until my back is to his front. Then he hisses menacingly into my ear, "Calm the fuck down. We're going to talk. Once we've done that, I'll decide whether you are ever going to see your son again."

The door might have closed, meaning I can no longer hear my son's hungry cries, but the echo is going around my head. "He needs me," I repeat. "I have to go to him."

"He doesn't need you. Just needs someone who'll take care of him, and he's got exactly that. You didn't care who'd be looking after him earlier, did you?"

"I cared. You have no idea how fucking much," I shout,

knowing I'm sounding unreasonable. "What do you mean he's got someone to look after him? Who's got him?"

"One of the ol' ladies."

That statement makes me feel no easier. The last old woman he had caring for him tried to drown him in a too-hot bath. I'm beyond frantic with worry.

"Calm down, woman. Violet, calm the fuck down. Answer my questions and maybe I'll let you see him, okay?"

I'm still struggling, my brain seems to have switched off, settling on only one thing. Now all I want to do is get back to my baby. I realise I've been in some sort of fugue since I left him; now it hits me how wrong it was, and maybe, just maybe, there's another way to sort this mess out. A way which means both Theo and I can be together. Trouble is, I have no idea how it could be achieved.

"Calm down. Breathe."

I'm pulled back more tightly. I can feel movements of a chest behind mine. A ribcage that rises and falls rhythmically. Unconsciously I find my lungs beginning to work in time with his.

"You're safe. I've got you. You're safe. Theo's in very good hands. Breathe, that's it. Breathe. You're safe, Violet. Safe."

It's his quiet, reassuring voice that breaks me. One minute I'm struggling to get loose, the next all the fight goes out of me. The last breath I've taken comes out on a sob, soon followed by another. Now he turns me, my arms go around him, my muscle memory seeming to remember the man who had comforted me when I was a kid, who'd held me at Nathan's funeral, encouraging me to let all my grief out. He's Demon no longer, but Dave, my brother's best friend.

I cry for ages. All the tears I'd held back as I survived my ordeal, pregnancy and becoming a single mother, all the despair I'd kept inside as my mom grew worse, all the fear and escalating horror, all the months when I couldn't allow myself to be weak. A hand is rubbing my back, a voice murmuring nothings into my ear. I've no idea how much time has passed before I've recovered enough to speak.

"He wants Theo," I tell Demon. "He'll stop at nothing to get him."

"Here is not the place for this conversation," Demon says gruffly as he lifts me up into his arms, carrying me bridal-style, as if I weigh nothing, to the door. He shows no signs of exertion as he carries me up the stairs. In the main room I look around eagerly, but there's no sign of Theo, just a few men drinking or with their arms draped around women who might as well be naked for what little they're wearing. A fog of cigarette smoke makes me worried for my son's lungs, but Demon might be the only person who can help me.

It's time I tell him the truth.

Up another stairway and I start to worry about his back, but it's as if he's carrying a feather, not a woman who could never be called skinny, and who's still bearing weight gained through pregnancy. Down to the end of a corridor, and then to a room on the left. He puts my feet on the ground but still keeps one arm around me as he reaches into his vest for a key. When he finds it, he places it in the lock.

"Worried people might steal your stuff?" After my initial surprise that he keeps the door locked, I don't wonder about it. The men here are criminals, after all.

"Nah, worried about Bitch making herself at home."

Well, the thought that Demon has to fight the women off shouldn't, and doesn't, shock me. But the fleeting pain the thought brings is unexpected.

Then we're inside. I have a second to appreciate the tidy, but very masculine, room, before Demon points me toward the bed. As I hover, unsure whether to stand or sit, he pulls up his desk chair, turning it around before he places his ass on the seat, his arms folded over the back.

"Vi. I reckon there's a lot I don't know. Supposition can be dangerous, so why don't I let you get it all out? I won't jump to judgement until you've finished."

"You did earlier," I tell him, as I perch on the edge of the bed, "and you're assuming there's judgement to be made." I've already been in front of a jury who didn't believe me. Why should Demon be different?

He actually looks chided, but then defends himself, "There's wrong things done for the right reasons, and right things done for wrong. Can't help but feel what you did isn't right, but I'm comin' to doubt you've got no feelin's. Tell me straight. How d'you feel about the kid?"

That's easy to answer. "I love him with all that I am. There's nothing more important to me than Theo."

He nods, slowly, as if re-evaluating everything he's thought up to now. Then he lets out a long sigh. "Think this is going to be a long session. You want a drink?"

"A water? I'm, er," I glance down, drawing his attention to my leaking boobs, so quickly look back up. "I'm still breastfeeding."

"The kid going to be alright with bottled shit?"

"*Theo*," I correct haughtily, "is going to be fine. He's a greedy little bugger; I supplement him with formula every day." I want to go to him, but Demon talking about bottles suggests at least he's not going hungry. Mind you, if he was, I'd expect him to be brought to me. When he wants to be fed, his cries soon become deafening.

"Theo," he repeats as though chastised. "Any particular reason you named him what you did?"

I shake my head as he stands, opens a mini-fridge and extracts two bottles. One of water, one of beer. "Not really. I liked the name. It means 'God-given'; I suppose that's what I think he is. Never expected him or..." *wanted him*, I complete in my head.

He reseats himself and nods as though he's plucked the words out of my head. "Talk to me, Violet. How much of what you told me the other day was a lie?"

"None of it," I reply, shocked. "It's true, I lost my job. Dad died, I came back here. I had been planning to return to New York, but I couldn't go straight back. I needed to find a new job first. Then, when I saw how Mom was, I knew I had no choice but to stay here instead. She went downhill fast when Dad had gone. She'd found him, you see, when he collapsed. I think the shock was the last straw."

"What's wrong with her?"

"Pre-senile dementia." Such innocuous words for something which sucks the soul out of a person, leaving behind nothing but an empty shell.

Another rise and dip of his chin, encouraging me to continue.

"I needed to find a well-paying job here. Vicky was already helping out, said she could do more hours if I was bringing the money in."

"You studied business management or some such shit, didn't you?"

It's my turn to nod. "I majored in art but realising I might find it hard to earn a living doing what I love, I took courses in business studies alongside. Anyway," I pause, gathering the strength to tell him the cold facts calmly. "I told you the other day I was taking what jobs I could, while looking for something more suitable. Thought I'd found something when I answered an ad for a manager, seemed something I could turn my hand to. By then I was starting to get desperate, I'd had a few interviews, but was never called back. I knew it wasn't the ideal job, but it was more like the kind of money I hoped to be earning."

His eyebrow rises as he sees me bite my lip. My hands clench together and begin to twist in my lap. I allow myself a moment to watch his throat work as he swallows his beer, then, when he puts the bottle back down, I resume.

"I had an interview with the person who introduced himself as the owner. It seemed to go well. A day later, I had a phone call, and he invited me out for a drink." Seeing his quick look, I hurriedly correct any mis-assumption, "It was a business meeting. The job was mine; apparently, he just wanted to go over some details."

The look on his face, his intense doubting eyes on mine, is familiar. No, the jury hadn't believed me, either. It makes me sound so naïve, which I was.

CHAPTER SIX

Demon

That it's gut-wrenchingly hard for her to tell her story is clear. That it's going to be equally difficult for me to hear is also true. So far I'm reading she was gullible, used. Why should she have street-smarts? She wasn't brought up the same way as I. Nathan and I shielded her, protected her, when perhaps we should have explained how the world works. When Nathan had gone, I should have kept tabs on her, should have fucking known she was back in town. Should have checked up on Nathan's kin, not assumed that, as they were the same age as my parents, that they'd have been jogging along just fine. I should have been there for her.

What she's been through in the past few months? I should have been there beside her. If I had known, what she's going to say next might not have occurred. One thing I've already changed my mind on, there's no doubt she loves the kid. She truly believes handing him off like she'd done was the best she could do. I'm beginning to suspect there's a whole load of pain on someone's horizon, but I'm going to have to coax her to tell me whose it is.

Her eyes are red and swollen, tears still glistening where they hadn't all dried, but it doesn't detract from her ethereal beauty that remains visible underneath. When I'd carried her, she'd melded perfectly to my body. When I'd held her against me, it was all I could do to keep my cock under control. It's getting harder and harder to remind myself she's Nathan's kid sister, someone completely off-limits. I suspect she'd be disgusted if she knew exactly how the man she looks up to really wants to comfort her. I'll push all those selfish thoughts out of my mind, then do what I can to help her. After that I'll send her on her way with a promise that I'll be there as a big brother, be an uncle to her kid. Now she's got no family to speak of, I can at least step up and do that.

But first I've got to know what I'm fighting. I wish she'd drink something stronger than water, it might help her get this painful memory out. That milk drying on her t-shirt, the reminder she's ripe and fertile is not a turn off for some reason. In fact, it's hard to keep my eyes on her face and not react like Theo would most likely do, and reveal my hunger for a taste. What the fuck is happening to me? A lactating woman with a kid attached has never attracted me in the least. I'd laugh if my mirth wasn't sure to upset her; if she guessed the real reason, that is.

"Go on," I encourage, croakily, having to cough to clear my throat.

"I went for the meeting." Her eyes close. In memory? Or does she not want to see my expression? "I dressed smartly, nothing sexy. I was looking for employment, not preparing for a night on the town. I wore a suit jacket matched with a knee-length pencil skirt. It was grey, and my shirt was white."

The unimportant details are either helping her focus or justifying what happened next wasn't her fault. I have no doubt in the matter. Girl can walk around naked, but if she says she's not interested, a man should take note. Even our sweet butts can refuse our attentions if they're having an off night and are not in the mood. Though, too many refusals and they'd be out on their ass; we're paying them to put out after all.

This time the pause is lengthy. "What happened?" I prompt.

"I accepted a small glass of wine, drank it slowly. He took me through business hours, the days I was expected to work. I asked a few details on what the job entailed, and that's when he became a bit vague. It didn't strike me as suspicious; he brushed it off as stuff I could learn on the job."

"Were you attracted to him? Show him any interest?"

"No, I did not." She sounds and looks adamant. "If you must know, I thought he was a sleaze. But beggars can't be choosers, and no one needs to like their boss to go to work." When I raise my chin in acknowledgement, she carries on, "I finished my wine. There didn't seem anything more that needed to be said. I stood to go, he told me to wait there as he was going to the bathroom, and that he'd be back and see me out to my car. Just sounded like a gentleman. He was gone before I could tell him there was no need. He returned shortly after, carrying another two drinks. Again, it wasn't a huge glass, and I knew I'd be alright to drive. I didn't feel I could refuse. I'd just agreed to take the job after all. He said it was a celebratory gesture."

A second drink which she hadn't seen poured. "He roofied you."

Her lips purse. "He did."

"Do you remember any of it?"

The blood drains from her face. I feel a bastard for pushing her, but I can't stop asking for details. "Vi, tell me."

"I don't remember. Not... not that part. I was sore the next morning. I, er, woke in his bed." Her face has paled even further. "I guessed what had happened. I accused him of rape. He said I'd come onto him, and that he'd done me the favour of taking me to bed. He wasn't bothered I'd accused him, he... he just laughed and said no one would ever believe it. That he hadn't particularly enjoyed it, and that after all that, I wasn't someone he wanted working for him and hadn't got the job. Then he booted me out."

He's dead. He's fucking dead. No two ways about it. I won't do it fast, nah, I'll take my time. When he's begging for death, I'll start all over again.

My fists clench and unclench, and I draw in a deep breath, then another, in a vain attempt to calm myself down. Eventually I can ask, keeping my tone even, "Did you report it?" If only I'd stayed close to her, we wouldn't be having this conversation now. *If I'd been around, the fucker would have been dead the next day.*

"Not then, no. I was in shock. I believed him, you see, that I couldn't back up my story. I was in a hell of a state. Vicki came the day after; I didn't think she was working until the day after that. I was as confused as hell. Must have been walking around in a daydream. When I eventually pulled myself together and could think, I realised I'd heard Rohypnol, or whatever he used, doesn't stick around in your system long. I was drinking with him voluntarily and left with him. No one knew I was interviewing for a job, there had been no other staff in the office. The bartender? What would he have seen? A girl who couldn't hold her drink. I got tested, I was clean, I thanked my lucky stars for that and that I couldn't remember the details, and promised myself never to get in that position again." Her voice is trembling. She'd been affected much more than she's letting on, but like she dealt with the death and otherwise loss of her parents, she's struggling to be practical and strong. My heart bleeds for her, my brain has new respect for her.

Now her lips purse, this time in determination. Unable to stop myself, I reach for her hand. "It didn't work, did it? However you tried to forget it, you couldn't. Shit like that stays with you, Vi." I've had my recent experience with Moira to realise it remains with you forever, that it never fades from your memory even after almost four decades have passed. The circumstances were different, but still the horror would be retained in the back of your mind. Especially with a constant reminder. Like I'd been there to remind Mom, Vi had Theo. I stare at her. "You weren't a virgin, were you?" At the side-to-side motion of her head, I continue, "You weren't a virgin, but you had sex against your will. By a man who should never have taken advantage of you. By someone who had to drug you to get you into bed." I tap her forehead. "I'd bet good money you still have nightmares."

Her eyes fix on me, surprised at my level of understanding. Perhaps a few months back I wouldn't have been able to comprehend how being taken advantage of like that, used without giving her consent, would make a woman feel. But I did know; it had happened to my mom. Only recently I'd had to come to terms myself that I was a product of rape, had had to delve down deep inside me to examine whether I carry any traits of my true bloodline, dealing with the knowledge the man who'd sired me was a rapist.

Having had to do it myself, knowing that Theo might go through something similar when he's older, briefly I wonder whether I could one day help her son come to terms with his background, then dismiss the notion immediately. Violet and Theo will probably be far away by then, living their own lives, having nothing to do with an outlaw biker. That's the gift I aim to give them, a chance to be free from fear, and a leg up in life. I've got some money saved—what does a confirmed bachelor who lives in the compound have to spend it on? I've three bikes already, that's more than enough when I can only ride one at a time.

A tear rolls down her cheek. My impulse is to wipe it away, but my fear is I wouldn't stop there. I gentle my voice as I ask, "When did you find out you were pregnant? And more importantly, how did he find out? Why did you tell him?" I'm burning to know who it was, my brain already questioning which method to use when I take him out. Not a bullet, no, that would be far too easy. But I need to know the extent of his crimes first. Once she gives me a name, it will be hard to refrain from immediate action.

Her head moves again, this time, up-and-down. "As I said, I tried to blank it out, tried not to think about it, tried to forget what had happened. Obviously I stayed well away from that part of town. I didn't want to risk seeing him, it would only have reminded me how stupid I'd been. Mom was getting steadily worse, even Vicky was having trouble dealing with her on the worst days, so I told myself I'd hold off on getting a job as she needed me. Vicky started to come in everyday whether I paid her or not. Dad had left some savings; I tightened my belt to eke out what I had. It wasn't too bad." A quick self-deprecating grin fleetingly appears. "I'd had enough experience of being a student, then struggling to maintain the apartment in New York on just my wage."

A quick blast of anger. I should have been there to help her. Nathan wouldn't have allowed her to struggle.

"I was so taken up by Mom. Taking her to doctor's appointments, desperate to find something that could help her, but whatever they could do wasn't enough. She continued that downward spiral. I was fit and well. When my next period was lighter I didn't take notice, just thought it was the change in diet —I'd cut out a lot of meat to save money. I had a second too. There was no warning signs at all. It wasn't until the third didn't appear that I began to get worried. Even then, I didn't consider I was pregnant, thought looking after Mom was stressing me out." Her mouth opens and closes. I wonder how much she's filtering, how much she doesn't want to tell me. "By the time I admitted it could be a possibility, I was four months along. Sixteen weeks." Her teeth worry her lip. Another feeling like a blow to my gut as I realise how much she'd gone through alone. "I didn't know what to do. Because I'd been raped, my doctor explained my options to me. It wasn't too late for an abortion, here it's permissible up to twenty-six weeks, but Planned Parenthood has a limit of nineteen weeks. I was so close. I had the thought in my head

I'd never be able to forget what had happened if I continued the pregnancy." A small smile crosses her face. "Then I saw Theo on the ultrasound. He was a baby, not an alien growing inside me."

Pausing, she picks up the water and drinks some. "I knew then, the only way forward was to suppress the memories of how he came into being. If I proceeded, Theo was going to be mine, no one else's. I would be a single mom." Another sip from the bottle, and a look of determination. "He carried my blood, his grandparents', and Nathan's. I was going to bring him up right. so nothing was there of his sperm donor. I told Vicky; she was great, really supportive." A short mirthless laugh, "Of course I told Mom, but there were only brief periods when she acknowledged she was going to be a grandmother. My pregnancy was easy. The birth? Well, I'd rather not go into that. Not something I'd undertake again lightly."

Why am I concerned at that? It's my turn to narrow my lips as I search for an answer. Nathan would have wanted his sister to have children, that's all. I'm looking out for her like a big brother.

"You told—him?"

"Of course I didn't," she snaps. "I wanted nothing from him. No money, no help, and definitely no involvement. It never crossed my mind. What woman would want such a monster to have any influence over their child?"

I can understand that. My mom certainly didn't. Not that she had the chance. Hellfire had wasted no time killing the man who had raped her. But it's not too much of a stretch to think had things been different, she'd have thought much the same way as Vi.

"But he knows now." My brow creases as she nods. "How and when did he find out?"

A mirthless snort of laughter. "By accident. One day he saw me heavily pregnant and approached, and quickly put two and two together. He knew I wasn't the kind of woman to sleep around, and, as part of the job interview process, I'd told him I hadn't a partner." Her cheeks grow red again, this time with pinpricks of anger. "I tried to lie, told him I was large for this stage in the pregnancy, that it was nothing to do with him. But he laughed it off. Said it was easy to prove with a simple blood test when the baby was born. I was so scared. The baby was mine, not his. Who'd want a man like that anywhere near a kid?"

Why the fuck hadn't she sought help? Come to me? But why should she? I'd had no physical contact for nine years, didn't even know she was in Pueblo. It follows she didn't know where I was either, and, as I hadn't followed up on my promise to Nathan, probably hadn't thought I'd care. She's so wrong. I care, too much. Her words are gutting me, and not just because of her relationship to my friend. What happened to her would be a nightmare for any woman.

"I went to the authorities then."

Her comment surprises me. So does the look on her face.

She nods to confirm it. "I hired an attorney. Not that I could afford the best, but Vicky helped. The first attempt was to get him convicted of rape. In Colorado, all parental rights are blocked if there's a rape conviction."

"But he wasn't convicted?" If he had been, she'd have nothing to worry about.

"No. His story against mine, just as I'd always thought. I had my whole personal history laid out in that courtroom. I'd been a student, Dave." I let her use of my government name pass. "Yeah, I'd had one-night stands, and he had the money to investigate me thoroughly. There were snide glances exchanged with the judge, which led me to believe there was something between them. The case was dismissed."

"With no conviction, you couldn't deny him parental rights?" That doesn't sound right to me. Okay, so if a man impregnates a woman he's got some responsibility and should pay for his mistake, but to claim rights to a child as a result of putting his cock where it wasn't wanted and where a pregnancy was never intended? Not only had he violated her body that night, but that violation continued for nine months as she'd carried his child. As it's still continuing, the now drying t-shirt bearing witness to that.

"I could, but only if I could prove his involvement wasn't in the best interest of the baby. It was easier to deny he was the father. With the background he'd concocted for me during the rape case, I thought it would work."

One look at her face shows me it didn't. "Who is he, Vi?"

She's reluctant to tell me. "Someone no one in their right mind would want near a child. Even my attorney backed off when he started looking into him. Yeah, I took him back to court. He came over as a well-monied and connected man, I came over as a slut with loose morals. The judge believed him over me and awarded him rights."

"With no proof he was the father? You have to share parenting with him?" My teeth grind together and it's hard getting the words out.

She gives that laugh again, the one lacking humour. "Wednesday, before I met you, I was served with notice. I don't understand why, but he's going for full custody."

I shudder at the look of total fear that crosses her face. Her teeth seem to clench before she continues, then the words tumble out one after the other.

"I couldn't let him have Theo, and after my experiences in court, knew he would win if he took me back there. Somehow he'd got hold of the story of my mother burning Theo. He had access to the medical records." Her eyes rise to mine. "He's a monster, Demon. That's what I've found out about him. Anyone else caring for Theo would be better than him."

"That's why you left Theo?" Her palpable terror had clearly led to her taking drastic action. What she'd done starts to make sense.

"I was in a hurry. Knew we both had to disappear, that Theo had to go somewhere where his parentage could never be traced. I researched on the internet, found a woman who'd take him; she knew a family who was having trouble finding a child through normal channels. A same-sex family. It seemed legit; we all know how difficult it is for people who live a different lifestyle to legally adopt. I didn't hand over his birth certificate, she didn't know his name. Once she'd taken him, even I would have had difficulty finding him again."

Violet loves Theo. She's assured me of that. I stare at her, unable to comprehend how scared she must have been. She'd give up her son, knowing that would be the last she'd see of him. Just who is this man that she'd risk the child's future like that? Biting my tongue, knowing she doesn't need me to point out the holes in her plan, that anything could have happened to him. Any story could have been fabricated and Vi in her desperation would have believed it. Theo could have been trafficked. The thought makes me go cold.

"I'm supposed to arrange an unsupervised visitation. I've been putting it off, obviously. How could I take Theo to him and leave him there? I was terrified his father would swoop in and take him away. I had to do something and fast. I suspected I wouldn't get him back." Her hands wave uselessly. "There was nothing else I could do. Just hope that whoever adopted Theo would be a good parent."

A cold feeling settles inside me. I've a feeling I don't want to know, but am driven to ask, "What were *you* intending to do, Vi? Where were *you* going to go?"

She's so quiet I don't think she's going to answer. Then when she speaks, I struggle to hear the answer.

"I was going to disappear and never come back."

That cold feeling becomes ice. "He'd have looked for you, found you if he'd had the contacts you're suggesting."

There's no attempt at evasion as she looks straight into my face. "I'd already got rid of my phone and got a new number. He wouldn't have been able to track that I'd gone to Canon City; he'd have no clue as to where to start looking for Theo."

"*You*, Vi. What were *you* going to do?"

She shrugs. "You can't get information from a dead woman."

If I'd felt cold before, now I'm completely frozen. This man cheated her, raped her, threatened to take her baby, and because of him, she was going to take her own life. My anger is so great I can hardly get the words out.

"His name, Vi. Tell me his fuckin' *name*."

CHAPTER SEVEN

Violet

Again, my shoulders rise and fall. I don't know if a biker moves in the same circles as the man who raped me. It's possible. I'm wary what he'll do once he knows. I'd been so delighted at being called for an interview, I hadn't looked into the man who was doing the hiring, hadn't known anything about the man who subsequently drugged and raped me. Then, immediately after he'd abused me, I'd tried to forget him completely. But my eyes had been opened when I had no choice but to take him to court. That dreadful experience where he escaped without a further blot on his black character while mine was forever tarnished. Angry, I'd wanted to know who I was dealing with, and had done my research. Enough to learn I'd gotten involved with the wrong man.

Demon going after him wouldn't do anything to help, and could make matters worse. The man's powerful, he comes from an influential family. I'd rather not tell him. If I do and he knows him, I daren't hope that he'll have the sense to walk away from a fight he wouldn't be able to win. I already know that kind of man isn't him.

There's a certain lightness, now I've told him everything that before only Vicky had known. I'd prefer him to remain in ignorance, but realise, having come this far, I can't keep the name secret. The court cases are a matter of public record, and he'd soon be able to find out for himself.

My eyes find his. He's so still, the only movement is his chest rising and falling.

"Demon, if I tell you, please, please don't do anything stupid."

"His name, Violet." His tone is persistent.

I take a breath, and a leap into the unknown, wishing I didn't have to involve him. "Angelino Silvestri."

I'd been hoping for a simple nod to register the name and put it into his memory. What I get is far worse. His statue-like posture changes in a flash as he leaps to his feet and starts pacing the room while saying 'fuck' repeatedly and increasingly louder. Then, sweeping back his hair, he rounds on me, his fingers pinching the bridge of his nose.

"What the fuck were you thinkin', Vi? Even going to him for a job in the first place? What fuckin' type of a job was he offering?"

Again, I raise and lower my shoulders. He's probably never been in the position I'd found myself in. Has never known what it's like to be unemployed or to exist taking jobs that may as well advertise their rates in cents. Having taken over the MC from his father, he's more likely to have been born with the biker version of a silver spoon in his mouth. His parents and siblings are all alive and healthy. What does he know about dealing with death and loss, and the struggle to put food on the table?

"I was going to manage part of his casino."

His mouth gapes. "You know what type of place that is?"

"Well, I do now." Like his, my eyes flare. "I never went anywhere like that when I lived here before. I was too young. You can't imagine how pleased I was to get an interview. I wasn't going to be working tables, the job was nine-to-five in an office."

It was only afterwards I'd looked it up, googling and reading old news articles. It doesn't have a good reputation, though nothing's ever been proven against the Silvestri family who run it. I continue to defend myself, "It was a chance to at least give a nod to my business degree. A day job, ordering supplies, dealing with staff issues. I wouldn't have been involved in anything else."

"Christ, Vi. You can pick 'em, can't you? He's one powerful man in Pueblo. The word 'shady' was invented for him. Do you know what they call him?" He shakes his head. "The man you..." His eyes meet mine. "Christ, Vi. You didn't have a chance. His name makes men shake."

"Then I'll go back to Plan A," I snap. "You think I don't know that now, Demon? Why do you think I wanted Theo far away from him? A man like that doesn't want a son, he wants a commodity."

Suddenly he's back, standing in front of me, then folding to his knees almost in supplication before me. "Shit, Vi, I'm sorry. Of course you weren't to fuckin' know. These are the type of lowlifes that *we* deal with, not someone like you. And you can put any thought of plans A, B or fuckin' C right out of your head. You and Theo are now under our protection, and I'll make sure nothing happens to you, or to him. Okay? I swear I'll keep you safe."

I stare at this man in front of me, the man I'd looked up to all my formative years. It's like seeing Nathan all over again, my big brother who'd tease me mercilessly, but had always been there when I needed him. *Could I trust Demon?* At least now he knows what I'm facing. "You'll help me get away? With Theo?" For the first time today, well, in weeks really, I let a little hope creep into my voice.

"Angel Silvestri has got a debt to pay, Vi. He's not going to get away with hurting you, or with making your life hell. You won't have to worry about him. I'll fuckin' kill him."

Rapidly I move my head side-to-side. "You can't, Demon!" I

cry out, envisaging him dead or languishing in prison. "Nathan wouldn't have wanted that. Either I run, or we find the right way to fight him. Maybe a better lawyer…"

"Vi, you can't treat a sub-human as anything more than an animal."

But all I can see is Nathan. He fought for this country, believed in the law. Surely, if someone was on my side, there's a way to do this? A right way. A good lawyer, though, that would cost money. I press my lips together, then back down. "I'm sorry, Demon. Of course, fighting Angelino would be expensive. There will be funds from the sale of the house…"

"You've got no money, Vi. Everything is going toward making your mom's life easier." He waves his hand. "You don't have to worry about money again. I've got enough for both of us."

Now it's me who's standing, pacing, then turning to face him once more. "Both of us? Demon, there's no you and me." But those three words have caused feelings I've not had for a very long time, dragging up a memory of him and me together being all I'd once dreamed of. Even in the depths of my despair, drawing forth an admission that I keep to myself, I still desire this man. *What kind of father would he make for Theo?*

"Of course I don't mean it that way." Demon's also standing, his dark eyes blazing as he dashes my embryonic dreams into smithereens. "I need to make good on my promise to Nathan. You might have lost one brother, but it's time I stood up and stepped up in his place. Nathan wouldn't have wanted to see you needing anything, you know that. So you treat me as you would have done your big brother. You want something? You come to me."

It's like a bucket of cold water being thrown over me. I'm twenty-five years old. Our ten-year age difference was massive when I was a child; now it's nothing at all. Yet I'll never be anything more than a little girl in his eyes. I'm not crazy, I'm not going to throw his offer of help back at him; I'd be a fool to do that, and I've my son to think of now, my pride can take a back seat. I need to grab the chance of Theo and I being together, accept Demon's help to rid me of the spectre of Angelino and his threat hanging over us. I must just never, ever lead Demon to suspect for one minute that I wish he would play a role very different to that of a big brother. He'd only laugh in my face.

Demon's got his head in his hands. I can almost see the wheels turning as he tries to work out what to do. All I want is to go to my son, who I'd thought never see again after I'd left him earlier today, to seize the opportunity to hold him again, the chance I didn't expect to have.

"I've told you everything," I start, in clipped tones. "You know everything I did was to protect Theo, not to harm him. Now I'd like to go to my son." And get him away from the old lady or whatever scantily-clad woman is mollycoddling him right now. My mouth curves slightly. While Theo is too young to be influenced by a nearly-naked female form, he wouldn't be averse to pulling down a revealing top and trying to find a nipple. Some whore might be in for a surprise.

Demon looks up, his hands dragging down his face. He considers for a moment, then nods. "Yeah. I'll take you to Theo. Gonna take a minute to decide how this is going to play out, but for now, Vi, you're staying put. Told you we'd protect you, okay?" He frowns. "Need to know what the fuck's behind this. Why you, and why the kid?"

Yes. Questions I'd been asking myself. I'd settled on that Angelino just wanted something he considered his, and only because I'd denied him. Maybe he wasn't used to being told no. But whatever the reason behind it, he wants Theo.

Now that Demon's given in, I'm suddenly uncertain about venturing into the clubhouse, remembering the looks of animosity that had been directed at me before. I don't blame them. Since Angelino had told me he wanted, and was going to get, full custody of my son, I'd been in a blind panic. Relaying my thought processes to Demon has made me see all the holes in what I had planned. My first impulse was to get Theo somewhere safe, and I hadn't been able to see how I could provide that safety myself. But if I heard of a woman giving her baby to strangers, without understanding her distraught state of mind, I'd be critical of her too. "Your..." *What do I call them?* "Men. They hate me."

He pulls himself up to his full, not inconsiderable height, and looks down at me. "Vi, no one hates you. I'm the president. You needn't fear anyone here. They'll do what I say, and if that's to treat you with respect, that's what they'll do."

He seems to have complete control over them. I'm not surprised, he's an imposing man. Strangely, growing up I'd been more in awe of his father. Now they seemed to have switched places, Hellfire being the more temperate one. My observation leads me to ask, "Are they afraid of you?"

He snorts. "They're afraid of losing their patch. Now come on. Let's go find the kid."

That's music to my ears. I wait impatiently while he goes through the ritual of locking his door, wondering again who this bitch is who would otherwise take up residence, suppressing the ridiculous instinct to discover just who and scratch out her eyes. By his side, together we retrace our steps back down to what is obviously their clubroom.

The first thing I see is Theo, sitting on a fully-clothed young woman's lap, twiddling her hair around his fingers. She's much younger than what I expected, then I stop thinking about her age as I wince on her behalf when I see him give a sharp tug, but admire the way she's not fazed and competently deals with it, gently prying open his fingers and pulling away the strands with a laugh.

Demon speaks quietly, "That's Jayden. She's Pal's. She's going to be training to be a nanny or some such shit. Got a lot of experience with kids. I know you'll want to do everything for Theo yourself, but don't be afraid to ask her for help. As you can see, she's a natural."

My first instinct is to turn any assistance down, but the events of today, the emotional wringer I've been through, the expectation I'd not be alive tonight and certainly not with my son, and, not least, the draining conversation with Demon, has taken it out of me. I want to hold my son, but if Jay's going to be around to help, I won't refuse.

As I stand by Demon's side, quizzical and assessing looks are being thrown at me. Demon clears his throat. "Brothers. Need to have church in a few. Violet's going to stay here with Theo." He then gives a pointed look toward the taciturn man who'd brought me here. He clearly gets an unspoken message and raises his chin back.

As the other men start to rise and move off in the same direction, I assume they're following Demon's strange instruction. I'd never have taken any of them to be religious. The man who'd tied my hands and pushed me into the car, though, he stays put, his legs apart, hands clasped behind his back. His eyes meet mine, brows raised in challenge. *Guess I've got a jailer*. Not that I care or would try to escape. At least here, and at least for tonight, Theo and I can be together, relax and feel safe.

Theo spies me, and his hands reach out. I start moving forward when Demon suddenly shouts, his voice full of panic, "Stop. No."

Perplexed, I halt, *He's letting me hold my son, surely?* Then, with a sigh of relief, I grin. He's not looking at me, his eyes are fixed on something else. One of the biggest cats I've ever seen in my life is approaching Jayden, who's holding my baby.

"Pishk, get out of here!" Demon urges, flapping his hands, but making no move forward.

Fickle as ever, Theo turns his attention away from me and onto the approaching feline, his chubby hands quickly changing direction as he clenches and releases his fingers in a 'come here' gesture the cat seems to understand. It inches nearer, rubbing its back along the side of the couch, idly flicking its tail left then right.

"Get out of here, Bitch." The young man sitting beside Jay, her man Pal, I take it, slowly, careful to make no sudden movements, gets to his feet and sidles away. Feeling concerned, I wonder why he's avoiding touching the cat. And why the hell he called it 'Bitch'. Can't he see it's not a dog?

Nothing can hold me back from Theo any longer. As I step forward, Demon's hand shoots out, but I'm too fast for him to pull back. Two more steps and I'm kneeling on the floor reaching out for Theo, while the cat closes the gap and, purring loudly, starts to rub its face against me.

Jay passes Theo over; he comes into my arms, immediately reaching out and grabbing a handful of fur. There's an audible gasp from all around the room, a silence as though everyone's holding their breath, then a general sigh as the cat sits beside us and starts licking her fur, daintily holding up one paw to clean it.

Theo is entranced.

Jay's grinning broadly, then chuckling up at her man. "Best you scoot along. We've got Bitch to protect us."

Now the name registers. Bitch? Is this who, or rather, what, Demon didn't want in his room? Doesn't he like pets? I frown. He helped rescue the squirrel all those years back, so that seems odd.

"See you later, Doll." Pal reaches over as though to give Jay a kiss. Immediately the feline stands, arches her back and hisses.

Pal doesn't complete his movement toward the girl, but steps away with his hands held up in defeat and a rueful smile on his face.

Then, one by one, the men disappear.

"What was that about?" I kiss Theo's head, holding him to me, breathing in that baby aroma I didn't expect to fill my nostrils again.

"Bitch," Jay giggles, pointing at the now settled cat. "She hates men. Women, and presumably babies, are fine. She can be really vicious with the opposite sex." She eyes me for a moment, then her hand moves from Bitch and indicates Theo. "I fed him a bottle, he took it well. Are you still feeding him yourself?"

Her attention draws mine to the dried milk on my clothes, realising I need a clean shirt, but that's the least of my worries for now. I answer her question, "He's fine with bottles. I can't produce enough so he's used to them."

"I don't know where you'll be sleeping, but I got the girls to get this..." She points over to the other side of the room where there's a portable crib. "They got blankets, too."

"Couldn't find any with motorbikes on, but I'll have a look online."

"Oh, Titsy," Jay addresses one of the women who's nearly naked. "I doubt he'll notice as yet."

"Got to start them young," Titsy replies with a wink. "He's an absolute sweetheart." She nods over at Theo who, blissfully unaware anything significant happened today, is dropping off in my arms.

Apart from Jay, there's an older woman hovering in a doorway looking at me curiously. The barely-dressed woman called Titsy is standing with two other under-clothed girls. Demon is presumably setting the men straight, it's up to me to make peace with the women.

"I didn't abandon him because I didn't want him," I tell them, my tone serious. "I didn't know what else to do."

"Hey, hon. Demon wouldn't have let you near him if there was any worry about that," the older woman speaks, crossing the room. "I'm Jeannie, by the way. My old man's Bomber. You don't need to explain yourself to us. We're," she points to herself and Jay, "old ladies. We don't need the details. And as for the rest," now she indicates the other women, "they do what they're told."

Titsy leans over to Jeannie. "Not much difference between you and us as I see it," she says, jokingly.

Jeannie, glares, then gently bats her with her arm, and her eyes fix on me. "Wealth of difference between an old lady and a whore." Then she winks. "But yeah, we do as we're told as far as the 'don't ask questions' goes."

"Club business," Jay starts.

Jeannie finishes, "isn't our business."

Whatever the reason, I'm relieved they're not going to give me the third degree. Right now I'm too worn out to go through it all again.

CHAPTER EIGHT

Demon

My brothers are curious, as they're entitled to be. I've brought Violet and Theo to the compound, and into their home, after all, and under extraordinary circumstances. But I can't leap as I want to and take Silvestri down without carefully thinking how best to handle him. There's no fucking doubt Violet has gotten involved with the completely wrong person, and I've promised to sort it, and that I will. But in between the time I got the story and now, while I've been waiting for the men to leave their businesses and return to the compound, I've had second thoughts. As they walk into church and take their seats, it dawns on me I'm unprepared and have called this meeting prematurely.

Tell them all of it, bring in my brothers, and there'll certainly be a war. One we're not prepared for.

I should have first considered taking Angel out on my own without getting the club involved, a hit for which I'd take full responsibility. If these men knew I was even considering that option, the club would not let me get away with it, and not just because I'm the president. They'd want to have my back. Nah, I think looking around, the only way I could do it alone is to leave them in the dark.

One thing I can't do is dismiss this roomful of men without saying anything. Though it's lame, to buy time, I decide to pretend it's just a normal meeting and that I haven't interrupted everyone's evening.

I bang the gavel. "Right, let's get this meeting started. When's the contract being signed for the new premises for the tattoo parlour? Any progress?"

"That's where you're starting?" My father, *brother* is sending me an incredulous look. "You call us in for a special meeting, then start as if it nothing unusual? Think we'd like to have an update on Violet and the kid."

Fuck. Of course that's the reason for this meeting, can't pretend otherwise. But not only am I belatedly considering tackling Angel on my own, looking around at their critical and inquisitive faces, I realise I'm also loathe to discuss Violet's painful truths and bring everything out into the open. I brazen it out, staring at Hellfire. "I'd say our new business, getting it up and running as soon as possible, is the most important item on the agenda. I propose we start with something that affects us all."

"As does the woman you've been questioning," Bomber, sitting beside Hell, insists.

"Yeah, Prez. Is she our prisoner or what?"

"You gave the kid back to her, Prez, is that wise?"

"Is this a meeting of MC members or the ol' ladies?" I snarl, ignoring the questions from Mace and Sparky. "Let's talk about business, and then I'll fill you in on what you need to know." I glare at Hellfire for raising it. He just shrugs, but one corner of his mouth is turned up. Yeah, he would appreciate not being in the hot seat.

"Any chance the kid is yours?" Thunder asks.

"No, there fuckin' isn't," I roar.

Unrepentant, he shrugs, holding up his hands. "Look, as your acting VP, I'm only askin' what everyone is thinkin'. Come on, Prez. I know there were personal reasons you wanted this bitch here. But you've brought her into our house. Can't blame us for being curious."

At the other end of the table, Hell raises his eyebrow. If I was to try to interpret the expression on his face, it's a mix between *I could have told you this would happen,* and *What are you going to do about it?*

Shit. I'm still finding my place at the head of this table. Someone has to lead the MC, and that's fallen to me. While I can well understand my brothers' curiosity, it's me who needs to take the helm. Heading into a fight, you can't decide which way is up by way of a democracy.

I'm just about to try and get the meeting back on track, when Bomber speaks.

"Prez, I speak for us all when I say we just want to help. All we know is there's a woman here who tried to abandon her kid. Not many of us are family men." He grins, that's an understatement. The only person who could ever qualify for that title is Hell. "But that doesn't mean we don't get concerned when someone walks away from a child." As I open my mouth, he continues without letting me speak, "Now, you've spoken to her, obviously decided she has good reasons. You might think we're getting up in business which you think is yours, but all we want to do is understand how we can make what's obviously a bad situation right."

I catch Thunder's eye. He's mouthing *VP* to me, but I shake my head, my own lips forming the words, *I've asked.* Yeah, I'd approached Bomber with a suggestion of him playing that role, but he'd turned me down, saying he wanted no such pressure at his age. He was content to ride at the back of the pack while he can still handle his big two-wheeler. Like it or not, Thunder will have to put up with sitting on my left for a while yet.

While he's there, I'd best listen to him. He thinks I need to explain. As it seems no one's going to leave the subject alone, I better just get on with it. Taking a deep breath, pushing my hastily aroused temper back into the box, I lean my elbows on the tabletop. As they settle in to listen, Mace gets out a packet of smokes, and lights up. When he passes them around, Sparky, Liz and Ink are the only other takers. Hell looks tempted but pushes the pack on when it gets to him.

"To understand, I have to give you some history," I start, as the air becomes tainted with smoke. "When I was a kid, I had a friend, a best friend, named Nathan Palmer. We were inseparable from the time we met and right through our teens, and remained close beyond that. At eighteen he signed up, joined the Marines. Wasn't a way out of a shit upbringing; he'd had a good family life. Being in the forces was all he'd ever talked about doing from when he was little more than a toddler. It was going to be his life, same way as all I'd wanted was to join the MC." I break off. Even though nine years have passed, getting out the next words remains hard. "He lasted eight years before a stray bullet took him out."

They'd been quiet, listening, but the silence becomes more intense for a moment, and serious looks come over their faces. If they hadn't done a tour themselves, most knew someone who had. Some of those hadn't returned, just like Nathan; some had, but as changed men. Ink's face has paled, his fingers tapping fast on the tabletop. His PTSD is mostly under control nowadays, but sometimes something can send him back.

"Nathan had a little sister," I resume, hastily moving on. "She was ten years younger than us, and an absolute pest." I soften my description with a smile. "She was fifteen, no, sixteen when he died. Well, to step back, when Nathan signed up, he wasn't stupid. Knew his life could be cut short. Made me promise to keep an eye on Violet if anything ever happened that meant he couldn't."

"I take it that woman out there is the sister?"

It's Hellfire who answers Bomber. "Yeah. That's Violet."

"So you've been watching out for her all these years?" Rusty, quite reasonably asks.

"Not closely enough," I admit, then come clean. "Actually

after the first few years, and when she moved to New York, I lost touch with her completely. Didn't know she'd come back to Pueblo a year and a half back. Not until I ran into her by accident, last Wednesday. When we'd been at the mall, Liz."

Lizard nods. "So that's why you hurried off. What, you met her, talked to her, knew something was wrong immediately, and put a prospect on her?"

"That about sums it up. I had a feeling, okay? Things just didn't seem right. I admit, it was part guilt from having been out of touch with her. I didn't know she'd returned, didn't know she had a kid, and while I was there, the way she treated him seemed off." Now I know she was pulling away, trying to do the impossible, turn off a mother's love. A gut reaction to a threat she'd received only that day.

There are frowns, anger. I realise I need to bring them up to date. They hadn't all been down in the basement when Vi had blurted it out. From my reaction, Thunder and Mace would have kept it to themselves. "Theo, the kid, was the result of a rape."

"Jeez," Pyro strokes his hand down his face. "Can understand why it might be hard to accept a kid..."

"She couldn't cope with the thought?" Bomber's eyes flare as he cuts into Pyro's statement. He glances toward Hell, then at me.

Before they all start joining the dots and coming up with the wrong picture, I cut them off. "That's not it. Problem is, the rapist walked free, and has claimed parental rights to the child." I go on to qualify it as Vi had explained to me. "If he'd been convicted, he wouldn't have been awarded anything. But, as he was cleared, he has every right to co-parent. Violet's view is that he's the last person on earth who should raise a child. Wednesday, just before I met her, he went one step further. Told her he was going for full custody. Served her with a court summons for the week after next."

Bomber's sucked in air. "Club has a history of dealing with

rapists," he says before I can stop him. "Reckon our way is best. When we going to kill him, Prez?"

His comment is echoed around the table. The night Moira, my mom, had been raped, Hellfire had been patched in, and Blackie had taken his last breath. But I'm going to have to tell them who they're dealing with. When I do, they'll vow to be behind me. What's most concerning, this battle may be one greater than we can afford to take on.

I glare at Bomber to silence him. "Violet's had a hell of a time of it recently. Her father died; that's why she came home. Her mother's brain has gone, she doesn't even recognise her daughter anymore, and has spells where she can be violent. She's all but homeless, as her house is up for sale to pay for her mom to be properly cared for in a home. On top of that, she had to deal with a rape and a pregnancy alone." I break off, then realise they need to know the full story. "She's lost twice in the courts: once when he was cleared of rape, and the second time when he was awarded co-parenting rights. She thought he'd be successful a fuckin' third time and declare her an unfit mother. I think you can say she wasn't thinking straight. Rather than let him get near Theo, she arranged a private adoption, one that couldn't be traced. Not doing things legal meant there'd be no paper trail to follow. Even she wouldn't know where Theo had been taken." As it had when I'd first heard it, a chill runs down my spine.

There's silence. "She'd prefer an unknown stranger to care for him, instead of his sperm donor?" Rusty asks at last, the first to break it.

"That plan has more holes than a piece of mesh," Pyro puts in.

Paladin, who I have to remember comes from a club where babies are the norm not the exception, is looking disgusted. "Her story's a sad one, but there must have been something else she could do. How the fuck can a woman give up her child? She could have gone out of town, hidden herself and the baby."

"As I said," I start sticking up for her, "she was fuckin' desperate."

"That little girl's had so fuckin' much on her plate," Hell glares at Pal. "Her mind must have been all over the place."

"If this fucker's as bad as she thinks, could well be he'd find her, and use her to trace the kid. No one disappears completely," Cad puts in wisely.

I lower my head into my hands. "They do if they're dead."

Stunned silence greets my words.

"He'd kill her?" It's Hell who tries to clarify my meaning.

My eyes meet his. "She was going to do the job for him." *Dead women tell no tales.* I shudder, remembering the chilling way she'd said it. My eyes meet Paladin's, who seems to have been shocked into silence. I nod. "You were right, Pal, she knew she couldn't live without her son. But she thought she was doing the best for him. His sperm donor wouldn't have been able to find her and beat the truth out of her. If we hadn't been there, it would have been as if Theo had disappeared off the face of the earth."

No one speaks for a while as that settles in. Knowing my brothers, these fiercely protective men, they'll think as little of the solution Violet had come up with as I do myself.

"She gonna be yours?" Ink, quiet up to now, asks. Taking out his own pack of cigarettes, he passes them around.

I sit up with a jolt. "No, I told you. She's Nathan's little sister. Completely off-limits to me, and anyone else here. So get any ideas out of your head before they get planted." *As I should get it out of mine.*

"The question none of you are askin' is the one bit of info that the Prez should have started with," Hellfire states, his voice as deadly as when he used to sit in this chair. "Who is the piece of shit that got that little girl pregnant?"

As all eyes land on me, I'm not surprised it's my father who's gone straight to the heart of the matter. I raise my chin. He's not goading me, just taking me where I would have gotten to eventually.

"Hesitated to tell you this, Brothers, as this is a personal matter. Due to my debt to my friend, Violet's under my personal protection. I know you'll want to have my back, and this is somewhere I hadn't planned on asking the Satan's Devils to go." I pause, I've certainly captured their interest. "We have to be smart about this. No raiding party, we're circling the wagons until we have an airtight plan, and one that's a fuckin' improvement on Violet's. The rapist is Angel Silvestri." As I let the words leave my mouth, I look around the table, worrying I might have signed any of my brothers' death warrant. Or worse, the whole club's perhaps. The Silvestri organisation is not one any sane person would approach head-on. It's the local Mafia. Already mouths are forming the handle Angel goes by. *The Angel of Death*.

"I've wanted an excuse to go after that little shit for years," Rusty pronounces, his eyes gleaming as he nods at Bomber. His response is exactly the one I hadn't gone looking for or wanted.

"Hold up." I bang the gavel to get their attention. "No one's going after anyone."

"How can you say that, Prez?" Cad sits up straighter.

My fist hits the table. "This isn't a small street gang we can use our muscle on. This is organised crime. I'm not proposing stepping back and doing nothing. But think for a second what happens if we go after Angel? They'll come for us. I'm not convinced we can handle them."

"Prez is right," Mace puts in. "They heavily outnumber us. We know they've been itching to get rid of the club and take over our territory. One sniff that it's war, and we'll have a fight on our hands that we might not survive."

"This would have come to a head anyway, Prez. I was going to bring it up at the next church. They've been getting blasé, stepping on our toes. Found a load of needles behind Tits Up the other night. I have no proof but wouldn't be too much of a stretch to think someone's dealing inside. Been on the lookout, but not spotted anything yet." Ink looks annoyed. Since Taser has gone, he's taken over running the strip club.

"Hate to say it, Prez. But that might go for Devil's Pins too."

Dealing at the strip club was something that we've come up against and had to knock on the head before. The bowling alley, though, I like to think that has more of a family vibe. We pride ourselves that women feel comfortable enough to bring kids there on their own. Get a reputation for drugs and we'll lose a large chunk of our clientele.

Pinching the bridge of my nose, I ask, "They're crossing the boundaries?"

"We have an arrangement with them," Mace reminds everyone. "Goes back to the days when Furnace sat in that chair, Prez."

Hell raises his hand. "Sorry, Demon. Knew I was going to have to deal with them, but, well, other shit blew up and it took a back seat. If you want me to lead on this, I will. Shouldn't have left that shit for you."

There's the strange dynamics blowing up again. Hell's stepped down from the head of the table, but he's still here. If I accept his help, am I showing weakness that I'm not ready to be in the hot seat? Or am I failing if I let that possibility influence me? Hell has a wealth of knowledge and experience which I could tap into. As the previous VP and his right-hand man, I'm not entirely ignorant, but there are still matters where he probably knows more than me. I make do with raising my chin toward him. *Offer acknowledged, but not outrightly accepted.*

"I was stopped and searched a couple of days ago, Prez," Sparky interrupts. "Obviously wasn't carrying anything more than a bit of pot, but they were looking for something different."

"You suggestin' it's not just us noticing increased activity? You think there's more product moving into town?"

He might be our road captain, but when he thinks to use it, Sparky's got a good brain, and not just for planning routes.

"Heroin's cheap at the moment. So, yeah. Think the Silvestri might be upping their game."

Possibly getting ballsy with it.

Thunder's fidgeting and looks like he's trying to get my attention.

"Yeah, VP?"

He grimaces when I use the title. "Like Hell's handed the reins over to you, I've heard word Lucio has tapped Angel to take over from him. Out with the old, in with the new. Old man's getting on now. Could be the reason why we're seeing more movement. New hand might be flexing his muscles. It's likely if your girl hadn't given us reason to go up against the gang, might have had to put them back in their place in any event."

I raise my eyes to Hell. He shrugs. *Get on with it, boy. I'm not at that end of the table anymore.* Jeez. *Thanks a lot, Dad.* It's times like these I remember I really hadn't expected to have my ass in this chair for at least another few years. A moment of self-doubt while all eyes are on me.

Hell buys me the time to think. "Way the Mafia works is similar to us. Old man can put his weight behind his son, but it's the captains, the *capos*, that have the final say when they cast their votes for the new boss. Angel's underboss now, doesn't necessarily mean he'll step into his father's shoes."

Ignoring Hell's words, which are just useful information for now, I consider what the temporary VP's just laid on me. I don't like what he's said but admire the summation. Not for the first time I wish Thunder would take on the role permanently, but sergeant-at-arms is the most he wants to rise to. I could do with a good man by my side, as I'd been to Hell all these years, and Thunder would fill that spot admirably. His refusal, though, is final.

"Cad. Any more news about the new police chief?" While Sparky's stop could have been a coincidence, we can't rule out the MC could be the intended target.

"I've been keeping an ear to the ground. Nothing more has

come up. Like when I looked into his background, I reckon he's pretty straight. Nothing to say he's out to take us down. Any focus on us could just be incidental. If there's more product moving around, eyes could look our way for being responsible."

Raising my chin, I take the plunge, "We're clean. We don't run drugs. Well, not hardcore." We might dabble in a little weed, but Colorado was the first state to make that shit legal; there's no need to keep it under the radar unless we're shifting in quantity, which we don't normally do. It's in our charter, the club runs clean. Don't want members hooked on the hard stuff; men like that become unpredictable, their loyalty to a white powder topping that to their brothers. But we would have been happy enough to turn a blind eye to someone else's business. Up to the point it starts affecting ours, which seems to have now arrived. Dealing on our premises is a no-go.

"Leaving aside for the moment Violet and her problems, we would have respected the boundaries drawn up between us and the Mafia in Furnace's days, unless they bring trouble to our door. Looks like us and the cops might be on the same side wanting to halt the increase in flow."

There's an audible gasp around the table. "Team up with the cops?" Bomber half laughs and half scoffs. "And that would help your girl, how?"

A reasonable question. "If it can be proven that Angel is not a fit father, he'll have any parental rights taken away. And doing shit legally would mean Satan's Devils weren't going up against the Silvestri alone."

A general mistrust of the citizen world means my suggestion isn't jumped upon. But neither is it dismissed out of hand. They're right to be cautious. Talking to the cops could lead to them getting into our business, places we don't want them to go. It wouldn't normally be my go-to position, as I decide to explain.

"To help Violet out of her situation, we have to take Angel Silvestri out of the equation. Yeah, my preference is to send him to meet Satan. But I might have to wait for that satisfaction. The alternative is proving his criminal activity."

"Both brings risks to the club, Demon."

Thunder's right. They do. "That's why I said at the beginning, this is personal. A debt I need to stand up to and repay. My proposal is I take this on without club involvement."

"You're the prez, Demon. Don't see how you can do that. No one would believe you weren't speaking for the Devils."

"So, I step back down. Temporarily."

A strangled laugh from my left. "You don't have a permanent VP. I ain't going to be fillin' in for you."

My eyes automatically go to Hell. He shrugs and shakes his head. "Getting pretty comfortable sitting down this end of the table, Brother. Don't look at me."

Thunder's moving quickly. "Motion proposed that we're behind Demon. He ain't going to be doing anything alone."

"Seconded, Brother." Mace is quick on his toes. "We help Demon sort out this mess. And he ain't stepping away from anything."

All hands are suddenly raised in the air and one word is shouted and repeated "Aye".

A warm glow wars inside me with the cold of concern, a fear about what I might be leading them into. But slowly a smile glides onto my face. "Lemmings," I tell them, "fuckin' lemmings."

"Hopefully we won't reach the edge of that cliff," Thunder grins.

"Can I ask a question, Prez?" Cad looks thoughtful.

"Sure."

"We're talking about the fuckin' Angel of Death. How the fuck did he get off the rapist charge, and furthermore, prove himself such an upstanding citizen he was awarded parental rights? You proposed trying to do things legal. Seems the girl's already tried that and failed. Why do you think that route might work? How can we succeed when she didn't?"

I sigh. "She failed because everything was against her. It was a fucking date rape. Violet was drugged, only realised after. She was ashamed. She tried to put it out of her head until she found she was pregnant. It was only when he started making a play for the kid that she tried to fight it through the courts. Not reporting it at the time didn't work in her favour. Then Angel dug into her history, made the most of what he'd found. She's a normal red-blooded woman, had a couple of one-night stands." I frown, not liking that thought, but realise I'm being ridiculous. I never spend more than one night with any woman, but as I'm male, it doesn't count against my character.

"Why the fuck did she tell him it was his kid?"

"After money, I suspect," Buzz answers Pyro.

My hand hits the table. "You're wrong, she didn't. Wouldn't have taken his dirty money. She didn't say anything. He saw her pregnant and fuckin' guessed." And that's something else to worry about. Why he knew it was possible. *Fucker didn't use a condom.* "Made the assumption. To date, she's refused to have a DNA test done, but there's no doubt he's his. She hasn't been with anyone else. Bastard knows that even though she's told him different."

"Why don't you step up, Demon? Claim her and the kid."

CHAPTER NINE

Demon

Hell's suggestion seems to ring in the air after he said the words. The immediate response that comes to my lips is to tell him not to be so fucking stupid, that I've never heard anything so inane in all my life. Luckily, I snap my mouth closed before I can voice it. After all, isn't that what he did? He stepped up when Moira had been raped and became pregnant. Okay, so our father had been responsible, but I have a feeling it wouldn't have mattered. The big difference, though, was that Moira was already his though he hadn't yet officially claimed her.

He'd raised me as his son for thirty-five years. It's only in the last few months I'd discovered the remarkable truth. My reaction had been to replace that pedestal he'd always occupied by reason of being my father with one even higher. To step up like he did requires a very special type of man, setting the bar too impossibly high for anyone else to reach.

It's why I'd not given voice to my immediate response. He's proposing I follow in his footsteps. Because of his actions, I can't follow my first impulse and dismiss his suggestion out of hand, or not without giving it some thought. There's no similarity between the circumstances. I might be attracted to Violet, what man with a working dick wouldn't? Though my cock wouldn't turn any offer down, I know me, and all I could offer is a one-night stand. Anyway, she looks on me as a brother; she'd be horrified to know what's on my mind.

Violet isn't the woman I'd earmarked to be my partner in life —I haven't yet met the woman who'd fill that spot—whereas Hell had already been in love with Mo. I owe nothing to Vi but a promise I'd made to her brother. I, at least, carried the same blood as Hell. He might have raised me as his son, yet I'm his true sibling. Hell also carried guilt that it was his and Moira's connection that had made her a target for Blackie, whereas I played no part in Violet's abuse. Except, if I'd been looking out for her, maybe I could have stopped her making that mistake. A big if, and one I don't feel I should be standing up and taking responsibility for.

Nah, the circumstances couldn't be more different.

Becoming confident that by rejecting his suggestion, I'm not negating anything that he'd done, I finally allow words to come out, "I hear what you say, Hell. But it wouldn't be right."

"Don't dismiss it so fast," Bomber interrupts. "You say you don't want a war, and maybe you're right. This could be one way to avoid it."

I'd grown up with these men. Most had joined along the way, but Rusty and Bomber had been like uncles to me, there from the time of my birth. I'd always respected their views.

"Angel needs to pay for what he did," I respond through gritted teeth.

"Yeah," Bomber continues, "I agree with that. But there are ways and means, and sometimes revenge is best served cold when it's least expected. If he really wants the kid, you stepping up and claimin' it would at least throw put a dent in his plans."

"Kid has dark brown eyes, just like yours," Rusty puts in.

"That's because he's half-Italian," I respond. "Could be he'll grow up to look like his sperm donor." But he'll have Violet's and Nathan's inherited features too. Could be that he'll remind me of my friend who left this earth far too soon. Can't deny I'd be claiming a part of Nathan, his nephew the only thing he'd left behind.

I feel like slapping myself around the head. Fuck, this whole idea is ridiculous, even if you leave out the part where I've no desire to be a husband or a dad, and probably wouldn't be good as either.

"It's a crazy suggestion. For a start, we all know it's a lie."

"But a lie for all the right reasons," Lizard speaks up. "Angel wants the kid. At least Violet has it right that he's the last man suitable to be a father. What I don't understand is why he's going after her so hard. Do we know why he wants full custody? Could we get him to back down to visitation rights?" He breaks off and frowns. "And why Violet, and why the kid? If he did it to her, man like that's probably done it before. Why's it her he's messing with?"

From what Violet said, I doubt if Angel could be persuaded to reverse his claims. Anyway, even co-parenting would be bad enough with a motherfucker like that. I wouldn't trust him as far as I could throw him. There seems no reason he'd want the kid. Unless he could profit from him.

"Why Violet, and why he wants Theo so badly, I've no idea, Liz. You're right to ask, but my first concern is his bid for custody's right around the corner, and that's what I'm focused on dealing with."

"As far as I can recall, Angel's married, but with no offspring." Hell's rubbing his brow. "I'm sure Lucio said as much during one of our meets."

"From choice or circumstance? And what's he doing raping a girl with a woman waiting for him at home?" Bomber's been faithful to Jeannie since the day they wed, well, so I'd been told. They'd gotten together before I was born.

Buzzard leans forward. "Why don't you step up, Demon? You could claim the kid, then divorce or whatever after Angel backs down. Violet would be safe..."

Cad barks a laugh. "Yeah, he could. But paternity can be challenged for eighteen years in Colorado. Unless Angel is taken out of the picture, Prez would have to carry the lie until the kid reaches maturity. He'd be close to his sixties before he was free."

I raise my eyebrow at him. "You seem pretty handy with that info, Cad. Something about you we don't know?"

He shrugs and turns away from my inquisitive stare.

"You got a secret kid somewhere, Cad?" Pyro asks gleefully. I'd be surprised. Man's pale as the cadaver for which he's named, as he barely comes out of his computing cave.

"A virtual one, maybe," jokes Sparky, on the same wavelength as myself.

Cad's glaring. "Had to look into some shit for my sister, alright?" He satisfies our curiosity but isn't comfortable doing it.

It was useful him knowing what he did. If I step up as Hell suggested, it wouldn't be a short-time affair. Which brings me back around to eliminating the threat to Theo.

"I didn't suggest we wouldn't off Angel eventually," Bomber smirks, showing he's on the same page. "But we wait until he least expects it. We go head-to-head with him about the kid, he'll be watching out for us comin'. Get that shit sorted, Prez and Vi playing happy family, then we off him. Prez can step away then."

I find myself nodding. Yeah, a few months. A year. I could do that. *A platonic relationship just for show? Hell, no.* My fist slams down on the table. "No way, Brothers. We find another way around this. I am not getting hitched. There's no way Violet would agree to it." Christ, sure she's a pretty girl, nice pair of tits I wouldn't normally turn down, good rounded ass that a man could hang onto. But she'd see it like incest, and that's how I should look at it, too. She's Nathan's sister, for fuck's sake, not some hangaround looking for a good time.

If she wasn't, would I be considering it? Of course I wouldn't. Yeah, my dick's more than interested, but one fuck, maybe two, is as far as I'd go, I've never had a yearning to be saddled with a wife and kid.

"What alternative are you proposing, Prez?"

I swear my father gets a thrill each time he calls me that. It's not just pride his son has risen through the ranks, it's relief he's no longer in the hot seat. Narrowing my eyes, I think fast. "I'll try and get a meeting with Don Lucio. See if he can bring pressure on Angel."

"Prez, I love ya," Thunder starts, "but that's just going to raise a red flag. You know what these families are like. You doing that admits the kid is Angel's and isn't going to help Violet's case. The only way to get them to back off is for it to be claimed by someone else."

I'm starting to hate that they refer to Theo as 'it'. But I'm not crazy enough to admit it. But my temp VP has a point. "I need to meet anyway about the product floating around. That gives me an in. Ask them politely whether the increase in product is down to them, and if so, will they please stop dealing in or around our premises. Or words to that effect." I smirk.

"You'd face that head-on? They'll just deny it, Prez."

"Yeah, they will, Bomber. But it seems a good way of getting them to show their hand. Could be new dealers not aware of our old agreements. At least let them know we're aware of what's going on."

"They're deliberately stepping on our toes," Mace observes, seeming adamant the Silvestri are to blame. "Flexing their muscles, testing our strength."

Hell is nodding at the end of the table. "I agree with Prez, and what the rest of you have said too. Don Lucio's not the best poker player, and his reaction would be interesting, to say the least. If they are deliberately coming into our territory, then they're the ones declaring war. Want me at the meet, Demon?"

Seeing the meeting is a go, I decide fast. "Hellfire and Thunder," I propose, seeing as my dad's offered and his relationship with the don goes back years. "Thunder, set up the meet, and the three of us will go. Yeah, Buzz?"

"You're assuming Angel will be present?"

I nod. "It's likely. He's not only the underboss, but if the rumours are correct, the son being groomed to take over."

"Maybe even his *consigliere*, Lucio's counsellor, will be there, or one of his trusted *capos*." Hellfire shakes his head as Mace shows him his pack of smokes.

Buzz hasn't finished; he waits for Hell to stop speaking, then says impatiently, "So you have Angel as a captive audience. Of course, he won't know we have Violet and the kid. Are you going to bring it up? Come right out and tell him to back off?"

My hastily constructed plan hasn't gotten as far as that. I speak my thoughts aloud, "I've met Angel before. He's not someone I care particularly about one way or another. We all know the type of shit the Mafia's involved in. Don Lucio comes across as more of a gentleman; Angel loves nothing better than getting his hands dirty. Earned his nickname from the up-close-and-personal wet-work he likes." While the don would order a hit from afar, Angel would carry it out himself. Or would in the past before he was promoted. "What worries me most is their other side-line."

It's Mace who puts it into words. "Trafficking." His eyes meet mine. "Hate we turn a blind eye to that shit."

"Couldn't stop it, Brother." Thunder's brow furrows. "Too many of them, too few of us. Could, and have, thrown the odd monkey wrench in the works when we heard of somewhere women and kids were being held, but on a large scale? Nah. And if it wasn't the Silvestri, it would be someone else."

Thunder's right. Cad's managed to discreetly pass on info a couple of times to the cops. Feds have come in and the Mafia's lost one of their houses. But while none of us like it, there's too much money to be earned for people like us to step in and stop it for good.

"If that's what he has in mind for the kid..." Liz breaks off. His hand smacks down on the table.

"He wouldn't do that to his own blood?" Skull speaks for the first time, his eyes opening wide.

"Not sure how that would work. He gets custody, kid can't just disappear." I'm grasping at straws. There was a reason for Violet having taken such desperate measures, and I wonder if she suspects what Angel's capable of. But then, even just knowing he's a drug dealer, a pimp and a people trafficker would be enough to know he's not the man to raise her kid. I raise my eyes. "Look, my intention is to get the measure of the man at the moment. I've avoided getting close in the past, but now the more we know, the easier it will be to take him down. This meeting is going to be about club business, not going to mention more than that."

But Buzz is looking thoughtful, there's something on his mind.

So I press, "What? You're seriously suggesting we tell them outright Violet's here? Show our hand?"

"Fuck, no. That would be war." Rusty's looking aghast. "Don't want to give them a reason to fuck with us."

I jerk my chin to acknowledge Rusty's comment, but my eyes are still on Buzzard. He shrugs. "Could just get friendly-like, talk about families, and your woman and kid."

It takes a moment for the penny to drop. When it does, I snarl, "I am not laying claim to Theo."

Buzz's sharp eyes meet mine. "Could lay the groundwork, that's all. Put doubts in his head that he's the dad."

For fuck's sake! My eyes go wide. My fingers pinch my nasal bones and I bow my head for a moment. A burst of anger has risen as I realise he's not letting Hellfire's suggestion drop. *Nope. Not doing that. No way. Never.* Trying to tamp my sudden rage back down, I snarl, "Moving on to other business, or back to where we started, when are we signing the contract for the tattoo parlour, *Treasurer?*"

My voice, which, when I want it to, can be every bit as scary as Hell's, gets Buzz to focus. It's not long before we agree on some dates. Devil's Ink is going to be moving premises soon.

The decisions we've made, a meet with the Silvestri and

progress on Liz's new business venture, are recorded, then I can bang the gavel and bring this uncomfortable meeting to a close. At fucking last.

Why am I not surprised when the others file out, Hellfire stays in his seat at the end of the table?

"You got something to say?" I'd be surprised if he hadn't. Not that I expect him to interfere with the way I run the club. He'd made it clear from the moment he stepped down it was mine now. I'd prefer his comments to be about club business, but I doubt they will be.

"What are you going to do about sleeping arrangements?"

Well, not quite where I thought he was going to start. We're full to the seams already, and he's right, I hadn't considered where Violet and the baby would bed down. Or more to the point, where I would go. I wouldn't be staying with them, and if anyone was sleeping on a couch, it wouldn't be her.

"They can have my room," I tell him, as though it had already been decided.

"Nah. You stay where you are. Not much point when there's my old bedroom staying empty."

When Hell had been the Prez, he'd slept there more often than not. While I don't know the details, for some reason he'd avoided sleeping at home over the past year or so. Since he and Moira have gotten on the same page though, he's right, the room has rarely been used.

"If she's going to be stayin' a while, and my suspicions are that she will be, tell her to get it set up as she wants. Or," he pauses, and his eyes land firmly on my face, "she could move in with me and Mo. Your mom would love having a kid to fuss over."

Yeah, she would. I haven't provided her with grandkids, nor have any inclination to do so in the future, a pronouncement which hadn't gone down well. It's a good suggestion, but if Mo got a whiff of what Hell's been suggesting, she might take a hold of the idea and not want to give it up. There's also a valid reason why I should turn the offer down.

"I'm not easy with bringing Mom into it, Hell. Sure, your house might be more comfortable for Violet, but what if Angel finds out where she's staying? Mom could end up right in the firing line. He's going to be angry she's dropped out of sight as it is."

"It wasn't picked up on in church, but how did he know she was pregnant? Just luckily spotted her and put two and two together, or has he got eyes on her? And if so, why?"

Hell's as sharp as he ever was.

I rub my nose. "Can't deny I'm not worried about that."

"So he might already know exactly where she is."

Yeah. He might. "I think, if he does, we'll soon hear about it. As far as the Silvestri know there's no connection between us and the Palmers, no reason for loyalty to Violet. I'd put money on him talking rather than an attack on the compound to try to take her."

"You don't think we need to be prepared?"

"What would you do, Hell?" I've taken his place; doesn't mean I'm not going to take his advice on the direction I'm steering.

He bows his head, his hands pushing back through the hair that's more silver than black nowadays. "They outnumber us, that's the problem. They have the muscle, but we have the brains. We co-exist because we're useful to each other. We control this part of town and they know it. Angel might want his son, but what benefit is it to the family to take us out? He might end up with the kid, but the fallback would mean they left bodies stacked up to achieve it."

I agree. I can't see how Theo can be that important, to anyone other than Angel.

Hell resumes, "Meeting with the don is the right way to go about it. I think the odds are low he has eyes on them, otherwise they'd have taken the kid when Violet had handed him over.

That's where the fight would have been. Could he track her by her phone? Might need Cad to look into that."

"She got rid of it, changed her number and bought a new one."

His lips press together as he nods. "Then that's one less thing to worry about."

"We play the meeting by ear, Hell. See if they show us their cards."

"You going to be okay with that, Demon? You going to be able to keep your hands off Angel when you see him, knowing what he did to Vi? If you can't control yourself, you're going to have to step away and let someone else go."

"I can keep myself in check. Yeah, so it's not right what he did. But he's not the first to date rape a woman and won't be the last." I shrug, trying to brush off the fact it was Violet who'd been his victim. "Can't go around offing all such bastards, I'm no fuckin' Robin Hood."

A glance at Hell's face shows he's not buying it. An indrawn breath let out as a sigh shows a father's exasperation. "Demon, I know you didn't like my suggestion. Can appreciate you have reasons. We have a few days before we can get a meet with them; don't dismiss the option out of hand. I still think you putting your name on her is a good way to get Silvestri to back off. Without DNA evidence he can't claim the kid. You claiming her puts her under our protection, it will be them declaring war if they want to object. Might not be important enough to them. Angel might be out on his own with no support."

"He's clearly not frightened of the courts, Hell. They've decided twice in his favour so far. He can go back and demand DNA testing. Don't forget he's already been cleared of rape and has been given co-parenting rights."

"Seems to me someone else has to step up and claim to be the father. Only thing to prove it's not so would be DNA tests. And that, someone like Angel wouldn't want to provide. He gives a sample? His DNA would be in the system."

"I'm not particularly keen on my own being taken either. You're forgetting, it's also mine that wouldn't be a match. In the end, what you're asking me to do is a complete fabrication, Hell. You're asking me to live a lie. I can't do that." Angrily I stand, sliding my chair into the table, a sign I won't be sitting back down. "Convince him I'm in love with her? That I had an affair with her? That the kid's mine? Fuck, Hell. How the fuck do I do that?"

He stands too. "You've had an example right there in front of you all of your goddamn life. You copy your mom and me. Shouldn't be that difficult." His face has reddened. "You treat that kid the same way I fuckin' treated you. You think living a lie isn't worth it if it's done for the right reasons?"

"You really think I should do this?" I round on him, furious. "Throw the next eighteen years of my life away on something that wasn't my mistake?"

"I invested the last fucking thirty-six years in doing the same thing," he rasps back.

I send a wary glance toward his hands bunched into fists. A throwdown with my father isn't what I want to get into, but the way this is going, I may need to take the old man on.

"You loved Mo from the start," I throw at him, taking a warning step closer. "Don't compare Vi and me to you and Mom."

"Perhaps I just needed something to make me step up and claim her! To show me what was right in front of my eyes."

My fist rises, but instead of hitting him, smashes down on the table. "I'm not marrying Vi to make a ready-made family to satisfy you and Mo's desire for a grandkid, *Dad*. The circumstances are totally different."

For an answer he throws up his hands, a very similar gesture to that when I was a teenager; a parent's *I can't talk to you while you're in this mood* dismissal. Then, with one last glare, he leaves.

Christ. We get on so well it's been years since we last argued. At least he'd walked out before it had come to exchanging blows.

He might have twenty years on me, but I'm not sure who'd come out the winner.

Pulling out my chair, I sink down onto it, lean forward and put my head in my hands, rage slowly seeping out of my body. *I am not my father.* Definitely not my real one—I've never had any inclination to put my dick where it's not wanted. But I don't resemble Hell either, never wanting to settle down and be a family man, and not prepared to play dad to a kid I hadn't fathered.

If I forced Violet into a relationship to fight alongside her, I'd not be able to go with the whores, the hangarounds who come to our parties, the booty calls I rely on in town. Fuck, my cock couldn't go anywhere. I've not gone without sex for more than a day in all of my adult life. Fucking's a hobby for me. If I was to be faithful, I couldn't be celibate. Fucking Vi wouldn't be any problem for me, but there's no chance she has reciprocal feelings. She's clearly outgrown her teenage fascination with me. How does she see me now? A man, much older than her, who leads an MC. She doesn't want me like that, but pretending, being close to her, being celibate when all I'd want to do is strip her clothes off? Would desperation lead me to press my case just like my sperm donor? And would she simply comply, lay there and take it, because it's all to protect her son? Angelino's already ruined her life, I can't add to her woes.

Fuck, there's no chance she'd agree even if I asked her. I'm an outlaw biker with no knowledge of parenting. Not much different to the criminal who's fighting her for custody.

CHAPTER TEN

Violet

When I'd been introduced to Jayden I'd taken to her almost immediately. My admiration for her grows the more I speak with her. She's shown she possesses a wisdom, and a knack for looking after children, that belies her years. Quite calmly she told me a little of her background, so much worse than the one-night stand I luckily have no recollection of. Sharing our confidences has begun to forge a connection between us. So much so, that when she took a fussing baby from me and he immediately quieted, I didn't feel jealousy, just relief.

"You have a way with kids," I observe.

"Practice." She grins, then grimaces. "I just wish I could go down to Tucson and see my new niece, Faith, but it's too dangerous for me to show my face there. And Ella doesn't want to travel here with a newborn. Hopefully it won't be long before they visit. Mo's already assured me Ella and Slick can stay with her." As she places a kiss on Theo's sleeping head, the faraway look in her eyes suggests she's dreaming of holding her niece the same way.

"Any kids in your future?"

"Huh. Not yet. Eventually, I suppose. But I'm in no hurry. Pal and I are just enjoying getting our relationship established first.

I'm only seventeen, I can afford to live that much again before I even start thinking I'm running out of time."

It's not the first instance that she's had to remind me. Her maturity makes me feel like I'm talking to someone my own age. I'd already place good money on a bet that if I stay here, I reckon we'll become good friends. That's not even a possibility though; Theo and I need to move away, start afresh. I can't, and don't want to, presume on Demon's hospitality, or not for too long. With my carnal thoughts about him, it bugs me he looks at me as nothing more than the sister of his old friend.

Eyeing the direction he'd gone off in, I ask, "Do you know what time the men will get out of their meeting?"

"Church? No. Could be any time. Depends what they have to discuss."

'Church'? That word again. "I didn't take Demon as a man much for prayers."

Jay giggles. "It's just what they call their meetings. Bikes could be a sort of religion, I suppose."

A brief shared moment of mirth, but my merriment soon disappears, knowing what the men are discussing will be me. While I don't like the story of my stupidity being shared, I do hope Demon's finding a discreet way to let them know I'm not a bad mother. I hated the way they all looked at me earlier. Understood it, of course, but they didn't know that the last thing I'd do is leave my son unless I saw no other option, that I'd been at the end of my tether, seeing no other way out.

As the baby sleeps on and Jay seems happy enough to hold him, I relax back and think less of my predicament and more of Demon, the man who's swept in and turned my life upside down. He's given me hope for the first time in what seems like forever. I remember him better as Dave; the man he is now is like a stranger, wearing a similar, but not exact, exterior to Nathan's companion of the past. He's broadened and muscled up, his chiselled face gotten more defined. There's no doubt the extra years suit him.

The only thing I'm having difficulty processing is his new name. I could never see him as demonic and hate the handle passing my lips. He seems to insist on it, though. Maybe there's a compromise?

My stomach growls loudly interrupting my thoughts and making Jay chuckle. She bats my arm. "Look, I have Theo. Why don't you go get something to eat? You'll hear him if he wakes."

I certainly would. No one could say he didn't have a good set of lungs. I glance to the kitchen, hearing the female voices, hunger fighting with reluctance. She's expecting me to take her up on the offer, so I lean into her conspiratorially, admitting, "Jeannie scares me."

Jay gives a small laugh again, softly so she doesn't wake Theo. "Yeah, she scared me too, at first. But she's okay once you get used to her."

Nevertheless. While they haven't yet interrogated me, I'm still expecting an inquisition, and I'm not sure how much I should tell them.

"I'll wait for D," I decide out loud.

"D?"

Yes. That had been my inspiration, and to me, my reasoning is sound. "Always knew him as Dave growing up. It's hard for me to now think of him as Demon—he doesn't like me reminding him of his real name, so my compromise is to call him 'D'."

"Pal's real name is Dominic. I quite like that. But he's been Pal to me forever, don't think I could call him anything else."

The sounds of a door banging open and loud voices interrupt our conversation, alerting me that church—a misnomer for their meetings, rather than any religious assembly—is out. I look around, hoping to see the man I've been waiting for. I have questions to ask about what's going to happen to my son and myself. I don't see the one I want to see most, and my face starts to burn as each man walking through the clubroom looks at me as he passes.

Their expressions are mixed, but mostly, that disapproval

they'd shown earlier is thankfully missing. Some look sympathetic, some inquisitive, and a few, for some reason, are nudging each other and looking amused.

I try to keep my head down and ignore them but can't prevent myself looking up from time to time to see whether Demon has emerged.

I sit, fidgeting, wishing Theo would wake to give me something to do. But after a good feed of formula, it's not uncommon for him to sleep like the dead for a few hours. My hands twist in my lap; I stare at them, not wanting to meet the eyes of the men milling around, nor wishing to be their audience as they start to get over-familiar with the scantily-clad women who've emerged from wherever they've been hiding as though summoned. Bottles are clanking, voices are getting louder, but still my son sleeps on.

I risk another glance toward the hallway; this time I find a man making a beeline for me. It's not the man I'm waiting for, but his father. He still has the ability to make me feel like a little kid, his presence sending me back in time to when I was a young child hanging around with the boys in his house. I find myself automatically standing.

"Er, Mr Black."

"Fuck, girl. Call me Hellfire or Hell." He smiles as he says it. "You got a moment?"

I half turn; Jay's already nodding. "You go ahead. I've got the little man."

"Come." Without explanation, Demon's dad, Hellfire, strides off toward the stairs without checking to see that I'm following him, which, of course, I am. He takes me down the same long corridor where Demon has his room, passing that one, then pauses at a door at the end. Taking out a key he unlocks it. "You been warned about Bitch?"

"The cat, er, yes." I found the bundle of fur quite cute and wouldn't mind her entering my room. My only concern is with Theo, thinking I'll need to watch him carefully around her. He's not been in contact with animals before and I'll have to be on the lookout for any allergies.

"Well, remember to always lock your door. Can't be too careful with that one around. She has a knack of opening handles if the door isn't locked."

"Have you thought of turning the handles up the other way?" He shoots me a look with his eyebrows raised. *Guess they haven't.* It's an easier topic than any other we might land on, so I pry for more information. "Why's she here?" It seems odd, if she hates men so much, why do they keep her?

He chuckles, a sound which comes from deep down in his throat. "Like all of us, she walked in, seemed to like it, and made her home here. Tolerate her as she catches mice. Well, occasionally." His grin broadens. "Fuckin' shame we couldn't make her prospect, she'd wouldn't have gotten her patch and we could have parted ways with her."

"That's mean, Mr er, Hellfire."

"But true," he insists.

Bitch seems to like women and children. I'd like Theo to grow up with a pet, but perhaps one with a more child appropriate name. Luckily he won't be here when he starts to talk. I could just imagine how that would go down at school when the teacher asked for the name of his cat.

I stop daydreaming when I realise Hellfire's talking to me.

"Right. This is my room, but I don't use it anymore. Haven't for a few months now. There are clean sheets on the bed, and more than enough room for you to set up a crib. Bathroom's through here." He opens another door while I'm standing bewildered.

"I'm going to stay in here?"

"Yes. That's the proposal. You can get it set up just how you want. Do what you like with it." He turns to face me and there's a twinkle in his eye. "Or were you expecting to stay with Demon?"

Just what is he asking? I blush. This is the father of the man I secretly lust over. He can't be asking if I want to sleep with his son, is he?

"Er, no." I cough to cover the fact my voice has come out as a squeak. "No," I manage in a more normal tone. "If you're sure we're not imposing, this room will be fine. But I won't be here long enough to rearrange it. We'll be gone as soon as we can."

I look around the room that seems more than adequate, knowing my son and I could certainly be comfortable here. But I can't view it as anything other than temporary. I'll give myself a break, a moment to process that today's plan hadn't worked. But soon, I'll need to make a fresh one. Maybe Demon can help me get a new identity and move out of state? There's no one I need to stay in contact with, so no reason to hang onto my birth name. Theo and I can start a new life somewhere different. Unfortunately, it's not as if I need to visit my mom, she wouldn't know whether I was there or not. That's a fact which hurts, but a true one.

"Stay here as long as you need. Exactly how long, you'll have to work out with Demon." A friendly, paternal hand rests briefly on my shoulder, while I bristle, thinking what I do is none of his son's business. But I can't be annoyed with Hellfire, especially when he says, "You can relax here, Vi. You and the kid. We'll keep you safe."

It's tempting, but I can't impose. And a biker club is no place to bring up a child.

"There you are!" Demon's deep voice booms out from the other end of the corridor.

"I'll leave you two to it." With that, Hellfire turns abruptly, leaving us alone.

God, but Demon's a handsome man, I think, and not for the first time today. Tall, dark brown eyes which look sinful, his hair long enough for me to run my fingers through. High, well-defined cheekbones. The only thing marring it is a slight crookedness of his nose when you look at it right, suggesting it's been broken at some time. It gives his face character and stops him being pretty. An intentional five o'clock shadow, which has fascinating possibilities... My hand covers my face as I feel my cheeks burning again. *I should not be thinking about what he could do with that scruff on his chin.*

There's a clonking and banging sound, accompanied by swearing, coming up the stairs. Peering around Demon, I see a man struggling with the crib, which while not heavy, is awkward.

"Er, it's collapsible," I tell him, trying to smother my laugh.

"Well, I didn't know that, did I? Hey, we haven't been introduced." He puts down the crib and stretches out his hand. "I'm Ink." So he might be, but where he might be tattooed I've no idea. His skin looks completely unmarked to me.

"Thank you, Ink."

After eyeing the crib for a moment, with a smirk Demon flicks the catches, folds it, and easily manoeuvres it through the door. Then he reverses the process and sets the crib up. Ink huffs and walks away with his nose in the air.

"You gonna be okay here?" Demon examines the room with a critical eye.

I cross to the large king-size bed which dominates the room and sit on the cover, taking a moment to look around me. It has everything I need. A television to keep me amused while Theo's sleeping, a closet, drawers. "It's great, D. Thank you."

"D?" he asks, sounding amused.

I could go into an explanation, I don't bother. I'll use it unless he calls me out on it.

"Be a bit like the old days, you having a sleepover. Fuck, you were a pain in the ass when you insisted on tagging along with Nathan. Spoilt rotten as I remember, twisting your parents around your little finger."

The reminder is like a slap in the face. He still sees me as an extension of Nathan, not as a person in my own right. This isn't a favour to me, but a debt owed to my brother. I lower my eyes. Whenever I look at him carnal feelings arise. It's unflattering my reaction is no way reciprocated.

Of course, he misunderstands my dejection. "I know I'll never fill the hole left by Nathan, Vi, but look to me as you would him, okay? Whatever you need, I'll help you get it."

He wants me to treat him as I would my big brother. Problem is, I'm not quite sure how I can look at him that way. Not now I'm grown, and have the desires of a woman. As Demon walks around, occupying himself by checking that the drawers are empty, I take a second to wonder what my relationship with Nathan would be now, had he lived. Last time I saw him I was fifteen. He hadn't grown out of the habit of pulling my pigtails and teasing me; in retaliation, I'd pull up his sweat pants when he wasn't expecting it and give him a wedgy. A small smile curves my lips at the memory, somehow doubting if I were to treat Demon the same as I'd acted toward Nathan it would be the way to get on Demon's good side. There are much more adult things I'd prefer to be doing with him, but I expect, if he knew that, he'd be horrified.

Having completed his inspection, Demon pinches the bridge of his nose. "Jay mentioned you needed feeding."

That's a safe enough topic. "Yeah, I could eat." My stomach, which earlier had rolled at the thought of food, now reminds me again that I'm hungry and that I hadn't eaten at all today. "I need to go get Theo and feed him first though." I drop my eyes to my breasts which have become full once again, threatening to dampen the borrowed t-shirt Jayden had found for me earlier.

It's like he snaps to attention. "I'll get him for you."

"There's no need..." I'm not an invalid or helpless. I don't need him doing things for me. He starts to protest when a figure makes a timely appearance in the doorway.

"Hey, Violet. Theo woke and started fussing so I brought him up. Do you want to feed him, or shall I do a bottle?"

I'm full of relief Jayden has saved me from a conversation I was finding awkward. Having had to cope mostly alone, I'm used to doing everything for myself. Demon offering to get my son for me had been blown up out of proportion in my mind, an indication he'd thought that after the bad decisions I'd made today, I couldn't do anything for myself. Gratefully I take Theo from her, nuzzling his head and breathing in the baby smell that's even more precious after I'd come so close to losing him. "I'm going to feed him myself, thanks, Jay."

The borrowed t-shirt is a bit tighter than the clothes I usually wear. As I work out the best way to manage this, I notice Jay has disappeared, and while Demon has stayed, he's averting his eyes. I shrug. To me feeding my baby is the most natural thing in the world, nothing dirty or disgusting about it. I've fed Theo in public before, discreetly covered with a blanket; the snide looks and comments have never bothered me. So why should I feel awkward giving him sustenance in front of Demon?

Because I feel maternal, decidedly non-sexy. Feeding another man's baby is no way to attract a man.

"How about I go get you a plate of something for you?" Demon offers, his back turned toward me.

An escape for us both. I jump at it. "Yes, please."

I suspect he was in no hurry to return. A good half-hour passes, during which I've fed and changed Theo, and there's still no sign of him or the promised food. I've started to wonder whether to stay in this room, or go to find him. The main thing which keeps me rooted is his men, and their differing moods as they came out of church. Sympathy, I can handle. Curiosity too. But those smirks, half-smiles, or outright laughing? Why am I the butt of a joke I don't understand?

Perhaps if I got to know them, I'd find they weren't so unnerving. But maybe leave it; I won't be here long enough to need to make friends, and tonight, well, I just want to enjoy being close to my son.

Laying Theo on the bed, I go sort out the portable crib, then pull it close to me and settle him down. Then, tired, I lean against the pillow, thinking over the terrible day I've had, and the emotional wringer I've been through.

Lying on my side, I watch Theo sleeping. It's hard to think

when I awoke this morning, I never expected to have him with me tonight. I might have been rescued by Devils, but God must have had a hand in it. Maybe Nathan's watching over us and had sent his best friend to help. Now at least there's someone on my side to keep Theo hidden from his sperm donor. It's a comforting thought that, for tonight at least, we're safe.

I call out when a knock comes at the door, "Yeah, come in."

Demon walks in carrying a tray. On it there's a delicious smelling plate of food. Some kind of stew, but as my stomach growls once again, I couldn't give a damn what sort. Sitting up, I waggle my fingers in a 'give me' gesture.

He laughs. "Fuck, Vi, I remember you doing that when you wanted our candy."

I roll my eyes as he defines our relationship yet again. To him I'll never be more than Nathan's little sister.

I dig in and eat as though I haven't eaten all day, which is the truth. I'm so hungry, and the food so good, I'm unaware of Demon watching me eat every mouthful until I'm almost finished. Then I notice his eyes transfixed on my spoon as I move it between plate and lips. To test him, I take time over the next morsel, making a show of sucking it into my mouth, then licking the utensil.

His eyes catch mine. Swiftly he turns his back. *Hmm. Perhaps not so immune to me as he'd like to think.*

"That was great, D. I'm stuffed now."

There's a slight groan, then a chuckle. "Christ, Vi, you've emptied the plate."

"So?" I shrug. "I was hungry."

I'd like nothing more than to go to sleep, but having eaten so much, I need to let the digestion process start to work. Putting the plate to one side, I sit up, propping pillows behind me. They'll have discussed my situation in their meeting, and I want to know what conclusions they've made.

"What's going to happen? Where do I go from here?"

The last is a metaphorical question, but he answers literally.

"You go nowhere, for now," he says sharply. "You and Theo, you'll be staying here."

I don't bother protesting. He must know we can't stay forever.

"Can I get our things?"

I'd packed a few things in the suitcase, so Vicky wouldn't become suspicious. Going to visit my fictional friend without taking anything with me would certainly have aroused some misgivings. Distraught, I'd not put much thought to what I'd thrown in. Most of my stuff I'd left behind. Theo has no toys, and I'd like him to have them.

"I'll get the suitcase brought up from your car; should have thought of that earlier. But if you're referring to shit from your home, no, Vi. Can't rule out someone will be looking for you, and the house is the first place they'd go. Have to tell you now, you're not going to be leaving the compound, so don't even ask. The only way to keep you safe is to make sure that no one knows you're here."

He's being so heavy-handed. I'm an independent woman, used to doing stuff for myself. He might be right, but his arrogant attitude is annoying.

"But..." I start to protest for the sake of making a protestation.

"No, Vi. The girls can go buy whatever you need."

I don't have enough money to replace everything Theo requires. "I can't afford—"

I was going to say 'much' but he interrupts, "Vi! For fuck's sake. I told you, I'm stepping into Nathan's shoes. Anything you need, I'll pay for it. I'm good for that, I promise you."

My cheeks flame. "I can't ask you–"

Again he cuts me off before I've finished. "You're not asking. I'm telling. Nathan would never have let you go wanting..."

Suddenly I've pulled myself up on my knees, my finger prodding him in the ribs, my voice as angry as I can make it without risking interrupting Theo sleeping.

"Look here," I hiss. "I'm a grown woman. I can look after myself. Whether Nathan is here or not, whether you somehow think you're his proxy, I'll make my own way in life. I've done well enough on my own so far."

He's there. His hand captures my fingers, he pushes both our joined fists against my chest, pressing me back against the pillows. His temper has risen as fast as my own.

"And you make some great fuckin' choices, don't you? You say you don't need looking after? You're a single mom with a kid and without a penny to your name. Not to say, without me, you don't have a place to stay, either."

The words ring in the air.

A movement, a snuffle, we both freeze, then I sigh as Theo goes silent.

"Remind me," Demon hisses. "Where would you be without me, Vi? Where would you fuckin' be right now?"

He knows the answer. I'd be somewhere where I wouldn't care about anything, content my son would be well looked after. Dying inside, if not physically. Maybe already dead. I wonder if I'd have had the guts to go through with it, driven by despair.

He backs away, stands and starts pacing the room. Suddenly he turns my way.

"Tell me, Vi. Would you prefer that? Get back in contact with the woman again, hand Theo over? Is there a way to restart that process if you absolutely think that's in his best interest? Tell me Vi." He runs his hands back through his hair, his head moving side-to-side. "How the fuck do I know what's best for you and the kid?"

"D?" My voice sounds small, weak, as if I've reverted back nine years, and oh, how I wish I could. Nathan home on leave, back at the house, me sneaking in and trying to flirt with Dave. Both men rolling their eyes. I'm sure Dave found my naïve teenage attraction to him amusing. I'd give anything to turn back time, to tell Nathan not to go on that final tour, or to keep out of the path of that bullet. But I can't go back. I need to deal with the present.

"D." I repeat his name. "I haven't said thank you, and I should have. I want Theo with me. I got so caught up in getting him out of his father's hands, I couldn't see any other way out. I just need a minute to get my head around things I never expected to be; a chance I didn't expect to have. I am grateful to you letting me stay until I get sorted."

There's a strange look on his face as he turns. His voice is gravelly as he says the last thing I expected him to say.

"Never, *ever* refer to that fucker as Theo's father again, you hear me?" His eyes flare as they fix on mine. "You fuckin' got me, Vi?"

I can't remember ever seeing him so serious. Not even earlier when he'd started questioning me.

Why should it mean so much to him?

Then it dawns: he's schooling me. Giving me a lesson I should take to heart. If I'm going to stop Angel getting custody, or any rights at all, I have to deny his parentage, even out of his hearing. That starts today.

"Got you, D."

CHAPTER ELEVEN

Demon

Fuck! I shouldn't have lost my temper with Violet. After the day she's had, I should back off and give her space to realise what I'm offering her, the chance for her and Theo to stay together. My support to enable that. How long is it since she's been able to rely on anyone but herself? It's been well over a year since her father died, and while her mom was there physically, mentally she'd have been no help at all, only adding to her burden. Christ, I can't believe how the little girl I remember has grown up to be such a strong woman. Just half of her problems would leave most women reeling, but she stood up straight and handled everything life threw at her. She'd done the best that she could, and that includes the actions that had shocked me today.

She'd had to deal with the aftermath of being raped, is probably still doing that. Had to cope with giving birth alone, raising a child as a single mother, caring for her mom who was losing her mind. Topping all that off, facing being homeless and penniless. And all that's without considering the court cases and that Theo's sperm donor had been making threats. Under the circumstances, with no home, no money, and with records of the hospital visit when Theo had gotten burned, Angel could very well have been awarded custody.

Even I'd have found all that hard to deal with, but I wouldn't have had to go through it alone. I'd have had my brothers behind me. Well, she might not yet appreciate it yet, but from this point forward, so has she.

When I'd brought her dinner, I'd wanted to have a conversation, but things hadn't gone the way I'd planned. I wasn't going to share all our discussions at church with her, especially not some of the more far-fetched suggestions, but I had been planning a longer talk about her expectations now. I'd been going to explain our offer of hospitality to her, that we'd be there to support her trying to get the millstone of Angel off her back.

My plans had gone awry. She'd been in no mood to listen. Why doesn't she understand I'm gladly stepping into the role her brother would have played were he still alive? Nathan would have expected nothing less. Of course, I should have stepped up earlier, but too wrapped up in my own life, I admit, Violet had been put to the furthest recesses of my mind.

I'd taken her empty plate back downstairs and had left her, giving her time to herself. Tonight, I can give her the luxury of being with her kid and not having to worry about where her next meal's coming from, or where to lay her head. Hopefully she'll relax and get the sleep she's probably not had for weeks.

Now, she needs the help I can give her, and I'm going to step up to the plate. As a brother. I don't have it in me to be anything else. There's no way in hell I'm going to marry her. Why Hell had come up with that suggestion, I've no idea. Except... that's what he'd done, wasn't it?

But my feelings for Vi don't come close to resembling what he felt for my mother. Fuck Vi? See her naked?

I could have gotten a glimpse of her tits when she'd been feeding Theo if I'd turned around...

Nah, the thought makes me think of seeing Kennedy, my own sister, naked. Nope, no way. Never want to do that. *Eww.* Well, that's what that idea should make me feel. Unfortunately, it doesn't.

What would Vi look like under her clothes? Would her body bear the marks of the miracle of childbirth? Would her ass feel as good in my hands as my eyes suspect? Would her tits...

Fuck it. That's why I have to keep reminding myself that she sees me only as a Nathan substitute.

She's not helping. Mentioning my brotherly concern seems to be some kind of a trigger. Leaving aside my unwanted sexual attraction to her, her predicament has rekindled the affection I'd had for her as a kid. Sure, she'd been annoying, but Nathan had loved her despite all that. And I, as his friend, had copied his example, treating her much as I'd treated my own little sister. But Vi seems to hate any reminder of our relationship in the past. I can't read her at all.

Maybe it's that I don't understand women, and that's why I'm a happy single man.

"Prez."

The sultry tone gets me turning. "Hey, Breezy, how you doing?" Automatically my arm goes around the sweet butt's waist, hugging her to me.

Moving around to my front, she places her hands on my chest. "Want some company tonight, Prez?" She licks her lips suggestively. "Titsy's available if you want both of us. You know we know how to take care of you."

She's right. They do. But I make it worth it for them. It's give and take. Citizens don't understand the whores in the club, why they're there of their own volition, thinking we must coerce them in some way or that they are so down on their luck they have nothing better to do. The 'nothing better to do' part is correct, but only as far as the girls are concerned. They are right where they want to be. They like to fuck, love sex. As long as they're getting those needs met, they're satisfied. They get food and a roof over their heads for doing what they enjoy. Are they all trying to become a biker's old lady? Maybe, but more often I think not. A nice idea in theory, but in practice I believe it would be as hard for these girls to stick to one cock as it would be for the man they were snagging to keep to a single pussy. Who am I to blame them for that? As long as everyone's clean and takes precautions, it's satisfying all our healthy appetites, both ours and theirs.

"Well?" Breezy's hands start inching slowly downwards. She isn't trying to hide she's reaching for my cock.

Covering her fingers with my own to halt their journey, I realise I've too much on my mind to pay the girls the attention they're wanting. "Nah, sweetheart. Not tonight, okay? Maybe tomorrow." I wink over her head to Titsy who's watching our discussion with interest. "Got some shit to do," I explain.

A brief flicker of disappointment, then she nods toward the bar. "Want me to get you a beer instead?"

"With a shot of Jack. Thanks, babe." I nod over to the table where Thunder and Mace are sitting, indicating I'll be joining them. Seeing me approach, the enforcer kicks out an empty chair with his foot.

"She settlin' in?" As I sit, Thunder jerks his head in an upward direction in case I might not have a clue who he's referring to.

"Seems to be. She's had a fuckin' hard day." And isn't that the understatement of the century. "She's not up for a serious discussion, that will need to wait until the morning."

He nods. "Understandable. Got that meet arranged next week, Prez. With Lucio Silvestri. Wednesday suit?"

My brows rise. "That's quick." My concern had been that the crime boss was going to make us wait.

The temporary VP shrugs. "Maybe he's curious why we want to see him. You got any problem with going to his house?"

I'd have preferred neutral ground, but it takes guts to walk into a lion's den. No sign of weakness in meeting him on his territory. If he thinks it will give him the upper hand, it won't. "Nah. That's okay, VP."

"Christ, Demon. When you going to find a permanent second hand?" Thunder shakes his head.

"We've gone through this." I rub the bridge of my nose. "Look, Bomb is the obvious candidate, but he doesn't want it." Mace is shaking his head and holding up his hands. I grin. "Okay, so Mace is cool with what he's doing now." My smirk widens as the enforcer makes a mock show of wiping his brow, then I grow serious again. "Ain't moving Buzz, he's too good with figures. Sparky's too..."

"Flaky?" Thunder helpfully supplies.

"Yeah, with anything other than bikes or routes." The sides of my mouth turn up again. "So who do you suggest?"

"If Rusty was in a civilian role, he'd be winding down for retirement." Mace has got it in one. "Who does that leave? Pyro, Ink, Lizard..."

"Paladin, and of course, Hell or Skull," Thunder lists.

"Hell would be my choice."

"He would be mine, Mace. But he won't take it; he's given enough years to this club. Mo's his focus now. As for Pal? He doesn't have enough miles under his belt." I don't bother mentioning Skull. He's only been patched in a couple of months.

"Pal would be good though. I like his way of thinking."

If it wasn't that I've also been impressed with the transfer from Tucson, I would be thinking Thunder was naming anyone just to pass on the new patch that doesn't sit easy on his cut. But my vision is of someone older, someone who's learned more of the ways of the world. Trouble is, with Pal, his youth shows on his face. Sure, could mean he'd be underestimated which in some circumstances could be a plus, but my VP needs an ability to step into my shoes when I'm not around to wear them. Not sure Pal's there yet.

"Well," Thunder resumes, seeing my dismissal of his suggestion without me having to say it, "look at it another way. You put me into this role permanently, where you going to get a sergeant-at-arms from?" He replaces his glass on the table, then sits back, his thumbs through the loops of his belt.

He's made a good point. There's not one brother still here

that I don't trust to put the club first. But a couple of months back I'd have said the same for Taser. Yeah, his betrayal blind-sided us. Certainly made me wonder more about the rest of the men around me. Maybe that's why I can't see the man I'd want at my right hand, apart from Thunder. But he's right, a sergeant-at-arms has his eye out for any risks coming for the club. No man could do it as well as him.

"Get a transfer in?"

"Boys won't like that," Thunder warns. "It's a promotion opportunity. Should go to one of our lot first."

"Anyone got their eyes set on being VP?"

Thunder shrugs. If someone threw their hat in the ring, maybe I'd consider them. But no one has. Like Thunder, no one wants to step up. Likewise, there's been no noise about filling the sergeant-at-arms role, either.

Mace seems to have lost interest in filling officers' posts. When Titsy approaches, answering a summons from his crooked finger, I understand why. He raises an eyebrow at Thunder, who nods. My shot glass might be empty; my bottle of beer isn't. As the two men rise and walk off with the club girl, I sit back to finish my drink, while contemplating how easy life is here. We understand each other without having to use words much of the time. We've melded together and formed a family. A strange one at times, but one which isn't driven by the rivalry that comes from blood siblings you have to accept. This is a family of brothers who've chosen each other. We don't let anyone join without a unanimous vote, nor without serving their time.

"Another drink, Prez?"

As soon as my empty bottle touches the wood, Dan appears to offer me a fresh one. Yup. Prospects know their role and make sure they do it if they want to get patched.

"Nah, thanks. I'm calling it a night. Hey, grab Vi's suitcase out of her car, will you? Leave it outside her door."

Glad I remembered, I walk up the stairs to my own room where I take a quick run through the shower. As I collect my clothes from the floor to throw into the laundry bin, I pause as I inhale a waft of faint musky perfume. *Must have been from when Vi was hugging me earlier.*

A final thought. *Perhaps I should have called a whore to my bed, or at least jerked myself off in the shower.* For some inexplicable reason, now my cock decides to come to life. *Oh fuck. Admit it. It's Violet.* Sooner we can get her situation sorted out, the better. Just look at the state of me, all I can think about is her.

The wrongness of the thoughts I'm having about Violet make me wary of being alone with her. At the back of my mind is the thought that Nathan would probably have put a bullet in my head if I laid a hand on his little sister. Not that he'd have thought I wasn't a good enough man, but he knew my lifestyle. It would be a crime to draw someone like her into this life, particularly as I wouldn't be able to make a long-term commitment.

Why can't life be easy? Why has she taken this step into my world? Why hadn't she stayed in New York? But if she had, our paths wouldn't ever have crossed, she wouldn't have Theo, and I wouldn't be planning the death of the man who raped her and fighting this insane attraction for her. Instead I'd be fucking a sweet butt without not a care in the world. Well, only those of an MC prez.

The following morning Vi surprises me yet again. She emerges from her room, seeming to take a biker compound as much in her stride as she has anything else life has thrown at her. She's not nervous or scared, but interested and, despite the circumstance, upbeat and cheerful. Whether she's had a good sleep, whether it's that she has someone else to share her burden, there's a new confidence about her, and an obvious joy in being able to spend time with her child. I gain a new respect for her, which for some reason, makes me even more wary of spending time alone with her.

Instead I watch from afar. Jay's happily been out spending my money, and the floor of the clubroom now has baby toys strewn around. There's an elephant which flaps its ears and sings some fucking song that gets stuck in my head. Doesn't take long before my brothers have an intervention and restrict its use to times when men weren't around. *Thank fucking God. If I ever hear a song about ears hanging low once more I swear I'm going to get out my gun and shoot that toy.* There's a colourful mat that can be placed on the floor and something that's apparently called a baby gym. Even I smile when I see Theo kicking at it and giggling.

Jeannie, I'm pleased to see, has taken Vi under her wing. Identifying she has a need to be useful, she has her helping in the kitchen. I suspect Vi needlessly thinks she's found a way to pay us back for our hospitality. She's wrong in that, she owes nothing to us. I owe her.

So I apply no pressure. For four days I give her space to just be a mother.

If I've been avoiding her, she's likewise kept a distance from me. Word's reached me she's not going to be leaving anytime soon, has accepted at least for now, here is the safest place she can be. But if I pocketed her keys to her car, well, that was just a precaution.

I tell myself I'm just giving her time to settle in and time for me to put my attraction back into the box where it belongs. At the back of my mind, and, I suspect in hers as well, is the understanding we need to face up to her problems. Angel might have lost her, might believe she's disappeared, but she can't hide forever. He'll be doing all he can to find her. The only way I can keep her out of his clutches is to keep her prisoner. As a temporary solution it's fine; long term, it would be ridiculous. The kid will have doctor appointments, at the very least.

The options, as I see them, are either facing him in court and clearing her position legally or starting somewhere far away from his reach with a new identity. The former seems unlikely. The latter? Well, that's something I don't want to face.

When I'd brought her here, Violet had taken extreme action because she couldn't see any other way out. Since Theo had been born—even before that—she's been dealing with one thing after the other. Here, she has support, even if it's just another pair of hands more than happy to take Theo for a moment. That first day I'd seen a reduction in the stress lines on her face and had been unwilling to remind her of the problems she's facing. While evading her issues and giving her space isn't a permanent answer, I'm loath to remind her of the shit she needs to face up to.

Each day she's here, she relaxes a little more, and each day it becomes harder to worry her. I've been unable to give her help before; providing her with a safe haven, putting her problems in abeyance for now, is what little I can give her. Doesn't mean I'm not doing the worrying and planning on her behalf, though.

Before I know it, Wednesday has come around. I enter the kitchen to find my father already there.

"So how do you want to play this, Prez?" Hellfire takes a piece of toast and starts to slather a low-fat butter substitute onto it, while I'm tucking into a full fried breakfast Jeannie's just prepared.

"You already eaten at home, Hell?"

He grins but shakes his head. He also takes a cup of coffee and foregoes his usual cream and sugar.

Seeing how much his habits have changed drives me to point at the meagre plate in front of him and ask, "Is it worth it?"

This time he grins wider, having no need for me to explain I'm referring to him having given up smoking, cutting down on the whisky, and now taking more care over what he eats. "Hell, yes," he replies, chomping on his toast as though it's the tastiest snack he could have. "Yeah, I get to..." Whatever he was going to say, he decides better of it, and makes do with a shrug.

The smile I notice more on my mom's face nowadays could provide a pretty good clue as to what he's alluding to, but this is my mom and dad we're talking about. If I've jumped to the right conclusion, I don't want to have confirmation. Mom's certainly been happier lately.

Hastily, I return to his original question. "We go meet the

don, suss out whether someone just needs to be given the facts of life or whether they have deliberate intentions."

"What if Angel is there?" Thunder walks in, catching our conversation. He, too, takes a loaded plate from Jeannie. "Had any more thoughts about letting him know Violet and the kid are here?"

"Definitely not. Won't show our hand unless we have to."

But I will be very interested to meet the man if he turns up. Up to now, I've dealt mainly with Lucio. Sure, Angel's been around in the background, but it's only recently he's become the underboss. I have several reasons to regard him as more than part of the furniture. Now I need to get the measure of the man, or reptile, that he really is.

"The product? What if they're doing it deliberate? Yanking our dicks to get a reaction?"

"We don't react," I tell Thunder, firmly, remembering he's new at being my VP. As sergeant-at-arms he'd have stayed back, watching, listening, his posture showing he had our backs. Now he may well need to interact. "In that case, he'll put forward a proposal. We don't comment other than anything needs to come back to the table."

"That's what he'll do," Hellfire confirms. "I've known him long enough to know the rules he plays by. Way he'll play it, if he's gonna step on our toes, he'll stomp until we take notice, then admit it was him doing it. From there he'll take it to where he wants to go and leave the ball in our corner."

"Fight or give in will be our only options." Thunder's face looks set.

"That's what he'll expect. So no sign, not one flicker of our intentions." I don't really have to warn them. We all know the score. And we're used to playing shit close to our chests. There's no way we're giving up territory to the Silvestri or allowing them to deal drugs around our businesses.

An hour later, we're heading out to our bikes. While we all know it's risky, since there's no requirement to wear a lid in

Colorado most of us ride without helmets, particularly in the warm summer months. I simply wrap my bandana around my forehead to keep the sweat out of my eyes and hair off my face before slipping on my shades.

By the time I've completed my meagre preparations, Hell and Thunder are also ready to get moving. The prospect slides open the gate, and then we're off. Our route will take us in through the city, then out the other side.

I've had a lot of experience riding at the front of the pack. As VP, I took lead position if Hell wasn't with us, but times like today, I have to stop myself standing aside and waiting for him to precede me, only just remembering in time it's me who's the prez. I set the pace, not too fast, not too slow, and enjoy the morning sun on my face, the cooling breeze rushing past, and the clear blue sky overhead. At least, for the moment, it's not going to rain.

None of us have been to the don's lair before. Oh, we've had meets, in their clubs, ours, in neutral territory, but never have we been to the very heart of the crime family. As I ride, I run through what I know of them. Lucio Silvestri has a few years on Hell though they both stepped up to the top spot around the same time. New blood, new deals forged. Since that time, things agreed in an unwritten contract have been abided to by both sides. Of course we know the Silvestri are into some shady shit that we would never touch, hence my concern for what Violet was potentially getting herself into. Drugs we know about, trafficking, too, but as long as they stayed their side of the invisible line, we weren't going to get up in their business.

Unfortunately, with heroin now flooding our part of town, we need to make a stand. Especially with our plans to take the tattoo parlour upmarket. We get a bad rep? We'd never live it down.

I'm unsurprised when we're faced with gates that we have to wait to be opened, then the need to ride our bikes up a long driveway. Crime obviously pays a lot more than can be earned by an MC trying to stay the right side of the line. We park, backing in so our rear tires are facing the house wall, as always, prepared for a quick escape should we need it.

My expectations continue to be met when we're asked to hand over our weapons on entry. You don't get to last long as a Mafia boss without being cautious. It's something we would do were we inviting an enemy into our clubhouse. A quick pat-down, then it's sorted.

Lucio doesn't leave us hanging around. We're immediately shown into a pleasant reception room. Whatever he's into must be lucrative, I muse to myself, looking around. Could be imitation, but I reckon not, and there are some genuine antiques here. Not that I'm any expert.

"Gentlemen." The man who hasn't entirely lost his Italian accent steps forward. He glances at Hell, who stands just a little behind me and to my left, then his eyes examine his cut, before settling on mine. "So, are congratulations in order, Demon?"

I grin. "Not sure if it's congratulations or commiserations right now," I reply, mimicking his friendly tone. "Time will tell."

He nods, then turns to Hellfire. "And you, old friend. You are well?"

"Just about managing to keep the shiny side up," Hell replies. They grasp hands for a moment and exchange respectful nods.

"Retirement agrees with you?"

"Not sure I'd say I'm completely retired, but passing over the gavel, well, that I can recommend."

Don Lucio looks thoughtful. "Might take a page out of your book one day soon. Perhaps before my *capi* get impatient."

A dutiful laugh comes from behind him where two other men stand waiting. One is Angel, I'm pleased to see. Surreptitiously I inspect him. He's not much to look at, older than me, balding, slightly overweight, as if he indulges in too much pizza and pasta. Not the type I'd expect Violet to have gone with voluntarily. My fingers curl into my palms as I remind myself I have to keep my hands off him. For now.

The don has moved on and now reaches out his hand to Thunder. "VP," he nods respectfully.

I'm glad this is one person Thunder doesn't correct with the word 'Acting'. We're here to present strength, after all, and identifying a gap in our ranks would do nothing to serve our purpose.

Lucio stands back and indicates the men behind him. "My underboss and son, Angelino probably needs no introduction. And this is Ferri, one of my *caporegimi*." After we've all exchanged chin lifts with his second and captain, he asks, "Can I offer you refreshment?"

"Not for us," I take the lead. "We're here on business."

Lucio shrugs as though in his view mixing in pleasure would be quite acceptable, but he turns and opens a box, taking out a cigar. He offers them around, but only his team take them. It's enough so the room fills quickly with a sickly-sweet smelling fog.

He draws in smoke, holds it, exhales, then shakes his head. "Friends, you are missing out. This is the best Cuba can offer. But come now, please sit. I was intrigued when you asked for this meeting. You have me at a disadvantage. I have no idea why you requested we sit down together. The Devils and *la famiglia* Silvestri have always been friends, have we not? So I am more than happy to listen to what you have to say. I doubt this is just a social call."

Rumours are he rose up from the slums of Naples, in which case, I wonder where his cultured accent comes from. And kudos to him and his forebears from escaping poverty and immigrating to the US. The Silvestri family has certainly done well for themselves over the decades they've been here.

Bringing my thoughts back into focus, I take the seat indicated, perching on the edge rather than getting comfortable. "You're right. It's not. Something has come to our attention, and I thought perhaps you should know about it."

"Is that right?" The don frowns. "Do continue."

I nod, and do so. "Dealing. White shit. In and around our businesses."

Lucio's eyes open wide. "You don't deal in drugs. I know this. Our agreement states we stay out of the areas you operate in."

"Exactly." I smile widely, showing all my teeth. "Which is why I thought you'd like to know. Whoever it is, we'll come down hard on."

"Of course you will. And after you've finished with them, I hope you'll let me know so I can deal with any pieces that may be left. If someone new is bringing product into the area, it's an activity they'll fast come to regret."

"Prez?" At my raised chin, Hell takes over, "Don Lucio, we wondered whether you'd taken on any new dealers, who perhaps don't completely comprehend the terms of our agreement?" I suppress a grin, seems Lucio's polite way of talking is rubbing off on my old man.

The Italian crime boss' eyes open wide as if that thought hadn't occurred to him. He glances behind him. "Have we?"

"I can look into it," *Capo* Ferri offers, his brows knitting together.

"Yes, please do. If we turn anything up, we'll inform you immediately, Hellfire, Demon. If someone needs to be better educated, we'll make sure it's a lesson they take to heart."

"I would most certainly appreciate that." *Fuck, this politeness is rubbing off on me, too.*

CHAPTER TWELVE

Demon

So far so good. War hasn't been declared, and we haven't come to blows. But I'm hearing nothing more than the platitudes I had expected. Rather than focusing on the words, I've been watching facial expressions, the movement of their eyes, and the relaxed or otherwise stance of their bodies. But they're as well-schooled as us. I observe nothing to suggest they're leading us on, not even a twitch to indicate our troubles result from their ploy to gain ground. Doesn't mean that's not what they're doing, just that they're good at hiding shit, and not ready to come clean and admit it. Except... My gaze lingers a little longer on Angel, noticing a tic in the corner of his eye. *Does he know something the others don't?* I put it to the back of my mind to think on later.

"If we catch anyone dealing on our territory, there won't be much left for you." I warn him he's not going to have everything his own way. If they are indeed his dealers, he'll end up short of a few men. "If there is anything remaining, I will, of course, let you have it." It will save us having to bury corpses.

"I hear you. It may be we have a joint problem." Don Lucio still admits to nothing. "In which case, we could do well to work together."

A suggestion he'd make if this is indeed the first he's hearing of it. If it's true the Silvestri family are not behind the sale of drugs on our turf, I'd be a fool to turn down their offer of help without at least giving the idea some consideration. I'd be happier to know it was him. Know thy enemy and all that. If he truly isn't involved, then we have someone else organising it, an unknown gang with a pipeline that's coming into our town. "If that is the case, I will, of course, welcome your involvement."

"Angelino, Ferri, see if we've identified a similar issue," Lucio instructs, without glancing behind him. He's confident if he did, he'd be seeing the nods just like I am. "If we find we have, I will let you know. The Devils and *i Silvestri* have a relationship going back a very long time. We understand each other, yes?"

I'm viewing this conversation in a similar frame of mind that I'd have were I to be facing a snake I've never come across before. I don't know whether it's going to fight or slither away. And if it bites me, whether it will be harmless or have deadly venom in its fangs. We've reached a sort of agreement. No point in extending this meeting.

"We understand each other," I agree, telling him nothing. "I believe we both know where we stand."

I stand. When he does likewise, I extend my hand. "Thank you for your time, it's always helpful to discuss matters face-to-face."

"Indeed, and I'm grateful for you coming here," he replies, copying the insincere smile on my face. "But before you go, there is one other matter you can help us with. My son has a question to ask you. Angelino?"

There's no change to my features, nothing to give anything away, my expression totally blank as my eyes firmly meet those of Angel, who's stepped forward to stand by his father's side.

Equally emotionless, he asks the one question I'd hoped not to hear. "How is Ms. Palmer?" he inquires. "And my son, young Theo? I am hoping they are both well. Please inform Violet I am looking forward to seeing her in court next week." His voice hardens. "I fully intend to pursue all my rights as my son's father."

It's like I've been struck by a thunderbolt. This meeting, in this house, displaying wealth earned through feeding habits of kids and the trafficking of unwilling women, men and children. These men who I wouldn't rub shoulders with unless there was no choice. One split second is all I need to know there's no way in hell I want this slimy man anywhere near Nathan's sister, nor to lay claim to his nephew. My mental processes work so fast there's been no discernible gap between the question being asked, and the answer that comes out of my mouth.

Worthy of the performance of a best actor on the world's biggest stage, my brow creases as I give him a look of confusion. "There is a mistake." I even shake my head as though perplexed. "Theo is my son, and Violet and I will be getting married. I hope, under the circumstances, you don't expect an invitation." My eyes harden in warning.

Angel looks like he's going to explode. His dark skin glows, his eyes flare. As he takes a step closer, Lucio's arm shoots out and holds him back. "You lie! Theo is mine. He carries my blood."

I don't pretend I don't know what he did to Violet. I might want to kill him, but now is neither the time nor the place. But I'll hurt him in the only way I currently can. I shrug. "Seems we both fucked her. But the kid's mine."

"You're lying," he repeats. "Violet would have mentioned you..." His eyes look wild as his hand makes a slashing movement. "She never said a word, even when she was in court."

"Violet's an independent woman. She wanted to handle everything alone. She has denied you are the father, hasn't she? She just didn't mention an alternative." I shrug. "Violet hoped she could keep me out of it. Bikers, and," I wave to include him and his father, "the Mafia avoid contact with the law where we can."

His eyes meet those of Lucio. "Father..."

"Angelino!" Lucio snaps. "There's a proper route to getting custody of your son. One we've already started. You know this." While Angel wants to respond with his fists, Lucio is using his brains. "I don't know what game you are playing, Demon. But there can be no truth in what you say. The possibility has never been raised."

"Has she ever confirmed you are the father, Angel?" I challenge. "Because she's told me I am." I know she hasn't. That's why Angel's going to have to get the court to demand a DNA test. The proper route that Lucio mentioned.

My head's trying to have a conversation while dealing with the major issue. *How the fuck does he know where she is? Have we got a leak? Could anyone in the club be a traitor?* Before Taser, I'd have staked my life on the answer being 'No'. Now? A brother? Christ, another one gone rogue? That would be unthinkable. A whore? A prospect? I'm going to have a few questions I need answered when I get back to the club. For now, I won't give Angel the satisfaction of asking how he knows.

"I don't understand why you are pursuing this, Angel. You won't get anywhere. Violet will not be turning up at court next week or any other. There is no chance you'll get custody. Any DNA test will show you are not the father." If I could, without them noticing, I'd be crossing my fingers.

Something flares in his eyes. *Doubt?* If it is, it means my sacrifice of taking a wife who I want to fuck but will have to live with those feelings being unreciprocated might be worth it. Maybe it means he'll finally leave Violet alone. I push my advantage. "Why you are tormenting my ol' lady, I have no idea. I suggest you drop it. You won't succeed, Angel. Theo is my child, not yours. I am his father." There, I've said it. I've claimed them. Now I've just got to find a way to tell Violet and manage the fallout.

Lucio puts his hand on his son's arm, his fingers digging in tight. "Not now, Angelino," he warns him again, presumably not wanting blood on his expensive carpet. Then, to me, in a tone with all pretence at politeness gone, "Whatever game you are playing won't succeed. My son is seeking his proper parental rights in the courts. I don't know how you think you are going to beat us. What you're saying is pure fabrication. Marry her, have the bitch. But the child is ours."

I feel Hellfire's presence at my left side, but it doesn't stop me. I spit out at Angel, "You raped her and now think you're entitled to her child? A child that is mine?" I'm really getting into this lie, but if I can't convince myself, I won't be able to pull the wool over anyone else's eyes.

Angel steps closer, one arm behind him as Lucio won't let go. "She willingly came to my bed, then tried to accuse me of rape. But with a reputation like hers, of course the court believed what I had to say, and I was cleared. There is nothing to stop me getting custody of my son." He sneers. "You, however, seem to lay claim through some immaculate conception. When did you come on the scene? And why have you so recently laid claimed to my child?"

I don't back down, using his own words against him. "Like you said in court, she has a reputation, the same reputation that cleared you of rape. I, too, took advantage of a young woman's healthy appetite for sex. She didn't tell anyone she had a child. When I found out, I claimed her. Theo is mine." There. I have a child without all the messy sex that goes along with it. Unfortunately.

"Angelino! He's lying through his fucking teeth." Now I have Lucio swearing; he must be riled. "A DNA test will sort this out."

Yeah, I'm fucking worried a court could order that. But I never roll over and submit. I'm going to fight this all the fucking way. We have to be taken to court first. As soon as I'm back at the compound, I have a list of things I need to be doing. Get a good lawyer for a start, get the court case postponed rather than my original plan for Violet just to not turn up. That won't work now Angel knows where she's hiding. Then see if we can stop this before we're in front of a judge.

Find the fucker who gave Violet's presence at the compound away, and if all else fails, kill Angel before he can swab his mouth.

"Come, Demon. There's nothing more to discuss here." Hellfire's hand is on my arm, an unconscious imitation of Lucio, pulling me, his son, back. Thunder's stepped to my other side.

"You'll be hearing from my lawyers!" Angel's parting comment reaches me as I'm hustled through the door.

"Say nothing," Hell hisses to me and Thunder, in warning.

Quickly reclaiming our weapons on the way out, we make it out of the house. We're on our bikes and moving before they decide using guns instead of words might resolve the problem faster. Once we're a good mile away, I hold out my left arm, then bend and swing it toward my shoulder, the signal they understand means I intend to pull up.

Once we do, I've kicked down the stand and am off the bike, bandana ripped off my head.

Thunder's looking, well, thunderstruck as he follows me. "What the fuck was that, Prez? Thought you tossed that idea about claimin' her on its head when Hell suggested it. You really going to step up and marry her?"

I throw my best president's glare at him, then turn to Hell. "What are they up to?"

"That was them fuckin' with us," Hell replies.

I kick some scrub; a disturbed lizard runs off, his tiny feet leaving a trail in the sand. Bending, I place my hands on my knees and breathe deeply. Leaving aside probably the most disastrous decision I've ever made in my life, I have another ginormous fucking problem.

"How the fuck do they know where she is, Hell? Who the fuck told them? Who's the fuckin' traitor in the club?"

"That's right, Prez. Let it out here." Thunder's in front of me. "You go throwing those accusations around in the compound? You know what you'd fuckin' do? Lose the trust of the motherfuckin' lot."

Still bent, I raise my eyes. "We hadn't seen Taser's betrayal coming."

"One fuckin' man, Prez. No one has the motive he had. Motive, that's what you need to think on. Who'd have fuck-all to gain from doing a favour for the Silvestri?"

"He has a point, Demon."

That's why Thunder would make a good VP, even if he doesn't know it. Slowly I stand, but turn my gaze to the barren desert in front of me. Motive. Well it wouldn't be the same one driving Taser. He'd seen himself with an officer patch, murdered to make sure there was a vacancy, went off the rails when he wasn't selected to fill it. Now there's an empty top spot, and none of the remaining members wants to step into it. But what other fuckin' motivation could be driving anyone?

"Could be a mole. Someone working with the Silvestri. In their pocket perhaps? Money they're offering, too much to be turned down?"

"You got anyone in mind, Hell?"

"Can't see anyone going after that. Can't say any of us can afford antiques and fancy ornaments, but we do alright." Interesting, Hell had also noticed the flagrant display of wealth. It shouldn't surprise me. He wasn't the prez for twenty years by not being observant.

"The girls?" Thunder puts in. "They think Demon's off the market?"

"Huh!" A startled laugh leaves my lips. "My cock that important?"

"Not sure I want to know what you do with your dick, son, but unless you have some magic technique..."

I shake my head. "Even if the whores want me to remain single, they couldn't have known I was going to claim Violet."

"And that there's the next problem, you have." Hell shakes his head. "Fuck, man, I know I suggested it, but didn't expect it like this. Thought you'd approach it different."

I'd had no intentions to approach it at all until I blurted it out. Now I'm wondering what the fuck had made me say it. Now that I have, I have to follow through; take a woman into my life who has no desire to come into my bed. A woman I'll need to treat like a sister.

I try to create some sense of the words coming out of my mouth. "It works, though. That fuckin' custody case is next week. Of course Vi isn't going to go, but as Angel knows where she is, he would have the law on his side to come drag her there. I need to have good grounds to get it legally kicked back. Now I've made plain his paternity's in question." I shade my eyes from the sun and turn around to look at them. "Which brings us back to, how the fuck does he know where she is?"

Thunder makes a VP-type comment again, "You knew it was a risk Angel had a man on her. Could have followed her to the compound. May not be a leak at all. Or can track her with technology."

"She's replaced her phone. Not sure the piece of crap she's got even has GPS."

"Thunder's made a good point, Demon. Talk to Cad, for fuck's sake, before you piss everyone off. You go in all guns blazing accusin' people, even look at them odd, you're risking your president's patch. Brothers earned trust the hard way, we've all been there and done that." He's right. Even I, his son, had spent twelve months doing shit to get patched in, days I'd prefer to forget than remember. "You give them one inkling they've lost that trust, you might lose it yourself."

Again, he's not wrong. Brothers, God help them, look up to me. If I start viewing everyone with suspicion, they'll be casting their eyes around, too. Best way to break a club or lose a good member, if twos and twos are added with the wrong result. We'd all but killed Skull for circumstantial evidence which pointed the wrong way.

"I'll speak to Cad. The question we need to ask is how he knows. Not to come out directly and demand to know who told him."

"You're focusing on the wrong problem." Hell gets my attention again. "Whatever, however, he has that information, you've claimed a woman who probably has no desire for a claimin'. That's what your head should be working on. She refuses? You don't follow through? You've just made things ten times worse."

"You basically told him she's a whore, Demon."

Fuck. Have I? Jesus, he's right. I told him, given her supposed immoral background, it wasn't unlikely she'd jump into my bed after leaving him. He wants to prove she's an unfit mother? *Maybe I've just handed him more ammunition. Shit.*

Hell's hand lands on my shoulder. "Let's get back."

I'm not ready. But this plan I've set in motion has to be kicked off. One last deep breath and I follow the others back to the bikes. Slipping into the lead, I ride on autopilot, thoughts whirring around my head. *Why the fuck did I publicly claim her? How could I not?* Something had to happen to put doubts in Angel's mind and get him to back off. I couldn't have said anything else, could I? I needed him to worry his wasn't the only dick near her. Christ, the idea of that slimy bastard laying his hands on her is abhorrent. The thought I'd been inside her, the fiction I'm going to need to get people to believe, is disappointing, I admit, only because I have not.

Now I've claimed her, maybe there's a chance I'll be able to rectify that frustration. *What would she feel like? Is she tight, inexperienced? What does she like in bed? Are there things I could teach her?* For fuck's sake! She's like my little sister. I would not be having these thoughts about Kennedy, so why am I about her?

Because I'm a man. She's a woman. And I'm having problems getting my head around that I've just sentenced myself to being faithful to someone I'll have to live with platonically. If I want to save Theo, I can't go back.

"My office." I barely wait for the engines to be switched off.

"Try and keep me a-fuckin'-way," Hellfire mutters as he swings his leg over the saddle.

Heads turn as we storm through the clubroom, but I hold up

my hand to stop questions being thrown my way. I do notice Cad's not in his usual corner. "Prospect. Find Cad. I need him." I don't bother to ask which of them will respond, content one of them will.

"So," Hell asks, as he sits on the visitor side of the desk, "you had any further thoughts on the way back?"

As Thunder kicks out the other chair, turns it around and straddles it, I sit, pinching my nose, then meet his stare.

"Whether it was wise or not, I've said Violet and the kid are mine. If I back down, Angel will smell a rat and come after her harder. No doubt about it, I've no option other than to carry this through."

There's a quirk to his lips when Hell says, "You're going to make your mother very happy."

Ain't that the fucking truth. A grandkid for her to fuss over. She'll be the last person to worry that the kid's not really mine.

The immensity of what I've taken on hits me. Words start tumbling out. "I presume she put 'Father Unknown' on the birth certificate. Need to get that changed to my name. Need to get the wedding organised. Get a lawyer to tell us our rights. Get next week's hearing postponed..."

"Whoa, hold up, son. You're forgetting one thing." As I raise my eyebrow, he continues, "She has to agree."

She can't afford not to. I have to make her see that. "Violet will do anything to keep Theo safe. If I tell her this is the plan, she'll go along with it." She'll take my advice, she thinks I'm her proxy big brother. She'll do what's best. *Big brother, yeah. One that wants to put his cock in her. Nothing wrong with that. Shit!*

There's a knock at the door, followed by Cad putting his head around it. "Heard you wanted me?"

"Yeah."

Thunder stands, indicates the chair he's just vacated, then steps back and leans against the wall, folding his arms across his chest. Quickly I explain to Cad.

"How the fuck did he know she was here?" The question

Cad's just asked must, for now, overshadow the personal ramifications of what I'm taking on.

"That's what we want you to find out." I'm proud of the patience in my tone.

The implications hit him fast. "We need to talk to everyone. See who could be in contact with the Silvestri. See who could have opened their mouths and let anything slip to the wrong person. We've been sending the girls out to buy baby shit, Prez."

"Wouldn't mean much unless he knew Vi and Theo were here."

"Before we alienate everyone in this club, Cad, any technical way he could have traced her?"

I notice my temporary VP has gone still, his brow furrowing.

"Thunder?" I encourage him to continue.

"Just hit me, Prez. What if they found out accidentally? I mean when they were listening for something else. We have product moving around our businesses. For all Lucio spouted, I still think his crew is behind that. What if they've found a way to watch us? Bugs in the club? Hell, I don't know, but I'd rather look for an answer before we start throwing accusations around."

It takes no more than a second for the implications of that to sink in. Then I'm blasting at Cad. "Could we be bugged? Watched?"

"Whoa." Cad holds up his hands. "Back up a bit, Prez. Someone would have needed to have planted shit like that. It would take a mole."

"Hangarounds coming to the parties? Couple of the guys have brought chicks back, too."

Cad's lips press together, his hands rub his temples. My fingers drum on the table, wondering why he's not jumped up and is tearing the club apart. "I'll do a sweep, Prez. Check it out. But this Angel has an obvious interest in Violet. He could have physical eyes on her, or virtual ones."

"You think he's tracking her? Thought of that, Brother, but she ditched her phone long before she came here."

Cad grins, leaning forward. "How about I tell you how I'd do it? What's the one item a woman always has with her?"

Hell's the one who answers. "Her fuckin' purse. Mo won't leave the house without it."

Could it be that easy? I was about to tear the club apart and she might have brought the Silvestri bug into the compound herself? Completely unknowingly, clearly. Placing my palms on the table, I start to push myself off the seat.

"Where you going?"

"To get her purse."

"Demon, sit down. You plan to walk in and take it?"

Of course, why not? "Yeah?"

"Well you might need to do some explaining when taking a woman's prized possession."

That's one reason why I never wanted a woman. The explaining myself part is not what I'm good at.

"Then," Hell continues, "you'll get into where you've been and why. Scare the shit out of her that Angel knows her location. And then have to tell her the decision you've unilaterally made. Think you need to plan how to approach it a bit more carefully."

"What do you suggest?" I glance out of the corner of my eye and see Cad listening intently.

Hell jerks his chin toward Cad, then his gaze comes to me. "How isn't the most important thing right now. Dealing with the implications is." Hell's face looks pinched. "Not the way I'd have wanted you to get hitched, Son." For the moment, he's my father. His lips press together, then he continues, "But this has to look right if you're going to fool Angel. You need to get everyone on-side to back up your story, which, if I'm allowed to point out, is as full of holes as a fuckin' sieve. It has to be water-tight, so you need everyone behind you. You also need to know how to approach this legally. Marriage, paternity rights. You're already talking about changing the birth certificate. When you talk to Violet, you can't be all ifs and buts, you have to know what you're doing."

Cad looks at Hell, his eyes going wide, then he turns back to me and nods. He's added all that data together fast. "I, we, will be behind you, Prez. Whatever you need. We will all have your back. Tell me what you want and I'm on it."

For a moment I stare at the ex-prez who I'm thinking should rightly still be sitting in this chair. He's right. To pull this off, I need to convince her I have a plan, and that it will work. Knowledge, that will be my weapon.

"Order of play, then. I'll start to look everything up."

Christ, I don't even know where you get a marriage license or how long it takes to do things right. But I will. Before I see Violet.

"Her car's in the compound, isn't it, Prez?" When I nod, Cad continues, "That's where I'll start. Could be as simple as he's put a tracker on it."

"Then we have church. Bring everyone in..."

"Before or after you tell Violet?"

Right now I don't know which is worse. If it comes down to it, I'd far rather be explaining my plan to my brothers than trying to convince a woman to tie herself to me in a loveless, platonic marriage.

Cad and Thunder disappear. Hell stays with me while I try to work through the mire of legalities, getting everything straight in my head. We could marry today, it would seem, not too much formality. I've a phone full of notes that will override any objection she has by the time Cad reappears.

"Car's clean, Prez. If she has anything on her, I'd put money on it being in her purse. I've just seen her in the clubroom. She has the kid with her, she's engrossed with the women. Couldn't see she had any bag with her except for the kid's stuff. If we're going to search her purse without her knowing, what about now?"

"Good call. Let's do it."

CHAPTER THIRTEEN

Violet

"He's gorgeous, Violet. You can see Nathan in him, he has his nose."

Frowning, I respond, "Not sure that's a compliment, Mo. Poor kid."

"Nathan was a handsome man, Violet."

Now I'm laughing at Demon's mom. "He was my brother. You'll have to excuse me if I don't think of him that way."

She smiles, and leans over, smoothing her hand gently over a sleeping Theo's head. "He grows up like your brother? I assure you, he'll be fighting all the girls off."

"Or not." Jayden slumps down beside us. A grin accompanies her next words. "If he's anything like the men here, he'll be lapping all the attention up." Reaching over, she pulls down the blanket that is covering Theo, so she can get a good look at him. "Seems he's out for the count, Violet. Want to put him in his stroller and I'll watch him for you? Give you some time to yourself?"

I've just changed him; he's been fed. *I could use a few moments to myself.*

Moira's been bombarding me with questions since she arrived. Does he feed well? Sleep well at night? Had his shots?

Any issues? Her friendly concern and interest isn't anything I haven't experienced before, but coming from Demon's mother, a woman I knew well in the past, makes me wish it was my own mom making such enquiries.

It doesn't seem right that my mom wouldn't remember him being born. She isn't able to understand she is a grandmother. I'm torn between guilt that I should check in and see my mom for myself, and the knowledge even if it was safe for me to go see her, it wouldn't do anything but upset me. Even if I could go visit, I don't know what I'd achieve.

The last few days have at least given me a chance to catch my breath, to concentrate on being Theo's mom, putting the rest to the back of my mind for a moment. Theo's benefitted from my less-anxious state; he's sleeping better at night. Of course, I haven't stopped worrying. Angelino won't have given up, but he doesn't know where I am. This has become my safe haven.

No one seems to be in a hurry for me to leave, but I won't be able to stay here forever. Sometime soon I'll need to speak to Demon and work on my future plans.

I put my hand to my mouth to cover a yawn. Theo's sleeping better, but that still means he wakes early for his first feed. Jayden's suggestion of some time to myself is very welcome, and something I haven't had much chance to indulge in since Theo's birth. I've no qualms about leaving my son with Jayden, and Mo's hovering around, desperate for him to wake up, if I'm any judge.

A long soak in the tub? Yeah. Maybe. Perhaps, first, some fresh air. I've been cooped up inside for days.

"Thank you, Jayden. He should be down for a while now. Mo, it was lovely catching up with you again."

"You go and relax. I'm happy to watch him with Jayden." Demon's mother's eyes have a maternal gleam to them. For a second my stomach clenches. What would it have been like if Theo were Demon's son, and Mo his real grandmother? *Don't go there, Vi. Theo's yours. It doesn't matter who his sperm donor was.* But it does. I force my mind away from the immensity of problems his parentage has caused.

Nodding to them both, I stand, then, with one last glance back, reassuring myself that he's in good hands, I walk across the clubroom to the kitchen, and out through the back door. I haven't had a chance to explore outside before. The ground is damp, but steam is rising as it's heated by the sun, which has reappeared after a sudden heavy downpour of rain. Seeing the area with a mother's eye, I notice the grass, but also dangerous lumps of concrete lying around. Spying picnic benches, I wander across, worried when I see a huge, deep pit. Inside there are grills, which must be for when they have barbeques. I doubt I need worry; I'll be long gone before Theo starts running around, but it seems dangerous for a youngster.

Was this where Demon and his brother and sister played? Or didn't they come here as kids? I only remember their house off-compound. Whether children have run through these grounds before is nothing to do with me. My future is starting over in another state, not here.

The industrial history of the buildings housing the club is more pronounced from the outside. I spend a moment looking around, intrigued, as well as enjoying the sunshine and the solitude.

"They used to melt down trains in there," a deep voice sounds from my side. Looking around, I see the man they call Thunder.

"It's not big enough for a train," I scoff, thinking he's pulling my leg.

He walks closer and looks down into the pit. "They'd saw it in half first. It's true. What you're looking at is the furnace."

I look at the pit again. Yes, perhaps half a train would fit. Seems he could be telling the truth. "How long since it was worked?"

He shrugs. "Getting on forty years now. Steel mill closed when the industry crashed."

"And the club's been here since then?"

"More or less."

"Demon's grandfather was the president back in those days, wasn't he?" I'm sure someone told me. Nathan, perhaps.

Thunder glances my way, then quickly averts his eyes. "What you doing out here, anyway?"

It's a quick change of subject. I don't understand why Demon's relationship to the initial president is a touchy subject, but it certainly appears to be. I don't press; it's none of my business. As my relationship with the club will only be brief, I have no need to pry. "I just wanted some fresh air," I explain. "Jayden and Mo are watching Theo for me." I add the last hastily, not wanting him to think I've abandoned my baby again.

Thunder laughs. "Mo will be in her element. She loves kids."

He's got that right. It's a bit awkward. My solitude has been ruined. I barely know this man. Don't know how to speak to him.

"You should be safe out here, Violet," he says, suddenly. "But you shouldn't wander around alone."

"No one can get into the compound." I'm viewing the high brick walls that surround the old factory. Where the wall has fallen in, there's high chain-link fencing to keep people out.

Thunder touches my shoulder and turns me around. He points around my arm. "Sniper could take you out if he wanted to."

My eyes go wide. "Why would anyone want that?"

"Because if Theo has no other parent, Angel gets what he wants."

I go cold. I truly hadn't considered that I could be in danger, that killing me would pave the way for Angelino to get what he wanted. As chills run through me, I wrap my arms around my stomach. "Angelino doesn't know where I am, does he?"

He hesitates, then shakes his head. "Nevertheless, pet. If I was you..."

"I'll go back inside," I say quickly.

"Best you do. Demon wouldn't want you exposed. And I need to get off to work."

As Thunder waits, expectantly, I realise he'd only come out to make sure I was safe. All Demon's men seem to be looking out for me, and now I'm holding him up. I know they have my best interests at heart, but it makes me feel a bit like a prisoner. Thinking I really need to make some plans about moving on, I turn and make my way back inside.

I return through the kitchen; a long soak in the bath is sounding more and more attractive. Noticing Mo and Jay talking, I presume Theo is still asleep and not stirring and go over to check. Cad walks past, giving me a nod.

"Hey, that was no more than five minutes," Jay grins.

"Go on, shoo. All moms need time to themselves."

Thanking them both, but still feeling guilty, I slip across the clubroom and up the stairs.

Entering Hell's room that he's kindly allowing me to use, I grab a clean towel. Soon I'm watching steaming water fill the tub. Having Theo, quick showers are normally all that I can take, so I'm longing to have a good long soak. There's no bubble bath, but just being able to lie back and relax is enough. When it's full, and I might have over-indulged with the amount of water I've used, I ease myself down with a sigh, feeling my brain start to unwind.

It's sheer enjoyment, a luxury I've missed. I take my time, ignoring that my skin is wrinkling; it's just so nice to lie back, knowing Theo is in good hands. I didn't know how much I needed this moment to myself until I had it.

Mmm. This is so nice. It's a shame I'll need to get out soon; I swear, one by one, my muscles are unknotting as I let my arms drift weightless to the surface. In a state of total relaxation, I hear voices coming through the door. There are men in my room.

I come back to myself. My heart beats fast, then my brain kicks in, reassuring me. I'm safe in the compound. The men outside will only be Demon's men. But what are they doing in the room that's been assigned to me? Not really afraid, more curious, and slightly indignant, I rise from the bath, water cascading off me, then realise I've nothing to cover myself with but a towel. Having thought I was alone, I'd left my clothes outside, so they wouldn't be dampened by the steam. Luckily, it's a large bath towel. I wrap it around me. Then pause at the door, listening.

"Where the fuck does she keep it?"

They're searching my room for something? I've no idea what, I've very little possessions here at all, nothing worth stealing. My temper rises. If they wanted something of mine, why didn't they come and just ask?

Right. One, two… On the mental count of *'three'*, I throw open the door, hard enough so it crashes against the wall before bouncing back. Three men jump, three faces carry identical startled expressions.

After a second, each shows a different emotion.

Cad is holding my purse, his hand rummaging inside. He looks guilty. Demon's standing next to him looking annoyed, and Thunder is smirking. When Demon glances his VP's way, he hurriedly steps forward, putting his body between me and the other two men.

Peering around him, I glare at the man holding my purse. "What are you doing with that? And you," I prod Demon in the back. "I want the truth. What's going on?"

He swings around, then averts his eyes as they land on the damp, bared skin above the towel tightly knotted over my breasts.

"Cad," he tosses over his shoulder, "take the fuckin' purse and get out. You too, Thunder."

"Hey, that's mine." I try to go past Demon to stop Cad leaving the room with the bag holding all my personal possessions, but Demon moves to block my way. My glare has no effect, and my feeble attempts to budge him don't work.

As the two men leave, Thunder tosses, "Good luck, Prez," over his shoulder. That smirk I don't understand and find myself wanting to smack off his face is still firmly in place.

"Speak. Now," I demand, my temper getting the better of me as the door closes behind them. "What the hell are you doing with my purse? If you wanted something, you could just ask for it."

I've little enough in there. But it's personal. My face burns at the thought of Cad finding my tampons. Like any woman, I don't carry much around. Only a few notes in my wallet, a couple of bank cards, my driver's license. A spare diaper, pens, of course. A bit of makeup. An appointment card for Theo's shots, a spare pacifier, a mirror, hand sanitizer, notebook, lip balm, tissues, band-aid, a few hundred receipts I just chucked in there. A few photographs of me and my mom in happier times, and God knows what else. Lots of things I'd be lost without. Oh, and my car keys, of course. Not that I can remember seeing them. I bet they've just gotten buried at the bottom; I'm always having to rummage to find them.

"I want it back, Demon."

Demon pinches the brow of his nose, then says, wearily, "Put some clothes on, Vi. Didn't know you were here, else we wouldn't have disturbed you."

"Obviously not," I toss back angrily. "You'd prefer to come thieving when there was no one around."

"Thieving? What the fuck, Vi? Cad's not going to steal anything. You'll get all your shit back."

I snort. "That 'shit', as you so kindly put it, is private. No one should go into a woman's purse."

"Clothes, Vi," he reminds me impatiently. "Got things I need to tell you, and I'd rather do it when you're dressed."

"Why?" I strike a pose to taunt him. "Can't resist me?"

His hand slashes down through the air. "Vi," he growls, warningly.

"Okay, okay." I go to the drawer and extract a tank top and a pair of shorts that had been lent to me. I hadn't bothered to pack much in my suitcase. "Which reminds me, Demon. I need clothes."

"I'll take you shopping soon, Vi. Promise."

Back up. Two things there. One, that I'll be allowed to go out, when I thought there was too great a risk of anyone seeing me, and the second he's implied he'll take me himself. Even my brother would have found some excuse to avoid clothes shopping. But knowing there's some reason he won't talk to me until I'm wearing less than the towel covers, I return to the bathroom, quickly throwing on my clean clothes, and tying my hair into a messy bun.

When I emerge, he nods approvingly and seems to relax, as if being in my room with me wearing only a towel discomfited him.

"Where's Theo?"

"Out for the count. Jay and your mom have him."

He startles when I mention Mo, but then recovers himself before I can think anything of it. "So, we've got time to talk."

When I nod, he raises his chin as though pleased I've agreed. He starts to pace.

I'm not going to give him time to think of excuses. "Tell me, D. Why have you stolen my purse? I'm not going to be making a run for it." Not that I'd get far with little more than loose change in my wallet.

"Vi, look. I didn't want to worry you." Again, his forefinger and thumb meet at the top of his nose. It's a gesture he seems to use when he's uncomfortable or when he's thinking.

He's going to worry me? Okay, so now I'm concerned. "I suggest you start talking."

I perch on the end of the bed, pulling my legs up under me. Seated, I can better ignore the great difference in our height. With me in bare feet he probably has a good foot over my just below average for a woman height.

But instead of towering over me, he sits down by my side. Not close enough to touch or invade my personal space. *If I was brave enough, I'd inch closer.* My anger at the loss of my purse is starting to turn into something else as my heart beats faster at the realisation the man who attracts me so much is on my bed with me. The situation I've so often dreamed about. But that was back in the days when I was in my early teens, and him unobtainable. Now? I'm a woman. He's a man. My son's in good hands... For a second, I wonder what would have happened if I'd had the nerve to drop that towel. Would Demon have lost control at the sight of me?

Christ, who am I kidding? My body can't compete with the likes of Titsy or Bella, or any of the whores come to think of it. They won't have the baby fat I'm still carrying, nor the stretch-marks. *He's out of your league, Vi, forget it.*

I sigh. Misinterpreting my action, Demon takes it as a sign of my impatience. "I met Don Lucio this morning. Angel's father." When I raise and dip my head, he continues, "A meeting to discuss club business." His eyes flick to mine carrying a warning that I'm not to ask for more detail than that.

There's a pause, a clenching of his teeth, then the admission, "Angel was there."

My gut clenches like it always does when the name of my rapist is mentioned. I look away, then back. *There's a reason he's telling me. He wouldn't be bringing it up if it wasn't important.* I raise my gaze to meet his.

"I wanted to handle this without you knowing, Vi. Still could, I suppose; come up with some shit to keep you in the dark. Shit, I don't know."

I've not seen him like this before. Demon's usually in such control, never at a loss for words.

"Just tell, me, D."

A quick look, then, "No easy way of saying this, but he knows where you are, Violet. Where Theo is." As my hand goes to my mouth to cover the gasp that comes out, he carries on quickly, "That's why Cad's looking through your purse. We think he might have put a tracker in it."

My initial thought is that I don't give a damn about the how. I feel like I'm going to be sick, the knowledge Angel knows I'm in the compound has swept my feeling of comfort and safety away. I drop my head into my hands as realisation hits. *He's been tracking me.* If that's true, there's no way I could have gotten away from him. Nowhere would have been far enough. I'd gotten rid of my phone. How the hell did Angelino...?

"I dropped my purse." It comes back to me in a flash. "After the court hearing. One of his men bumped into me, everything spilled out. He picked up the stuff, shoved it back in and returned it. I didn't think twice." *Damn it!* "I thought I'd been clever, D, getting the new phone, changing my number."

"I think odds are, knocking into you wasn't an accident and he slipped something in at the same time. He obviously suspected you'd skip town once you knew he was after Theo and wanted to be able to track you. You weren't to know, Vi." Briefly, his hand touches mine. A brotherly gesture of support.

Raising my head, I meet his eyes again. "So it's back to plan A. Cad destroys the tracker, and I disappear out of state." I wouldn't be able to visit my mother, ever. But she's being well looked after, and it's not as if she would know whether I was there or not. I think for a second, then get excited. "Or, can one of your men go on a long drive, take the tracker with him? Leave a false trail? Have him chasing his tail trying to find me while I'm going off in the other direction? That would work, wouldn't it?"

His eyes grow dark, his cheeks pinched. He doesn't seem as excited about the idea as I am. "Not going to happen, Vi. On your own, with a kid? Not going to happen."

"But, Demon. Look, I researched him. I know how big the Silvestri family is, they're the Mafia. And if they know where I am now – oh, hell. I have to run, get out of here today..."

"I said no." He stands and walks to the door. He doesn't open it but turns and leans his back against it. "I promised Nathan I'd look out for you, and that's what I'm going to do. This morning, words were said, put a plan into action."

"What words and what plan?" My eyes narrow. *What's he talking about?* I'm in a blind panic here, knowing I have to get away.

For a moment Demon seems more interested in his feet, then he looks up, meets my eye, then looks away again.

"I told Angel that Theo was my kid."

"You did what?" I shout incredulously.

"Told him Theo was mine," he repeats, patiently.

"He bought that?" My heart leaps for a second. *As easy as that to get my rapist off my back?* I'd always denied his parentage, but never thought to substitute another name. But there had been no man in the running, no friend I could call. I'd been out of state too long. "He believed you?"

"Nah," Demon shakes his head. "But it has to have sown a seed of doubt. And..." he pauses. He straightens, walks over, and sits by my side again. "Vi, hear me out, okay? Give me a chance to tell you everything before you interrupt."

Confused, I nod, wondering what else he's going to tell me.

"I'm claiming Theo." He says it as if it's a major announcement.

"If Angelino thinks there's a chance Theo isn't his, then it can only help. D. I'll happily say you're the father if you're sure you're okay with that? Of course, I won't ask you for anything, we'll keep the lie between us. Perhaps Angelino will put less effort into getting a child that he must now doubt is his." I begin to breathe easier. Yes, this help I can accept.

Demon puts his finger to my lips. "I asked you to hear me out, Vi."

I nod and say nothing. I don't know what else he has to tell me, but I'll listen. He's trying to help me after all.

"Did you put a father's name on the birth certificate?"

I stay dumb.

"Vi, I asked you a question."

"I thought you said I shouldn't speak?"

He 'humph's exasperatedly. "Vi," he growls.

"No, of course I didn't," I answer.

"Then we can get it changed. Add my name. There's no problem if we both say the same thing. I've checked it out. Won't take much to change it." Again, he pinches his nose. "Vi, listen carefully. Whatever Angel threw up about your supposed background in court, it was evident he didn't believe you'd jumped from his bed to mine. It was also clear I'd have to do something, say something, to convince him."

Okay. I nod. Sitting forward, I wonder what he's going to say next, interested to hear his idea.

"I told him we'd be getting married. We'll do that this week. You can change the birth certificate to name me as the father at the same time. It will be harder for him to contest..."

My brain picks out one word on which to focus and I don't hear anything else. *Married. Married to Demon? Married to Dave, my brother's best friend, who sees me as nothing more than a sibling? Married to Demon, the president of an MC?*

My horrified answer comes fast. "No."

"Vi, think about this."

Now I'm the one throwing myself off the bed and frantically pacing the room. On my second pass, I halt and look directly at him. "I don't need to think about it, Dave. You're out of your freaking mind. Angelino isn't going to fall for a sham of a marriage. We'd have to make it look real. We can't pretend, it would have to be official. I don't know how quickly we'd be able to divorce, either. You don't even like me that way."

"I don't have to like you 'that way'." He uses air quotes. "It's just pretence, Vi. We'll live here in the compound, only my brothers will know we don't share a bed. And there'll be no divorce, not until I'm certain Angel's no longer coming after the kid. If that's until Theo is eighteen, well, that's what I'll be signing up for. I'll be giving him protection until he no longer needs it. It's what Nathan would have wanted. Me to make sure you were looked after."

Moving a step closer, my finger prods him in his chest, punctuating every word. "Problem is, Dave, I'm not Nathan's little sister any longer. I'm a grown woman. As a woman I have needs. You expect me to stay here, living in the compound, watching you go off with whores while I what? Lie in bed with a vibrator?"

"Vi!"

His jaw drops and his face grows red, but I'm not letting him get a word in. Not now. This is my turn to have the floor. "There's better solutions, one which doesn't tie me to you, or you to me. I'll need your help to do it properly, but I've told you, I'll change my name and leave." It would break me. But to stay here in a sham of a marriage with a man I want who doesn't want me? That's an even worse alternative.

He grabs hold of my hands, strong fingers around mine, stilling them. "Marrying me means you can come out of hiding. Visit your mom. You really want to leave and never see her again?"

It seems he's going to bring out every weapon in his armoury.

"No, of course I don't. But as she doesn't even remember she has a daughter, it's not as bad as you're making out, Dave. Look, I'm grateful to you for giving me breathing space to get my priorities straight. But I'm not going to marry you and that's final. And don't bring up this stupid supposed debt you owe to Nathan. I don't need you stepping into the big brother role, I've done okay by myself up to now."

He's standing, towering over me, fury raging from those eyes which seem to be glowing, providing an insight as to how he got his handle. I wrench my hands out of his grasp and take a step back, and then another. He stalks me. When my back hits the door, there's nowhere left for me to go.

"You've done alright? First you put yourself in the position of being raped, Vi." I gasp, but he relentlessly continues, "If I'd been there for you, it wouldn't have gone down the way it had. If you'd spoken to me, and I'd checked who you were proposing to work for, I'd have told you the lay of the land before you put yourself in danger."

"Stop right there!" I cry out. "No woman, ever, puts herself in the position of being raped. Nothing she does excuses a man. Is that what you're doing, D? Absolving Angelino and putting it on me?"

"Fuck, Vi, I didn't mean it like that." His eyes roll. "I'm not blamin' you, I'm blamin' myself. Angelino should never have been able to get near you. I should have been there for you. If I'd known you were in financial difficulties, if you'd come to me, we could have sorted that shit out. But you lost your home, Vi, ended up homeless, with no money and a kid to support. Because I wasn't there for you, your only option was to give him away to strangers. Should have fuckin' been there. If Nathan had been alive, he'd have helped you out. So don't try and tell me there's no debt to repay."

I make the mistake of looking at him. He's leaning over me, one hand balanced on the door to the left of my head. I smell his breath, a mingling of mint and coffee. Feel it as he exhales, a warm huff against my cheek. I'm scared of the beast I've taunted and enraged, while I know he'd never hurt me. Even if such violence was within him, the respect he holds for my brother would hold him back. What frightens me is how much he's made me aroused. My breathing is coming in pants, his chest is rising and falling as fast as my own. Momentarily we stare into each other's eyes. Me, willing him to lower his lips and...

I come to my senses.

He's never going to do something so intimate, and all because of the long past relationship between him and my brother. I may be hot for him, but he's never going to have the same feelings. How could I exist in a loveless relationship, knowing he's fucking other women when I'd rather he was fucking me? Never in a million years could I do that.

"No," I tell him again.

He ignores me. "We both need to go to the Marriage License office to get the license. You'll just need your birth certificate; if you haven't brought with you, I'll go get it from your house.

Then we'll get married immediately. We'll go down today. No point in wasting time."

"You're not listening to me," I growl.

"No." Once again his hand makes that slashing through the air gesture. "You're the one not listening. We're getting married, Vi. I'm giving you my name, my protection. That makes Theo safe. I'm doing everything I can to stop Angel getting his hands on the kid."

I erupt. My hands push him roughly. If he hadn't let me, I wouldn't have had the chance of pushing him away, but he steps back.

"I am not marrying you!"

His voice is icily cold as he asks, "You really want to risk Angel getting custody of Theo? Cause that's what he's going after, Vi. He won't be satisfied with visitation or joint parenting. He wants everything. He wants to break you, Vi. He wants Theo with no strings attached. You'll be cut right out of the picture. Do you want to risk that? Even if Angel died, don't you think his family would move Heaven and Earth to get hold of his son? Don Lucio is quite clearly backing him. And you—if you died, there would be no one in his way."

Deep down I think I'd known it, but it's not something you want to admit. A brief recollection of my conversation outside with Thunder. A bullet, my death, and, if Angelino insists on a paternity test, there'll be nothing to stop him taking my son. Even if I'm alive, he'll probably get his way. With his access to the hospital records, he'll twist the truth and make out I'm unfit to look after my son. That's why I took the drastic actions I had. My few days in this oasis are over; it's time to face reality again and remember I'll do anything, *anything*, to protect my son.

I turn around, resting my forehead against the door. Demon and his bikers would protect me. If I left, I'd be alone. Could I really hide? Where could I run? What reach do the Silvestri have? How does one go about getting a new identity? It would certainly cost money, something I don't possess. I couldn't even start without Demon's help. If I did manage to get somewhere safe, every day for the next eighteen years I'd be looking over my shoulder, viewing each stranger with suspicion, panicking each time I heard an Italian accent.

Just days ago, I was going to take the drastic action of handing my son over to strangers to keep him out of Angelino's hands. I'd already decided I would then have nothing to live for.

Is what Demon is offering really worse than what I had planned?

CHAPTER FOURTEEN

Demon

I wait with bated breath for her answer, hoping for acquiescence, expecting another refusal. I don't know what else I can say to persuade her; I've already used every argument that I can think of. Giving her my name and protection is the only way I can see of fulfilling my promise to Nathan. His blood runs through Theo. I'll happily bring up his nephew as if he were my own.

I've never wanted kids.

Seems like I'm about to acquire one. If she says 'yes'.

If she says 'no', I can't force her.

Christ. Standing so close to her, my cock's been hard to keep under control. When she's riled her chest heaves, and it's hard to stop my eyes from focusing on those breasts which she keeps unintentionally bringing to my attention. She's small, petite, but well-rounded. Fuck, there's part of me that would definitely enjoy consummating the marriage. *Knowing she was mine for the taking whenever I wanted? Wouldn't be any hardship in that.* Something suggests that once I've had a taste of that pussy, I could forego all others.

Can't go there. She's Nathan's sister. He'd turn in his grave if I took advantage. As for Vi? She'd be horrified at the direction of my thoughts. I have to keep my dick with a mind of its own behaving. Christ, she's already been through a rape, she doesn't need more pressure on her. Nah, until Angel's finally out of the picture I'm going to have to get super-friendly with my hand. This marriage isn't about getting my dick wet, though I suspect at times I'm going to find that fact one hell of a challenge to remember.

Though I keep telling myself that's all she is, it's getting harder and harder to think of her as a sister. My cock's never swelled around Kennedy, thank fuck. But Vi? Around her, my dick has a mind of its own. Thank fuck here in the compound we won't need to pretend and can keep to our separate rooms. If I was to have to sleep in the same bed as her, I don't know how I could keep my hands off her. Would try every trick in the book to persuade her.

I close my eyes, roll my head back, and try to think of another line of reasoning I can use to convince her. Anything to get my mind off the throbbing in my groin. I realise she's gone silent. Wondering why she's given up arguing, I glance back down to see her shoulders are slumped. It dawns on me that all the fight's gone out of her. *Thanks to me.* Fuck, I hate I've done that. That look on her face? I never again want to see her so defeated. I vow there and then, while I'll never be a husband to her in the true sense of the word, I'll do everything I can to make her happy and content, to give her the security to bring her boy, our son, up right.

"Babe." I place my fingers under her chin and turn her face up to mine. "I promise I'll give you a good life. Within reason, everything you could ask for. I'll be a dad to Theo. Neither of you will want for anything."

Her eyes close briefly. Hopefully, from her position I'm painting a picture of a utopia. What more could she want? I suspect I'd go to the ends of the earth to give her anything that she desires. That's what Nathan would have done.

She's quiet, then shakes her head sadly. "What if I want more children, D?"

Oh, fuck, no. She had to go there. The one place I couldn't follow her. My head moves sharply side-to-side; that's one thing I'll have to deny her, confident she doesn't mean with me. While we're married, she'll only have access to my cock. As it's the last one she'd want, it's not going to happen. She's struck me speechless, she takes it that I need persuasion. Nothing she could say will change my mind.

"I didn't have a say when Angelino raped me." Her voice is monotone. "And now I've apparently no say in who I'll get married to. Angelino wants my son. What makes you different? You're saying you want him too, want to co-parent. You don't want to go through the fucking, the pregnancy, the birth of your own children—you just want what is mine."

"Hey, Vi. How the hell did you come up with that? Just thought it would be easier if I was there with you, sharing the burden." As her mouth opens to protest, I quickly add, "And the joy. But if you want, I won't interfere at all. Leave his care all down to you. You can make all the decisions on your own. I can be his dad in name only if that makes you feel better. Never, ever, compare me to that asshole again."

"You even like kids?" she remarks scathingly.

"From what I've seen, I like Theo," I admit, cautiously. "I've not been around others." *And that's the truth.* "Say yes, Vi. Let me help you. Please."

I think it's my pleading that diminishes the sudden burst of anger. "You said you told Angelino. How did he react?"

At last, an easy question to answer. "I think saying he was angry would be an understatement."

She nods and adds a little smile of satisfaction. "To see another man bringing up his kid? That will hurt him."

I take advantage. "He took something from you, Vi. Take something back."

She pushes me away and starts to pace, her teeth biting her lip as she thinks. Then she lets me into her thoughts.

"If he insists on a DNA test, he'll still have rights."

I pinch the bridge of my nose. "Yeah, Vi, he might. But if Theo has a stable homelife with me and you, the worst will be parental rights and visitation, and I'll be right there beside you making sure Theo is safe. And don't forget, a court has to insist on a DNA test. I'll get the fuckin' best lawyer I can. See if we can convince them there's no doubt I'm the father so they won't order it in the first place."

She huffs. "A court decided he wasn't a rapist. I've no faith in the law."

"See? The court made an unexpected decision that time. There must be some way to sway them to your side. Angel blackened your character, but with the right lawyer, we can disclose the truth about him." I'll get Cad digging, see if there's a trail of evidence to child trafficking. Angel wouldn't have a cat's chance in hell with that on his record. Or, if something comes to light, he wouldn't want that business to come up in court. Yeah, there are things I know to do that she wouldn't have dreamed of, or have been able to do by herself.

I haven't much faith in the law, though. Show me a biker who has. If it starts to look like she's no chance of winning, then whatever the repercussions, Angel will be close to breathing his last breath.

I press, now that she's listening. "I've fuck-all idea why Angel is so set on getting the child, Vi. At the end of the day, he might realise he's losing the battle, and his interest will fade. You have more chances of success with me beside you. Sweetheart, I know you think I'm forcing you, but you do have the choice. Can't do anything without you saying 'yes'."

If she insists on doing it herself, I'll help her. I'm not such a bastard as to throw her to the wolves, or even use that as a threat. If she refuses, so be it. I'll get her the best fucking fake identity money can buy. Set up an allowance so she's well-supported. Send her to where we have another chapter to keep an eye on her. But that's the last resort. I want her close so I can personally protect her, so I'm going to do my damnedest to persuade her.

Of course, if she insisted on moving away, that would mean I'd have some backpedalling to do with the Silvestri, some explaining, some made-up fight that meant we hadn't made it to the courthouse, and that she ran off instead. But I'll come up with something; that's the least of my worries.

"The way I see it," her voice has gentled, "is that you're making more sacrifices than you're expecting me to. I can't ask you to do that."

"You're not asking or forcing me to do anything I don't want."

Would I have made the offer if I was a different person? If the man who raised me hadn't taken on another man's son? At least he killed my mother's rapist. That's what I'll do in the end, though I can't admit that to her. Angel signed his death warrant when he first laid his fingers on Vi. We'll both have our freedom when the motherfucker has drawn his last breath. But it needs to be done carefully, any suggestion the Devils were involved and Vi stands to lose more than her kid. It would end in a bloodbath, the likes of which Pueblo has never seen.

The Silvestri wouldn't take kindly to us killing one of their own, and now I've stepped up, unless it can be done without fingers pointing in our direction, we'd be the first culprits in line. The loss of his son and heir? Lucio might decide to take us out just to make a point, even if there was no evidence found.

Revenge, as someone at church had said, in this case is best eaten cold and with very careful forethought and planning.

She's crossed back to the bed and is sitting with her head in her hands. If she was any other woman I'd be there with her. Pushing her back down, using my mouth and my cock to persuade her, to show her what pleasures I could bring her if she'd just agree to take me as her man. *If she was anyone else, I wouldn't be in this situation.*

Instead I go over, sitting beside her, careful to keep my body from touching hers, just reaching out my hand and giving a brotherly squeeze to her shoulder. I can't think of more words I could use to convince her. To me, this is her only sensible option. Here she has support and friends; anywhere else she'd be on her own, trying to maintain a fabrication of a past so nothing could fall back on her, not knowing who to trust. I don't want that for her.

She's deciding the fate of the next weeks, months, years of her life, I'll give her time. While I've no intention of keeping her tied to me longer than necessary, to present the right front we have to make outsiders believe this is for real with no expiration date. Am I prepared to make that commitment?

Nathan gave his life; what's being asked of me is nothing compared to that sacrifice.

When someone knocks, she startles. I go to open the door, not surprised to see it's Cad. He hands me her purse.

"Went through it, Prez. Took a bit longer than I'd expected, there was a lot of shit to go through. But, yeah. I found it. That's how he knew where she was. Dropped a fuckin' tiny tracker in there. She probably wouldn't have noticed in amongst the other junk."

"Did you find my car keys?" A little voice comes from behind me.

Cad raises his brow. He wouldn't have found those, they're in my custody. I nod and dismiss him. That's one mystery solved.

"I have your keys, Vi," I admit, when I've closed the door behind him. "From when the prospect drove you here."

She shrugs as though it's of no importance. "At least we know, now. Angelino knew every step I took."

"He did." *Thank fuck I hadn't come back and accused all and sundry.* I stand, unsure whether to go back and sit beside her, torn between giving her more time and pressing her to give me the answer I want to hear, wary of leaving her alone to overthink it. "I'll never hurt you, Vi."

"Know that. It just proves it, doesn't it?"

She's lost me. "What proves what?"

Her hand waves toward the closed door. "Angelino putting a tracker in my bag. I wouldn't have dreamed of looking for it. I wouldn't survive in your world. In his world. Not without someone who knew how to protect me."

Cad's news seems to have changed her opinion. I hardly dare breathe, hoping this is going where I want it to go.

"You say you won't hurt me, D, but I don't care about me. You must promise never, ever to hurt Theo. Never to raise your hand to him whatever he does. Never raise your voice without good reason. If you're going to be a father to him, you must never make him believe he's any less than your son. If we change the birth certificate, you'll be all the father he'll ever know."

If I hadn't had a similar upbringing, I might have hesitated. But how can I when that was exactly what Hell had done for me? "You ever think Hell treated me badly, Vi?" She doesn't know my story, not yet. One day she will. If she becomes my wife, there'll be no secrets between us.

"Of course not."

"He's my role model, Vi. I had a good one. From the moment you say 'yes', Theo's my son. I'll be the same father as Hell was to me." One day, soon, she'll realise the significance of my words. But not now. She has enough to think about without me laying my troubles at her door on top of everything else.

"Then..." she pauses. "Christ, D, I thought this would be a bit more romantic, dreamed of having a man go down on one knee. But in the circumstances, you're offering more than I could have hoped for. So, yes, D. I'll marry you."

My gut churns at the thought of what she's missing out on. A man declaring his undying affection for her, a ring, a proposal done properly. I've a sudden impulse to take her into my arms and kiss her, our tongues entwining, her taste becoming mine. But that's not how this marriage is going to be.

I lean in and my lips touch her cheek briefly. "I do love you, Vi. Always have."

Her face turns toward me. She shakes her head and bites her lip. "I love you too, D."

I nod, accepting her declaration. She means like a brother. She'd be horrified to think there was any other interpretation to my words.

I squash the burst of elation inside me. *She's mine.* Or at least, very soon she will be.

A wail from the hallway gets Violet moving and running to the door. When she pulls it open, Jayden's outside, a bawling Theo in her arms. She shrugs apologetically; Vi's quick to take her son. That smile on her face speaks volumes, love emanating from her, the kind of look part of me wishes she'd give to me. *Not going there. Remember Nathan.*

She thanks Jay, brushes off her apology, and brings the wriggling bundle into the room. There's an unpleasant aroma accompanying it.

"Sorry, D. I need to change him." She takes him to the changing mat.

I'm the president of an outlaw MC. There's not much I've not been able to handle. I'm going to be a father; how hard can it be?

Going over, I put my hands around her waist and ease her to one side. "If I'm signing up for this, I better start as I mean to continue," I say softly, while popping the studs on the all-in-one thingy Theo's wearing. "You're a stinky one, aren't you?" I say, gruffly.

My deep voice catches Theo's attention; his cries ease away as he stares intently at me.

"D, do you know what you're doing?"

"I can work it out."

She stands back, a look half-concerned, half-amused on her face, her arms held as though ready to step in and take over.

Fuck, the stench! But I soldier on.

I pull off the dirty diaper, wishing I didn't have to see what was inside, and fold it. She's there, a bag ready, held open for me. *Have to remember to get prepared in the future.* Taking the handful of wipes she's holding out, it's natural to try to catch hold of the legs that are kicking and, eventually successful at that, wipe his ass.

Theo starts giggling when he manages to get one leg free. I wonder whether he always does this, or he's testing me. Whatever, I have him handled.

"Gotcha, little man," I grin, catching the flailing leg while just about managing to keep hold of the other.

"D, watch..."

Quickly I grab the tissues she's now passing over. "You trying to piss on your old man, son?" I try it out and hear a gasp at my side.

Managing to keep myself dry, I clean him up again. She hands me some sort of lotion. Competently, or so I hope, I rub it on in the right places. The fresh diaper? Well, I've never passed up a challenge in my life. It takes me a while, but at last it's on.

When I've refastened his clothing, I pass a clean, and fresher-smelling baby, back to his mom.

Vi takes him. On her face is one of the strangest expressions I've ever seen.

CHAPTER FIFTEEN

Violet

Oh my God! I cannot believe what I just saw. I think my female parts convulsed when I watched this big strong man being so tender and patient with my baby. Which is a pity, as he told me he didn't want kids, or at least, with me. I suppose it's the 'going to bed with me' part that puts him off. The way he's handling Theo suggests he'd be a natural at the parenting role.

I'd said yes at his insistence, but watching him now, maybe he'd have been better with a woman he did get the hots for, and have children of his own.

I never expected he'd step up so fast, and once having made his decision, dive headfirst into being a dad. And calling Theo 'son'? I just about melted on the spot.

I couldn't have predicted my reaction. When Angelino had referred to Theo as his, every fibre of my being objected and I wanted to be sick. When Demon had said it? It had the complete opposite effect: a relief that here was going to be someone to lean on, to help share not only the joys of having a child, but the trials that come with that too. Okay, so all he's done so far is change one diaper, but it was a pretty horrendous one, at that.

Theo's rooting expectantly, his little hands finding the edge of my tank top. "I'm, er, going to have to feed him."

"I'll give you some privacy. I need to get to church anyway."

You don't need to. But I don't say it.

As he swiftly turns to go out, I satisfy myself with a nod to his back. A dirty diaper is fine, a woman feeding her baby, apparently not. Taking Theo to the bed, I lean back against the headboard and allow him to suckle. I'll have to get him a bottle too; I know my milk's starting to dry up, or at least isn't enough to satisfy him. I look down proudly at my son, he's becoming a big lad, and already very handsome, at least in the eyes of his adoring mom. Now he's acquired a father. A man I can trust, not like his sperm donor.

The room seems silent after an afternoon of arguing, the only sound a slurping coming from Theo. It seems empty, too. Demon's such an imposing presence, an energy has left and gone with him. I have space to think for the first time in what seems like hours.

Have I done the right thing? I've been handed everything on a platter. But I have the man of my dreams for all the wrong reasons. How I wished we'd met as strangers, became attracted to each other, dated and fallen in love, then agreed to take that step into marriage as a consolidation of what we felt.

We do, however, respect each other, and there's a sibling-type love. But is that enough? Can we pretend for Theo? Or will he grow to suspect? Exactly how long will we be together in this sexless relationship? If Angelino continues to press his case, it could be for years. By the time Theo's eighteen I'll be forty-three and verging on, or even over, the line of being able to have any more children. Demon will be fifty-three, not many years younger than his father is now. The best of both our lives will have passed.

Will Angelino give up? I'd never wish death on anyone, but I hope he dies an early gangster's death. That's the only way I'd ever truly be rid of him. In his grave is exactly where Demon wants him, but I don't want Demon to spend his life behind bars, or, worse, if the Silvestri live up to their reputation, bring danger to all his club.

Theo's finished, but his fist going into his mouth shows he's still hungry. Straightening my tee, I stand up. "Come on, little man. Let's go get you topped off."

Carrying him carefully, I descend the stairs, my attention on the next step, not on the people below. When I near the bottom, I realise the chatter in the room has quieted. It's the silence that makes me falter and look around. The men, apart from the prospects, aren't in sight. But all the women are watching me.

Jayden and Mo are sitting on the couch, frozen in tableaux, Jay with a cup halfway to her mouth. The club girls are in a group by the bar, and Jeannie has paused halfway across the room.

The prospect Dan has a smirk on his face and Wills looks puzzled.

"Er, I'm just going to get Theo a bottle." For some reason I feel the need to explain my appearance. Then I quickly look down to make sure I remembered to pull my top down and my boobs aren't hanging out, but everything seems to be fine.

I start moving again. You could hear a pin drop as I cross the clubroom, but no one impedes me on my way through. As I take a bottle I prepared earlier and put it in some hot water to warm, I hear the murmur of conversation start up again. I shrug, maybe I'd been clanking down the stairs and had disturbed them. Still a little uneasy, I decide I've done nothing to upset anyone and take Theo out to give him his milk.

As soon as I sit, I notice once again the chattering has stopped and I'm the centre of attention. I settle Theo on my arm, he eagerly grasps the bottle and starts drinking. I steady it with one hand, then look around.

"Okay, have I grown an extra eye or something?"

Jeannie steps closer and takes the seat at the opposite end of the couch. "Something, definitely."

"You been holding out on us, Vi?" Jay raises an eyebrow.

"Knew there was something going on with Demon," Mo states.

He couldn't have told them, could he? He wouldn't, surely. Not without letting me come to terms with it first.

"You really going to marry Prez?" The sweet butt called Titsy —why she bothers to get dressed I'll never know, it's clear she's not wearing a bra or underwear—leans over the opposite sofa.

Okay then, he has.

But what on earth has he actually told them? It's best to ask so I don't put my foot in it.

"What's he said?" I'm staring at Mo.

"For all of us to get our finery ready as we'll be going to the courthouse as soon as he can arrange it."

What?

Breezy joins Titsy and waves the other sweet butts over. "Can't see it myself," she announces conversationally. "Prez likes variety. Never shown an interest in settling down. There must be more to it, unless you have a magic pussy."

As my face starts to burn, Jeannie claps her hands. "That's enough now. Think you better get your head around the fact that Prez is off the market. No one wants to know your views on that."

Titsy straightens reluctantly and shrugs. "Can't see how she's gonna keep him satisfied, that's all. Even if her cunt's made of gold."

Tulia taps her on the shoulder as they follow Jeannie's instruction to make themselves scarce. "Wouldn't that be uncomfortable?"

"What?"

"A pussy made of gold?"

"For fuck's sake, Tulia. I didn't mean it literally." Titsy gives a loud sigh as she rounds the bar. Playfully she slaps Tulia around the head.

Jeannie's narrowed eyes follow them out of the room. When

they disappear and their voices fade, she theatrically mimes taking something off her head and holds out her empty hand to me. For some strange reason mine automatically reaches out as though she really was giving me something.

My hand hovers in mid-air. "What?"

"I'm passing it over. Seeing as you're the Prez's old lady."

My face scrunches up showing my confusion. "What? And I'm not, yet."

"Responsibility for them, the club girls. I've been chasing their butts for too many years now, I'm more than ready to hand them off. And that, my dear, comes with being the club's first lady."

Still confused, I jerk my head toward Mo. "She was the prez's old lady until recently, yet you say you've been doing it for years."

Mo shrugs, Jeannie answers for her. "Well, Mo didn't come to the club much, and someone had to keep their asses under control. But now I'm ready to pass the baton over."

"I'm not his old lady."

"You soon will be," Jayden says with a grin. "Bet they're agreeing it now in church."

"Yup." Jeannie sees my confusion. "Even a prez's old lady needs to be voted in by the club."

"Especially the old lady of the prez," Mo confirms. "Everyone's got to be happy with it. You're going to be Queen Bee, dear. You think you're up to it?"

No, no. This marriage is just for show. It isn't for real. Yet they seem to be sitting here taking it seriously. "You mean there's a chance someone might object, and I won't have to marry Demon?"

"Have to?" Jeannie says sharply.

My eyes close. *Damn.* Poor choice of words.

"Knew there was more to it. Spill." Mo sits forward. When I stay silent, she lowers her voice. "Prospects aren't listening, it's just us here. We're all old ladies, we know how to keep our mouths shut. You and Demon getting together? Can't say I think there's anything wrong with the idea. But something tells me there's something not right about it, either. In which case, bottling it all up isn't going to help. You need women around you." She breaks off, glancing at Jeannie. "Jeannie's kept secrets for me for many, many years. Secrets which no doubt you'll be hearing, but not from my mouth, so don't bother asking me. Owner of the secret can decide whether to tell it or not."

"Mo's right." Jeannie narrows her eyes. "I know how to keep my mouth shut." She indicates first Mo, then Jayden. "You can tell us shit you don't want others to know. And she's right again, isn't she, Violet? This isn't some crazy-fast lovefest come to its conclusion. Tell us or not, as you want. But there's something that's not so straightforward about how you came to be here, and what Demon's achieving by marrying you." She stops for a moment. "He hasn't forced you to do anything you don't want, has he?"

"Hey, Jean. You're talking about my son."

Before Mo and her friend come to blows, I blurt out, "Of course he hasn't, and won't. That's part of the problem." Christ, I should be watching my tongue. "Look, the short story is I was raped. The man who got me pregnant wants Theo. He's Angelino Silvestri, part of the Mafia family, and I wouldn't trust Theo with him, even for a visit. Demon thinks marrying me, saying Theo is his, not Angelino's, will keep him off my back."

Mo's face has gone tight as if something's pained her. She seems to be at a loss for words. *Something's wrong.* That's confirmed when she stands, her body jerking as if she's a puppet being raised by strings, and then she walks off.

Jeannie's watching her carefully. When I go to ask what it was that I said, she shakes her head, then, as if to distract me, "Why is Demon stepping up?" she asks, her brow furrowed, "Why not someone else? Someone a bit younger, perhaps."

I can't explain I wouldn't want anyone else. Wouldn't be pushed into a sham of a marriage even if someone else had offered. It's only ever been Demon. I'm saved by answering when

Mo comes back, carrying a glass of water. I notice she seems to have gotten herself under control.

She sits, sips from her glass, then leans forward, clearly having overheard Jeannie's question. Her brow, which had been creased, begins to smooth as she finds her voice. "It's because of your brother, isn't it?" Quickly she fills them in on what happened. "Those boys were as thick as thieves. Demon's doing it for him, isn't he? Taking on Nathan's nephew and his sister."

I glance around. Mo I like, always have. Jeannie I'm coming to respect. Jayden's already a friend. I need women in my corner, so I confide in them. "And that's what's wrong," I supply. "He'll never think of me as anything other than Nathan's sister."

"Do you want him to?" Jayden, who's been quiet for a while, asks.

I put down Theo's empty bottle and settle him on a mat on the floor. Jayden reaches over behind the couch and the baby gym appears. He starts to kick happily.

"I've always liked Demon," I admit, realising it's his mother I'm speaking to. She's grinning, probably remembering how I used to embarrass myself, it's impossible to hide much from parents. "I've grown, but he can't get the image of Nathan's annoying little sister out of his head. He doesn't seem to see me as I am now."

Mo still has a smile curving her lips. "Presumably his intention is that you'll stay married until he's sorted out this Angelino for you."

"It might take years," I glumly agree.

"Then you have time to change his mind, Vi. No need to rush, take things slowly."

Jeannie laughs. "That's one thing the whores said right. Demon's enjoys a good..." she breaks off as Mo's frantically signalling her, grins, then resumes, "Shall we just say he has a healthy sex drive." At that, Mo nods primly.

"So he'll be unfaithful," I say. They are so not making this better.

"No," Mo's the one who contradicts fast. "Demon won't step out on you; I brought him up much better than that. But he might get a little desperate."

Jayden giggles. "He might need a... helping hand, shall we say?"

"Let's not," says Mo. "I'd rather not have that image in my head. It's my son we're discussing. I'm not going to give Sex Ed to my future daughter-in-law."

Jeannie reaches across the low table and pats her friend's arm. "Nah, we'll just have to find a discreet way of getting the lowdown on whether they've fucked yet or not."

Mo throws back her head, clearly exasperated, but amused at the same time. "As long as you don't talk about opening a book," she says when she looks back down.

"Now there's an idea."

"I'm not freaking telling you when, *if* we have sex!" I cry out. My cheeks couldn't go any redder if they tried.

The sound of heavy footsteps and loud voices drowns out any reply. Dan reappears from wherever he's been hiding and slips behind the bar. Demon comes out from the direction of their meeting room, a number of men slapping him on the back as they pass on their way to get a drink. The man himself, however, is heading straight for me.

"What you all been gossiping about?" He crouches down, and stares at Theo, watching him play, then reaches out and tickles his tummy, making Theo laugh. "You been getting at Vi?" He keeps his voice gentle, but his eyes, flicking between Mo and Jeannie are hard. "Girl's gone red. What have you been saying to her?"

"Old lady business," Jeannie quickly replies. "And none of yours."

The look on his face is priceless. When the others burst out laughing, it's not long before I'm joining in.

CHAPTER SIXTEEN

Demon

Fuck, but it's good to hear Violet laugh, a genuine chortle right from her belly. Jeannie's comment had taken me by surprise, but I suppose I, and my brothers, deserve that. On purpose I stand, glaring. That just makes them laugh harder. Vi's wiping tears from her eyes, and I'm happy she's getting some relief from the tension I laid on her earlier. It warms me that she's getting on with the other old ladies. Jay, used to club life, had settled right in, deferring to Mo and Jeannie as the senior women in the club.

To Vi, though, this is all new and strange.

As my old lady, she'll be at the top, and expected to enforce her position when there's a need to. I've been worried about that, whether she's too young, too genteel, so seeing her right in the thick of it warms my heart. Maybe this will be easier than expected. Well, accepting herself as an old lady part.

That she definitely is, boys just agreed to it, and Buzz wrote it in the book. Signed, sealed, and delivered. Soon she'll have my patch on her own cut.

It's their other suggestion that I've just agreed to that I think will come harder. How I'll persuade her I've no idea. They think it will help protect her from Angel.

I wait until the laughter dies down, then approach. "Jay, you okay to take Theo for a while?" I make sure I cock an eyebrow at Vi, a silent question to check she's okay leaving her, our, child. She glances down at him happily kicking his feet and nods.

"Yeah, Prez. We'll take care of him." Her gaze encompasses Mo, deferring to her. In a second I find out why.

"Seeing as he's my grandson, I'll be here too." Mo challenges me. A mom-stare that hasn't lost its power over the years.

It startles Vi as much as it does me. But when Hell raises his chin, I take it as a sign all the men and women here will have my back. This marriage might be something only on paper, but outside these walls, no one else will know that. It starts here, inside. With us all committed.

Vi stands. I jerk my head upward, she comprehends my meaning. Following her up the stairs, I wish for a moment I'd taken the lead, the way her ass cheeks flex is too fucking enticing, and predictably, has my cock interested. Discreetly I adjust myself in my jeans. Why is it the one woman I can't have who gets my engine revving? *Is that it? That it's not her, it's that she's unattainable?*

Oh, shit. She left her door unlocked. There, in the middle of her bed, is Bitch. Vi laughs; my cock deflates. On seeing me approach, the cat gets to her feet, arches her back and hisses, making Vi giggle more. Of course, when she approaches, the darn thing relaxes, and rubs up against her and purrs.

"Can you please put that fuckin' animal out?"

Violet's eyes flash. "Don't call her that." She makes no move to do as I ask, instead she lets the cat settle on her lap. She's wearing it like a suit of armour. "Time for an explanation, D."

I sigh deeply. It is. Made more than one decision without her input.

Unless it involves the club where everyone votes, I've only had myself to consider. I've always felt I've known best. A niggling thought at the back of my mind warns me a woman, a wife, might not be so easy to convince.

"It's all agreed, Vi. I've officially claimed you as my old lady. We'll get the license tomorrow morning and be married the next afternoon. There's no need to wait."

"I hear you told everyone they're coming." Her voice is bland.

Shrugging, I explain. "When the president of the club gets married, it's a big deal, Vi. Word gets to Angel we've sneaked off as though we want no one to know about it, he'll be suspicious we're doing it for all the wrong reasons."

There's another factor, too. I want all my brothers there, a show of strength, just in case Angel decides to use violence and take Theo by force. It's also for that purpose we've decided to invite guests from the other chapters.

"He'd be right," she snaps.

I take a step closer. That fucking cat growls, but it doesn't stop my rising temper. "We're doing this for the right reasons, Vi, never fuckin' forget that. What's more important than keeping Theo safe and out of the clutches of the Italians?"

Her hand strokes the cat's fur vigorously. When she looks back up, I swear I see a tear glisten in her eye.

"I know that, D. There's no other freaking justification why I'd be marrying you. But I always thought I'd be heading toward that altar for love."

No altar. Just a desk. But still.

"You are," I tell her. "You're marrying because you love Theo. Because you want to give him security. That's what I can offer, babe." And a home, though I'll not tell her that part yet. Until the immediate danger is removed, she can't live off-compound. But I'm already making plans to get us a house.

She's looking back down at Bitch, her hands moving automatically. "I've said yes. You've told me your plans. I can see your reasons, and I'll go along with it. I just didn't appreciate the extent you'd go to, to make this a mock celebration. I thought we'd sneak down to the courthouse alone. Telling the women to break out their best dresses?" She shakes her head. "I've never felt more deceitful in my life, but yeah. Okay. So there was thought behind it. Now you've said your piece, I don't think there's anything more for us to discuss, D."

I risk perching my ass at the end of the bed. Green eyes flick my way warily, a low warning growl not to come any closer. When she sees I'm currently not a direct threat, Bitch's hair around her neck flattens again. Once the cat relaxes, I prepare to tell Vi the rest.

"There's one more thing. A suggestion proposed, discussed and agreed to. One more level of security."

Her head dips up-and-down. She's accepted the inevitable. *She's ready to agree to anything.* Anything, except what I'm about to demand.

"We're going to keep you safe, Violet. I swear that to you. Angel might make a play to get hold of you, may try and prove my claimin' you isn't real."

She flinches as though I've hit her. But that's what we discussed. Though I suspect his desire for the kid will fade over time, we're still unsure of his motive. If that's strong enough, he might wait his chance for years. Yeah, my plan is to put him underground, but it's what happens in the meantime that I'm worried about. So this is just another precaution I'm taking.

"He'll already know I'm yours by your ring on my finger. I am getting a ring, aren't I? If not, it might be a good idea to get one. Just something simple."

She sure is getting a ring. Pyro's out choosing one now. A good wedding set that's probably going to set me back a few thousand dollars. But it's another sign to Angel how serious I am. Nathan, of course, would have wanted her to have the best; I could imagine his disgust if I got her a plain band. Of course, I don't tell her that, I just settle for, "You certainly are."

Her head tilts. Her brow creases. *What more, Demon?* She doesn't need words to communicate.

Pinching the brow of my nose, I strengthen my voice. I'll not be making the normal demands on her during our marriage, but this is one time where I'm determined to get my way. The decision's been made and recorded.

"Rings can be removed, Vi." Not much of an explanation so far. "You need to wear my property patch too."

Her facial features relax. "Oh, that's all. Yeah, I saw Jay's vest. That's not much of an ask, D. I suppose as your old lady, it will be expected I'll have one, too."

My eyes sharpen, find hers and hold them. "Not a patch on your vest, Vi, though yeah, you'll certainly get one of those. Nah, a tattoo."

"A tattoo?" Her voice stretches out the word, starting low then rising an octave on the last 'o'. There her head shakes rapidly side-to-side. "Not going to happen, D."

"It is, Vi. I want my mark on you." I stand and start to pace. "When this club started, it had its own bylaws. When we became Satan's Devils, we accepted theirs. But kept some of the old club's too. One of those archaic rules was if a man took an old lady, she was to get a 'Property of' tattoo."

"Angel won't know that. He won't know your rules," she scoffs dismissively.

"They're not exactly top secret, Vi. Hell says he knows; recalls a discussion once back in the day when he and Lucio were closer. Don't know the ins and out of it, possibly some discussion about women. But he's certain they know. If Angel ever takes you, and looks for one, he needs to find it to show how seriously you—we—take our relationship.

"Does Jay have one?"

"She'll get one when she's eighteen. She could get one now but needs a parent with her."

"Jeannie?"

"Jeannie and Sindy have them. Mo has a small one too. Vi. You having the tattoo will cement that we're permanent."

Now she stands, the cat in her arms, going to the door and putting Bitch outside. I'd be thankful if I wasn't wary of her reason. She closes it behind her and locks it. For a second all that can be heard is that darn cat jumping up at the handle from the outside.

"That's the motherfucking point, isn't it, D?" Her use of the profanity shocks me. I hadn't expected it to come from her innocent mouth. "This isn't forever. This is all make-believe. You're asking me to have my skin permanently marked. What happens after we divorce? Who'd want me with your fucking name written on my body?"

I stand, march toward her, my body closing on hers, pinning her to the door. My arm thumps the wood above her head. "I think you need to know who you're dealing with here, Vi. I'm not asking, I'm telling."

Instead of backing down, her eyes flare. "No."

"No?" I let my echo hang in the air for a few pregnant seconds, before continuing, "I'm giving you my fuckin' life, Vi. Letting you into my world. Giving it to you. Giving me to you."

"No," she repeats.

"Then I remove my protection." I step abruptly away from her and hold up my palms to face her. "I'm doing the best I can, Vi. If you won't give anything in return, then we're finished. Tomorrow you can take Theo and go do the fuck whatever you want. We're finished."

When Liz had suggested the tattoo, I'd dismissed it. But the more the boys discussed the idea, the more I found I was getting onboard with the notion. Her skin marked with 'Property of Demon'? A permanent sign she was mine. No man would ever mess with the property of the Satan's Devils MC president. If the thought made my cock stand to attention, that had nothing to do with it.

Her protests only serve for me to want it more. Just for her protection, of course.

Her face has paled as she thinks through the ramifications of what I've just said. Turning she starts to pace the room, her teeth worrying her lip, her face going through several expressions. So many emotions conveyed by the arrangement of her eyes, brow and mouth, it's hard to take any reading. I've used every word I can think of to persuade her. Fuck knows what I'll do if all she does is refuse.

I don't push, don't add any more argument. I just wait for her answer, hiding my impatience, giving her time to make her decision.

When, finally, she speaks, it's not a weak capitulation. Her voice is strong, steady. "You're right, D. You're giving me everything. Your name, your reputation, your support. What am I giving you? Everything you never wanted. A child and responsibility. If this means so much to you, I'll do it. But on two conditions."

She'll do it? Despite my threats, of course I wouldn't have turned her out if she'd refused, but her acceptance fills me with relief. But I'm cautious about her stipulations.

Warily, I demand, "Name them."

"First, I design it."

"With Liz's help," I tell her, uncertain of her talents. "And the second?"

Her eyes come to mine. Her eyebrow rises. Her voice, defiant.

"You get one too."

I rear back. She's taken me by surprise. I hadn't expected her to request that. I'm no stranger to tattoos. On my back is the Satan's Devils patch, the grim reaper standing over three devils. Amongst others, high up on my right arm, I've dog tags with Nathan's name and the date that he died, that fateful day and month I lost my friend forever. Again, my forefinger and thumb press above my nasal bones, as I think of the implications. It doesn't take long to come to the conclusion; I have her brother inked on me. Why shouldn't I have her, too?

"Okay."

If my easy capitulation surprises her, it astounds me. A woman's name on my body will cause questions to arise with any woman I go with in the future. But the only person I'll owe explanations to will be a woman I intend to stay with for life. Having Vi's name on my body won't be a burden, easy to dismiss as that of my first wife. Yeah, that's how I'll explain it.

"You will?"

"Looks like we'll both be seeing Lizard tomorrow. In his professional capacity," I tell her.

"I want to draw yours, too." Her voice sounds lighter, almost as if there's a bubble of excitement. If sketching something out takes her mind off the implications, I'm happy to go along with it.

Fully expecting to throw her design in the bin and go with a suggestion Liz is bound to put forward, letting her think she's getting her way is the easiest thing to do. "You do that. I'll consider it."

"I'll go get Theo, get him settled, then start."

I stare. I've not seen her this animated about something other than her son since she's been here. "You'll need to do a design around 'Property of Demon'," I warn her. "And mine isn't fuckin' includin' the words 'Property of'."

As a response she snorts a laugh.

I look in on her briefly later that evening. Theo's asleep, adorable little snuffling noises coming from his crib. She's seated at the desk where, for so many years, Hellfire used to sit working on club business. She's biting the end of the pencil she's using. When I try to see what she's coming up with, she covers the paper with her body.

Contenting myself with a reassuring touch to her shoulder, I leave her with only an inadequate wish for a good night.

Back in my own room I indulge in a very long shower. Fuck, if thinking of her having my property patch inked on her skin gets me this hard, how will I be able to control myself when I see the real thing?

CHAPTER SEVENTEEN

Violet

I've never considered getting a tattoo. Not that I've a particular reason for being against it. The thought of needles doesn't upset me, it's just never been the right time or place, and no design I particularly wanted. When Demon first suggested it, I was horrified. Me, having his name permanently inked on my body? A constant reminder that it was all fake?

He'd threatened me, but I know him. He'd never have followed through. Might have rescinded his offer to look after me personally, but he wouldn't have sent me and Theo away penniless and exposed. Not down to the nothing he feels for me, of course, but his promise to Nathan.

I'd bargained for two things. There were a couple of thoughts driving them. Firstly, I've always found intricate tattoos intriguing, and have often fancied trying my hand at that style of drawing. Indeed, during some of my lectures I'd doodled a few designs. Secondly, the women had told me if I wanted Demon, I should go after him with every weapon I could bring to bear. If his only objection is that I'm more like a sister to him, then I need to replace that thought in his mind with the fact I'm all woman. How better to have him reminded time and again that I'm his? That I've lusted after him all my life made giving in easier. I can't think of finding a man who'd match up to him. The substitutes I'd gone with previously had all been failures. There's never been anyone else, and I can't imagine there would be anyone in the future, whose name I'd agree to carry forever. If, when this marriage ends, as it will do, I'll have the tattoo to help me remember that once, even if for only a short while, I was Demon's.

He'd agreed fast to reciprocating. He's going to see that tattoo, know he's wearing my name on his body. Any other woman he goes with will see that as well. He might not think of it in that way, but I'm claiming him just as much as he's claiming me.

With that idea in mind, I've designed the tattoos with matching elements. A bunch of violets, surrounded by barbed wire, to me representing a love that is trapped, unable to break free. On mine in fancy script are the words he wants; on his, my name, with the flowers less prominent. I'd borrowed Jay's tablet, and had done some searches on the internet while Theo had slept. I'd become intrigued by tattoo designs, the artist in me animated by the unlimited possibilities.

The following morning I wake with no doubts, instead partly excited and partly nervous, knowing I'm going to experience a tattoo, which some people find very painful. Others say it hurts at first, but then as the body releases endorphins, it can become almost hypnotic. I'm hoping the latter is true. Guess I'll soon be finding out.

Demon comes to collect me. I keep my designs folded up, hoping to discuss them first with Lizard. We're taking the club's SUV, which has blacked-out windows. Lizard and Demon sit in the front while I'm in the back seat. The tattoo parlour isn't far away, and both men remain silent as we drive. There's almost an air of seriousness, and I don't feel encouraged to start a conversation.

We go to a parking place around the back, and Demon tells me to wait until Lizard has the door open. Then, with his arm barely touching me, he guides me inside. The furtiveness of the arrangement brings home he's not a man excitedly putting his name on his future bride. No, he's clearly reluctant.

Lizard holds out his hands once inside. When I pass over my sketches, he views them with a critical eye, while I look around in disgust.

"This place is really seedy, D. It's like something out of an old film."

"It might be a dump, but it's clean, sterile, Violet. Don't worry about that." Lizard looks up for a second at my criticism, his eyes still creased in concentration.

"We're actually moving premises, Vi." Demon waves his hand indicating the room. "A bit more upmarket and definitely more modern."

"What's this?" I walk over to some equipment. Lots of different size needles sealed in clear plastic.

"Shit for piercing."

"You do piercing too?" I find I'm fascinated.

"You getting ideas, Vi?" Demon looks amused.

"You got piercings?" I'm intrigued. Very intrigued. But he shudders. "Fuck no. A tattoo needle's enough for me."

Smothering my unnecessary disappointment—I was very unlikely to benefit from any he might have in any event—I notice no comment has been made about my proposed tattoos.

"Is there a problem, Lizard?" Up to now, he's just been staring at them.

"You done this before, Vi?"

"No, but I studied art."

"She has a degree," Demon says proudly. "Are they any good, Liz?"

For an answer, Lizard passes them over. I look down at my feet, wondering whether it's too much, whether my name in really small letters was all Demon thought he'd agreed to. After Demon's looked at them, his expression unreadable, he catches Liz's eye.

"They're not good, Prez," Lizard starts, and my spirits begin to fall. "They are fuckin' fantastic for shit done freehand." He looks at me sharply. "Ever worked with ink, babe?"

"No, but I was reading up on it last night. I loved drawing those."

"Hmm." He looks thoughtful but says nothing else. "Prez, mind making some coffee? I'll make a stencil of Vi's design."

"And Demon's." I don't want mine done and him to avoid getting his.

"He'll get his tat. Don't worry." Liz, seeming unbothered he's just given his prez an instruction, gets to work. I'm fascinated watching him, taking in every step. He gets out both tracing and carbon paper, then looks at me. "You got any tats, Vi?"

"Nope, virgin skin."

"Right, so this is what we're going to do. Well, why don't you do it, as it's your design?"

"I thought you'd just copy it?" As he gets up from the seat, I take his place.

"Sometimes I do, if it's something I've drawn; sometimes I do it this way, it makes sure I get exactly what the client wants." He proceeds to talk me through the process, which sounds a little laborious, but I soon get sucked in. I use tracing paper to make a copy of my drawing, then, using the traced image as a guide taped down over carbon paper, repeat it again. Time ticks by as I steady my hand and concentrate. When I've finished, Lizard looks pleased.

Two cups of coffee have been made and drunk by the time I'm done.

Then he asks me to lie face down, raise my shirt and lower my shorts when Demon points out where he wants it to go.

"It's a tramp stamp," I object.

"Vi..."

"No. I thought high on my thigh where no one will see it, but there?" It seems seedy to me.

Demon pinches the skin between his eyes and exchanges a

glance with Lizard. "I'll make a bargain. If you place your tat where I want it to go, you can say where mine goes, too."

"Over your heart," I respond fast.

He rears back, "Vi..."

"Fair's fair," I challenge.

"Fuck!" He slams his hand against the wall, then rests his forehead against it. The clock on the wall loudly ticks over a few seconds before he comes to a decision. "Go ahead, Liz. I'll have the fuckin' tattoo over my heart."

Liz grins widely, then tells me to lie down and relax. There's a whirring sound, then he starts working. The only way to describe the sensation is that it feels as though I'm constantly being scratched, like... like Bitch's claws.

"Sorry," Lizard tells me when he's working on the middle bit over my spine. "Over the bone is never nice."

"You're doing great, Vi." Demon's crouched down at my head, his hand brushing my hair back from my face. The constant sting of the needle indeed becomes hypnotic. When Liz has finished, it takes a moment for me to realise the tattoo gun has been switched off. I'm marked as Demon's property.

I'm told not to move as he finishes up, then offers me a mirror. My lower back looks red and raw, yet the pattern can be seen clearly. It's not overly large, about five inches by three, the wording needing someone to get close up to read it. When I've admired, if that's the right word, the permanent evidence of Demon's claim on me, Lizard covers my new tattoo.

When it's Demon's turn, I look on with interest, watching Lizard's every move, admiring his steady hand and concentration. I ask questions, he answers. After he's explained everything he's doing, I'm surprised when he looks up and enquires, "You sound interested, doll. This something you think you'd like to do?"

Looking on eagerly, I nod.

"Prez, you know I was thinking of taking on more staff. How about an apprentice?"

"You talking Vi?" Demon's eyes widen and he looks at me thoughtfully. When he sees my face brighten with interest, he shakes his head. "Vi, this isn't for you. Can't see Nathan liking..."

"Don't you dare!" I hiss, ignoring our audience. "I'm not going to live my life with reference to my brother. Even had he lived, I wouldn't have allowed him to influence me. I'm my own freaking person, D. You'd do well to remember that."

Liz's eyes are flicking from me to his prez. His eyes sharpen. "Why the fuck not? She's a fuckin' natural. I saw the promise in her designs. Want to do it, darlin'?"

"You don't have to work, babe," Demon reassures me fast. "I can support you."

Why should I lean on him for everything? What I've seen here today has intrigued me. A chance to be an artist rather than use the business part of my degree? Hell, yes.

"I'd love to Lizard. If I can sort out childcare."

"Vi, not so fast. Don't forget the little problem of Angel."

Lizard looks at me with sympathetic eyes. "We have time, hon. Got to get the new place set up first. Maybe by the time that's in hand, we'll have sorted out Angel for you."

Demon, though, looks like it's not going to be as easy as that. But he's wise enough to wait for a better time and place for our argument.

Strangely, now we're both adjusting to the thought that we have tats of each other's names on our skin, it makes the next part, getting the marriage license, just a formality. The soreness of my back is a reminder of what I've gone through today. But I'm excited, too. I have the prospect of employment in the future, doing something I'd never considered, but something I think I could get into. Jayden's so good with children, perhaps she could be my nanny? There's just the little problem that I'd be earning just to pay someone to take care of my child; I doubt apprentices make much of a living. Deep down, though, I know I'll make a better mother if I have something else to do than being a fulltime mom.

I'm still thinking it all through as we arrive back at the clubhouse. It takes me a moment to realise there are more bikes here than there were when we left. Demon notices the additions with a nod of appreciation.

The clubhouse is full. Dan and Wills seem run off their feet trying to keep hands filled with bottles of beer. The room is loud, and I look anxiously around for Theo.

"Jay's taken him upstairs," Jeannie informs me, correctly reading my look of concern.

As I turn to go find him, Demon's hand takes hold of mine. "Vi, I want you to meet some people. Theo will be fine for a few minutes longer." He leads me to the bar and exchanges backslaps and manly hugs with three men, followed by a round of those strange handshakes where they grab forearms, then finally he introduces me.

"This is Snatcher, he's the Prez of the Utah Chapter. With him is his VP, Thor, and Piston. And this is Violet, my wife-to-be."

"I'm the road captain, sweetie," Piston says as he shakes my hand. "Had to come along to make sure they rode in the right direction."

His prez slaps him playfully around the head, then nods at Demon. "Thumper and Rascal are around somewhere too."

"Thanks for coming along."

He's interrupted by a roar of bikes from outside and turns expectantly as the sound cuts off. Shortly after the door opens, in walk five more strangers. Seeing Demon, they head straight to join us.

"Drummer, welcome, Brother." Then to me. "Drummer is the president of the mother chapter in Tucson." He does that back-slap man hug thing again with Drummer, then to the men with him. "Thanks for coming, Wraith. Hey, Beef, Rock and Joker."

"Beef. Heard you were dead. Fuckin' corpse walking," Snatcher says, with a grin taking the sting out of his words.

Drummer's hand lands on the big man's back with a force that sends him reeling a step forward before balancing himself with his hand on the bar. Beef just gives his prez a smirk. "Nah, Beef here is a fuckin' medical miracle. Thought we lost him last year, can't keep a good man fuckin' down."

"Satan probably sent him right back," the man introduced as Thor observes, causing a burst of laughter. Beef joins in as though he agrees.

Snatcher's mouth changes, the corners curving downward. "Heard you're a man down, Drum. Any news on your firefighter?"

Drummer shakes his head; he too has lost all mirth. "Still hanging on, Brother. Looks out of the woods now but refuses to see anyone. His firefighting buddies or us. Seems like Truck will recover, but how bent or broken, we don't know yet."

"Bad fuckin' business."

There are a few murmurs of assent at Demon's words, then the subject of men I know nothing about is dropped. The topic of conversation changes. I notice Joker and Piston bumping fists. "Got here okay?" They walk off discussing journeys, times and problems along the way.

Drummer leans into Demon. "Lost and Dart wanted to come, but that journey, man. Too far, I'm afraid."

"Be all done and dusted by the time they'd get here," Demon agrees. "They're the San Diego crew, Vi," he addresses me.

Quickly his attention shifts as the door bursts open again, revealing yet five more strangers. He shouts, "Red!" enthusiastically, waving the new group of men over.

As I'm wondering how many more people are coming, I'm introduced to the Vegas president, his VP Crash, and men called Indian, Twister and Shadow.

To be honest, all the names seem to blur into one.

Having been polite, I tug Demon's arm. "I'm going to see Theo."

He excuses himself from the crew around the bar. "You okay, Vi?"

"Why are all these men here?" I hiss.

"I'm the prez, Vi. When I get married, it's expected that representatives from other chapters will attend to pay their respects. There'll be a big party tonight."

"You expect me to be here? I'm slightly outnumbered, Demon, in case you haven't noticed. Why are there no women with them?"

"I'll take this, Demon."

I start a little, not having realised I'd been overheard. Drummer is imposing as I suppose a national president should be. When he focuses his steely blue eyes on mine, I find I've automatically reversed a step, my back against Demon's chest. Demon steadies me by placing his hands on my shoulders.

"Demon's filled us in, Vi. Not going into the rights and wrongs of it, or what I think. He's made a decision, so our chapters will support him. We're here as a show of strength to make sure nothing goes wrong tomorrow. We'll all be protecting you and your kid. I have an old lady, two kids at home. Most of my men have. Yeah, it's a wedding, they're women, they'd love to be here, but under the circumstances, it felt right to leave them behind."

I'm not stupid. I can read between the lines. *The women aren't here because their men won't put them in danger.*

"You think Angel's going to try to take Theo?"

Drummer's gaze moves over my head. It's Demon who replies.

"There's a chance he'll try. That's why we're taking precautions. Not putting you or Theo at risk, Vi. Doing what I have to do to keep you safe."

CHAPTER EIGHTEEN

Demon

I watch Vi make her way through the room, which is heaving with bodies, until she reaches the stairs and disappears from sight. The number of men presents a problem I hadn't considered before. Just where the fuck were we going to put everyone tonight? We're pushed for space as it is.

"Drummer's crew have booked into a hotel. Prospects gonna sleep out here, and the rest of the boys are doubling up." Thunder appears at my side.

He's read my mind and solved the problem before I had a chance to mention it. "You sure you don't want that VP spot?"

In response there's a chuckle. "Nice try, Prez. Happy to lend my organisational skills, but not to be second-in-command. Too much fuckin' responsibility for me."

You can't blame a man for trying.

Turning back to have a word with Drummer, I see Pal's already there, catching up with his Tucson brothers. The lad's settled in here well, though.

"How's the new patch working out?" Wraith, having grabbed himself a fresh drink, asks in my ear.

"Skull? Yeah, he's doing okay. He and Pal are about the same age and have hit it off. Doesn't seem to bear any bad feelings for what went down."

"You trust him?"

I can see why Wraith might be suspicious. "With my life, Wraith. Boy won't fuck this up. He has no other family. Had a long chat with him when he returned. Spun it how we were protecting the club. Think he's looking at it as an extreme right of initiation."

"Word of advice?" At my nod, he continues, "Keep your eye on him. Now," he changes the subject, "what's going on with this woman and kid you're taking on?"

I knew someone would ask me. Crash wanders over; Thor, too. The four of us had been VPs together for a very long time. I am still not totally comfortable with my recent change in rank, and to be truthful, am more comfortable with an inquisition by them than by Drummer, Red and Snatcher. I indicate a table in the corner of the room, jerk my head to the men seated there, who get up and move, then we take the places they vacated.

"How much trouble are the Silvestri?" Thor leans back in his chair, the front two legs coming off the ground.

"Bad news," I sum it up. "They're big. Control the drug scene in town. We jog along with them well enough, they know not to step on our turf. But they're growing, and we're not. It was only a matter of time before we butted heads."

"Like the Herreras?" Wraith asks, referencing the crime family back home. I know of them, have been down to Arizona when the Tucson chapter had had to take them on.

"Similar. Though their links are to the cartel, the Silvestri are a branch of the Mafia. Don Lucio is the boss, the underboss is his son, Angelino, Angel. There are at least ten *capos* that we know of, maybe more. That means at least a hundred *soldatos,* and then there are associates."

"Associates?"

"Men not of Italian descent. You can't rise in the ranks unless both your parents are Italian."

Wraith nods at my explanation. "Ever thought about taking out both Lucio and Angel? Would it crumble?"

"There'd be some disarray, but someone has to run the product through town. The *capos* would just elect someone new to take their place." Not that I like the idea of drugs and personally steer well clear of them, but where there's a demand, someone's going to step in and supply. "Don't like Angel for more than one reason. But Lucio's always played it straight, down the line. Cut him out, maybe the next boss won't be someone so easy to deal with."

"Your long-term plan must be to take out this Angel," observes Crash.

"But you want to avoid war." Drummer and the other presidents have drawn up chairs to join us. For a moment there's a bit of shifting around to make space. "Understand your problem, Brother." He would. His crew have had issues with the Herreras in Tucson for decades. It's the reason why Jayden had to come to Colorado. For a moment I wonder whether sending Violet away would have been a better idea than going through with this plan to marry her. *She has my ink on her now.* Fuck, who am I kidding? She belonged to me long before that. That knowledge, though, I'll need to keep to myself.

"Does it end with one man, Brother?" Red asks, his eyes lighting briefly on Titsy who's on her knees in front of Twister, his enforcer. From what I remember of the Vegas prez, he'll be itching to go and join in. I hide my grin as he holds up a finger to Twister. An unspoken message passes between them.

I answer his question, "That's the only one we have issues with. Lucio is old-school, reasonable."

"He has just one son?"

"Yeah, now. Lost his other son years back."

Red raises his chin and continues, "So who does he groom to take over when Angel's taken out?"

With a shrug I respond, "Way I understand it, it's not his

decision. Sure, his son's the underboss, but that's just the way it happened. It's not a succession."

Wraith's head is tilted to one side. "Your woman Italian?"

"No," I say, shortly.

"Lucio must be pleased his son's risen high. Presumably on his own merits. Angel got a kid to do likewise?"

"Married, no kids." I have a feeling I know where the Tucson VP is heading.

"Hmm," Wraith pauses. "But your woman's kid. He isn't pure Italian."

"He's not," I confirm. My eyes meet Wraith's gaze, then that of each of the men at the table. I don't need to spell it out. The worry that's been in my head. The question I'm constantly asking. *What the fuck does Angel want with Theo?*

"You got plans, Demon?"

"Yeah, Drum. Need to get eyes off us first. Get him to drop his play for the kid. Then, when we apparently have no reason, kill him."

"He raped your old lady, Demon."

Returning Drummer's stare with one of my own which, while not as well-practiced, is just as deadly, I say coldly, "I assure you, of that I'm only too well aware." I tap the table in front of me. Dan runs over with a fresh beer, eyes up the state of the other bottles, assessing, then quickly returns to the bar and comes back with another half-dozen bottles. I wait until he's left once more, then inform them, "Angel's word is that it wasn't rape. That she made up a story to cover her guilt for giving in to her urges."

"You're not buying that?"

"Of course not," I snarl at Crash. "But I let him think that I am. We have meets set up to deal with our drug problem. I want him to think business is the number one priority and my focus. Make him believe I don't care what happened prior. I ended up with the girl and my kid."

"What's happening about the DNA test? You lawyered-up yet?"

"Alex is sorting out a good family lawyer, one who knows his shit better than the crap guy who lost the rape case and access hearings for her. Soon as the wedding's behind us, we'll see where we stand legally." Alex is the VP from San Diego, Dart's old lady, and the club lawyer. She's specialised in the criminal side but has good contacts in family law. I've no doubt she'll find us a good local person to deal with.

We thrash ideas backward and forward but apart from assurances of support, which are welcomed, we come up with no other plans. Eventually, with a wink, I remind them it's my wedding day tomorrow, and that I need to get a good night's sleep. But they know where I stand, that I'm doing a favour for my dead friend's sister, so there's none of the usual leering and leg pulling. Drummer and Wraith gather the Tucson boys and leave for the motel around the same time.

As I make my way to the stairs, pushing through a party that's getting rowdier, Thunder stops me. "Girls are working well tonight." I follow his stare. The Tucson lot all have old ladies; I'd even heard someone mentioning Beef had found a woman, but don't know whether to believe it. Apart from them, the other visitors are single. All the sweet butts seem to be enjoying riding different cocks tonight and seem to have no worries that the lack of accommodation means they're performing their roles out in the open. I nod, glad that the men who've ridden here to support me are getting the best of our hospitality. And I was right; Red has wasted no time joining in with Twister and Titsy.

"Don't forget Snatcher has your room tonight."

My chin rises and falls and I take a step forward, then, just as fast, a step back. *What the fuck?* "What did you say, Thunder?"

"I told you earlier, apart from the prezes, we're all doubling up. God help me, but I'm in with Mace and he snores like a fuckin' bear."

"Where am I fuckin' sleepin'? I'm the fuckin' *Prez*." I had expected to go to my own bed.

"Planned on you sleepin' in Hell's room."

"Violet's in there," I hiss.

"So? You say she's just like a sister. Thought you wouldn't care."

I shouldn't, but I can't trust my cock around her. Can't tell him that, though. "I'll sleep in my office."

"Nah, Thumper and Piston are in there."

God dammit.

Thunder's standing relaxed, his thumbs through his belt loops as if there's no problem. Well, fuck. Seems like I've got little option. What Vi will have to say about it, I've no idea. But she'd have had no problem bunking down with Nathan; time after time I've explained my brotherly role to her. Sharing a room isn't something we've never done before, though the three of us sleeping together was when she was only a little girl, and I'd had no idea what an attractive woman she was going to grow into.

She looks on me just like a sibling.

I'll sleep fully clothed, and on the chair.

Thunder's watching me, his eyes narrowing. "You okay there, Prez?"

Pinching the bridge of my nose, I say ruefully, "Yeah, just worried about the kid waking me up every few hours."

His face brightens in understanding. "With you there, Prez. Forgot the fuckin' kid. Sorry."

My excuse offered and accepted, I turn and finally complete my journey to the stairs. With one hand on the banister as though I need it to support me, I carefully make my way up to what I expect to be an uncomfortable and sleepless night.

Whether Theo wakes up or not.

Passing my own door with a rueful glance, I walk on, making my way to Hell's room. I hesitate far longer than necessary, only getting the nerve to knock lightly when Pyro and Cad, who are presumably bunking down together tonight, come up behind me. I nod as they pass, then turn to the door, which is opening a fraction.

"D?" Vi yawns as she speaks.

"Sorry, I didn't mean to wake you."

She moves her head side-to-side, then changes the action to tilt it toward the corridor behind me. "Not exactly quiet out there."

I hadn't thought how much sound from the party would travel up here, but she's right. It is noisy. "Theo being disturbed?"

"No, thankfully. Once he's asleep, he's gone. I'm lucky that way. What can I do for you, D?"

Not the right question Vi. Not when I'm sleeping in your room tonight. Could I find somewhere else? Go to a motel, maybe.

"Rooms are being used for the visitors, Vi. I, er... don't have anywhere to sleep."

Her eyes crease, then she smiles widely. "Well, come in here." With that, she throws open the door.

Years back, she'd flaunt herself in front of me wearing tiny sleep shorts and a tank. Her choice of sleepwear hasn't changed, I'm unhappy to see. Whereas in the past I'd been able to ignore it, now my cock jerks as I see the tantalising curve of luscious ass cheeks as she turns away from me.

"Bathroom's in there." She pauses, and giggles. "Of course you know that, better than me. What am I thinking, blabbering on?"

I think she's finding this situation as difficult as I am, but for completely different reasons.

"You get into bed, Vi, I'll sleep on the chair. I'm sorry to have woken you."

"Oh, I wasn't asleep, I was just reading." She pauses. There's a moment of quiet, then she says, "Now you're here, D., could you do something for me?"

I'll do anything she fucking wants. Preferably, stick my cock inside her. I'm hoping all she'll ask for is to get her a glass of water, perhaps. "Yeah, what?"

"Can you check my tattoo for me? I've not had one before. I put some ointment on about dinner time; do I need to use more?"

Yeah. That would have been hours ago. "Best you wash it and put some more on."

She nods and disappears into the bathroom. Good. Last thing I need to see right before I settle down to sleep is my name on her back.

Two seconds later she returns with a washcloth in her hands. "Could you do it for me, D?" she asks, her eyes wide and innocent.

Fuck, woman. If you only knew what I'd really like to do to you... But how can I refuse? It's a brotherly thing to do, right?

"I'll get on the bed. It will be easier."

Sure. My eyes widen as she does, but instead of lying on the edge, she eases into the middle of the king-size mattress, her head on the pillow. There's no way I can reach her, unless...

Instead of asking her to move closer, I climb on, too. The easiest way to do this is to straddle her.

She reaches her hands back and pushes at the elastic of her sleep shorts, moving them down, unintentionally now giving me a view of the curve of her upper ass cheeks, revealing her crack. *Jeez.* For a second I'm unable to move, or to breathe. *Fuck me, but she's perfect.* Some men like tits, for me it's a nice rounded ass. My cock starts to thicken and lengthen, my jeans far too tight and constricting.

If she was one of the club women I'd think she was coming on to me. But this is Violet, Nathan's sister. She's doing this artlessly, just as she'd do if her real brother was here.

But I'm fucked. She has my name written on her back, the words telling me she's mine.

She fucking belongs to me.

CHAPTER NINETEEN

Violet

What do I have to do, D? Strip off naked and have a neon sign flashing over my head?

I'd known the place was going to be short on beds for everyone, so many extra men were here, so I wasn't surprised when Demon had asked to share. My brain had immediately gone back to the conversation with the women earlier, about making D see me as a woman, not as a little girl. Well, I'm not quite sure how to approach it, but I'll give it my best shot.

His hesitation, his obvious reluctance to look at my tattoo, suggests he's maybe not so immune to me as he pretends. That's something to work on. I've positioned myself so he's no choice but to get close to me, and I wriggle as enticingly as I can. Using his hesitation to be even more brazen, I then hook my fingers into the waistband of my shorts for the second time.

"Can you see all the tat, D?" I push them down another inch. "Is that enough?"

"No. Yes! Stop, Vi. I can see it." His voice sounds strangled. But at last he starts dabbing the washcloth and cleaning the tat. "Right, that's done. You can pull your shorts up now, Vi."

"It needs to dry, doesn't it? And what about the lotion?"

"What?" he croaks.

"You might as well rub the lotion in while you're there. You can see what you're doing better than I can."

I feel the bed dipping, then hear sounds of water running in the bathroom as he washes his hands and dries them. Then he's back, and for the first time ever, I feel Demon's hands caressing my naked skin. Sure, it's sore over the new tat, but his fingers stray outside the boundaries, moving across the top of my ass. It's almost as if he can't quite control them.

Yes!

I was already turned on by the thought of spending the night with him. Now my stomach clenches and a groan comes out of my mouth.

"Sorry, I didn't mean to hurt you."

"You didn't, D, but my muscles are so tense. Give me a massage while you're there, will you?"

There's a sharp intake of air, then his hands start to rub and circle around my shoulder blades, further down my back, then back up again. As I murmur and press my head into the pillow, my body's reaction showing my appreciation, his hands sweep around the edges of my rib cage, inadvertently touching the outsides of my breasts. I arch my back upwards.

"Vi," he says, warningly, and lifts his hands. I hear something plastic tearing, then feel a slight pressure as he applies the new dressing. "Vi," he repeats my name, in a voice that again sounds slightly tortured. "It's done now. You can cover yourself again."

Wondering whether I can summon up plans B, C and D now plan A hasn't worked, I sit up and turn to face him. As he rests back on his haunches, he tries to turn away when my eyes trace his body.

"Vi," he says again, this time warningly, when he sees where my gaze has landed. "I'm a man," he says, and shrugs dismissively.

"Pretty certain my brother wouldn't have had a hard on for me."

"Fuck, Vi. I'm sorry, okay? Last thing you fuckin' need is a man's desire in your face."

I go to my knees and shuffle closer to him. "Not sure you understand my needs, D."

"What? Vi, stop."

Subtle isn't working. Perhaps I should make myself clear so there's no misunderstanding. My hand reaches forward and grasps his cock through his jeans. He hisses and covers my fingers with his. He doesn't pull them away, which I take as encouragement.

"Pretty impressive package you've got there, Prez."

"Vi," he growls. "You're going to get more than you bargained for if you keep that up. You have no fucking idea what you're doing to me. You're playing with fuckin' fire. You wearing my name marked on your skin? You showing me you're my fuckin' property? You're already my ol' lady, I fuckin' claimed you. One last chance, woman, and you're going to see what I'm packing close up."

"Show me," I taunt him, my eyes rising from his groin to his face and locking onto his eyes.

"No," he retorts suddenly, in a fluid movement throwing himself off the bed and landing on his feet. He's breathing heavily as though he's run a marathon. "You know the fuckin' rules. You're..."

"If you bring Nathan into this bedroom one more time, D, I'm going to scream. You're not my fuckin' brother, got it? He cannot be replaced."

"Vi, I'm sorry."

"The wedding's off, D. I can't do it."

My words take both of us by surprise. The party below must be finishing up as the sounds coming up through the floor have diminished, and my adamant statement rings in the sudden quiet.

"Too late for that, you're wearing my property patch," he offers sneakily, smirking.

I stand. I stalk him. Only halting when I'm up close. Unfortunately, it's him who looms over me, my not impressive height totally unimposing. But quickly I move, ripping off the tank top, and shrugging out of my shorts. I've foregone panties, so I'm now standing naked before him.

"So, claim me then."

His hands clench and unclench at his sides. His body is quivering with tension. "You've no idea what you're asking for."

I decide to put it plainly, in words he can't misunderstand.

"I don't want a brother, D, I had one of them and I keep him alive in my memory. I want a man. A husband."

He's staring over my head, refusing to look at my body.

Again, I reach out and trace the shape of his cock with my fingers. "You might act like you don't have the hots for me, but this says you're lying, D."

"You can't want me."

"But I do." *I always have.*

His head rolls back. It looks like he's having an internal struggle, alternating between the obvious needs of his body, and doing what he believes is right in his head. I've done everything I could do, offered myself to him on a silver platter, and now, once again, he won't even look. I start to feel awkward, knowing I've failed, read the signs wrong. But how can I misread a rock-hard cock? I can't see how it's possible. From the way his head is moving side-to-side, I've lost this battle. I can only hope for my ongoing sanity that I haven't lost the whole war.

Dejectedly, I start to bend to pick up my discarded clothes when two strong hands come around my waist and lift me. Next thing I know I'm standing, my feet on the bed, steadied by his arms, putting me at an equal height.

"You asked for this, Vi. Remember that."

Then, with an arm around my waist, he moves his other behind my head, forcing me to come to him. Within seconds I know I've unleashed the beast.

Our first kiss isn't gentle, it's not an exploration, a polite getting to know each other's taste. It's forceful, it's him claiming ownership, as if he's waited for this as long as I have. As his tongue sweeps into my mouth, his lips press hard to mine, our teeth clash together. He's in complete control, I can do nothing but hang on and try to keep up. He leads, I follow. He's everything I've ever dreamed of.

I'm being pushed back, over his arm. The hand holding my head captive comes down and sweeps up my legs, then I'm on my back, on the bed, and he's kneeling over me. His mouth recaptures mine, then his hands are on my breasts, kneading and plumping them as though, now he's been given permission to explore, it's beyond him to take his time.

Suddenly he rears back, his hand wiping his mouth, our kiss so frantic it's messy, his saliva on my lips, mine on his.

"Theo," he gasps. "We can't do this in front of the kid."

"Theo's asleep," I tell him, then grin. "And he's far too young to care what we get up to."

It seems to be all the encouragement he needs. He kisses me again, the demanding slide of his tongue already familiar. Then his mouth moves down, laving one nipple and then the other.

"I can't take my time, Vi. I've been rock hard since you came back into my fuckin' life."

"I've wanted you since I first saw you, too."

Not just since we reconnected, I've wanted him all my life. All the nerves in my body come alive as I realise all the dreams I've ever had are about to come true.

"Fuck, Vi." He pauses in his task, his eyes meeting mine, his expression so earnest. "I wanted you when you were jailbait. Your brother would have killed me for the thoughts I had about you then. That's why I stayed away."

"You never said... I never knew..." His admission has taken me by surprise. "I never dreamed you thought of me that way." My heart leaps with the knowledge my feelings for him had never been just one way. "You gave me no sign..."

"I never dreamed you'd want me. I thought you saw me the

same as you saw Nathan." His mouth's moving down, trailing kisses across my stomach.

"Never," I cry out. Then realise exactly what he's doing. "D, I've, I've had a baby." It's only now I'm self-conscious, reminded of the baby fat and the silvery lines across my skin.

But his tongue has already begun to trace them, and he murmurs solemnly, the words vibrating across my flesh, "Shows how amazing you are, Violet. Never, ever be ashamed of them. You've done something incredible." For a second he looks up and his eyes meet mine. "You've given me a son."

My gut clenches hard as our gazes lock and the wealth of information in those five words is shared between us. To Demon it doesn't matter who fathered Theo, he'll bring him up as his own. It's then I really believe every word that he's said.

Then I can't think any longer as his mouth closes around my clit. He raises his mouth only to inform me, "Christ, Vi, you're so fuckin wet for me."

Then he's back showing his expertise and experience again. Fingers inside me working, his tongue, fuck, he's talented. I pull the spare pillow toward me, holding it over my mouth as I scream through the orgasm he's just given me.

Spasms and aftershocks are still shaking my body when he rasps out, "Got to be inside you, Vi."

Hearing a tearing sound, I realise he's opening a condom. I'm glad he remembered; I'd have forgotten.

But his head is there, next to mine, his voice in my ear. "You want more kids, Vi? I don't mind taking the chance."

Jeez, he's giving me palpitations. *Another baby this quickly?* I always saw myself with a big family. *Why wait? Why not do it properly with a man, this man, beside me? But shouldn't we have some time together first?*

"Vi?" I can feel the big head of his dick rocking ungloved against me. It would be so easy for him to just slip inside. *What does he want?*

"You decide." I've run from giving an answer; I can't make my mind up.

There's a slight hesitation before he replies.

"It's not that I don't want a baby with you, Vi. Fuck, you growing round with my seed? Make my world perfect. But it's not been long since you had Theo, and life's not been easy. We need to extricate you from this mess, take some time to settle, then do shit right. For now, I'm going to glove up."

It's the right answer. I think I fall in love with him even more as he smooths the latex down his cock.

Immediately he thrusts into me. It's been a long time. I'm tight, I feel the burn, but I'm so wet, so well-lubricated he's in with one glide, then waiting for me to adjust and relax. He uses that time.

"You're mine, Violet. There will never be another man in this cunt. You're it for me, you hear me? Been fuckin' waitin' for you all my life. Been waitin' for you to grow up. You have my property patch, tomorrow you'll have my ring on your finger." He starts punctuating his words with little pumps. "You feel me moving inside you? You better fuckin' like it. That's the only cock you're ever going to have in you, babe. From this moment and for all of your fuckin' life."

It isn't just his tongue he knows how to use. He's finding something inside me no man's ever found before. He adjusts the angle when he hears my gasp.

"Yeah, that's it, right there, isn't it, darlin'? That's the spot."

A slow slide out, then he hammers in, the changes in rhythm starting to drive me wild. No man's cock has ever felt so good; why would I ever want to feel another man's touch?

"Ain't gonna come before you, Vi. And you feel so fucking good. I can feel your muscles clenching me. So fuckin' tight, so good, babe."

I don't think anyone's ever given a running commentary before. Luckily, he appears not to expect an answer as I'm incapable of forming words. Especially when his fingers find my clit and start strumming.

"D, oh, D."

"You like that? I can tell. Fuck, your cunt's like a vice. That's right, you come for me, girl. Like that. Christ, you're going to take me right over."

As I grab the pillow for the second time, he begins to speed up, his thrusts coming faster until he pushes himself all the way home, holding himself as he grunts his way through his release.

We're still, silent except for breath being drawn into starved lungs. My eyes have squeezed closed; I slowly open them to find his dark ones staring into my own. "Vi," he says softly as he lowers his head, his mouth with the taste of me on him softly brushing over my own. The urgency has gone now, he takes his time, still the one in charge, still controlling, but there's emotion that was missing before. When he draws away, he moves slightly to one side, his cock still inside of me.

"Don't want to move, Vi. It feels like I've come home."

CHAPTER TWENTY

Demon

My cock is softening, slipping out of her. Her juices are making the bed wet. I'll have to move soon; I don't want to. For a second, I regret I hadn't played Russian roulette and had forgone the condom.

I wait for regrets to sink in. Wait for my head to say what I've just done is the most stupid mistake I've ever made in my life. I've fucked Nathan's sister. While my head's in turmoil, Vi's quiet, snuggled into my side as if she's meant to be there. The place she never should have taken. I wait for that voice saying what I've done is wrong, but it stays quiet. No regrets? None at all.

I should never have made her get my name inked on her body. From that moment on, I was fighting a battle I'd had no chance of winning. It hadn't helped that she'd wanted me, too. One thing I'm learning about my soon-to-be wife, if she desires something she goes after it. Once I came into this room I didn't have a fuckin' chance. Seems I'm the lucky bastard she wants.

While I'm loathe to lose the connection, my cock, now flaccid, leaves the warmth of her body. Leaning over, I kiss her forehead. "Gonna go clean up, Vi."

She turns, her face unreadable. A cold feeling settles over me, wondering if she's the one having regrets, fearing I might have taken advantage of her. Then she smiles, her hand reaches out to caress my face, a little tentatively, as if unsure of her welcome. Taking it in mine, I turn it over, placing my lips to the palm. Then I leave the bed.

It's only then I realise. "Fuck, Vi," I start with a self-deprecating laugh. "I didn't even take my clothes off. Sorry, hardly romantic, was it?"

Her hand stretches out but she can't reach me. Her eyes are half-hooded but match the smile on her lips. "Think it shows I drove you crazy."

Out of control, I'd call it. But crazy? Yeah. That's a good enough word for it. "Reckon it won't be for the last time." As I say it, I mean it, and I'm not just referring to in bed. Vi's a strong woman, and we'll end up butting heads. But the make-up sex? Yeah, that will be out of this world amazing. I start to take a step away, then remember. "Hey, Vi. How's your back? Didn't give it a fuckin' thought?"

She wriggles. *God, that body!*

"Neither did I," she laughs. "But now you mention it, it is a little sore. How's your tat?"

"What tat?" I smile down at her. I'm used to being inked. And that small tattoo I got earlier today was nothing compared to when I had my back patch done. Nothing to distract me from the incredible feeling of being inside her. Leaning down, I place another light kiss to her head. "Hang on here for a moment."

"If you think I have the energy to move, you're wrong," she groans.

Then I've done my job right.

It's only a moment before I'm back from the bathroom with a washcloth. I tap her legs, pleased when she opens them for me, loving that she's not shy and she lets me clean her up. I'm momentarily distracted by her glistening cunt. I want to experience that time and time again.

Part of me wishes I'd tried to make her pregnant; the

thought that I was an inch away from doing so doesn't disturb me. Not for one second. My decision had been right. Need to get shit put behind us before we move forward. What is worrying is how far I've let her in and how fast.

Nah. Always had feelings for her. Just, now she's old enough to act on them without me ending up in jail.

"You ever going to get undressed?" Her voice sounds lazy as she stretches, in much the same way as Bitch does.

"Thinking about it."

I smirk, realising how ridiculous this is. I can't remember the last time I was in bed with a woman forgetting myself so entirely I'd done nothing more than slide down my zipper. She stares as I at last get down to business, ripping my tee over my head, then sliding my jeans and boxers off, toeing my boots away so I can remove them entirely.

Then, as she moves her finger in a circle, I turn a full three-hundred-and-sixty degrees. I keep myself fit. Even at thirty-five there's not an ounce of fat on me. When I'm facing her again, I relish the appreciative look in her eyes.

When her arms open in welcome, I lay down beside her, chuckling as she shifts away from the wet spot and pulling her into my arms. Nuzzling my lips against her hair, I grow serious.

"Gonna need to rethink a lot of things, Vi. Gonna take a moment to get our heads around this step we've just taken."

"Don't you see this is right, D? You and me?" She bites her lip.

"I remember the day you were born, Vi. Even then, Nathan was so proud that he had a sister. You became ours to protect from that moment on. It was only a day or so later, I first got to hold you. You opened those blue eyes, looked straight into mine, and I fell in love with you."

A small frown darkens her face. "A different type of love, D."

I lean back onto the pillow, the arm that's not around her covering my eyes as I prepare to tell her a truth I'm only just now admitting.

"I remember how you clung to me at Nathan's funeral, Vi. Seeking my comfort and support as we shared the loss of that person so important to us both. You were sixteen; I, of course, ten years older. I know the feelings I had then that a man shouldn't have for a child. I wanted to hold onto you forever."

"But you didn't stay in contact."

"I stayed away but watched from a distance. I knew every step you took until you were settled. I let you move on with your life but made sure you were okay until you were through college and started out on your career. I'm an outlaw biker, darlin'. You seemed to be on another path. Didn't want to pressure you to step off it."

"You never spoke to me. Never picked up the phone, never asked how I was doing."

I ignore her, needing to get this off my chest. "I suspect I knew what I'd feel if I saw you up close, Vi. Like I did that morning we went for coffee. I wanted to step into your life and take over. You were no longer a girl I had to stay away from, you were a mature woman who I could pursue."

"But you didn't."

I turn over, stare down into her beautiful eyes, the colour only deepened since I'd first held her as a babe in my arms. "I'm the prez of an MC, Vi. What have I to offer but my protection? You were not of this world, Violet, until circumstances drew you into it. I thought I could do best by being a proxy brother."

"I don't need another brother."

Raising her fingers to my lips, I suck them into my mouth one by one, my tongue curling around them. She sighs, draws in a sharp breath, starts to turn to me...

Theo's sharp cry interrupts.

A quick grin for me, then the concerned glance of a mother. Quickly shrugging a wrap around her, she lifts her—our—son into her arms, then takes him to the changing table and has a fresh diaper on him in a quarter of the time it had taken me. I determine to get in more practice; whatever I take on, I'll learn how to be the best. Clean and dry, she now brings him to the bed. Unconcerned, she opens her wrap and puts him to her breast, then frowns as he suckles.

"That painful?"

"It sort of is and isn't? Pinches a bit. In some ways it's the best feeling in the world, but my milk is drying up, and now his teeth are starting to come through, it's time to stop."

I watch, my gut clenching. It's the most beautiful sight in the world. Doesn't matter how he came into my life, that's my son she's feeding. The child I'll guide to be what he wants, just like Hellfire had done me. I'm transfixed, but from the little frown on his face, I don't need her to translate the situation.

"Want me to get him a bottle?"

"Please."

The clubroom is covered with bodies sprawled out over every available surface. A few seem to have passed out on the floor. In the kitchen there are signs of life, Shadow is getting a glass of water. He watches as I heat the bottle, a grin covering his face.

"Bit domesticated there, Prez."

A swift glare stops any further jokes. But he's got an excuse to watch me wide-eyed. There are no babies in the Vegas chapter, as there were none here. Seems I'm not uncomfortable with it at all. Perhaps a new generation will be the making of us. New life to protect, the signs of a future. All of a sudden the new tattoo parlour, other businesses we run, are not just to give the brothers a comfortable existence, but for providing for our families and giving us something worth fighting for.

There's a spring in my step as I return to Hellfire's old room. "It's our wedding day," I tell her, noting Theo, now taking the bottle, looks more satisfied.

"Your mom said she got me a dress. I didn't think it important." She frowns. "I hope she has good taste, D."

"Mom will do okay."

What happened last night has given this day more significance. I'm not surprised Vi's gone from not caring to now wanting to look her best. The vows are no longer just words we have to say, but on my part at least, a real commitment.

"I've already claimed you, Vi. In front of my brothers, and last night…"

"Was incredible. Everything I ever dreamed of." She shifts Theo to make them both more comfortable. "It was always you, D. Always."

The tone of her voice tells me her words are the truth. I slide something out of my cut and approach her. "Want to give you something."

Her hands point to my crotch and she grins. "Again?"

My mouth quirks, then I grow serious. I turn her around so her back is toward me, then fasten a chain around her neck. She looks down; her fingers raise the heart I've just placed around her.

"You had this made for me?"

"It's our wedding day, Vi. It seemed appropriate."

"Even before we admitted what we felt?"

I don't tell her how special that heart-shaped jewellery is. Whatever reason I initially had for giving it to her, the gold engraved with an entwined 'D' and 'V' now seems right for more than one reason.

As weddings days seem to go, it starts as it continues, everything going so fast it all seems a blur. Mom has indeed done Vi proud. She's wearing a blue satin dress that hugs her lovely curves, with a knee-length skirt that flares as she moves. The women of the club have grabbed the opportunity to wear something other than shorts, and even the whores look halfway presentable.

Of course, my wedding attire is simply clean jeans and a fresh shirt covered by my cut. It doesn't take me long to get ready. Once dressed, I leave my room and am caught up with organising the escort to the church. Guns are checked in case the Silvestri family decide to call a halt to the proceedings.

When at last everyone is ready, engines start with a roar. The sound of almost thirty motorcycles is deafening. With Drummer in the lead, me behind riding alongside Red, followed by Snatcher, Thunder and the rest of the VPs and officers, then the various combined rank and file, we make our way to the courthouse. In the midst of our procession is an SUV bringing Vi and Theo. The rest of the women are up behind their men, even Mo riding pillion with Hellfire. The club whores hitch rides where they can.

"Did you spot the black limousine?" Drummer says quietly, taking me to one side when we park up.

"Sure did."

"Get inside, Prez. I've got this." Thunder waves at the SUV, now surrounded by numerous men in black leather.

"Come on, you're a target out here." Drummer takes me inside.

The limousine wasn't the only thing I'd noticed. I'd spotted a few of Silvestri's men as well. My caution in having invited the other chapters here today has been vindicated. Not only does it give the impression that this is a real president's wedding, but our show of force may well have deterred an attack. I won't settle in my mind until Vi's safely back in the compound.

She stunned me, that now-wife of mine. My vows were hurried and not thought through. Hers, though? She must have rewritten them since last night. No one could be left in any doubt of her love for me. I'm guilty I hadn't reciprocated, but shit, that's woman's stuff, and this is the marriage that wasn't meant to be but feels... perfect.

The kiss, though. In public, I demonstrated just what she means to me to the accompaniment of cheers and wolf whistles, and more than a few tears from my mom. Even Hellfire was sniffling.

"Proud of you, Son." My father's eyes glisten as I take Theo from Jayden.

I make him a vow, as earnest as any I'd just said to Vi. "I'll bring him up right, Hell. Got a fuckin' good example to follow and live up to."

His hand squeezes my shoulder. We both know I'm alluding to the fact he brought up another man's child. He points to the baby who's smiling in my arms. "Not his fault the way he was spawned. What he'll turn out to be will be shaped by you as his old man. Never look to see anything else there." Wise words from a man who's lived it.

A quiet moment to ourselves. A question needing to be asked. "You ever have any second thoughts, Hell? Ever wondered if it was the right thing to do?"

"Never." His voice is sharp, his rebuttal fast. "Mo was it for me. Whatever she came with was mine, too."

I nod. That's exactly what I feel about Vi, though I'd had my head in the sand too long and had tried to deny it.

Hell's wise, proves it as he sums up, "You loved a child, Son. You stepped back when she started to grow. That love resurfaced when you connected again as man and woman. The only fucker who couldn't see it was you. You've been fighting a battle you had no fuckin' chance of winnin'." He breaks off and grins. "Luckily, she's a strong girl, wouldn't let you run."

I chuckle, then grow serious. "Is she strong enough, though, for this life?"

"She will be, with your help, Demon."

I might have struggled with drawing her into my world, but I'm a selfish bastard. Now she's here, I'm going to keep her.

She is walking toward us, her progress slow as she stops to accept congratulations. Mo hugs her, secret smiles exchanged, making me frown, wondering what they are plotting. Mo and Vi? Yeah, reckon I'll need to watch my step with Mom and my old lady. Eventually she breaks through and is by my side.

Reaching me at last, she glances down at the new shiny ring on her finger, then up into my face. "It's perfect, Demon."

A moment of guilt. "Pyro chose it."

"Well, he has good taste. I love it."

Making a note to thank him again, knowing I don't regret spending those few thousand dollars if it puts such a smile on her face, I pass her the baby as she indicates she wants to take him.

I lean down, covering Theo's ears with my hands. "When we get back, I'm gonna fuck you hard. Ask Jay to take him. I want to hear you scream."

Her pale skin blushes a lovely shade of red. "Mo's offered to take him for the night."

"No way, Vi. Not letting him go off the compound."

She gives me a look which speaks volumes. It reads, *What the hell do you take me for, D?* "Hell and Mo are going to stay in your room."

So that's what they were just discussing. Seeing Mo's eyes catching mine, I raise my chin. Silent thanks that she's giving me a wedding night. At least we'll have more space once Vi's safely back at the clubhouse; most of our visitors will be returning home.

Drummer and Red approach, Snatcher not far behind. "About ready to go, Demon?" Their cautious eyes keep scanning the environment, all uneasy now we're outside.

I don't waste a moment. Whistling loudly, I raise my hand over my head and circle it around. Time to get this show back to the compound.

Conversations quiet, men start moving in the right direction. Mo's herding up the bitches, and Jay comes to take Theo from me. Vi might not be dressed for the slide, but it's only a short journey back to the compound, and I'll be taking it easy, so hopefully she won't end up with road rash.

I take position at the head of the ride. This is our time and taking prime spot shows it. On such an occasion as this, Drummer, the mother chapter president, typically gives up his pole position to the groom.

A very lucky groom as it happens, I think, as I watch that skirt twirl. *Can't wait to get her out of that. She's all mine.* She might have thought I'd given her my all last night; she's going to learn I haven't even started showing her my kind of loving yet. *Yeah. I can't wait.*

Getting on behind me, Vi takes a moment to make sure her skirt is tight under her ass and squeezed between her thighs so it won't be caught in the spokes, then, a helmet on and her arms around my back, she rests her chin on my shoulder. "Love you so much, D," she sighs.

My smile is wide. Jeez, how the fuck did I get so lucky in my life? She's my one, I admit it. Never been anyone else for me but her. I'm one lucky motherfucker.

Then, with a press of the start button, my engine starts with a roar, followed by all the bikes behind me. If I could hear over the exhausts, windows would probably be rattling. Feeling as happy as a fucking man on his wedding day, I pull away, a sense of pride in leading the column behind me. While Pueblo is used to seeing our bikes around, it's not normal that so many of us are riding together. People stop and stare with various reactions. Some wave, some watch, some hurry children in the opposite direction. I couldn't give a flying fuck.

Then we're through and driving through the outskirts.

Fuck! What the hell? I glance in my rearview, hastily applying my brake. Some fucker's come out of a hidden driveway off to one side and has driven straight into the bikes behind us; there are men and parts scattered over the road. I pull my bike to a halt and Vi immediately jumps off as I kick down the stand. I've started running back when I hear another squeal of brakes.

Turning, I'm already pulling my gun out of my cut as I see Violet scooped up and thrown into a car, which speeds off.

My bullets do nothing but bounce off the bulletproof bodywork.

CHAPTER TWENTY-ONE

Violet

I was blindfolded in the car so I've no idea where they've brought me, and no way of telling the outside world even if I did, as I haven't got my phone. I don't even know who they are, though I've my suspicions, of course. Who'd want to take me except for Angelino?

I've not been tied up. Apart from a little rough handling when I was shoved into the car, they haven't been violent to me. The room I've been left in is pleasant enough, clean, but with a locked door and window.

Was it Angelino? Or does Demon have enemies I know nothing about? I am, after all, the president's old lady. The only thing I find puzzling, but am grateful for, is that I'm here, but Theo is not.

I was expected. There's a plate of sandwiches covered in saran wrap, and a bottle of water. Huh. Won't be touching that. I've already learned my lesson, I'll be eating or drinking nothing while I'm here. Truth be told, I couldn't eat anything even if I was hungry. I'm worried sick, and not just about myself and who's kidnapped me. The carnage I saw first in the rearview mirror, then for a brief second before I'd been taken away had been terrifying, men and bikes all over the road.

Had anyone died or been seriously hurt? Drummer, he was definitely down. *Christ, he can't be badly injured or worse, he has kids and an old lady back home.* Red was on the ground, too, the big red-haired man who I'd only met briefly but who'd had a devilish twinkle in his eye. I'd seen him go down, his colouring unmistakable. That I had been the target was clear, I just hate that anyone else was hurt or worse in the process. *Please let them be alright.*

Demon. He must be beside himself. In my head he's no longer D, the mix of present and past. Now it helps to think of him as the man with eyes blazing like a devil from hell, who'd stop at nothing to rescue me. To take me back where I belong. With my son and my husband.

There's a couch, I sit on it, twisting the chain around my neck, fingering the locket which Demon had given me only a few hours ago. Fighting back tears.

Demon will come. I just have to stay strong.

Why am I here? Angelino wants Theo, not me. But who else could have wanted to kidnap me?

Will he use me as a bargaining chip? Me in exchange for Theo? It wouldn't work. Demon would never put my son in danger. *Would he?* If he did, there's no way I could ever forgive him. But what a choice to put on my new husband. Me or my son. If he's forced to make a decision, it will destroy him. *Sacrifice me, Demon.*

To wound-up to sit for long, I stand and walk across the room. I peer out of the window, trying to get some clues as to where I could be, but empty desert stretches out in front of me. The walls of my room are solid wooden planks, like that of an old ranch. There's a slight musty smell betraying its age. I eye the food again, not that I'm going to touch it, but taking it as a sign I'm not going to be mistreated. Or not yet.

Never one to be patient, I find the waiting, the knowing something will happen, that eventually someone will come, hangs heavy on me. I want to get on with whatever it is. Find out who's taken me and what they expect to achieve by it.

I'm obviously at the back of the house and can't see what's happening out the front. But I hear the faint sounds of a car, and downstairs, loud voices. Moving toward the door, I put my ear against it.

"*Questo è stupido. Quello che hai non ottiene niente. Era tutto finito anni fa, Angelino. Non puoi vendicarti di un uomo morto.*"

I don't recognise the voice, don't understand the language, but do pick up on the name. *Angelino.* I was right. My worst nightmare is here. My rapist. The man who wants my son as his own.

It's then I hear his voice, speaking in English, "Revenge is never over, old man. Debts have to be paid."

The first voice again, "*Non così. Non lo permetterò.*"

"You won't permit it?" Angelino's voice again. The sound sends shivers down my spine.

The other speaker switches to English. "The alliances..."

"Are old. We don't need them anymore. You've seen how easily we can corrupt their businesses. The don is a weak, old man, hanging onto the old days when a handshake was a man's bond. The same goes for you. It's time for you both to... retire."

There's silence. I'm trying to work out what I'm hearing. The Italian speaker seems upset with whatever situation this is, what I'm part of. I get a sense that he's in danger from Angelino. *Who is he?*

I think I've gotten my answer when Angelino speaks again, "*La tua giornata è finita, Sanna.*"

Sanna? The last word was sneered, said sarcastically, as though it was a name. *Who is he talking to?* He'd mentioned the don being weak. Is Angelino making a play to become boss? The more I think about it, the more sense it makes. I try to think back over what Demon had said, how bad a villain I'd been conned by. Does the underboss get an automatic promotion if he gets his father out of the way? The Angel of Death arguably would become one of the most powerful men in this part of Colorado. Or at least, where the underworld is concerned.

How the hell did I get involved in all this? Growing up, I was the normal child of a normal American family. I wasn't even aware of the gangs walking the streets. Oh, I knew drugs were around, but none of my friends had done more than dabble in weed. It seems laughable I've gotten myself tied up in this. Why on earth did I answer that ad and jump at the chance of an interview? Where somehow I'd ended up raped, abandoned and pregnant.

My father would turn in his grave if he knew what I was mixed up in. My mother? Well, for the first time I believe that it's best she knows nothing about it.

"I miei uomini sono ancora fedeli."

I hear doors slamming and a car departing. Then it either returns, or a different one arrives. Voices are shouting. A sudden crash followed by gunshots has me throwing myself behind the only shelter in the room, a worn sofa. Then there's an ominous silence. *Has Angelino killed the man he'd been speaking to?*

Am I an unwilling witness to a power struggle? And if so, which side won? For a moment I'm hopeful that Angelino was on the wrong side of the gun, but doubt I'd be that lucky. Staying in what my body seems to think is a safe place, though my head tells me nothing here meets that description, I stay crouched down, trying to interpret the sounds from below. Bangs, scrapes, and what sounds like something heavy being dragged. An 'oomph' of protest sounds. My mind conjures up all manner of things which are, from what I heard, not far from the truth. Bodies being moved. Is Angelino's father one of them?

One thing's for certain, it's not a rescue by Demon's men; I hear no Devils' voices which gives me some relief; hopefully my man is alive. But all's not well in the Mafia family, that's clear.

When I hear footsteps on the stairs, I stay crouched down, hoping they'll pass by my room. A snick of the lock and the door opens. I hunker down, trying to make myself invisible. Then two pairs of feet appear, one at either side of the couch. At least one pair of shoes appears to have fresh blood on them. One of the men has some kind of device in his hand, and he waves it toward me. One side of his mouth turns up, and he nods at the other in satisfaction.

The other stares at me, his eyes raking down my body, making my skin crawl. Then he issues an instruction.

"Take off your necklace."

I glance up, my hand protectively covering the locket.

"Take it off," the man repeats. "Or we'll take it off for you."

I'd have no chance against them. I need to save myself for a bigger battle. I'm going to lose a symbol that I'd like to cling onto, but it's not worth being hurt or incapacitated for. Maybe they want it to prove to Demon they have me captive?

As the man starts to move a step closer to me, with shaking hands I reach behind my neck, undo the clasp and pass it over.

The first man examines it, then nods. It appears to be all that they wanted. The door closes behind them and is relocked.

Cars come and go, but I'm left alone. Gradually light fades from the window. Since the argument and fight I've heard little more, just the murmur of voices and the odd sound letting me know I've not been left alone. I'm grateful Angelino hasn't renewed our acquaintance; he can wait until hell freezes over as far as I'm concerned.

But what is he waiting for? Has he contacted Demon? Is he demanding my son? Does he realise I won't be any part of that? That I'll leave Theo where he is, not even the empty promise of being reunited would make me change my mind.

Will Angelino be coming?

Time passes. Not only does Angelino not come, but no one else checks on me either. I'd be content to stay in this room forgotten forever. Except for one thing. The demands of my bladder. I try crossing my legs, but know that's not going to work, I'm becoming desperate. I'm surprised I've lasted this long, but fear must have overridden my body's needs. Now, though, it can no longer be denied.

Unwilling to draw attention to myself, I look around for a

handy receptacle, but can see nothing, and, even scared as I am, the thought of using a corner of the room is disgusting. Pulling my stiff legs under me, I rise to my feet and approach the door. Banging on it feebly isn't going to summon help, I realise quickly; the wood seems solid.

But I heard them. Maybe they'll hear me.

"Is anyone there?" I call out, unsure how to summon a kidnapper to escort me to a bathroom. "I need help."

It takes one more call before I hear the sound of footsteps on the stairs, then a key turning in the lock. I hold my breath, dreading to see Angelino, but it's not him. It's a man with a rifle slung over his shoulder.

"What?"

"Er, I need the bathroom."

A resigned shrug, then he steps aside. With his hand on my arm he leads me down the short hallway and opens another door. I step inside and slide the bolt. It's old-fashioned, but functional. One look out the window shows I've no chance of escape, but my business is too pressing to linger.

When I flush, a voice sounds, "Hurry up."

Quickly I wash my hands, then open the bolt. Without a word I'm escorted back to the room I'd been in.

They forget me again. Darkness falls. My stomach growls, but I refuse to touch any food or drink.

I shouldn't be here. This is my wedding night. I should be exploring, exploiting the new step we've taken in our relationship. Not here.

Demon will be climbing up the wall. The thought of how worried he'll be doesn't help me at all.

If only there was some way I could get out of here, but I haven't a clue about how to pick a lock, my education in that subject had been lacking. Send a signal from the window? It won't open, and there's no one to see anything anyway.

Theo. Will he be wondering where I am, or happy that he's being changed, fed and amused? That's one worry I don't have on my mind. His new grandmother, Mo, adores him, and Jayden has been a perfect find. Such a natural with children. Despite her youth, sometimes she seems more competent than me.

Though I presume this was a bedroom, there's no bed, just the lumpy couch which has clearly been well-used. As the house fell silent some time ago, I try to make myself comfortable. I should be really tired, not having slept much last night. As I remember exactly what kept me from sleeping, I have to stifle a cry. *It's not fair. Just when Demon's admitted his feelings for me, I've been stolen away.* In the still and quiet darkness, I allow myself the horrific thought I might never see him again.

I need to remain positive. Can't afford to think like that.

A sound disturbs me. Just a coyote howling, followed by a night owl. *Is there anyone in the house at all? Have I been left here alone?*

My throat feels parched. The room is stuffy and I'm feeling lightheaded. *I need water.* If there's no one around, would it hurt to try what they left? My hands find the bottle and trace the lid. It appears sealed.

To escape I need my strength. I won't eat, but... I twist the cap, feeling it catch as the seal breaks, and then take a sip, then another. Soon half the bottle is gone and I feel... fine. Slightly refreshed, I put the rest aside for the morning.

Dawn breaks. The room faces east, so I get a bird's-eye view of the sun rising over the horizon. Not that I appreciate the beauty of it. This time yesterday, I was waking up with Demon, feeding and changing Theo with no inkling that my hopes and dreams were going to be taken away. With nothing to do, I sit by the window, staring out, noticing clouds starting to gather, the sun slipping behind them. I watch the first raindrops fall. Then hear the patter, then the heavy roar of a monsoon. Thunder rumbles, lightning flashes.

In the midst of the storm the door opens.

I jump, startled, the heaven's drumroll having obscured the sound of the lock being opened. I fear Angelino, but it's not him, it's a woman instead. She walks in with a graceful movement, almost gliding into the room. She's tall, elegant, but not that young, perhaps in her early to mid-forties. Though she's kept herself in shape, there are age lines around her eyes, and silver streaks in her carefully coiffured hair. She immediately intimidates me, just with her haughty stare. *But I'm the one being wronged here.*

My dress, so carefully chosen twenty-four hours ago by Moira, has suffered from the length of time it's been worn; now it's decidedly crumpled and creased. While in itself it's stylish, beside her I feel scruffy. But I force my back to straighten and stand as tall as I can. "Why are you holding me prisoner?"

"My name is Vitalia. I am Angelino's wife."

With that pronouncement I freeze. Then my temper blows up. "Your husband raped me!"

"Rape? I don't believe force was involved. Or that's not what the court said."

As she refers to her husband getting off scot-free for what he had done, I take a step closer. "You don't care if your husband plays away from home?"

"There are matters you don't understand, *piccolino* Violet."

There's a damn lot I don't understand.

"Well, why don't you fill me in?"

For a few seconds I'm not sure she's going to reply, then she gives an exaggerated Italian shrug as if it's no matter to her whether I know or not.

"Angelino and I have remained childless, a sad situation as you can understand. To Italians, family is everything. He has no heir to groom, no one to follow him. Until now. Do you understand?"

He wants my son because he could have no children of his own. I place my hands on my hips. "He won't get Theo."

Her lips curve in a most unattractive way. A half-smile, a smirk, leaving an impression there's something she knows that I don't.

CHAPTER TWENTY-TWO

Demon

Christ, what a fucking mess. Bikes down, men injured. The truck that had mowed them down had done what it needed to and then zoomed off. Perfectly timed to separate me and Violet from our escort. Now she's been abducted.

As I start running back to my bike, Hellfire comes limping up, Thunder beside him.

"Where the fuck are you going?"

"After my wife!" I scream back, wasting time stating the obvious. "Angel fucking has her."

"You're right, he has. But you don't know where, or how many men he has guarding her. You rushing off now will only get yourself dead."

Thunder steps past Hell and yanks the key out of the ignition.

"What the fuck?"

"Hell's right," he growls. "All you'll do is leave us without a prez. He won't harm her, what good would that do him? I'd bet money that he'll want to exchange her for the kid."

Of course that's why he'll have taken her. But he could hurt her, torture her, send her back to us piece by piece until we give in and give up Theo. Which would kill her anyway, so I could never do that.

"I have to get to her," I cry out in desperation.

Drummer appears rubbing his fist. "We need to get back to the clubhouse. Get this mess off the street before we attract the cops. Get your prospects here with a fuckin' crash truck. A couple of these bikes aren't rideable." His steel glare is icy. "Get your head out of your ass. Know you're fuckin' worried, Demon. I'd be the same in your place. But you can't rush off all guns blazing, not until we know where she's been taken and how well it's guarded."

Having the mother chapter prez shout in my face has brought me back to my senses. I'm a husband, but I'm also Prez. My fingers go to the bridge of my nose. "Injuries?"

"All minor." Yeah, Drummer will have gone to the men first, while I hadn't spared them a thought. "Think Snatcher might have hit his head a bit too hard, but he says he's okay."

Thunder's already on his phone organising to get the stricken bikes back to the club.

"Anyone who can't ride?"

Drummer shakes his head. "We'll double up and get back. Get some talk going." His eyes soften slightly, and his hand rests on the shoulder of my cut. "We'll get your woman back, Demon." Then his expression hardens again. "You have fifteen extra men at your back, and we'll be here as long as we need to. But I don't want to lose any, so we do this right."

"I know where she is, Drummer. Or at least, I will when we get back. Gave her a necklace this morning. Cad put a tracker inside."

"As long as she's still wearing it."

Now, that's a doubt I don't want put in my head.

Where we are is luckily not far from the clubhouse and the prospects appear as we're still sorting out which bikes are still roadworthy. Scrapes and dents on most of them. Snatcher's and Crash's appear to have borne the brunt. Snatcher, trying to stem the blood from his head, is furious. Crash, having escaped with bruises, is red in the face.

"Mom alright?" I belatedly ask Hellfire.

"She's fine, son. She's checking out the other girls, but they all seem to have escaped injury."

"You?"

"Caught my leg under the bike when it went over. Bruised but I can walk and ride. Nothing broken."

By the time we've finished talking, the prospects have already started loading bikes onto the crash truck. We leave Wills and Dan there, then make our way back to the clubhouse.

I use the few minutes' journey to sort out what I'm going to do next. First is to get Cad to trace where she's been taken, then hold church and come up with a fucking fast plan of action. With fifteen extra people, there's no way we'll fit into our meeting room so we'll have to hold it around the bar.

I don't even need to tell him. As soon as we enter the club-room, Cad races over to his spot, opening his laptop and firing up a PC beside him. By the time everyone's parked up and come in, he's given me a sharp nod. He's found her.

Standing on a chair by the bar, I whistle loudly. Within seconds the individual conversations have died down. "We'll hold church here due to the numbers. Women and sweet butts, make yourself scarce."

Mo glares as she passes me, but she's been an old lady long enough to understand. She pauses to hiss, "You bring my daughter-in-law back." In return she gets a roll of my eyes; as if I'm going to do anything else.

Drummer lithely jumps up onto the bar, his loud voice bellowing, "Get chairs, drag up tables, anywhere to sit your asses down."

For a moment the main sound is wood scraping against wood, but at last there's a double row of men circled around. A few remain standing, mostly from my chapter, like me too agitated to sit.

"Cad?" I waste no time.

"It's moving. I'm tracking it. Seems like she's in a car."

She's been driving all this time?

"Looks like it might be a circuitous route in case we were following, but it's only the other side of Pueblo."

The room's gone silent. Cad's voice is the only one. Suddenly he exclaims loudly, "Well, fuck me, it's stopped. They're not being shy about it. She's fucking at the don's house."

Thank fuck for that tracker. But, Lucio's house? That's not what I expected. At least we know where she is.

"You know the place?" Drummer butts in.

"Hell, Thunder and I were there last week. Yeah, we know it, Drummer." I bend my head; my fingers find my nose. "It's well-defended, but there are weak points to attack. And, of course, we have the numbers."

"Need explosives?" Pyro asks. "Got some C4 in the shop. Want me to get it?"

I glance at Hell, then look back to Pyro and nod. "Yeah. We may need to blow the gates."

"Or a distraction would be good," puts in Thunder.

"You know how many guards he's likely to have?" Drummer snaps.

I think back to what I remember. "Half-a-dozen, I reckon. But if that's where he's holding Violet, he may have brought in more."

Hellfire's frowning. "Why there? I would have thought Angel would have taken her to one of his properties. Wouldn't have expected Lucio to be involved in this."

"He wants his grandson, so presumably he'd help. They don't know we're able to track her. May assume we'd think it's the last place we'd look, and that dwe'd waste time chasing our tails all over the city." Which is what we would have been doing, had she not been wearing a tracker. Thank whatever god is watching over us for that.

"What are we waiting for?" Snatcher pulls yet another bloody rag away from his head, seeming unfazed that his wound has not yet scabbed over.

My phone rings. I take it out, not recognising the number. Drummer's hand covers mine. "If that's him, mind your words, Demon, mind your words. We need to maintain that element of surprise."

Of course we do, but the reminder to be careful keeps my head sharp. I raise my chin, then accept the call.

"Demon."

"This is Angel."

I put the phone on speaker. "Angel. I believe you have something that belongs to me."

The room is so silent a pin dropping would seem loud. "Oh, have you lost something?"

"You fuckin' know I have," I growl. "I want my wife back."

"So careless to lose her on your wedding day."

"Cut the crap, Angel."

"I want the baby, Demon. I'll exchange your woman for the kid."

"Not going to happen, Angel. And if you harm one hair on her head..."

"You'll what? Harm the baby? Even I know you wouldn't do that."

He wants the child of his blood, just as I expected. My only usable threat would be to kill Theo, and I can't even voice that.

"No exchange? Well, that's a shame. Your woman and I will just have to get reacquainted instead. I rather enjoyed her the first time." Suddenly his voice changes and his mocking tone disappears. "I'll give you twenty-four hours to decide what to do."

The call ends.

"Something's wrong," Drummer says.

I don't follow him. It was exactly what I'd expected. A call for the kid in exchange for my wife. A bargain I can't make. It would kill Violet if I do, and if I don't, Angel might kill her himself. Or make her life a living hell and traffic her.

"You're not thinking clearly," Drummer insists. "His tone, his words. He didn't sound desperate for his son. He didn't demand him immediately, he's giving you time to stew, Demon. It doesn't sound right."

Hellfire steps forward. "Nah, Drummer. He's makin' us sweat. He thinks we'll be weaker tomorrow when we can't find where she is."

"Don't fuckin' care about the reason," I snarl. "What he has given us is time to get her back. Now we tool up and go on the offensive. By tonight, I want my old lady safe."

"What you got in your armoury, Demon?"

It's Thunder, wearing his sergeant-at-arms hat, who answers Red, "AK-15s, grenades, probably anything you need, Red. And Pyro's got explosives, as he just said."

"I have plans of Lucio's mansion." Cad stands and brings his laptop over. Thunder, Wraith, Crash and Twister crowd around it. There's no point all of us trying to get a look, we'd just end up blocking each other's view.

After what seems an inordinate amount of time and mumblings and gesticulations from the three men, at last Thunder turns around.

"Our suggestion is, we use explosives to breach the walls at these three points." He turns the screen around, his finger pointing to the locations. "Hopefully that will get the guards running in all directions. We'll have three groups of men waiting to take them out. You want extreme prejudice, Prez?"

"Only if necessary," Drummer puts in quickly. "Disable, disarm if we can. We're talking about a fuckin' bloodbath and all-out war if we leave too many dead bodies around."

Thunder glances at me. I raise my chin to confirm my acceptance of Drummer's sensible proposal. Then he continues.

"There's a back entrance. One group should aim for that. Another team—I suggest that includes you, Prez—will go in the front once the walls have been breached. Hopefully they'll be looking the other way when we do."

"Remember, we have the element of surprise. They don't know we're coming." Thank fuck I put a tracker on Violet.

The lair of the lion himself; I never would have expected her to be taken there. One of their properties we know nothing about, yes. But Lucio's house? I still can't believe he's made it so easy. Well. He's going to be left with a fair bit of damage both to his property and to his men. "How long to get your supplies, Pyro?"

"Give me an hour, Prez."

"Go get your shit, then." I jerk my head and he leaves immediately.

I hate any delay, but know I have to curb my impatience. We do this right or we won't succeed. I try to put to the back of my mind that Violet will be going crazy with worry. She doesn't know the pretty piece of jewellery I gave her is probably going to save her life. When Pyro's gone, we get down to discussing who's going where. There are five here from each of our other chapters; they decide to stay together, having been brothers so long they know how each other will respond. I will be leading the Colorado boys in from the front once the explosions have caused the sufficient confusion. When it's clear, Drummer, Red and Snatcher will lead their men through the back entrance. Our pincer movement should catch Lucio and Angel unawares.

Christ. Waiting is killing me. Beers are passed around, being consumed in moderation. I watch my brothers, from my and the other various chapters, and wonder how many of us will be returning. There's always the risk Angel will hurt or even kill Violet rather than let me take her. Drummer may want to disable the foot soldiers, but Angel? Well, he's signed his death warrant by touching my woman. This business between us ends today.

Cigarettes are passed around; I notice Hellfire taking one and I don't blame him, almost ready to take one myself. Conversations are subdued as final arrangements are made and discussed, any weaknesses identified and strengthened.

Cad goes back to his computers. Before too long he's returned. "There are camera feeds in and around the house. Once you're in position, I'll disable them."

I can't leave the clubhouse unguarded. I'd like Hellfire to stay, but one look at his set face and I know I'd have an argument if I asked him. In the end, I call Mace, Ink, Lizard, Rusty and Bomber to me.

"You keep Theo safe, you hear me? One whiff of fuckin' trouble and you get in touch."

They look at each other, then back at me. Sharp nods come my way. I know they'd rather be in the thick of the action but are also aware I'm giving them an important task today. Angel might be expecting us to put all our efforts into finding Violet, leaving my son unguarded. With Cad, that means six men are staying behind. Eight, including myself, are going. With the men from the other chapters coming as well, it should be enough to take Lucio and Angelino by surprise.

At last, Pyro returns, handing out bundles of explosives and detonators to each of the visiting VPs.

"Peg and Blade will be annoyed they're missing out on the fun," Wraith tells Drummer as he secures his dangerous cargo in his saddle bags.

"Ain't that the truth," replies his prez.

"Don't worry, Son. We'll get her back." Hellfire slaps my back as he passes.

"Too fuckin' right. Need my apprentice." I jerk my chin at Liz who continues, "Just make sure you bring her home." His statement needs no answer.

One by one my brothers pass me, well aware of the risk they're taking. A lump comes into my throat, wondering whether all these good men will be returning. Wherever they're keeping Violet, it's going to be well guarded.

At last, we're ready. With a loud chant of "Ride, Satan's

Devils; Satan's Devils ride together" accompanied by fists bumping over hearts, we prepare to set out. Four groups representing four chapters. Some of my boys will be going with the visiting teams to show them where they're going. I spare a special word for Sparky, heading out with Red; Paladin, going with Drummer, his old prez; and finally, Buzzard, who's going to be guiding the way for Snatcher. As they're providing the distractions, they head out first.

We're right behind them. I'm in the lead, Thunder and Hellfire riding behind me, Pyro and Skull having our backs.

Hold on, Vi. Won't be long until you're in my arms, darling. Just hold on a little longer. We're on our way.

CHAPTER TWENTY-THREE

Violet

Speculating what type of woman would be married to someone like Angelino, I stare at Vitalia, wondering what she knows that I don't. Whatever it is, isn't going to be good news, at least where I'm concerned. I immediately dislike her, and not just because of her relationship to the man I despise. Momentarily I wonder if I can bitchslap that smarmy look off her face, but I doubt it. I'm not a violent person, but her? She looks like she'd easily get the upper hand in a catfight. There's just something about her that warns me to keep my hands at my sides. My first clue is that she came in here alone. That means she can't see me as any threat. I'd love to act like a heroine in one of the novels I read and go on the attack, but I wouldn't be able to best her.

She even turns her back on me, walking to the window and looking out. "You've been here before," she says conversationally. "Well, not this room, but in this house. It was where your son was conceived."

"He's Demon's son." I can say the words quite truthfully. Demon's claimed him.

"A DNA test would prove otherwise," she throws back.

"Well, we'll have to wait and see. First you have to get a court to agree." I cross my fingers, hoping the fancy lawyer Demon's going to engage finds some way to stop that from happening. Demon's name on Theo's birth certificate will, hopefully, count for a lot.

"Whatever." She shrugs, then reverts back to what she was discussing before. "You stayed in this house for a few days."

I gasp. *What?*

Suddenly it all falls into place. My strange confusion about the day when I had returned home. I'd put it all down to the effect of the drugs in my system.

"You didn't know that, did you? Angelino wanted to make sure."

I approach her, my gut churning. "What are you saying?"

She spins around so fast I take a step back. "You're just a pawn, you know that? Angelino wants a child, and what better than one with the blood of his enemy."

"What the fuck are you talking about?" My head whirls. "I didn't even know who Angelino was when I met him. I answered an ad posted by a stranger. I had nothing previously to do with him." If I had known who he was I'd never have put in an application. "How can I be his enemy? I'm the one who's been wronged here. Your husband drugged me, had sex with me, and you don't even care?"

Again, she raises and lowers her shoulder. "My husband does many things which I find distasteful, but having a child will be what I always wanted. Sacrifices have to be made." Now she sighs. "Of course, at first, we didn't think it had worked. You're so stupid, it took you so long to realise you were pregnant. We were going to just take the baby when it was born, but then you dragged us through the courts and made it impossible for him to just disappear."

"You're never getting your hands on Theo. I'll die first." Okay, so plan A might need to be resurrected again.

"It's no matter. We've got you. Unlike me, you're fertile. You can just have another child. One where there's no doubt of his parentage."

Two things, good and bad, hit me at once. One—the unthinkable—that it sounds like Angelino has brought me here to rape and impregnate me again, and the other, hope that they do indeed believe Demon to be Theo's father. In which case, Theo is safe. That's what's important.

"What are you saying, Vitalia?" I speak slowly.

"You really have no recollection of what happened, have you?" She suddenly moves forward, making me step back. "It would have been fine, except Angelino's guard, who was supposed to be looking after you, decided he'd like to also get his cock wet. He's dead now, of course; was, the moment my husband found out."

Jesus! As the implications of what she's just said hit me, I reach behind me, needing to grasp the back of the couch for support. Not only was I raped by Angelino, but by another man as well? No wonder they don't want to press the DNA case, it could prove Theo wasn't his. For a moment I want to demand they do test, right here and now, as that might put an end to it. Then I realise there's still a fifty-fifty chance.

When I'd first realised I had been raped I'd gone into a state of shock; was a living zombie for days, weeks, trying to come to terms with the extent of my violation. Now I know it's so much worse than I thought. *Not once. Multiple times, and multiple men.* For days I'd been there for the taking, unable to protect myself or say no. Blood rushes away from my head and I start to feel dizzy.

"This time you'll be watched more carefully. There won't be a chance for anything to go wrong."

I shake my head, trying to clear it. I try to make sense of what I'm being told.

"This is absolutely ridiculous. You can't really mean what you're saying. Vitalia, I can understand how you want a child, but this way is absolutely crazy. You could pay a surrogate to have a baby for you."

Her cruel stare fixes me like a butterfly pinned to a board. "You are misunderstanding the point. Angelino doesn't want any child. He wants one with you. As the ultimate revenge. He finally gets what he's been seeking, and I get my reward."

This doesn't make sense at all.

"I don't know Angelino," I say, picking my words as though I'm speaking to a child. "Our meeting was accidental..."

"You're wrong." Her lips curve and not in a nice way at all. "Who gave you the leaflet about the vacancy you applied for?"

I purse my lips as I think back. "It was on a table in a café I used to go to."

"The waitress gave it to you with your coffee. Only you. He'd been watching you, knew the types of jobs you were applying for, so he made up one which would entice you. As expected, you fell for it and applied."

My brow creases. I don't understand. I'd never previously crossed paths with Angelino nor any of his family.

"But why? Why was he watching me?"

She sighs deeply, as though she's becoming impatient with all my questions.

"Because by the time the pieces came together, your father had died. Your mother was, let's say, incapacitated. At first, Angelino was going to kill you, but what good would that have done? There was no one to miss you, no one to appreciate the revenge that had at last been served. We needed a child, and you were a suitable incubator."

My head moves side-to-side, then I repeat the action. Not one word out of her mouth gives me any answers.

"What are you talking about my father for?" I rack my brains for anything that adds up. "He was an accountant." I think back to the man who I'd loved, wondering how he could have so angered the Silvestri family. I can't see how he could have been involved with them. Unless, "Did he do the accounts for one of your businesses? Is that what this is about? Do you think he lost you money?" If so, he wouldn't have done it on purpose. But even the best accountant can get caught out with an unexpected drop in the market at times.

"Lost us money?" She barks an incredulous laugh. She comes closer, placing a perfectly-manicured fingernail against my chin, forcing me to look up. "You really don't have a clue, do you?"

"He killed my brother."

Moving my head rapidly away from her touch, I turn to face the door where Angelino is leaning, his arms folded, his back against the wooden frame.

A chill settles in my gut just seeing him. "My father wouldn't have killed anyone," I protest, racking my brains. Was there a car accident or something I hadn't heard about?

"He thought he was clever getting out of the game. Covering his tracks. We could never discover his new identity. But we knew he was out there, weaving his magic from behind a curtain, like the Wizard of Oz." Pushing off the door, he walks into the room. "I didn't give up, unlike my father. I couldn't forgive. My brother bled out in my arms; you never forget that. I had to get the man responsible. Had to find out who he was. Well, lo and behold, he was your father. But by the time I came into possession of that knowledge, he was already dead."

I open my mouth to repeat that my gentle father would never do anything like that, when he steps closer.

"I went to the funeral to spit on his grave. But what did I find instead? A dutiful daughter. I nearly killed you right then and there. But then circumstances changed."

Vitalia gives a pained look to her husband. "We tried, but I can't give Angelino a child."

"Your father took someone I loved. So I came up with a better way of hurting him in return. I would have his daughter give me a son, and then take the boy from her. Marco, my trusted *soldato,* fucked that up. Theo might be mine, but again, he might not. He's with Demon. An outlaw MC president who'll spend his life thinking he's bringing up a mafioso's kid. Let him worry and watch his back, never being able to relax. While Violet, you'll give me another, one I can be assured is my own child. This time I won't make a mistake. You'll stay here until you've given me what I want. After that?" He raises and lowers his shoulders and leaves me to guess at what's in my future.

I hate him. I disliked him when I first met him, but you don't need to like your boss. I could have done my job without letting my animosity show. But to allow him near me? To allow him to touch me, knowing he's already had what I didn't give freely? There's no way I'd do that.

"You're wrong about my father." I make my voice as strong as I can, trying to hide the quiver of fear in it. "You have the wrong man. Whatever your investigations told you, the answer was wrong. As for me? I'll never let you take me again. You'd have to kill me first. And—" I think fast, wondering whether a lie could put him off. The expectation of the expression on his face makes a hysterical laugh burst out of me. "You'll have the same uncertainty again. Demon and I have started trying for a family. I might be pregnant even now." My hands cover my stomach protectively.

Angel's face changes. I never seen such an expression of rage. I rear back but can't evade the hand that hits my face, so hard it snaps to one side. Gingerly, my tongue touches my teeth; none feel loose.

Surprisingly, it's Vitalia who puts her hand on his arm. "There are ways to make sure she's not carrying a bastard kid. Our plans will just have to be put on hold, if what she's saying is the truth."

His anger is fading, his emotion changing to something else. I can tell by the way he's leering, how his greasy eyes are examining me from head to toe. Once again, I wish I was wearing something other than the dress I'd worn to impress my new husband. Now, though, it's not designer gear I'd prefer, but something made out of armour plating.

Keep him talking. "What do you think my father did? Who do you think he was?" I try not to move away, try to face up to him, desperate to get his attention off what he intends to do with me and onto something else. "Why do you think he still owes you from beyond the grave, and what's it got to do with me?"

His hand snakes out, curling cruelly around the back of my head. "It's got everything to do with you. He took my blood away from me, I'll take his. If you were a man, I'd kill you. As you're a woman, I'll keep you alive. For now, at least, while your useful."

I remember the voices I heard yesterday. The shots. That Angelino's here makes me think he was the one pulling the trigger. He'd mentioned the don. Is that where he's been? Is 'retiring' an euphemism for assassination? "What about your father? Did you kill him?" Maybe if I remind him he's a murderer too he won't keep blaming my dad.

"Kill my father? Oh, no, I didn't do that." He exchanges a strange look with his wife. If I didn't know better, I'd say he looked satisfied. "No, but yesterday I did have to dispose of a *capo* who did not see things my way."

Such cold words delivered in such a chilling tone. I shiver, realising I can't call on his better nature: he doesn't have one. Instead I voice my hope out loud, framing it as a certainty.

"Demon won't stop looking for me."

My words don't faze him at all. "He won't find you. You won't be here long and then you'll be moved. Once I know you're pregnant with my child, you'll be sent to another location until you give birth. Then you'll have outlived your usefulness to me. But I'll still get my money's worth. You see, I have an interest in another trade, and I'm sure to find a buyer for you."

It's not as though I hadn't suspected when he first indicated I only had one purpose as far as he was concerned. But I'd prefer death to what he has planned. I shiver again. Despite the warmth of the room, goosebumps arise.

I have to convince him I don't deserve the fate he has planned. "You're wrong. Daddy would never hurt anyone. He wouldn't, he couldn't. If he was involved in the death of your brother, it was an accident of some sort."

"My brother was tortured and killed."

I can't hold back my gasp. "Daddy would never…"

He gives an incredulous laugh. "Just because he might not have wielded the knife doesn't mean he wasn't responsible."

His fingers have relaxed. Taking the opportunity I pull away, moving around the sofa, putting it between him and myself.

"You're wrong," I tell him again. "All this is a great big mistake. And I'm not going to pay the price for a crime that was never committed, or at least, not by the man you're accusing."

Angelino tilts his head, his eyes narrow. "I'll make a bargain with you, Violet. If I show you the proof that you never knew dear daddy at all, will you come to me willingly? Or at least, not fight. I'd prefer not to drug you again. You were, shall we say, not an active participant last time."

He can't have proof. But if he shows me what has misled him, I'm sure I'll be able to prove it's untrue. There has to be some way to get out of this. Maybe stringing him along will buy me some time. Time for Demon to find me.

There's nothing that could make me voluntarily agree to let him violate me again. If I were to refuse to even consider it, he might just go ahead and rape me. I turn away, but watch him out of the corner of my eye. He's smirking. He knows he's going to get me anyway. He thinks no one is going to find me. He could be right. Demon might never discover where I am, but there's always the chance. A possibility I need to hold onto or I'll go crazy with grief.

Turning back around, feeling like I'm making a deal with the Devil, while knowing what's coming out of my mouth is a lie, I take a breath, then agree, "Yes."

It's childish, but I have my fingers crossed behind me.

CHAPTER TWENTY-FOUR

Demon

My phone vibrates. Cad's sent me instructions, I follow them religiously with the result that I and the other prez's can talk to each other. If we're to keep getting into situations like this, I'm going to have to invest in some of those earpieces the feds use. Cad had warned me you can only have five people on one iPhone call. He'd called it old-fashioned. I hope we won't be doing this shit again, but maybe we should be prepared and have a better way to keep in communication. I must have said some of my thoughts aloud, as someone responds.

"Get Cad to talk to Mouse," Drummer suggests. "He knows about that shit." I'd forgotten we're now all on the same call.

"Everyone in place?"

"Yeah, but I'm taking over from Snatcher, he's just been sick," Thor informs us.

Damn, I'd suspected he had a concussion from being knocked off his bike. Now is not a good time to have it confirmed.

"I'm all right," Snatcher himself informs us. "But yeah, to be on the safe side, deal with the VP. Don't want to keel over when it's all going down."

"Explosives in place," says Red, his statement copied by two other voices.

"On your count, Demon."

"Five," I start, and continue, "four, three, two, one."

Three explosions go off at once. Guards flood out of the house, unsure which way to run, rifles held across bodies. Well, I say 'flood', but I can see only four. Immediately they start gesticulating, and one's on his radio.

"How many coming your way?"

"Two came out the back, they seem reluctant to... ah, stay put. Let them come closer..." Red's giving us a running commentary.

A shot is fired. "Winged one," I hear Wraith through Drummer's phone. "There were two on our side, the other's just put his hands up."

Red sounds both pleased and puzzled when he confirms, "Fuck. Mine are surrendering too. Who the fuck are we dealing with?"

Not bothering to try to find an answer, I take the advantage offered to me, that Lucio's men aren't putting up much of a fight. "I'm going in. Keep them occupied."

At the sound of the shot, two of the guards who'd ran out the front door had turned tail and run back inside. The others dispersed around the side of the house.

"Got another couple here, Demon, just appeared from your direction. Sounds like we have the ones brave enough to fight back. We'll get them secured and come in and meet you." Thor doesn't seem worried.

Eight guards in all. In the process of being locked down.

Pyro's not only our explosive expert, he's a sniper, too. I leave him and Skull with rifles to cover our backs, then Hell, Thunder and I go to our bikes. There's a few hundred yards of driveway to cover, and that is the fastest way, even though it's hardly a discreet approach. I'm hoping that the holes in the walls and other three points of attack will keep any guards we haven't yet seen occupied and confused. I hear a burst of rapid fire and hope it's Devils doing the shooting and not getting shot. But there's no way back. Whatever we've started, we'll see through to the bitter end.

Engines started, stands up, pull clutch back, shift into gear, twist throttle, release clutch: actions performed simultaneously with me by Thunder and Hellfire, then our wheels are throwing up gravel as we speed down the drive.

Stands down, engines off, bodies thrown off sideways, and we're at the front door. A ping as a bullet hits a fairing, an answering shot from Pyro, and a swear word from Hell. Thunder shoots the lock and we're inside.

A guard holds up a gun, but faced with three others all pointing his way, he does the sensible thing and, with shaking hands, puts it on the floor. Thunder has his hands zip-tied quickly.

"How many of you?" I ask him sharply.

One glare at his face has him answering. "Eight *soldati*. six are outside," he grimaces as he hears more shots firing, "one more in here. He's stayed with the don."

So, not as many as I'd feared. They hadn't expected an attack. As for the *soldatos*. I study the man in front of me. The way he'd been holding his gun was as if he'd never had a weapon in his hands before. He'd broken easily, too. *What the fuck is going on?*

"Where's my wife?" I snap.

His eyes widen. "Your wife?"

"Violet Palmer." Well, she's technically a Black now. It's more important to find her than worrying about what to call her.

"American?" When I nod, he shakes his head. "There are no American females here. Only the staff, all Italian."

"Angel? Where is he?"

He looks confused. "He isn't here. Only the don."

Unsure whether to believe him, turning to Thunder, I order,

"Go search the upstairs. Hell, can you..." I break off as I see Drummer walking along the back corridor accompanied by Pal and the Tucson men. "Pal, go with Thunder will you?"

Drummer waves to Rock and Beef. "You two take this floor."

I add one last thing. "Tear the house a-fuckin'-part if you have to. But find her."

The Vegas enforcer is eyeing the man we've caught. "Want me to question him?"

"Later. Thanks, Twister," I decide. Searching will get faster results than torturing a man who might be prepared to take his boss's secrets to the grave with him. "Hellfire, Drummer and I will go see Lucio. Where's your boss?" I snap the last at the guard. A jerk of his head suggests the don's in the room where we'd met him only a few days back.

Pushing the soldier in front of me, I enter what appears to be an empty room. Yeah, not surprising. With bombs and gunshots, he's probably retreated to a safe room. "Where is it?" I tug the tied arms of the guard. Hell is already looking, in fact he's walked right over to a bookcase and is standing in front of it. Our captive stiffens, letting me know he's on the right track.

"Hell?"

"It's here. It was in the blueprints." *Of course it fucking was.* I should have spotted something like that, but I'd been too tied up with finding Violet.

"Open it," I instruct.

The soldier, who'd given up his gun so easily, shakes his head vigorously at the thought of giving up his boss.

"Open it!" This time I snarl.

"*Non c'è modo.*" I don't speak Italian, but his negative response suggests that he can't.

There's no time to waste. "Get the explosives from Pyro. We'll blow the room up. Don't care if we kill him."

"The Semtex should do the job. Spotted a weakness on the blueprints."

The soldier goes rigid again. His eyes flick to Hell, then back to me. As my father starts to walk past, he steps forward. "No." He stares at Hell, looking to see if he's bluffing or not.

I know he wouldn't have seen that level of detail on the plans Cad had shown us back at the clubhouse, but I also learned, early on, few people could come out the winner against my dad in a game of poker.

"Your boss comes out and answers our questions," I say, gravelly, "or we blow him to smithereens. Your choice."

He's gone pale. Loyalty to the *famiglia* will be as great as, if not greater than, that shown by the members of my club to me. If he makes the wrong choice, he'll be dead. And, for him, the wrong one is believing us.

"It can only be opened from the inside," he tells us, stiffly.

"Can he see, hear us?"

He answers through gritted teeth, "Lost the camera feeds before your attack. Thought there was a malfunction with the system."

The way he speaks again suggests they were in no way prepared for any confrontation. Minimal, in my view, guards for a man so important as the boss, and when they lost sight and sound around the building, they had simply put it down to circumstance, seeing nothing suspicious in it.

What the fuck is going on?

Hell catches my eye, his brow creases. He too, has picked up on the things which aren't adding up. Kidnapping Violet; potentially killing Devils in the process, not caring whether they did or not; holding her prisoner... Even if they thought we'd never come here to look for her, there was always going to be an outside chance.

So why weren't they ready and waiting?

Or are we the ones being set up? Lulled into a false sense of security before the actual attack. I don't need to warn anyone. My men know what to do. They won't be letting their guard down.

For now the questions must go unanswered; I need to

concentrate on getting Lucio out of that safe room. "How do you contact him?"

A moment's silence. Then, after Hell throws up his hands and starts to walk past mumbling, "I'll find Pyro and get that explosive," the soldier comes back to life.

"Intercom."

He seems less tall than he had before, the rigid posture now missing. He's resigned to his fate, should he fail to protect his boss. He walks over to the bookcase. "Behind the third book on the second to top shelf."

I move the book. Finding a button, I press it. The bookcase slides back. There's a solid door which looks like it should be guarding a bank vault behind it. Hell and I exchange glances. Even if Pyro had brought extra C4, the amount needed to blow a small hole in a brick wall would barely dent that steel. Lucky we have a man used to following orders, but not one used to thinking or issuing them.

To the side is indeed an intercom, with an old-fashioned phone attached to it. A clue that the guard had allowed some thought processes to work—the safe room must have been installed back in the sixties when the house had been built, and not updated. The date had been on the plans. He could have thought there was at least a possibility a modern bomb would destroy it.

"When I tell you, you explain to him it's safe to come out."

"Say it now. In Italian." Hell has his phone out, flicking to an app which translates.

"*Puoi uscire. È sicuro.*"

Hell glances at the screen, looks at me, and raises his chin.

"Not one word more. No explanation. You got me? No secret code. One wrong step and your boss will be blown to smithereens. You'll be picking up the pieces for the next week. We have enough explosives." My voice is cold, my delivery calm, leaving no room for doubt.

A sharp nod.

I take the handset down.

"Dial o."

When I do, I hear a ring, then a snick as the phone connects.

"*Puoi uscire. È sicuro.*" Immediately I replace the phone on the wall, then Hell and I stand to the side.

"Is the situation contained?" Lucio asks as he steps out. "I thought it was just a car backfiring."

The guard who's followed him out is immediately disabled by Hell.

"No backfire. You may have a few holes to brick up, but you won't be worried about that as you won't be breathing." Raising my gun, I point it straight at his forehead.

"She's not here." Thunder sounds out of breath as he enters, Rock and Beef close behind him. Without being told, Rock and Beef step up and take control of the two soldiers as Thunder continues his update, "We've searched every-fuckin'-where, Prez. Can't find her."

"She's here," I tell him. "The tracker shows this is where she was brought. There must be another secret room somewhere." I glance at Hell. "Somewhere that wasn't on the original plans."

Lucio raises his hands. "What are you talking about? A girl? Tracker? Secret room?"

There are sounds coming from the hallway. Turning my head so I'm still keeping him in my line of sight while glancing quickly behind me, I see Red poking his head around the door.

"We have the *soldatos* corralled out here."

"Damage?" Drummer snaps.

"Sparky was winged, but it was just a scratch. One guard dead, a couple wounded, but I'd say the boss wasn't guarded by the best men."

I'd turned back in time to see Lucio's eyes close briefly, and hear his mumbled words, "You got that right." When his eyes open, they flick between his two soldiers. "Get them out of here. We need to talk."

Talk. I want to talk alright. There's only one topic that interests me. But the don's reaction is not what I'd expected at all. Hell's confused too. Something tells me whatever the don has to say, I need to listen. His request to remove his men is reasonable, if he's going to divulge secrets he doesn't want his guards to hear. I jerk my head toward the door; Rock and Beef take their captives out. Thunder follows, and Red and Drummer stay with us.

"What girl?" Lucio isn't wasting time. Then he sighs and shakes his head and provides the answer, signing his death warrant. "Violet Palmer."

She's Violet Black now. But I don't correct him. "Where is she?" I ask again.

"I have no idea. But I can make some assumptions." His hand moves over his forehead as though he is in pain.

"There's only one way this is going to end, Lucio. I can make it quick and easy or slow and painful."

"Prez?" Both Drummer and I snap our heads around, but it's me who beckons Pal over. "There were two women in the kitchen. We have them tied up with the others. Prez, one of them, well, she was wearing this."

"What is it?" Lucio snaps.

I give a nasty grin. "The reason why we know you have her. It's a tracker she was wearing."

Again, his eyes close briefly. When they open, there appear to be even more lines around them than there were before. There's a world of hurt in them, pain, but no fear, resignation, not protest. It's not the reaction I'd expect from a kidnapper. No bluster, no threats and no swagger. *Because I've caught him red-handed?*

"Which woman? The older or younger?"

The question is directed at Pal, who replies, "The younger one." When I raise my chin, he understands and steps back out.

Lucio nods. "It is as I expected. Though I would suggest the outcome was not as planned." His eyes glance to the clock.

"Giuseppa would be leaving for home around now. You would have been expected to follow her, and kill her when she couldn't tell you what you wanted to know. That's what he would have done."

He could have said all that in Italian for how much of it made sense.

Lucio sees my confusion and continues, "Angelino was having an affair with her. Vitalia found out and put a stop to it. Giuseppa, how do you say? Wouldn't take 'no' for an answer. She would have been happy receiving a trinket such as that." He nods at the heart dangling from Cad's hand. "And Angelino would have been rid of a nuisance. But, as I say, it did not go as he planned."

"We're not in the business of killing innocent women," I tell him, feeling my teeth grind. "What we are in the business of is finding one. Violet."

Lucio's eyes go to Hell. "My old friend," Hell starts and glares as if denying any previous good sentiment between them could be called on now, but the Mafia boss is not put off. "We go back a long time. In your world, you can choose to step down. In mine? It is different. A power-play is messy, a boss killed by his enemies hands a cleaner way to clear the path to the top. Angelino, my underboss, my son, expects you to carry out that service today."

"If Violet is harmed, I intend to do just that." *There's no doubt about it, Don.*

"You may. If I was in your place, I would too. But Angelino has betrayed me..."

"You went along with his plans. Here, in this room, you were encouraging him to make a play for the child he claims. The baby that is my son."

"I did. I will always support a father wanting to stand up and parent a child." Lucio doesn't try to hide it. "But what he's doing now? It goes so much further than that." He attempts a smile; it doesn't quite work. "I have men loyal to me. Men suspicious of Angel's ambitions. Men who have presented me with facts. Facts you need to know."

CHAPTER TWENTY-FIVE

Demon

"All I need to know is where Violet is," I growl.

"That is information I do not have. I may be able to help; unless you prefer to shoot me instead," he laughs mirthlessly, "I would suggest you have patience. There are things you first should hear."

Hell gestures at me. My lips thin as I interpret he wants a quiet word. When I nod, he walks to a corner of the room. Drawing close enough, he speaks into my ear, "Lucio's right. We go way back. He plays it straight. Never known him to engage in cat and mouse. I'd listen to him."

"We're wasting time," I whisper back.

His hand grips my shoulder. "I know, Son. Know this is tearing you apart. But it appears we were lured here by a trick. All we know is that Angel has her, but more than that? We're in the dark. If Lucio can shed some light on it, I think we ought to hear what he has to say."

A sharp nod, then I'm walking back. "I'll listen. But make it quick."

"May I?" He points to a satin-covered couch. When he sits, Hell, Red, Drummer and myself remain standing. "I'm afraid a history lesson is in order. Or a refresh of memory in your case, Hell."

Drummer and Red exchange glances, their eyes sharpening with interest.

"When your club started, Hell, do you recall what it was like, then?" He doesn't wait for an answer but continues, "Unemployment with the closure of the mills. No work available, people wanting money, and who had time on their hands. They wanted an escape from their pain. It was an ideal bed of unrest, and the opportunity to get drugs pouring in."

That's not news to me. The club had been part of that; Blackie was always up for a quick buck. It might be his history, but it's my club's as well. After Blackie's death, Furnace had taken a move to the side, brothers who had become hooked on that shit found no sympathy in the club or supply and left. But we'd still provided safe passage for drug-runners, and accepted their money. Until Hell had taken over and made the agreement with the Satan's Devils that we didn't touch drugs in any shape or form and kept them out of our territory.

"The Devils were bit players," Lucio confirms. "Useful, but not invested. No competition. Someone needed to step in and take control."

"The Silvestri. But with all due respect, how's this helping me get Violet back?"

"Patience," Lucio snaps, telling me again. But before I can remind him who he's talking to, the man whose life, or more accurately, his death is in my hands, continues, "Not just the Silvestri, but another *famiglia* too. A family by the name of Parma." His gaze settles on my face, but I show no reaction. "The boss was Vittore Parma."

Now I can't control my body's slight involuntary jerk. *Coincidence?*

"I never knew the full name." Hell's face creases. "Demon would only have been a youngster, kept well out of the war."

"War it was. Two *famiglias* fighting over the same territory.

Foot soldiers, associates, only. Parma never showed his face, just sent in his men. It was over fast. We held the town, we were the victors. But it came at a cost. My eldest, Angel's brother, was tortured and killed. He was sent back to me in pieces. Revenge for his death has been a debt of honour unpaid for twenty years.

"Do you know what an associate is, Demon?" His change of tack takes me by surprise.

I nod my head.

He gives me the answer I'd neither requested nor needed. "They are not like your prospects. There's no trial period or initiation to go through. No, an associate is someone who works for us, fights for us, but can never rise up the ranks, as they are not of Italian descent. To become a *soldato*, a soldier, or progress higher, a person needs pure Italian blood."

Dots are joining fast in my head. Drawing an incredible unbelievable picture. "Angel believes Victor Palmer and Vittore Parma were one and the same? That Violet is a descendant of the Italian Mafia? That bird won't fly, Lucio. He's crazy if he does. Her father was as American as apple pie."

"We'd assumed he controlled everything from afar. But he didn't. He was here, living and working among us. Pulling strings."

Hellfire's shaking his head. "A coincidence, Lucio. I knew the man. He was an accountant. Meek and mild-mannered. Walked too far across on the right side of the line for me to call him a friend. But our kids got on well. I checked him out, as any father would, before allowing Dave, Demon, to get acquainted with his boy."

"He had you fooled. Us too. Not one of us looked in his direction or connected the name. An accountant, yes, ideally placed to cover many transactions which, shall we say, were far over the wrong side of the line you speak off."

"You implying he continued the war?"

"No. That ended with the defeat. His crew was either killed or disbanded, his businesses absorbed into ours. We confiscated, shall we say, his money. He had nothing, or very little left. He continued his cover, became his cover." Lucio coughs, a hacking sound. "I'd given up looking, had assumed Parma had died, or maybe had returned with his tail between his legs to Italy. But Angelino didn't stop. It became his religion. Although there was a large age gap—you may recall, my first wife died, and I'd taken a second later." I'm vaguely aware Lucio had buried two wives but hadn't paid much attention. "Angelino became obsessed with the death of his half-brother. It was about eighteen months ago that he discovered the truth and brought it to me."

Eighteen months? "You killed Violet's father," my statement made through gritted teeth.

Lucio's quick to deny it. "We would have done, yes. But he died of natural causes." Now it's his turn for his jaws to clench. "He died thinking he'd gotten away with it."

"Angel's going to kill Violet instead." Cold seeps into my bones.

"No," Lucio's quick to reply. "Killing's too quick. Too easy. For the way his brother was killed, he wants his revenge to last longer than that. To match the time he's been deprived of him. In case you're wondering, Violet's mother also is of Italian descent, a good woman with Sicilian blood running through her veins."

Which makes Violet Italian. *Fuck.* Then worry dawns. "Is he going to kill her mother?"

"She's already experiencing a living death. No, her, he'll leave to suffer."

I have sickening suspicions but need to ask. "What's he going to do with Violet?"

"The plan had been to take her son, adopt him. He would be no associate. He could become a soldier, rise through the ranks. With two bosses as grandfathers, it was likely he'd have inherited the brains. Angel and Vitalia were not blessed with kids. Seeing Violet suffer, knowing her child was denied to her, that should have been Angel's revenge."

"Should have been?"

Lucio puts his head into his hand as a low voice growls behind me, "We're getting no information as to how to find her, Demon. Hurry this the fuck up. I don't like what I'm hearing."

I nod over my shoulder to Drummer. I don't either. "Why did the plan change? And what the fuck does Angel want now?"

"The DNA test. My *consigliere*, the man who gives me advice, overheard a conversation. You'll have guessed by now, the vacancy for which she applied never existed. It was a ploy to get her into Angelino's hands. She was kept two days, drugged. I believe she thinks it was only one night. While she was here, Angelino wasn't the only man to take advantage. One of the *soldati*," he breaks off and a pained look crosses his face, a look of pure disappointment, "he also took her. The conversation overheard was him worried about the DNA test which could show the kid wasn't Angelino's."

"Is he dead?" *If not, I'll do it myself. With my bare hands.*

"Of course," Lucio growls out, smashing his fists together as though to emphasise it.

I realise there and then I never want to know Theo's heritage. My own father was the worst there could be, and I've survived. I might carry his blood but none of his character. I'm my own person, shaped by the man who brought me up. I raise my chin.

"He doesn't want Theo any longer?"

"There's a fifty-fifty chance he's not his. He won't go to court to insist on a test for obvious reasons. If he found he didn't carry his DNA, he'd still take him to hurt Violet, sell him, probably. But not to raise him as his. This time, he intends to do it right. Instead of a *soldato* he might not be able to trust, his wife is guarding her."

I snarl and jump forward. Hell just manages to hold me back, but can't stop the words I'm shouting,

"Where the fuck is she?"

Lucio gets to his feet; he looks nervous, but otherwise

ignores my outburst. "I tried to dissuade him once we knew you'd claimed her. I knew we'd start a war with the Devils and that, I wanted to avoid. Angel, though, he wouldn't listen. It's not just you who doesn't know the location of your woman, or my son."

"Too right he's started a fuckin' war," I snarl.

Lucio shrugs. "Unnecessary bloodshed is not what I would have wished, but Angelino knows that we'll win. We have more men."

"Not if we bring in the other chapters, and our support clubs," Drummer drawls, unconcerned by the threat. "At the end of the day, how loyal are your associates? They can't rise in your organisation."

Lucio tiredly replies, "That, too, was part of my reluctance to take your club on. There would be bloodshed. I might lose another son. But, Angelino is determined to come for you, Demon. Not just because of what you and the woman may or may not have done. That war confined to history? No, still all too recent for my son. The Devils stepped back and wanted no part of it back in the day. His reasoning? If you had added your weight, his brother may still be breathing."

Angel sounds like he's gone off the rails. "He's motherfucking crazy."

A look from Lucio suggests he might well agree. "He set me up. He expected you to come in guns blazing. He believed that because he acts without thinking. That nickname? It's well-earned. He'd rather speak to dead bodies than allow them to talk back. Hellfire, I envy you. Your son talks with reason."

"When I find Angel, he's dead." My tone is conversational.

Again, that hurt comes into his eyes. "I am still the boss. My men answer to me. My *consigliere*, my *caporegimes*, they follow me. We do not want war, we want no distractions. I thought Angelino might settle when he has a son to focus on, but..."

"If he rapes Violet, I'll hold the *famiglia* responsible. I won't stop until you are all wiped from Pueblo." *He could have already raped her. Fuck.*

"And we'll be right behind him," Red states.

Lucio nods, clearly taking that as a given. "I don't know where he is. That's the truth. All I know is that he and Vitalia will be there, along with his most-trusted *soldati*." His brow creases. "I don't know which *capi* are working with him." As my head tilts, he clarifies, "The *capo, caporegime*, is the captain. Each has a *decina*, a group of ten or more *soldati* who he oversees. I suspect at least one of my *capi* will be in the know, or, will be missing."

"Angel has been turning men? Turning this *capo*? Could he have turned all of them?"

Lucio shakes his head. "One, two, maybe. Sanna is trying to stay close to him on my instructions. I'm hoping that he can temper Angelino's plans, but whether he'll be successful, who can tell? And who knows who else could be enticed over to the other side? As you know, Angelino isn't exactly stable. His mother spoiled him; I did too. I'd lost Pompeo, his brother. You know what that name means? Five. He was to be the first of our five children. Instead I ended up with one. So yes, whatever he wanted, he was given. It's not helped develop his character in the right direction. Unfortunately, he can also be quite persuasive."

I need to cut through the crap. There won't be a chance for Angel to redeem himself, he won't have long enough while he's still breathing. "You can find where this *capo* is?"

"I can try."

"Locations, man," Drummer barks. "Where's he likely to have taken her?"

"Somewhere I don't know about, I assure you." Lucio's eyes harden. "Should your attack on me have failed, he will know I'd be looking for him myself. So it won't be a location I'm aware of. Maybe somewhere he's bought recently, maybe somewhere he has the owner tied up, or more likely, killed. Somewhere it will be almost impossible to find."

"Almost?" Drummer queries.

"People talk. People listen. You leave me alive, I'll question everyone. If it's only the direction they saw people heading, it will be a start. Angelino does like his comforts, and especially so does Vitalia. I suspect when Angelino's... with... Violet, she'll not want to be within hearing. What wife would?"

What fucking wife would be part of a plan to rape and impregnate a woman? Or force her to carry her husband's child?

"What are you suggesting?"

"That we get eyes out watching."

"I don't trust your men. I want information from you, Lucio. I want to know every fuckin' thing you find out. Even if it's what brand of toothpaste he uses and where he shops for it. Not leaving this to you."

"Best you leave me alive, then." Lucio stares at the gun I'm still holding.

"I will. For now. If Violet's hurt..."

"I do not want to see her harmed. She's the blood of my enemy, yes. But she had no hand in killing Pompeo. She wasn't even born then. I do not take the life of an innocent."

A hand settles on my shoulder, a familiar touch; I don't need to turn to see who it is. "I believe him, Demon. I've known Lucio for decades. He's always played it straight down the line."

"What are we doing here, then? Lucio. I need to know Angel's addresses and locations he might visit. His wife's too. I'll get Cad on to searching to see if he's bought or rented any properties recently." That's a long shot; as Lucio suggested, he might just have appropriated somewhere. The Angel of Death wouldn't give a damn about killing an innocent citizen. "Let's get this fuckin' ball rollin'." Sooner we start, sooner we can get Violet home. Hopefully, before his cock has gone anywhere near her.

"Wait," Lucio barks. Even I find myself momentarily standing to attention. "First, we need to arrange something."

"No delays."

"Not even something to help?"

"Let him speak." Drummer didn't get where he is without being a good judge of character. Something about Lucio has interested him.

Annoyed that we're not jumping into action, I gesture at Lucio. That grin appears on his face again, this time, more genuine.

"We need to arrange my death." I'd replaced my gun in my cut. Now I'm wondering whether I should just pull it out and shoot him to get it over and done with when he resumes, "Not my actual death, of course, but make it look like you've succeeded."

There are too many ways the truth could get out. "Your guards…"

"My *soldati*." He bows his head. "My normal guards had been replaced, their presence required elsewhere. A training exercise. Those you've captured, you may well have noticed their incompetence. One," he huffs a short laugh, "is my chef. They were no part of this. Pawns used by Angelino." He stares at me, then resumes, "There's a room that can be locked, in the basement. They can take down food, a TV; let's make them comfortable. There's even a bathroom down there." His concern for his men is touching. It makes me believe there's still a lot of loyalty to the old man. Angel would not garner the same respect. "I need my *consigliere*. I have the utmost confidence in him. He can spread news of my demise, and that the guards are dead and have been disposed of. By your men." He queries me with a look. I dip my head up-and-down in response. Don't mind a few more bodies added to my reputation.

"And that helps, how?"

"Angelino will get careless. He's hungry for power, but won't find it easy. Succession isn't guaranteed, though of course, he has a few things going for him. He's the underboss, my second-in-command. He's also my son, and I've always groomed him for the position. But the *caporegimes* have to vote on my replacement. If he's crossed too many of them, he might not win."

"Is there anyone else?"

"There are a couple of *capi* that are well-respected."

If I let him live, Angel is definitely facing death. Lucio might need to start preparing one of the others in the near future. I catch his eyes, there's that look of pain crossing it once again. He knows exactly what to expect.

Red lets out a short laugh. "You're buying us time."

"And," Drummer adds, showing he's not slow on the uptake, "forcing Angel out of hiding."

Of course! The old man hasn't stayed in top position for so long without looking at things from every angle. "When the *famiglia* hear of your death, Angel's going to want, need, to take charge." Thus, hopefully, putting on hold what he has planned for Violet.

I allow Lucio to take out his phone and place a call. A look my way, then after the word, "*Ciao,*" he continues his conversation in English. Without passing on a warning or giving a reason for the meeting, he requests the man, a Roberto, to come directly to the mansion and to use the rear entrance.

CHAPTER TWENTY-SIX

Demon

While we're waiting for Lucio's man to arrive, I and the other presidents go out to find our men. They're all congregating in the large hallway, circling the sorry-looking guards. The don comes out behind us, shaking his head.

One of the guards looks particularly sheepish. "*Mi scuso. Scuso.*"

We don't need a translation, the look on his face tells us all we need to know. Lucio walks over. A rapid-fire burst of Italian, then he turns to us. "I have given a brief explanation to my *soldati*. They know it is my will that they are kept out of the way for now and will give you no problem. Please, Luigo will show you the way. Then I'd appreciate those supplies we discussed."

I nod.

"We'll go check it out."

This time it's the Vegas prez I raise my chin toward. Yeah, we need to make sure there's no way out and no means of communication down there. There's only so far I trust Lucio.

"Luigo?" Having gotten my agreement, Red indicates to his men. When a man takes a step forward to identify himself, his hands still bound behind him, Red disappears with him through a doorway, Crash follows them through.

Moments later they reappear. "It's secure," Red assures me.

It doesn't take too long. Surrounded by the Satan's Devils, the men go to the kitchen and reappear carrying armfuls of food. The two women come along with them. There are also a couple of crates of beer going down there as well. Buzzard escorts one carrying a television and DVD player, along with a number of DVDs. Slowly the atmosphere changes. It's almost like they're preparing for a party. The injured ones are being helped down by their comrades.

I have to admit to breathing a sigh of relief once they're contained and I can focus on my next worry.

"It's not only Lucio Angel will want taken out," I tell Red and Drummer, bluntly.

"He'll be coming for us. He'll have to. Might be him who set Lucio up, but all his crew will know is that the Satan's Devils supposedly killed him. He'll attack the compound," Hell injects grimly, having overheard my words. "If he doubts the kid's his, he won't give a fuck about who he hurts."

"That's my thinking."

Looking around me, I send swift thanks up to some unknown deity that all our men have, so far, come through uninjured, with the exception of Sparky, who looks more annoyed than hurt. I take out my phone and place a quick call to Bomber, telling him to be on high alert, and to put the club on lockdown.

Then I turn back to Drummer and Red. "Need as many as possible back there."

"I'll stay. Want to know what Lucio's planning."

I dip my head at Drummer, glad to have his company. There's no way on earth I'm not sticking close to Lucio's side, needing to be the first to know where the fuck Angel has Violet.

"Don't like splitting our resources, but we're going to have to. While an attack might be imminent, we also need to be able to respond to whatever situation your girl's in. Need manpower for that." Drummer's hand tugs at his beard. "I suggest we send the

VPs back, but we'll stay," he breaks off to jerk his chin toward Red, "and perhaps half-a-dozen others."

"I'm going nowhere," says Hell. "That's my daughter-in-law we're talking about."

I'm happy to defer to Drummer and not make all the decisions myself. I'm torn as to what to do. If I rescued Vi, but lost the compound and Theo, well, that's unthinkable.

In the end, it's Pyro, Beef, Rock, Indian and Twister who remain. The VPs and Snatcher, who's looking paler by the moment, though he's trying to bluster his way through, will be returning. After catching my eye, as it's a multi-club front we're putting together, Drummer takes over, giving his precise instructions for how the lockdown is to be handled. Apart from being the national prez, Drummer's had a hell of a lot of experience with fending off attacks, and I'm happy for him to give advice which I might not have thought about. Face it, I'm not thinking straight about anything other than getting my woman back.

"You keep your fuckin' eyes peeled," Drummer warns the group about to leave. "If I were Angel, I'd have eyes on the compound."

"Could be an ambush," Wraith agrees, eyeing the men who'll be riding with him. "You keep your fuckin' guns handy. Any truck, SUV that gets too close, shoot the fuckin' tires out."

"You want us close formation, or spread out?" Crash calls out.

"Close. Don't want him to be able to pick us off one by one."

They're right to be cautious, but my money's on Angel not being organised yet. He doesn't know what's gone down, whether his plan succeeded. At the moment, he has no reason to instruct his men to attack.

Watching Wraith leave, Drummer turns to me. "When you going to get sorted and get a fuckin' VP, Demon? Once we're on the other side of this, make that your fuckin' priority."

He's right. Everything's all on my shoulders at present. While Thunder's more than capable, he's holding part of himself back. Unfortunately, it shows.

"Thunder will be okay," I tell him, pinching the bridge between my eyes.

"Sure he will. But your second needs to be able to take the helm, and I don't think Thunder will do that." His eyes soften slightly as his hand clasps my shoulder. "Not stepping on toes here, Brother, but told Wraith to step up. Do what's necessary if Thunder is lagging."

I don't mind. Don't mind that at all.

"Thunder's the best sergeant-at-arms," I tell him.

"He is. But the VP spot needs more than that."

"We have a problem," Red starts. "If Angel is watching this house, he'll be aware of this Roberto arriving. I don't like anything that might make him suspicious."

"No, he won't." Lucio, who'd stayed in the background until our men had left, comes over to join us, and picks up on the last comment. "I've got a secret access which very few people know. A tunnel under the grounds. I've warned Roberto to come in that way. The rear entrance is the code I used in our conversation. No one will see him arrive. Angel knows about it, but under the circumstances, I suspect it's highly unlikely he'll have a man looking out for anyone using it."

Only a few moments later, there's a sound in the hall, and a doorway opens. It's hidden in the panelling and impossible to see unless you knew what you were looking for. Hell and I glance at each other. *That wasn't on the plans,* he mouths.

Without waiting, Lucio introduces the newcomer as the mysterious Roberto. Then he wastes no time giving his *consigliere* an explanation.

Roberto's face goes through a range of emotions. At last he turns to me. "Your woman got in the middle of a mess which is not of her making. Angelino, well," he breaks off, turns to Lucio, his head shaking sadly. "Angelino's gone too far this time. I have warned you not to trust him."

Pain lines form on the don's face. He ages in front of my eyes. "As any father would, I hoped Angel would temper his ways with time. It seems it was a mistake to give him too much free rein."

"You made him the underboss, Lucio. It was then he started to get power-hungry. Wanted to take the *famiglia* in different ways. But now, it's time for action, not reflection. Time to bring the *capi* together. We both know who we can trust, and who have been swayed to Angelino's more violent ways."

Lucio nods. "You call them, Roberto. Get them here."

"Won't that be suspicious?" Drummer asks.

"No," Roberto replies. "If, indeed, Lucio was dead, that's what Angel would expect to happen. Much like yourselves, I suspect, we consider it no business of the authorities, and a council of war is the first step we'd take."

The *consigliere*'s face mirrors the misery on the don's. It seems both knew this day was coming, but hoped it was still a long way off. Sideways glances thrown our way also indicates they're uncomfortable airing their dirty laundry in public.

I'm sympathetic, sure, but despite the pain they're feeling, I have a different goal than who's leading the Mafia family. "I need to know where Angel is. Where he's taken Violet. What he's planning for my club. Other than that, we stay out of it." I'll fight for Violet, sure, but I'm not having the club brought into the Mafia power struggle.

Roberto's eyes come to mine. He pauses a second, then accepts the condition I've laid down. "Understood. We'll get your answers. I'm confident we'll have the majority of our men on our side."

I'm antsy, impatient. The men Roberto is calling together may well hold the key, the information I need on Violet's whereabouts. But I hate this delay with every fibre of my being.

I pace while he's placing his calls, arranging a meeting for later on this evening. Far too slow, but he needs time to get all the *capos* together.

My phone rings. It's Cad.

"Got a list of properties owned by Angel."

"How many? Can you text it to me?"

He gives me a number and a ping shows he already has. I end the call and pass the info to the others.

Drummer's stroking his beard, his steely grey eyes watching me, giving me the lead and letting me decide what to do. *Christ, what a fucked-up situation this is.* I curb my initial reaction to tear off and start searching because I need to be here, adding my thinking into how we're going to take Angel down.

"I'll get Mace, Lizard and Ink onto it."

"That enough?" Hellfire queries.

I let him in on my thought processes. "All we have are addresses of what we know he owns. Need to check them out, see where might be likely, whether there's been movement there. I trust those three to cross off those which are possibilities. If they're suspicious about one, they can call help in."

Hell nods. "I'll get onto it." He takes out his phone.

"Oh, and Hell? I want in if they think they've found the location."

Drummer, still listening carefully, nods at this instruction. Doubt if he'd be able to hold back if it was his woman who'd been taken.

"We could send more than one team out," Red suggests, his hand staying Hell from pressing connect.

Fucking decisions. On one hand, more men out searching could get results quicker. On the other... I shake my head. "We don't know whether Angel's going to make a play for Theo, or whether to launch an attack. I don't want to leave the compound short-handed."

"How about I go with them?" Hellfire offers.

"Need you here."

Hell's not happy, shooting me a look that says he'd rather be taking action. We're brothers, both sharing the same frustration at seemingly sitting on our hands while Violet's suffering. But Hell's experience with the Mafia might come in handy. I stare back steadily, letting him know there's no point in arguing. He sighs in exasperation and turns away. Shortly after, I hear him issuing my instructions.

A car arrives, shortly followed by another. Then more.

Ten men, each accompanied by one or more of their soldiers appear. Ten *capos*, each responsible for a *decina*. While they've not brought the whole lot with them, it strikes me how Lucio has at least one hundred men at his beck and call. Even with the extra fifteen at the compound, we're heavily outnumbered. If Angel had managed to turn them, we wouldn't have had a chance.

Roberto comes up beside me. "I didn't call all the *capi*. Just those who I'd stake my life on can be trusted. One, *Capo* Ferri, let me say is sympathetic to Angel's ways. Another couple I couldn't say either way and thought it best to exclude them. Even Sanna has a question mark over his head."

He has not made the situation better.

Lucio doesn't waste time, ushering us all into a large dining room. The table is enormous, can easily seat thirty. He sits at the head, Roberto beside him. Then beckons me to the seat on his left. I raise my chin in acknowledgement of the honour. Red, Drummer and Hell are also invited in, leaving the rest of the MC and the *soldatos* to mingle awkwardly outside in the hallway.

When everyone's seated, Lucio looks around the assembly, his glance landing briefly on each one of his men. My eyes follow his, waiting to see if anyone flinches or reacts when his assessing gaze settles on them. No one acts suspiciously I'm pleased to see. They're clearly curious as to why they've been summoned, and why three current and one former MC presidents are sitting around the table with them.

One man, whose grey hair betrays his age, is impatient. "What the hell is going on, Lucio? There are holes in the walls. Have these bikers..."

"Gallo. If you will give me a chance to explain." His eyes flick to Roberto, then he takes a breath to fortify himself. I'm not surprised. What he has to say will be devastating, for him to admit to his *famiglia*, and for them to hear. "I was set up. To be killed."

Growls and exclamations go around the table. "*Che cazzo?*"

I don't understand the phrase, but from the way it's snarled think I can make the right interpretation. The expressions of hatred being sent toward me, and toward my brothers at the opposite end of the table, make me rest a hand on the butt of my gun just in case.

Lucio raises his hand; his men go quiet. "I was set up," he repeats, "by my own son. By Angelino."

There are a few audible gasps. I'm watching all reactions carefully, eyes flicking away, faces looking down at the table, anything which might suggest one of these *capos* is in the know. But the expressions range from horror to surprise to resignation.

"But you are alive," Gallo observes.

"Because the Satan's Devils are not as hot-headed as Angelino. They speak first."

Roberto grimaces at the pain on Lucio's face and takes over as the don clearly is finding it hard to admit his son's failings.

"Angelino has taken a woman. He believes her to be the daughter of Vittore Parma."

There's swearing in both English and Italian at the name. I'm trying to work out whether they're praising Angel for taking Violet or upset at the name just thrown out into the open. My face must give me away.

"The woman is the wife of Demon, President of the Satan's Devils." Roberto indicates me. "For his sake, and the rest of his men, please talk in English only."

"Your wife?" A *capo* asks. "Why would he take your wife?"

"To get revenge on her father, *Capo* Lecce."

"The man who we suspect as being Vittore Parma is dead," Roberto puts in. "He died of natural causes eighteen months ago."

Now the expressions are of confusion.

"Angelino wants revenge on a dead man?"

"*Lui è pazzo,*" one says, tapping his forehead. Then for my benefit clarifies, "Loco, crazy."

"Don Lucio," the *capo* sitting next to Roberto starts, "how has he set you up?"

"Demon's wife was wearing a tracker. A necklace. He gave it to the woman on my staff who he was having an affair with. It led the Devils here."

A couple of the *capos* are nodding.

One puts it into words. "Angelino thought they would come in all guns blazing and kill you."

"I am sad and sorry to call you here today," Lucio rubs at his face tiredly, "to inform you of our underboss's betrayal. But there are two things on the agenda. One is dealing with Angelino and the second is finding Demon's woman."

"The evidence against Angelino is circumstantial," another *capo* observes. "The bikers could have planted the tracker themselves. There has been a change at the top spot as we all know, maybe Demon doesn't want to continue the agreement his club has with ourselves."

Whoa. That was unexpected. I eye the man suspiciously. Only a supporter of Angel would speak up like that.

Lucio clearly feels the same way as he suddenly snaps, "I'm his father. I've been pretending not to see what was happening. Who among us can deny that Angelino wants to lead this family in different ways? Napoliello had it right. He is crazy. I've tried to ignore the signs I see day by day that have been warning me my own son wants me dead." His voice has risen, he allows his last words to ring in the silence before he continues, "Angelino wants blood and violence."

Blood, violence, drug and gun running and slave trafficking are the bread and butter of the Mafia. But this group are all shaking their heads.

"He's getting careless," Napoliello says.

Ah. So that's it. Not disdain for the business they're in, but the way they do it.

The don nods. "We are respected. We have built relation-ships in this town, in this state. If we attract attention to our trade, then we all suffer. Angelino does not understand the necessity of discretion."

"We have proposals," Roberto takes over. "I have been Lucio's *consigliere* for three decades now. I have seen this approaching ever since Angelino was promoted. He is too eager to walk in the don's shoes."

"We would need to vote him in."

"You are right, Ratti."

"He wouldn't get my vote."

There's a moment of consideration, then a number of them echo the last observation.

"A show of hands. Who wouldn't vote for Angelino?" Roberto presses.

"One moment, *Consigliere,*" The *capo* called Ratti interrupts. "We are not all here. Do I take it there is a reason for that?"

For an answer, Roberto just steadily stares back. A second, passes, then Ratti nods. The reply, silence, was all that he needed.

The man sitting beside the *consigliere* reverts to Roberto's question. "Before today? I would have voted yes to Angelino taking over in the light of your—natural—death, Don Lucio. But under the circumstances, I could no longer support him. I would vote no."

"Thank you, Padovano," Lucio nods.

One by one, men stoically raise their hands.

"We are not all here. Of those who aren't, my view is Ferri and Sanna might support him. I suspect that was what Roberto hadn't said. They are close to him."

The *capo* called Padovano barks a laugh. "I was wondering about their absence. But I've also been wondering about their future with the *famiglia*. They've both been sampling the product a little too often." He stares straight at the don. "Both cocaine and women."

Lucio's face tightens. "We have a proposal. We need to draw Angelino out. Both to deal with him and to rescue Demon's woman. I do not want a war with the Devils on my hands. It's time I introduce you to the men at the end of the table."

"Let us introduce ourselves," Drummer suggests, then rests his steely eyes on each man at the table. "I am Drummer. I am president of the mother chapter of the Satan's Devils. Beside me is Red, who leads the Vegas chapter. We also have the president of Utah back at the Pueblo compound. We've other chapters, too. Our motto isn't just words. Satan's Devils ride together. You start a war with one, you're declaring hostilities against us all."

My heart warms at his promise.

Then Drummer continues. "We would also ask for support from our dominant, the Wretched Soulz."

I avoid giving him the sharp look I want to. Our charter exists by agreement with the Wretched Soulz, one of the main outlaw MCs in the States, fuck, in the world come to that. Drummer insists on all Satan's Devils chapters retaining a good relationship with their local branches for just such a reason as this.

An intake of breath, and that seems to clinch it. The dominant club is huge. The Silvestri family might be numbered over a hundred, but we're talking about the possibility of being able to summon up a thousand men. Men who, perhaps, would be a little more eager than us to take on some of the trade the Silvestris are running.

"We'll get your woman back." Gallo's looking in my direction. "Hopefully unharmed. Angelino cannot be allowed to come between the Devils and *il famiglia*."

I am not surprised. Bikers are mobile; our members are made up of large numbers of veterans who learned guerrilla tactics and have other military knowledge. I've a number of vets in my own club; Ink and Lizard are ex-Marines and Mace was in the Army, for starters. The Mafia's normal approach of bringing the fight into the open won't work while we're using speed and manoeuvrability to pick them off. Coupled with that, full-scale war would bring the Feds in pretty quickly. They'd just love an opportunity to bring down a RICO charge on our heads, and the group it would fit most would be the Mafia.

Catching Drummer's eye, I raise my chin. He gives back a quick nod.

"So where is Angelino holding the woman?"

I just about stop myself rolling my eyes. *If I knew that, I wouldn't be sitting here.*

"You have a list of properties?" Roberto, the more practical one, asks me.

"I do."

"Text it to me."

I take out my phone and send him the list. A few seconds later, every *capo* is taking out his phone.

"Check the list. I want to know of any other properties Angelino is linked to. Anywhere he might have rented or bought recently, or any person he may have intimidated to use their space."

They're allowed a moment to consider the list.

"You got this?" Gallo asks me, his jaw clenched. At my nod, he continues, "Not sure I like you getting all this intelligence."

I shrug. Must be recorded somewhere for Cad to have found it. Let them wonder how easily we can get the information we need, and just how much we know of their business.

"I know of a couple of places. Long shots." One by one a few more addresses get added to the list. I text them to Mace, confident he'll check them out.

I don't know his name, but one of the *capos* speaks up. "Checking known locations is all well and good, but doesn't deal with the fact Angelino might have gone off the radar. Why not bring him to us?" My eyes sharpen. I like that idea. "If he knows Don Lucio is still alive," the man continues, "he'll go on the defensive. Knowing him, he probably has a plan up his sleeve were he to find out the set-up failed. But on the assumption it succeeded, he'll be waiting on a summons."

The don sits up straighter. He's got them on board. "We let him believe it was a success, that I'm dead."

"And that we need our underboss to lead us," Roberto nods.

"He comes here, and what? We beat the truth out of him?"

Yeah, I like the sound of that.

Lucio sighs. "No. Not because I don't want my son harmed—I think his death warrant has already been signed; I for one could never trust him—but I think we need to consider his rationale for doing what he has. Angelino wants revenge. Yes, I agree, he probably has a backup plan up his sleeve, and probably more than one. He wants revenge on Parma, and on the Satan's Devils MC. In the event he doesn't return, I suspect he'll leave instructions for Violet to disappear. Which will mean she'll be alive, but wishing she was dead."

"Can't take that risk." My teeth grind together.

"Your idea?" another of the *capos* asks.

"I'm an old man," Lucio admits. "Roberto already has plans to enact when I am gone. A meeting, an election. The result of which Angelino thinks is a foregone conclusion..."

"You need Salvaggi here. He's in Sicily at the moment. All *capi* need to vote."

"So there's time. But as the underboss, he'll take over for now. Until a new don is elected." Roberto has taken over again. "You will meet to get his guidance. Then he'll return to where he's holed up with Violet. He has, shall we say, a personal interest in her?"

"That business about her baby?"

Lucio nods, then glances that way. "We will track Angelino back to his hide-out."

The plan will take time. My head rests in my hands. Time, I hope, that we have.

Fabbri suddenly raps his hand on the table. "You were asking about properties. I tagged along with Angel a year or so back.

He seemed interested in a property that was for sale. It's not on your list. Maybe he didn't proceed with it. Didn't think much of it at the time, we're always toying with properties to store shit or hole up."

I exchange a glance with Drummer, then look at the *capo*. "Where is it?"

As he reels off an address, I text Mace, and pass it on, telling him to get eyes on it and then wait. It sounds promising, so I want to be in on it.

"If anyone thinks of anywhere else. Let me know. I'll make sure the information gets into the right hands. And," Roberto's eyes come to mine, there's an iciness in them. "If you come across Angel before us..."

"Can't guarantee I won't kill him. He puts hands on my woman? He's a dead man."

The *capos'* eyes go to the don. Lucio closes his briefly, then opens them. "It if had been my Maria... Another had his hands on her? Raped her? I'd have gutted him on the spot. Can any of you say different?"

Like the club, the Mafia are all about family. No man objects. But they don't comment either. One way or another, whoever finds him first, Angel's dead. It's by whose hand that's in question.

The meeting is over. As the *capos* start taking their leave of their 'dead' don, going to put Roberto's succession plans into place, I know we won't be invited to attend any further gathering.

"As soon as we know where Angel's hiding, I'll be in touch. I guarantee it." I trust Roberto. He knows what's at stake.

"If I get any leads, I'll do likewise."

I'm impatient to be off. I might have sent Mace there, but I want to investigate this place myself.

Hold on, Vi, I'm coming. I just hope we don't arrive too late.

It feels good to be doing something. Anything, rather than sitting around talking. Joining the search at least makes me feel

I'm closer to Vi. Hell and I speed away from the don's house as fast as our bikes will go. When we catch up with the enforcer and Ink, Mace updates me on the places he's already visited, many properties Angelino might own, but wouldn't frequent, or, not personally. No, the drug dens would be supplied by his men. Likewise, the strip club, which certainly appears to offer no threat to Tits Up. The next house was in a residential area but set well back from the road. In the street there was a kid out chopping the next-door hedge. Ink, being the least threatening, had approached, asked, and received the information that nobody lives there, or no one he's seen.

"Where was it?" Hell asks.

"What is it?" The sharpness of Hell's tone catches my attention. Something's got him thinking.

"I don't know. Just a feeling."

His nose is spot on. The address matches the one the *capo* had mentioned Angel had thought about buying. Mace might have dismissed it; it's gone to the top of my list.

I ring Cad, asking for more info.

"Don't have much, Prez. Angel bought it a year ago. Nothing on who's living there now."

According to the neighbour's kid, no one at all. Or, someone who doesn't want to be seen.

"Any rear access?"

"Just pulling the maps up. Shit. Yes. A track. Google Earth shows it's possible to get an off-road four-wheeler up there."

That's enough for me. "Hell. I want to go to that house. You come with me."

"We'll all go," Mace says. "Prez, if I missed something..."

I clasp his shoulder and squeeze it. "You're trying to cover a lot of ground fast, Mace. Ain't nothing gonna fall back on you."

It's not that far. We park a discreet distance away, then proceed on foot. The house itself can't be seen from the street. As I view the driveway, it certainly does look unused, weeds growing up through the cracks. But there's an approach from the rear, Cad had said.

"Wait here. Hell, you come with me." Checking our guns are within easy reach, the two of us keep in the shadow conveniently provided by the bushes between this and the neighbouring property. When I reach the front door, Hellfire is right behind me. It's a quiet area; I hear an owl hooting and, in the distance, traffic moving. Nothing to raise suspicions.

Hell stands to my side, ready to burst in after me.

I raise my hand to knock. The slight pressure of my fist hitting the wood causes the door to ominously swing open. I exchange another look with Hell. *A trap?* I signal him to stay put.

Knowing my brother will have my back, I warily step inside. Darkness has fallen, moonlight coming in through the windows is the only brightness. Taking out my flashlight, I switch it on then look around carefully, my eyes taking in everything, the lack of furniture, the dusty floor. And the one set of footprints disappearing through a doorway, then coming back. Apart from those, the place doesn't look like it's seen anyone since Angel bought it.

Could Violet be upstairs? But how would they have gotten her there without leaving a trace?

"A trap?" Hell whispers behind me, his head peering around, taking in the same scene.

"Unless there's a back door, doesn't look like anyone else, apart from the person who left those prints, has been here." I listen again. I can't hear anything.

The shape of the shoes in the dust is compelling. It reminds me of Hansel and Gretel, but did that story have a happy ending? For the life of me I can't remember. Someone was cooked, that's for sure.

"Think we should search?"

"I'm going through there." I point to where the trail leads.

"Be fuckin' careful, Son," Hell growls "Remember, Angel likes a set-up."

I'm only too well aware. It's tempting to walk in the exact

same spot, but in my head, I'm running over any possible threat there could be. Explosives hidden under the boards? A pressure trigger just waiting for me? With hairs pricking at the back of my neck, gingerly I ease my way halfway between the footprints and the wall. My senses on high alert, I turn back, "Wait outside, Hell."

His face is full of concern, but he reluctantly obeys with a nod. I'd have the exact same feelings as him, I'd want to stay close, too, but there is no point us both dying together.

As carefully as a big man can, I move across the floor, my ears pricked for any sound, the tiniest snick of a bomb being primed, ready to throw myself back. But it's only silence and that damn bird 'whoo-o-ing' outside that I can hear. Two steps to go. I can now see I'm being led to a kitchen.

Am I on a wild goose chase? Is there really any clue to be found? Maybe it's just someone checking on their empty premises. There's nothing to be seen, the place clearly hasn't been lived in for a while. There are no pots, pans or anything visible. Just counters and cupboards. *And those footsteps leading to one in particular, then turning around and walking back out.* Perhaps someone just came in to look for something.

Wanting to move this along, I step to the cupboard, placing my hand on the handle and pulling it. Then I jump back so fast I slip and fall on my ass, my heart only just staying put and not leaping out of my chest. As maniacal chuckles ring out, my rage rises to the surface. *A fucking jack-in-the-box. Rigged to give a heart attack to whoever opened the door. Christ.* Wanting to kill something, anything, standing I return to destroy the toy when my eyes fall on a note behind it. Sweeping the offending object which almost caused my death through stopping my heart aside I take out the paper and quickly scan the words on it.

Don't bother wasting your time. I'm not so stupid as to stash Violet at any of my known locations. The woman's gone. Forget her. You'll never see her again.

"What the fuck, Demon?" Hell's come in. "What the fuck was that laughter and the crash?"

I point to the jack-in-the-box, now looking forlorn on the floor. "He was the messenger. And this, the message." I pass the paper over to Hell.

He takes it and reads it. His lips press together. "What do you want to do, Son?"

"We carry on. Might find a clue somewhere. Might be trying to halt the search."

"Or he could be telling the truth. He has her somewhere we don't know about."

"Already out of state?"

Hell considers for a second. "Nah. He needs her close, and if he's making a play to be don, he can't afford to leave Pueblo right now. She's here, somewhere."

But she's not. Mace, Ink, Lizard, Hell and I visit every location we know about, at one needing to call for backup and use our fists and the threat of our guns to get answers, but of Violet there's no sign.

CHAPTER TWENTY-SEVEN

Violet

"It would be easier just to drug her again."

Angel looks from me to his wife, then pointedly at the food and half-drunk bottle of water. "I think she'd rather starve herself than eat anything we give her, Vitalia."

"She has to drink. Or the *capo* could bring some heroin in. That's an idea. Get her hooked, she'll be more pliable, and she'll suffer."

"Not when she's going to be carrying my child. But after? Hmm. An idea with possibilities, my love."

I shudder, just listening to this discussion. It's time I stepped in. I can make threats of my own. "Demon's going to kill you, you know that, don't you?"

"Not now that he's given me even more reason to take him out first. Satan's Devils have started a war. Trouble for them, what they've done is brought *il famiglia* together. The Silvestri don't take the death of their boss lying down."

"You said you hadn't killed your father..."

His laugh is pure evil. "I didn't have to hold the gun to make sure he was dead. Your new husband did that for me."

Demon. What have you done?

I don't need to ask the question, which he takes great delight in answering as if I had voiced it. "Your locket led them to my father. Obviously you weren't there, so, in a fit of rage the Devils killed my father and all of his men."

"That's not true."

"You better believe it." He smirks. "It was my plan, and it worked like a charm. Not a single hitch. Out with the old boss, meet the new boss." He points to himself, "Me."

He's worse than I thought. "You're pleased your father is dead?" I ask incredulously, wondering if it can really be true and that Demon's committed mass murder. Something seems off. "But, your brother. All this is because you want retaliation for your brother's death. If he'd been alive, he'd be next in line; you'd have to have killed him too, to become boss."

He shakes his head. "Not necessarily." I notice he doesn't rule it out. "There has to be a vote. But with all the sympathy coming my way, and the strength I'll show wiping out the Devils and thus extending our territory, the vote will be a formality."

"Why are you talking to her?" Vitalia asks. She doesn't seem jealous at the thought that if he has his way she'll be sharing his cock with me, but she doesn't seem to like him paying me attention.

Hmm. Is there something I can use there?

"You must have come up with that plan very quickly. You couldn't have known the locket had a tracker in it. Even I hadn't been aware of that." I look down at my feet, knowing that Demon had tried to protect me. It had been a good idea but had failed.

"I'd already had a plan to lay a trail to my father. But as it turned out everything worked liked a dream. I suspected Demon may be tracking you. Our equipment showed we were right. Demon followed where that scrap of useless jewellery he'd given you had gone."

"Clever." The word almost sticks in my throat, but I get a sense of satisfaction when Vitalia throws an intense look full of hatred toward me.

"Boss?" A voice comes from outside the room.

Angel turns and opens the door. "Yeah?" There's a quiet mumbling in the hallway, half in Italian which I don't understand. But his wife does. Her expression grows concerned. When the sound of footsteps can be heard fading, and Angel turns, she puts her hand out to him.

"You go. You knew you'd have to take the reins. Now Lucio is dead, they need someone to lead."

"The *capi*..."

"Are on your side. You need to divulge your plans. You know how we discussed this. Hit back immediately. Show you're prepared when others are not. Don't let anyone try to seize control. Be the true leader you are, Angelino. Go. *Capo* Ferri will waiting for you."

Angelino looks almost loving as he smiles at his wife, then, with a sneer, he turns to me. "We'll have to continue this conversation later. Now I have to arrange a retaliatory attack on your husband's clubhouse. Seems a nice afternoon to blow something up.

My jaw drops in horror. "Theo?" I say fast. "Theo's at the compound."

He shrugs. "Collateral damage."

I fly across the room, my hands striking him, fingernails raking down his face. "You can't! You fucking bastard. I'll kill you." He staggers back with the unexpected force of my attack, throwing his arm out to catch the doorframe to regain his balance.

"Get off him, you bitch."

Vitalia's trying to pull me off him by my hair. A hard smack to my face combined with her tugs gets me falling backward, but not quickly enough to prevent the fist thrown hard into my stomach. Crashing to my knees, I bend double, gasping for breath. It's while I'm down, trying to recover, that they leave. When I can at last pull myself to my feet, I'm alone.

"Theo!" I scream at the top of my voice, tears falling down

my face. In my mind I'm picturing the clubhouse exploding, fire tearing through and my son, my lovely boy... Too young to protect himself. "Nooooo."

My lungs struggle to get oxygen, but not from physical pain, from the sheer terror of losing my son. I don't understand how Angel can be so callous; there's a good chance Theo's his too. His lack of concern goes to prove a son to him is a commodity, not something to be cared for and cherished.

Lightheaded, I collapse down to the floor, resting my head in my hands, trying to focus through my horror and mental pain. *What can I do?* I can't warn Demon. Demon's focus will be on finding me. *Surely he must realise the Devils are at risk now he's killed their leader?*

I thought marrying Demon had been the right thing to do. A way to protect Theo. Now it seems I was wrong. Angelino might be known as the Angel of Death, but Demon appears to be just as bad. *He killed many men, out of a fit of anger when he couldn't find me.* He's started a war. My perfect man hadn't turned out to be so perfect after all. Not the right man to be a father to Theo. Now his actions could get my son killed.

I'm the only one to know Angel's plans. What can I do? Angrily wiping my tears on the bottom of my dress, I look around the room with fresh eyes. If I call, maybe someone will come expecting to take me to the bathroom. If I can find something to incapacitate them in some way, maybe I can get out of this room. Or take their phone. I don't know anyone's number, but... While I know it wouldn't make Demon happy, I'll call the only contact everyone remembers. The police. Saving my son's life is an emergency. According to Angelino, Demon has killed his father, the don.

What does it matter that a murderer like Demon is locked up if it means Theo has a chance of life?

Theo alive, while my husband rots in a prison cell or dies at the hands of another prisoner. Or Theo dead, and Demon alive, wreaking vengeance on the Mafia family who destroyed the compound.

I'm Violet Palmer, Nathan's sister. Things like this just don't happen to me.

The thought I've pushed to the back of my mind resurfaces, the unbelievable story Angel told about my father. He has to be wrong. My father didn't have a secret life, hadn't lied to me all the years I've been alive. I would have known, wouldn't I? Would have suspected? Surely if he'd been a Mafia don there would have been some sign?

But if Angel is right, everything happening now started when Pompeo, his brother, had been killed. Had my father initiated the actions that led to me being here now, and the grandchild he never knew he had being in danger?

I have to escape. Got to get to Theo. Got to get him away. Revert to my initial plan and get him to safety.

I stand. There's a desk, but all the drawers are empty. The soft cushions on the couch offer no solution at all. I pry at the window frame, but it's not moving, and my fingers are bleeding trying to remove the nails which fasten it shut. *Break a window.* But how? And with what? And that would only bring men running.

Sinking down on the couch once again, my tears start falling. This time, I don't wipe them away. *I tried Theo, I tried. Mommy tried to come save you.* I weep, wailing uncontrollably, my cries bringing no attention. Eventually the tears dry. *If they'd already attacked, if that's where Angel went... If Theo is dead or hurt, wouldn't I already know it? Wouldn't I feel it like a hole in my heart? Wouldn't I have already started dying inside?*

I can't let myself give up. *But what can I do?*

It's only when I hear footsteps approaching that I realise I've been stupid. I do have a weapon, it's just that it didn't come in a box with 'gun' or 'knife' written on it. Racing to the desk, I tug hard on a drawer, it's old, and slides out without too much protest.

Moving fast to the side of the door, I hold it over my head.

Picturing Theo, imagining flames approaching him, I have no second thoughts as I raise it over my head and bring it down with all my strength on the head of the person who steps through the doorway.

But the man's too tall. All I do is knock his shoulder, but hard enough to make him stagger. He's one of Angelino's men; his eyes blaze as papers fall from his hands onto the floor.

"You're going to pay for that, bitch," he snarls, rubbing his shoulder. Then he wrenches the drawer out of my hands and throws it behind him into the hallway. Pushing me backward, hard, knocking me off-balance and onto my backside, he steps into the room, his eyes scanning quickly. Seeing the remaining drawer in the desk he goes and rips it out, turning to me with an evil grin. "There's no escape for you. Angelino wanted you to read that file. He'll be back once he's finished his business. He, er, wanted me to remind you to think on your bargain."

Kicking the file with the paperwork all away across the floor to me, he turns, slams the door, and disappears.

I hope his shoulder is hurting.

My bargain. Kneeling, I start pulling the papers toward me. There is nothing Angel can have left for me that will make me believe his fantastical story about my father. He hadn't led a second life. Involved in the Mafia? Never. It's a preposterous suggestion. I'll read the 'evidence' he's put together, find all the holes and find a way to rationalise them. Then I'll explain that he has it all wrong.

What happens if he doesn't believe me? Pursing my lips, I realise there has to be some way to convince him he has no reason to keep me. No reason to hurt Theo. There's no revenge to be had, my father wasn't the man he's describing, and no way was he responsible for the death of his brother.

He might rape me anyway. And Theo... Once more I stuff my hand into my mouth, biting down so hard I draw blood, unable to cope with the thought it might already be too late. The file drops from my hands, paperwork scattering.

No. Finding an explanation as to why Angel's wrong is the only chance I have to save my baby. My attempts at finding a physical weapon having been thwarted, I have to think on another way out instead, though all I want to do is curl up into a ball agonising about the planned attack on the Satan's Devils' compound.

Prove this evidence has no grounds.

I take a deep breath to steady me, and another. Then, having gathered the papers once again, I go to the desk and start reading.

A birth certificate is there. Vittore Parma. Same date as my father's birthday, but that's just coincidence, so is the similar sounding name. I flick through, there's a visa with a picture of a young man on it; sure, there's some resemblance around the eyes, but I only remember my father with dignified grey streaks in his hair, not with the jet-black mop this man is sporting.

My father had travelled for work. Some of the clients he worked for were based out of town, that's not unusual, surely?

Angelino's done his work thoroughly, or someone has on his behalf. There's a list of dates when things went down, a stolen shipment of heroin, a warehouse explosion, that drive-by shooting when Angelino's brother was captured and presumably subsequently killed. The last date was twenty years ago when Don Vittore Parma disappeared.

There's also a matching column of dates when Victor Palmer went out of town. I scoff at the way they conveniently correlate. This is no proof, Angelino could have written those dates himself.

There's one time I do remember, my fifth birthday. My father hadn't been around. I don't have many memories as a child, but that sticks out as one. At the time I'd been a spoiled brat, stomping my feet and wishing he'd stayed home for my party. But he hadn't. Quickly I check the date.

Arms that time. A shipment of AK-15s had been hijacked.

But this is wrong. Angelino and his father had money, they flaunted it. We'd lived a comfortable life, but nothing extravagant. A Mafia *famiglia* head like Don Vittore Parma would surely be well-off?

But a seed of doubt has been planted. I place my head in my hands, trying to rewrite my history in my head. He didn't speak with an Italian accent, though his pet word for my mom had been Bella. But surely, that didn't mean anything?

My confusion leads to disgust and anger. How could I live with the knowledge my dad, far from being a meek-mannered man and a good father, was someone who made his money from crime? Who had an elite team of men under his command? Who was involved in drugs, guns and murder? And whose nefarious activities had now put my son in danger? A son who only came into existence because of a desire for revenge.

I go back over the paperwork.

This isn't right. It's a fairy tale Angel's concocted, trying to find someone to blame for the death of his brother. He's found something and twisted it to make it fit, not least the coincidental name of my father.

Angel's lying. But why? Just to get me complacent in his bed?

He truly believes it. He must be mad. This is crazy. My father was not a bad man.

My concentration is on the papers in front of me; at first I don't hear the door opening. A shuffling of feet makes me look up. "You've read it then. Do you accept what I told you is the truth?"

"I'll never accept it." I've made up my mind. "The man who was my father wasn't capable of what you're accusing him of. You have the wrong person. And me, for no good reason." I stand, the chair moves noisily as I push it back into the desk, my action final, signalling I've had enough of this charade. "All the information is circumstantial. You've been clutching at straws trying to find the man who was responsible for the death of your brother.

Vittore Parma and Victor Palmer are definitely not the same man." My eyes flare as they catch his. "Everything has been a dreadful mistake. Let's salvage what we can of it. You let me go, go back to my son, that's all I want, Angelino."

Suddenly he moves. His hand reaches fast around my head, taking a bunch of my hair in his fist and pulling it painfully. "They call me the Angel of Death, the Angel of Misery, of pain and retribution. What you've seen of me is nothing yet. You're lying, just because you want to renege on our bargain. You could have come easily, but I don't give a damn if you fight me. I don't give a damn if you get hurt. You accuse me of lying, but everything I've told you is the truth."

At this point I realise I've never seen a man this angry. The room's small, nowhere to hide. But that doesn't mean I'm going to make it easy for him. Turning fast, I poise to leap toward the opposite wall just to put distance between us, but I've underestimated the tightness of his grip on my hair. My forward momentum means he doesn't stop me, but he's left holding a section from my scalp, leaving me shocked and screaming.

Hurt, I want to retaliate. As he crowds me again, I lift my knee, but I'm too slow. He grabs my leg and flips me so I land on the hard floor, winded. On hands and knees, I try to move away.

He reaches down, this time taking a larger bunch of my hair, he pulls me up by it, swinging me around in an arc, then throws me over the back of the couch, using his body to pin me in place.

I try to struggle, to kick, but he overpowers me. Still keeping me fixed in place by his grip on my hair, he presses his heavy weight against me. My brain registers the smell of sweat and the sound of him breathing heavily. It's not all from exertion. Through the material of his slacks I feel his hardness. I'm trapped, it's impossible to move him.

For a brief second that's over so fast that my brain doesn't register it in time to take advantage, he puts a small distance between our hips, but it's only so he can flip my dress up over my back.

"*Che cazzo?* What have you done?" His voice echoes in the sudden silence as I realise he's seeing the tattoo, Demon's mark of ownership. "You fucking stupid bitch." Then his voice comes closer as he bends to speak into my ear. "But no mind, I'll just burn it off, or flay the skin from your back. Of course it may decrease your value, but you'll still have a working cunt." He lifts up a little; turning my head, I can see him examining it. "'Property of Demon'? Wrong, you're fucking mine, bitch."

Then his hand rises and comes down to my face, slapping me hard. As I lie stunned, he shifts and frees himself. Then he's back, ripping apart the panties I'd worn to entice Demon on our wedding day.

"Don't do this!" I cry.

He laughs, then sneers into my ear, a parody of sweet nothings by a lover, "I love it when a woman begs..."

CHAPTER TWENTY-EIGHT

Demon

I'm not at my best waiting for news. My mood, my anger and fear, deepen every hour that passes. Roberto's been keeping in touch. The worst of it is, we have tabs on Angel now and we can't touch him. Not being able to bring him back and have Mace torture information from him is taxing.

The *capos* managed to get Angel to a meeting, but after that he returned to his home, no diversions along the way. I've been informed he wouldn't have Violet at his house—Roberto's assured me it's impossible. One of the trusted *capo's* men's women is Angel's housekeeper, and she's managed to discreetly search high and low and confirm there's been no woman brought there. I hadn't expected it would be that easy, it's too obvious a place, but it had been good to get confirmation.

But we have a plan. Knowing where he is is good, but it's where he'll be going that's most interesting. I have Ink and Pyro sitting outside his house waiting for him to make a move, but so far, he seems to have settled in for the night. *Celebrating the death of his father? Grieving, perhaps?* Whatever, it's now three in the morning, and my last report was the house is cloaked in darkness. Angel, it appears, has gone to bed. Which is where most people would be.

My hands itch to drag him out and question him. But there's a risk Roberto and Lucio were right. If Angel doesn't return to where he's stashed Violet, she could disappear. Too many women go missing never to be found again for me to risk it. One thing the Mafia does well is traffic people.

At least if Angel isn't with her, she's not being molested. For now.

The clubhouse is a mixture of activity and quiet. Some, dead on their feet, are giving in and taking the chance of a couple of hours rest. Hellfire and I, the other presidents and VPs, are all awake, surviving on nervous energy. I'm pleased to have such support around me, but it doesn't ease the choking feeling around my throat, or the dread in my gut. *Forget her. You'll never see her again.*

"Put it down, brother." Drummer points to the tattered note I'm reading for the umpteenth time. "We're going to find her. Soon as he makes a move, we'll be following."

"How's Snatcher?" I change the subject.

"Rusty, your medic guy, is with him. Thinks it is a concussion, but he seems to be a bit brighter now he's had a rest. Snatch is complaining about his bike being in the shop."

A sign he is feeling better, perhaps.

"Pyro called," I tell him.

"Anything?"

"If there was, do you think I'd still be fuckin' sittin' here?"

Drummer's eyes flare and my mouth snaps shut. I've heard it called his death stare, and now I know the reason.

"Nah. No movement. Seems the Mafia have sent a few of their men, too," I hurriedly start filling him in. "They went prepared with flasks of coffee, and they're fuckin' sharing it with my crew."

Luckily that causes Drummer's expression to change as his lips curve upwards. "There's a joke in there somewhere. The MC and the Mafia sharin' fuckin' java." Now his face softens. "How's the kid doing?"

"Okay. He's in with Mo and Hell. He's been a bit tearful, Mo said. Don't know if it's because he's missing his mom, or whether it's a tooth coming through." When we'd returned to the clubhouse earlier, I'd put my head around the door and watched him for a moment. He'd been squirming a little restlessly while he slept. I'd made him a silent promise that I hope to fuck I can keep: I'll bring your mom home, Son.

"Your kid's young enough he probably doesn't care too much what's going on as long as he's kept comfortable and fed."

Drummer's probably right. Hell, he has two kids of his own. He'll know much better than I do. What do I know about raising a son?

Son. My son. The boy I'll protect with my life. Observing him sleep, I suddenly knew why it had been easy for Hellfire to step into the role of my dad. It's not where they come from, it's the life you can give them, that will determine the person they'll grow into. I'm not a throwback to my sperm donor, I'm the man Hell taught and helped shape. I know for myself there's no point waiting for signs that Theo will bear any behavioural resemblance to his sperm donor. I'd had those worries myself. When I'd learned my true heritage, I examined my beliefs, my morals, and realised there was nothing of Blackie in me. I was more like Hellfire.

I don't think I'm a bad man, but whoever I am, I can do better. I will. To set an example to Theo.

I'll bring your mom back, I silently promise again. I have to. Else I'll be bringing up Theo on my own.

Three-thirty AM. If he's not moved by now, I doubt he will. He's bedded down until morning.

I drowse, on and off, on the couch in the clubroom, ready to leap into action the moment we get any news.

First thing in the morning I get a call on my phone, I've barely had time to say my name when the screen shows another's trying to reach me.

"He's movin'," Pyro says. "During the night we managed to

get trackers on all his vehicles. We'll follow to make sure he doesn't swap cars somewhere but will hang back out of sight."

I end the call. There's no need for me to say anything more. I'll only hold Pyro up. I answer the other call.

"Demon."

The don's velvety Italian tone reaches my ears. "Lucio. He's…"

"Movin'. I heard."

"My men are following." Christ. He's going to be leading a fuckin' circus at this rate. "I'll be going to wherever he is."

The best way is to do this together. "I'll meet you there," I tell the don.

Replacing my phone in my cut, I check my gun and take more ammunition out of my drawer. Then I go out into the clubroom. Smells of breakfast cooking are coming from the kitchen, but I couldn't face food. We're so close to getting to Vi now I can almost taste victory, and I anticipate the flavour of that will be far more satisfying than bacon.

I'm not surprised to find most of my men already awake and alert; news of the phone call had spread like wildfire. I whistle to get their attention. As soon as I tell them to get ready to be on the move, they are all checking guns and ammunition in preparation.

"We can't all go, Prez."

"Know that, VP."

Thunder flinches. "Said that wearing my sergeant-at-arms hat," he grumbles.

I whistle again. "Hold up." I wait until I have everyone's attention. "I need a prospect with a cage." *Just in case Violet's not up to riding behind me.* I frown, hating the thought she might be hurt but needing to be prepared for it. "I'll take five other men with me. But the rest have to stay here. There's still a chance Angel has something planned for the compound."

Drummer and Red step forward. "We'll come."

"Bomber and Rusty." They nod back when I call their names.

We don't know what we're heading into and another sniper could come in handy. There's also a good reason why the older red-haired biker might come in handy, though I hate to even think, other than he's coming along as a spotter for Bomb. He also doubles as our medic.

"Mace." The enforcer nods.

"Me, Prez?"

"No. Thunder. You stay here. And wear both your fuckin' hats."

I suppose I deserve the finger sent my way.

Eyeing the rest of my crew, I consider who else I'll be taking. As far as we know Angel has two *capos* loyal to him. That means he could have twenty men, maybe more, their *decinas* sometimes don't limit themselves to ten. The don will also have the same information. Deciding to pick a few more, I start calling out names. "Liz." He's an obvious choice given his experience, Ink, of course, will already be there with Pyro. "Sparky." He always tops everyone's score at target practice, and his injury yesterday wasn't much more than a graze. "Pal and Skull," I finish up. Time to see what the youngsters are made of.

"Prez..."

"Nah, Hell, Buzz," I address the two men who've spoken simultaneously. "Need you here."

My phone pings, giving a location. I don't need to say a thing. All the men coming with me are already moving, Red's moved fast and is out the door. I'm checking the coordinates as I go to the bike, picturing the location. Yeah, I know roughly where we're heading toward, or at least, the turn we'll need to take.

I indicate I'll take point, and get into position, Drummer and Red settling behind me, the rest falling into place behind. Then as the sound of exhausts starts rattling the windows, the eight of us ride out through the gates Wills has already opened, followed by Dan driving the truck.

Forty minutes later and my memory of the turn-off is all that I needed. Little more than a mile up there are cars and alongside, Ink and Pyro's bikes. It's Pyro who's waiting for me. "Ink's gone up on foot. Someone's used this place as a base to restore cars at some point. There's a residence attached next to a shop."

"Any sign of Violet?"

Pyro shakes his head. "Nah, but we reckon we're in the right place."

Lucio comes over. Without wasting time on greetings, he gets straight down to business. "We've been discussing this along the way. I suggest we surround the house."

"I don't want bullets flying." I want Vi safe, not riddled with holes.

"Understand your concern for your wife. There's no sign she's here," he confirms what Pyro says, "and no sign she's not. But if she isn't, Angel must be left alive to talk."

But not for much longer. I nod.

"Your proposal?" I'm confident he has one from his manner.

"You, I, and some of my men approach the front door. I will take the lead, you will remain out of sight. I would suggest you remove your cut."

My teeth grind. Not something I want to do but wearing it will make me an immediate target. Again, I raise and lower my head.

"I am taking the chance the men inside will be surprised to see me alive but won't want me dead. I'm banking on Angel's deviousness in trying to set me up. If he had his men behind him, he would simply have executed me himself."

What he says makes sense.

"Angel must know his plan failed, immediately he sees you."

He grimaces. "He will. So that's who my men will be taking down. With me there, I think *Capo* Ferri and *Capo* Sanna won't dare show their support for him. I don't see this as anyone's except Angel's coup." He looks down, then back up. "If I'm wrong, then your men and mine surrounding the building will be alerted by the shots. That will be the sign for them to make their attack." His eyes hold mine. "I'm suggesting you come with us to search for your woman. If you want to hold back..."

"Fuck no," I breathe out. "I'm one of the first inside."

He gives a quick grin. "I did not expect you would leave me to go in alone."

"We're wasting time." I want this over and done with. Angel is in there with my woman.

"My men are being briefed now. I suggest you do the same with your own. Five minutes for them to get into position. As soon as they are, we'll go inside."

I explain the plan. Drummer's eyes narrow when he sees me remove my cut, but Lucio's right. The men inside will be astounded seeing their don alive when they'd heard he was dead, and we'll be taking advantage of that surprise. But if they saw my cut, they might fire first and ask questions after. With the size of the family I'm banking on that they don't know every man under every *capo*, and with my colouring, I could easily pass for being Italian, especially with my deep summer tan.

With back slaps, fist bumps and demands to fucking take care, I watch my men, Drummer and Red move with the don's men to take up their positions. I can see Mace is particularly twitchy, knowing my enforcer would prefer to have my back. After a quick word with *Capo* Fabbri, Rusty and Bomber set themselves up hidden by bushes in front of the house.

"Anything?"

Rusty has his high-strength binoculars trained on the building in front of us. Without taking his eyes away from his target, he shakes his head. "Fucking curtains are pulled, Prez, on the upstairs windows. Can see men inside moving around. Hard to tell how many. Half-a-dozen, probably more. But no woman."

Then the don comes alongside. He points me to the limousine he presumably arrived in. "We drive up. It will be expected."

Angel will have warning. A buzz of nervousness settles inside me. All this hangs on Lucio being right, and that he'll be greeted enthusiastically and not killed on sight. For a second I appreciate how brave he is to take the chance and not send another man in his place, but then realise he'll be losing a son today, hell, has lost him already. He doesn't have much left.

It's not that much different to being prez of an MC. If the positions were reversed, there'd be no doubt I'd walk inside ahead of my men. Much like Red and Drummer being here with me today, Snatcher would have come along as well, had he not taken such a bang to his head. We'd never ask our men to do anything we wouldn't.

Six men, including myself and Lucio, get into the limousine, two up front. Another five squeeze into the second car. The atmosphere in the limo could be cut with a knife, no one speaking as we drive up. Not a muscle twitches, but no one can deny there's a chance both cars could be riddled with bullets even before the brake is applied.

The car's engines have summoned life. I see bodies in both front windows, and the front door opens. Angel is not in sight, but three of his men step out. They are all carrying rifles which point toward us.

Brave man that he is, with a deep breath, a handkerchief appears to wipe sweat off his brow, then Lucio tucks it back into his pocket, nods at us, opens the door, and is the first out. Split seconds later, the limousine empties, and he's surrounded by his men. *Capos* Fabbri and Salvaggi are with him.

I hang back, but close enough to see jaws dropping. One man falls to the ground, his hands over his head. When he looks up, his eyes are glistening. His mouth works, but he seems incapable of speech.

"We heard you were dead," another says.

"You did?" Lucio sounds surprised. He holds his arms out to his sides. "As you can see, I am not." He takes a decisive step forward; as he passes, he rests his hand momentarily on the kneeling man's head. "I am here to meet with Angelino."

As he's been speaking, we've closed the gap to the door. I let out a breath as I see rifles being slung back over shoulders. I'd rather see them disarmed, but that will have to wait. Lucio steps inside unimpeded, we crowd in behind him. Out of the corner of my eye I see Lucio's men using the confusion to subtlety herd those that had been here with Angel together and surround them.

"*Capo* Ferri," Lucio raises his chin toward the man who had first spoken. "Where is *Capo* Sanna?"

While I want to scream 'Where is Angelino?', I appreciate the don's concern. We don't want to be surprised by another captain and his men.

Ferri shifts awkwardly.

"I asked you a question," Lucio insists. Then, when he gets a mumbled reply, he asks for it to be repeated.

"Angelino said he was a traitor. He's dead."

Beside me, Lucio stiffens. I take it that's how Angelino deals with a man who won't go along with his plans. "And where is my son?" the don asks.

The *capo's* eyes flick to the stairs. At that moment, I hear a woman's scream. It's Violet.

Lucio's arm shoots out and holds me back as the *capo* says nervously, with another glance upward, "I'll go get him."

"No worries. I'll find him." Lucio looks around, nodding at Salvaggi and another man, and finally, with no emphasis, at me.

The men who'd already been here seem lost and confused as Lucio leads the way casually to the stairs. They're awed in the presence of their don, who is miraculously alive, but must sense this isn't the way things were supposed to play out. I can't forget they know very well what they are doing here, that in that room above, Angel is hurting a woman who's not here out of choice.

Or is it all in a day's work for the Mafia? I can't rule that out.

With my back decidedly itching, I follow Lucio up the stairs. There are only a couple of rooms here, one with the door shut, sounds of protest and a struggle the other side of it. I brace myself to kick it in.

Lucio turns the handle. It opens.

I don't hesitate. My woman is pressed down over the couch, her dress hoisted up, her legs naked. Angel is leaning over her... I tear him away. My fist to his face, then his stomach, then, almost in the same action I turn and pull Violet's dress down, not wanting her bared ass shown to these men. Seeing Angel's being dealt with, I'm now the one crowding her, leaning over her, letting her feel the warmth of my body, and soothing her fast.

"It's me, Vi. You're safe. I've got you." Gently, not knowing whether she's hurt or how badly, I put my arms around her to pull her up straight.

Instead of relaxing, she tenses up further. *Christ. What has that bastard done to her? Was I too late?*

"Theo..." As she stammers his name out, I reassure her. "He's fine. He's back at the compound..."

"Angelino's men are going to attack. They're going to blow it up. He's already arranged it, D, Theo..."

Jesus! Fucking son of a bitch. I grab my phone out of my pocket and place a call to Thunder. It rings out. Same happens when I try to get Hellfire. Nothing fucking works. Then, I notice, I have no signal.

No chance to give a warning. "You alright, Vi? Are you okay to walk? Need to get somewhere I can make a call."

She's overwhelmed for concern for her son. "I need to get to Theo." With no regard for her safety of what she might find outside, she's already making her way to the door.

I waste only the seconds it takes for me to growl, "You keep him for me, Lucio. We had a deal, remember." Then, my desire for revenge having to be put on the back burner, I steer Violet through the throng of Mafia men, some disarmed, some standing guard, and out of that house.

Thank fuck! Dan has had the presence of mind to drive the truck closer. I almost throw her inside.

"Bomber." I run to where he's hidden, taking my cut. "Get everyone back to the compound. Lucio's men can clean up here. Angel's arranged an attack."

Rusty's already moving to round the rest of them up.

"Shift." I motion for Dan to move over, then take over the driver's seat, throwing my cut onto the back seat. "Keep ringing everyone in the club, Brother. Need to know what the fuck is going on."

CHAPTER TWENTY-NINE

Violet

Angel's unsheathed cock is prodding at my backside. So close, I brace myself for the invasion, which despite all my efforts, I have failed to fight off. Though tensing will make the tearing worse, my body instinctively wants to continue the battle. I'm still trying to twist away, trying to do anything to stop him forcing his way inside when, suddenly, he's ripped away from me. I hear 'oomph's, a shout of pain, then, so fast I have barely enough time to take a deep breath, my dress is tugged down to cover my bare ass and another body is lying over me. My fear for myself immediately flees, the scent that comes to me telling me it's Demon.

He's found me.

He's here. Safe. Not at the compound. But, Theo? It was my first, my only thought. Ignoring whatever question he'd asked me, I cry out, "Angelino's men are going to attack. They're going to blow it up. He's already arranged it, D, Theo..."

He takes out his phone. I'm beside myself when it's clear he's getting no answer. Then he growls and asks, "You alright, Vi? Are you okay to walk? Need to get somewhere I can make a call."

I'd run out naked, right now I don't give a damn. "I've got to get to Theo."

While I know he must hate leaving Angelino among men I don't recognise, I'm just relieved when thoughts for my son's safety take priority over getting the revenge he must crave. He races me down the stairs and out to a truck. That he, himself, takes over the driving shows how much he shares my concern.

Dan keeps placing calls, but there's no answer, no response. My fears escalate each time he turns to Demon and shakes his head. *Theo.* My hand rests over my fast-beating heart, thinking again, if he was gone, wouldn't I as a mother know? Wouldn't my heart just stop? A cry escapes my mouth.

"Vi," Demon starts, then stops, his hands hitting the steering wheel, then hitting it again. There's nothing he can say. It's not just Theo. The club's on lockdown. Everyone who isn't with him is there. His mom, dad, and the men he calls brothers, as well as those from other chapters.

"God dammit!" Demon roars with frustration as he comes up behind a slow-moving vehicle. Then he yanks on the wheel and overtakes in a manoeuvre for which I'd usually admonish any driver. He's cut it close, there's a truck coming from the opposite direction; we slide past back into our lane missing it by just inches. A loud and extended angry honk sounds.

Dan's hanging onto the oh-shit handle, his face looks white as I catch sight of it in the rearview mirror. Neither of us say anything; I don't care how Demon drives. If Theo... If he's not there, I'd rather die without knowing.

We're on the freeway. Now Demon puts his foot down, and I watch the speedometer rising, looking nervously around to check there are no traffic cops near, relieved when at last we're off the main drag and heading toward the clubhouse. I start craning my neck to see and spot smoke rising.

"Shit!" Demon bangs the steering wheel again, then turns the truck violently into gates which are hanging off their hinges. There's a truck that's crashed into a row of bikes.

The place is a mess. For a split second we're all stunned. The front of the clubhouse seems to be missing, the doorway blocked by yet another crashed truck. Flames are leaping behind what were windows. Bodies lying all around.

"Stay here!" Demon barks. "You stay with her, Prospect!"

No fucking way! He must be mad. I reach for the door handle and throw myself out. Dan's just as fast, his strong arms come around me holding me back. Struggling in his arms with tears streaming down my face, I watch as men and women come running down the fire escape at the side of the clubhouse; I can see the club girls rushing down but no Theo.

I need to get to them, to find someone and ask...

"Hell!" Demon thunders, running forward.

I'm not proud of myself, but I'm a desperate mom. I kick hard at Dan's shins, surprising him. He loosens his arms and I run forward.

"Prez," Dan roars.

Swinging around fast, Demon catches me. I try the same tactic on him, but he's better prepared and avoids my feet. His arms are like iron bars imprisoning me. I scream, kick, flail, but I can't get free.

"Calm the fuck down," Demon snarls into my ear. "Theo's fine." I don't believe him. I need to see for myself. "Theo's fine, he's fine."

This time he gets through to me. When I pause my struggles, I look into his face, then into Hell's.

Hell is covered in dust, soot, and he's bleeding from a cut on his forehead. His earnest eyes stare at me. "Your kid's fine, Vi. Mo took him back to our house. Thought it was safer for him there. Jay's with her. Jeannie and Sindy too."

"You were on lockdown." I can't believe what he's telling me. *Theo's safe?* The clubhouse may be burning down around us, but those are the words I need to hear. Having been given the reprieve from my greatest fear, it's highly inappropriate but I want to laugh. "You moved him out of the clubhouse?" I haven't had enough confirmation as yet.

"Attack was coming for us, wasn't it?" Hell defends what

appears to be his decision. But it's not, as his next words tells us. "Snatcher's idea to get them out. Cad and Indian, the Vegas sergeant-at-arms," he adds, presumably to reassure me they're in safe hands, "are with them."

I feel like I'm going to collapse, but Demon's arms, still around me, are now supportive.

"Casualties?" he snaps.

"One of Snatcher's men. Thumper." Hell's face hardens. "He caught a bullet. He had no chance." He pauses to let that sink in. "Few walking wounded. Couple of burns. Yeah, coming." The last was directed over his shoulder at one of the men from the other chapters. "We need to get that fuckin' truck moved before the fire reaches the gas tank."

Only one man dead? For the first time I look at the bodies surrounding us, thankfully realising there's none I recognise, and selfishly pleased Demon's not lost any of his men.

"Dan. Keep Vi out of the way." With that, Demon quickly assesses what has to be done, then runs off. There are obviously men pushing from the other side, but as Dan leads me out around the clubhouse and out to the back well away from any possible explosion, I see them making headway.

Theo's safe, he's safe. Theo's safe goes around and around my head. After the last few hours thinking I was never going to see him again, the release of worry is almost disabling. If Dan's arm wasn't around me, I think I'd stumble and fall.

The rear of the clubhouse is out of a different world. Apart from the shouts, crashes and other sounds that reach us, and the smoke blowing up in the air, it would be possible to think nothing had happened. I sink down onto a picnic bench, facing the club, assessing whether it's really safe here. When I realise I'm in no danger, I let my head drop into my hands, relaxing for the first time since Angelino so callously threatened Theo. No, since long before that. When I'd been kidnapped coming back from the wedding. A hysterical burst of laughter escapes from my mouth. The most important day in any woman's life, and I hadn't given it a second thought. I stare entranced at my wedding band as though seeing it for the first time, wondering what's going to happen to Angelino, and whether I'll ever get a chance to have a normal life.

"Here." Dan taps me on my shoulder, his brow scrunched in concern. "Why don't you phone Mo and check the kid's okay? I don't have her number, but Cad will put her on the line. Want me to call him?"

Do I? That's not a question that needs answering with anything other than the fervent expression on my face. As Dan places the call, I glance around, for the first time noticing the other women. They are all the club girls. Bella's looking pale and shocked; Titsy's sitting with her arms around Sheila and Breezy, their heads touching. Tulia's looking stunned, staring at the unmarked side of the building in bemusement, tears sliding down her cheeks. None look hurt, just confused and dazed. And, half-dressed. Not in their normal state, but as though they just rolled out of bed.

"Here." Dan passes me the phone.

"Mo? It's Vi." She automatically knows what I need. She asks me no questions but talks in a grandmotherly way about her new grandson. I listen to her calming voice as she tells me he's doing great, how he's feeding, his diaper changes, who's entertaining him—that's Jayden, of course—and how he's been a bit fretful as his new tooth is emerging. Everything a mom needs to know. Finally, when she gets a chuckle from me, she hesitantly asks me what's going on at the club.

She's given me the time and the information I needed. My bout of hysteria has passed, replaced with the knowledge Theo really is fine. Cared for and wanting for nothing. "It's mayhem, Mo. They're trying to put a fire out, I don't know what's going on, whether we'll be able to go back in." A gasp shows me Bella's listening to my every word, her distress clearly visible. The sun glints off my wedding ring, and words that Mo had spoken come back to me. 'Queen Bee'. It may not have been my priority over the past—goodness, it's been barely more than twenty-four hours, it seems far longer than that—but I am married to Demon. With that comes responsibilities. Although I had thought I'd be eased into them, maybe I need to step up while Demon tries to save his club. I might not be good at firefighting, but I can at least see to the women.

"Mo, the girls have nowhere to go, and they can't do anything here. Can they come over to yours? At least for a coffee or something? They're in shock and distressed." I glance up at the sky. "Looks like a storm's coming and we can't go back inside."

There's no hesitation. I smile and nod, raising my chin at Bella. The look of relief on her face is precious. As I end the call, Titsy calls out, "Thanks for thinking of us." Her pleased smile suggests my unexpected action is welcome.

Dan has also been eavesdropping. "You stay here, Vi. I'll go check with Demon. But I can't see any reason why not. You want to be with Theo, and there's nothing you can do here." Now Angelino's presumably been put out of action, I can't see why Demon wouldn't agree, and this is the fastest way to get to my son. I eye the darkening clouds gathering, hoping we'll be able to get going before the monsoon comes.

It's not the prospect who reappears, but Demon. I stand and wait. I'm feeling awkward, suddenly realising I'd slept with him, married him, got taken, almost got raped, learned things about my father I still don't believe are true, and last but not least, am the cause of the destruction of his club. As he approaches I look down at my feet, unsure of what expression I'll see on his face. *I've caused so much trouble.*

He draws me into his arms, cradling my head with a hand so large it spans all of my skull. As my cheek rests against his cut I feel like I've come home. Despite all the sounds still going on around us, he seems in no hurry to release me. Perhaps words aren't necessary. If he blamed me for everything he wouldn't be holding me this tenderly. My arms snake around his waist; I'm holding onto him, too. It must be a couple of minutes before he starts speaking.

"Fuck, Vi. With the worry about Theo, the race to get back, the damage to my club, I just need one moment to get my head back on." His words are spoken quietly and murmured into my ear. "I'm as proud as fuck that you're thinking like my old lady. After the way I failed you, everything that happened—I'm so damn fucking proud of you."

I pull back. *He failed me?* I go to tell him there's no way he's responsible, but he hasn't finished.

"Vi, you've got my back, haven't you? Good call on arranging to get the girls out of here."

I realise dissecting what's happened and how it affects us will need to come later. Now's not the time. "Will we be able to come back?" I lean slightly so I can look up into his face.

Aware that ears are listening, again he speaks quietly, "On that I'm not sure, yet. The fire's not out, but we're winning on that front. Will have to assess the damage after we've dealt with the danger from that."

"You calling the firefighters?"

He chuckles softly, and not very nicely, "Got some trash to move first. Luckily, way out here, they've not come to investigate."

I shudder. By 'trash' I take it he means the bodies. "How many...?"

"Later, babe. It's all good on our side."

"Apart from Thumper."

"Yeah, Snatcher's cut up about that."

As his prez, he would be. "Is Dan...?"

"No, Dan's not taking you. Hellfire is. I want Mo to look at his cut. It's not serious but the stubborn man won't allow Rusty to doctor him. One thing I can do, now I'm the prez, is give him orders."

That makes me chuckle. A bit of a turnaround for a son to instruct his father.

"You ladies ready to go?" The man in question appears; his face darkens when he looks at Demon, who doesn't seem affected at all.

The club girls start getting to their feet, gathering up their purses and the meagre belongings they managed to pick up before they evacuated, and move toward Hell. As I take a step to go with them, Demon holds me back.

His eyes flare, then, with no warning, one arm goes around my waist, lifting me to him and his mouth comes crashing down on mine so hard I feel my lips bruising. His tongue sweeps into my mouth as he all but devours me. I feel heat pooling inside me as well as his hardness brushing against me. All too soon, he pulls back. Leaning down he places his forehead against mine.

"I'm so fuckin' sorry, babe. So sorry I didn't get to you sooner."

"You got there in time," I try to soothe him.

"Nah. Never should have happened. Not to my ol' lady."

"Hell's waiting..." I interrupt, scared he's going to say this life is too dangerous for me, when there are things he doesn't know. That it was down to me and my past that made Angel target me.

"Let him wait."

"D, your clubhouse." He raises his eyes to look at the building behind me. Then lets out a heavy sigh. "Yeah, I got work. I'll come for you later, Vi. We'll have a discussion then."

CHAPTER THIRTY

Demon

I'm jealous of my father, for fuck's sake, as he puts his arm around Vi when she nears him. Truth be told, I do not want to let her out of my sight. Of course she wants to reassure herself that Theo's okay, to hold him and love him. Trouble is, that's exactly what I want to do to her. The time we've been forced apart has been far too long. It's so fucking unfair, we've only just started on our relationship journey.

Being away from the compound is best for her. She's made the right call. When Dan told me she'd made arrangements for the sweet butts too, I was so fucking proud in that moment, all my misgivings about her being the right woman to stand by my side have fled. It hurts watching her walk away with Hell, but I couldn't go with her. I'm the prez, and now she's safe, my place is with my men. I allow myself one moment to think maybe the daughter of a Mafia don and a president of an outlaw MC maybe aren't so badly matched, then, as she disappears, bring my thoughts back to my current and pressing problems instead.

So far, I've found out the attack must have started about the time I was dragging Angel off Violet. By the time I'd tried placing my calls, the brothers back home had been dealing with Molotov cocktails being thrown into the clubhouse, followed by shooting as men tried to escape. Although at the time they hadn't known they were dealing with an imminent credible threat, Snatcher had treated the situation like an exercise, and had everyone ready and organised to protect the compound. The Mafia crew had headed into what was essentially a trap. Pincer movements by my men and those from other chapters had corralled them in the front, hence the crashed trucks. The enemy had been surrounded. It was over fast. By the time I'd arrived, they'd already made a start of clearing up.

Walking back inside, ruefully I eye the damage. The fire, now all but out. Pyro, having returned from where we'd found Violet right on my heels, is watching it carefully. Which is a joke, he's more likely to be laying them than putting them out. But he knows how fire behaves and its habits, where it's likely to find fuel and flare up.

"You doing okay? Got enough extinguishers?"

As though to answer, there's a short burst of fire retardant from one that he's holding. "Ink's just brought me a couple of new spares." He waves his hand toward them to confirm his words.

"Status report?" I stop by Sparky.

"Prez, electricals are fucked. Gonna have to do some rewiring all through this section. I can set up some breakers for now, just means we won't have electric at the front of the clubhouse. Should have everything else back on soon."

"Good man." I slap his back while eyeing where the front of our clubhouse was. Won't need electric when we're missing part of the wall and half the windows.

"Looks like a fuckin' bomb went off."

I roll my eyes as I turn to greet Bomber.

"Dead? Injured?"

I update Drummer, who passes a hand over his beard when he hears about Thumper.

"And them?" He points to a dead Italian.

"Got six dead, eight alive. Some injured, but not fatally.

They're down in the basement." I grin at Drummer. "Far as they know the place is burning down, with them trapped in it."

His sharp eyes meet mine. Then he gives a wicked grin. "They came here to kill everyone in the compound, women and the kid. Think a bit of mental torture is apt punishment." He pauses and looks around. "I'll get Viper up here to assess structural damage, and whether you need major work."

He has a whole construction company back in Tucson. We're not total strangers at a bit of DIY, but don't want to patch something up if it's in danger of falling down. "Thanks for the offer, Drum, a bit of advice would come in handy." I step closer to the hole in the wall; now the fire's out I can get nearer to it, warily eyeing the ceiling above my head.

"What you going to do with the dead Mafia crew you have lying around?" His mouth twists in distaste as he sees the bodies we've pulled inside, out of view of the street, piled up like cordwood.

My lips curve up. "Thought we'd get Lucio to collect them. He'll want to know who was involved in this, anyway, seeing he doesn't want to start a fight with the Devils."

Drummer laughs and slaps my back. "Fuck, I've no idea if the dominant would have come in on our side. Taking over the drug trade may have attracted them. But the threat of the Wretched Soulz having our backs worked, didn't it?"

"Like a fucking charm." My eyes convey how grateful I am. I don't have the clout of the mother chapter president. The same words out of my mouth wouldn't have carried so much weight.

I stand for a moment watching my men, and those here from the other chapters, getting to work. They're not waiting for instruction but assessing what needs to be done and getting on with it themselves.

"Hey, Prez. Just going out to get some boarding and sheetrock."

I raise my hand toward Bomber and Rusty acknowledging their self-imposed task. Wills and Dan are sweeping up the debris that had been blown inside, Skull is taking charge of a broom himself. Paladin seems to be sorting out bricks that can be reused, and Thunder and Mace are knocking out the remaining glass in the shattered windows. Slowly some order is being restored, the clubhouse looking less like a war zone.

A couple of Drummer's men, Rock and Beef are carrying burned tables and chairs outside to pile in a heap. And there's Twister and Indian from Vegas, carrying the couch that really has seen better days. Well, out of disaster rises opportunity. It was past time the clubhouse had new furniture, and it could do with a lick of paint. Only problem is, we obviously don't carry insurance. I continue cataloguing the losses as I slowly turn around. *Well fuck me, and dammit.* The jukebox obviously took the full force of the explosive thrown in. That had been a relic from the old days and will be missed.

"This going to hit our plans for the tattoo parlour, Prez?" Liz pops up from behind the bar and asks as he walks past, emptying a dustpan full of broken glass into a garbage bin.

"Have to speak to Buzzard, Liz. Once we can estimate the cost."

"Got any full bottles behind there?" Not that I want a drink now, but I'm not taking the chance on the bar running dry tonight. After the day we've had, everyone will want to get their throats wet.

"Surprisingly, yes." He grins. "Made fucking sure the flames were kept well away."

Ink chuckles beside us. "First thing Liz did was grab an extinguisher and stand guarding the spirits. Wanted to make sure he'd be able to get his whisky when the excitement had died down."

Probably just as well. Wouldn't have wanted the amount of alcohol we keep here adding fuel to the flames.

Having checked on everyone, I find a quieter corner and place a phone call. "Lucio, it's Demon."

"I am glad to hear your voice."

"Angel tell you what he had planned?"

Lucio's voice sounds weary. "Indeed. I presume, as you're alive, I've got dead men."

"Seven, yes. Six still breathing. They are yours if you want to collect."

A moment of silence. "I would appreciate dealing with them, Demon. And I'll take the dead bodies off your hands. No one would want to risk them being discovered."

I bristle slightly at the implied inference of us being unable to deal with a dead body, but him taking them means less work for my men. At the moment I'd rather they wielded hammers rather than shovels.

"Angel?"

"I'll bring him when I come to collect. I'll be there tomorrow."

I end the call, realising he hasn't confirmed whether Angel will be delivered alive or dead. I find I'm not too bothered either way as long as the threat has been removed. Revenge, it seems, isn't as important as Vi and Theo being alive, and safe.

"It'll be okay." Thunder's hand lands on my shoulder when I emerge from my corner. "We'll come back better than before. Now why don't you go to Mo's and check up on your wife and kid? Not much you can do here. Unless you got bricklaying skills I don't know about?"

I haven't. But I still can't walk out on my men. I tell him that.

"You keep telling me, Demon, that I have to act as your second-in-command. Well, how about you let me get on with the fuckin' job? You're stressed about Vi, hell, deserve to be. She was one step away from being raped from what I heard. Saved her, yeah, but she needs you, man."

Red, walking past, overhears. "You know what they say about too many cooks, Demon? Well, that probably goes for MC presidents too. More than enough of us here. Take a time-out, you need it." When Thunder slaps my back and walks off, brushing off my grunt of appreciation, Red leans in and adds, "Take a break. You've been living on adrenaline since your fuckin' weddin'. Thunder's right. You need some time with your wife and kid."

I can't just leave them, can I? "How's Snatcher?"

"Snatcher's fuckin' fine." I hadn't seen the man himself was behind me. Swiftly I spin, noticing today he has more colour in his face and seems to be holding up well enough.

"Look, fuckin' sorry about Thumper."

He meets my eyes, nods, but there's nothing else to say. No words can express the pain he'll be feeling, losing one of his men, and no words of sympathy adequate from me.

"Red's right. We can do without you here. Doesn't look like your men need their hands being held."

"If you're sure?"

"They're fuckin' sure. Now, scat."

Drummer's bark makes it a complete order. Outside I find Pyro, obviously happy the fire has been beaten, as he's with Wills. They're picking up stricken motorcycles and assessing the damage.

A tow truck appears with one of our trusted civilian mechanics from the shop. I'm glad he's acted fast and is looking to get us all mobile again. What good is an MC without its motorcycles?

He waves away my offer of help, saying he has extra hands coming along.

"You can trust them to keep their mouths shut?" This destruction, until we can get the place tidied up, is not going to help our reputation in Pueblo if someone with a loose mouth sees and starts describing the scene.

"I do, yeah. But I'll slip some extra in their pay checks. That'll do the job."

Satisfied, I at last mount my bike with a sense of relief that everything appears under control. Duty had kept me at the club-house, but with Vi is where I really want to be. As I ride, I realise I've been pushing myself to the limits since the ride home from my wedding was disrupted. The attack on Lucio's compound, the anxious wait to find where Angel was. While everyone had been worried, I'd had the additional burden of my personal concern about the woman I love, for twenty-five years as the sister of my friend, and more recently, as my wife.

She's here. Angel won't be a problem any more, and Theo is safe. That's the mantra that goes around my head when I pull up outside the home where I grew up. I stay on my bike for a moment, the ticking of the cooling engine sounding loud. Even from here the house looks like a hive of activity, people milling around in the living room.

Unable to hold back from seeing my woman any longer, I throw my leg over the seat. Walking to the front door, I use my key to step inside.

Mo and Jeannie have the club girls working. Plates piled with food are coming out of the kitchen, but the person I want to see most isn't in sight.

Hellfire walks toward me. "Update?"

"Fire's out. Clean-up's in progress as we speak. I don't think there's any structural damage, but Drummer has Viper coming to check that out. If he can get a seat, should be flying up tonight, so we'll know what we're dealing with soon. Windows are being boarded up. Pyro's dealing with the bikes."

"The Italians?"

"Are Lucio's problem. Got six alive, Hell." I brush my hand over my face. "I'd rather hand them over for him to deal with. Doesn't sit right to just take them out."

"They killed Thumper," he reminds me.

"But lost seven themselves. Thank fuck you and Snatcher were prepared for it."

Hell nods, then gives me an intense stare. "You holding up, okay, son?"

I spare him a quick grin. "I sure can understand why you passed over the gavel. But yeah, I'm okay. Just need to make sure my woman's alright."

He raises his chin fractionally, then jerks it toward the hallway. "Put her in your old room. She's in there with Theo. Son," his hand rests on my arm, "she's been through one fuck of a lot. May need treating gently. Focus on her. I know I didn't step up into the VP spot, but right now, I'm your father, and grandfather to that kid, and Vi is my daughter-in-law. Take some time with her. I'll go back to the club and get shit handled."

"Thunder's doing okay," I tell him.

"Nevertheless, I'll return and back him up if he needs it."

I nod gratefully. He's had twenty-years-plus experience of doing my job. There's no one better to stand in my place.

As Hell yells to Mo where he's going, I avoid other conversation and make my way down the hall.

My childhood bedroom is much as I left it before I moved into the clubhouse. At least it has a queen-size bed in it. I pause outside the door for a moment, hearing no sound, I quietly turn the knob and open it, then stand and take in the sight that I see.

Theo's in the portable crib by the side of the bed, asleep with his thumb in his mouth. He looks so cute a wave of emotion washes over me. *He's mine.* Then my eyes fall on his mother.

Violet's sleeping. My gut clenches when I see her red sore eyes which suggest she fell asleep weeping. Christ, everything she's been through over the past day, days, weeks—jeez, over the past year and a half. It's no wonder she needs a minute to cope with it. As I watch, her face scrunches, her hands twitch, and a sound comes from her mouth. She's dreaming, but it's not a good one. Vowing nothing will ever hurt her again, wanting to keep even her nightmares at bay, I shrug off my cut and shirt, then take off my jeans and boots, and lie down beside her.

As I pull her back against my chest, she stirs. "Hush, Vi, sleep. I'm here, I've got you. Sleep now."

The warmth of my body seems to soothe her. Without fully waking, she relaxes. Although last night I got no sleep either, I can't turn off my brain. I breathe in her perfume and relish in the feeling of just holding her. *My woman, my wife.* Christ knows what an ass I was to even try to deny my real feelings for her.

She's now sleeping so soundly, so when Theo stirs, I rise gently. With his changing bag slung over my shoulder, I pick him up from his crib and carry him out of the room.

"You okay, Dave? Want me to take him?"

"Nah, Mom. I got this. Can you get a bottle ready?" Knowing Vi she's probably sorted that shit out before settling down with him.

"I'll heat one up."

Ignoring that I have an audience, I open the bag, spread the changing mat out on the floor, then remove and dispose of Theo's dirty diaper in the bag I'd remembered to get ready. He wriggles and turns over, I tickle his tummy when I turn him back. "Behave," I admonish him gently. Taking a firm hold of his legs in one hand, I proceed to clean him, put his cream on, then fasten a new diaper around him. There's a fresh onesie in the bag which I put on him. As I fold up the mat and put it away, I realise the room has gone silent around me.

I stand, picking up my son, and take the bottle of warm milk from Mo's outstretched hand. My focus on Theo, I note, but can't interpret, the weird look on her face. As my intention is clearly to sit there, Titsy rises from the chair I'm heading to, and points that it's now free with her hand. I sit, settle Theo in my arm, then hold the bottle to him. He doesn't take a moment to suck the nipple into his mouth.

"Christ, I think my ovaries just exploded!"

Bella's statement rings out and seems to echo, then it starts a round of conversation.

"Mine fucking, too."

Glancing up, I see a look of longing on Breezy's face. When she catches my eyes on her, she giggles. "You're the prez, Demon. A rough, tough biker. I never thought I'd see the day when you changed a diaper and then sat patiently feeding a baby."

My eyes narrow as I look at her, then note the similar expressions of astonishment on the faces of the other girls, and then my gaze falls on my mom, who's smiling broadly. I shake my head and return my focus to Theo. His bottle empty, I put him over my shoulder to burp him.

"Here." Mom's handing me a cloth.

Thanking her, I lift him slightly and put it between him and my shirt. I can't for the life of me understand why changing a diaper and feeding my son is such a big deal for the women. Like anything, it was a job that needed doing, and now, it's done. Content, happy, burped and clean, I put Theo on my lap and start bouncing him gently. Not too much, I don't want his feed to reappear.

"You're a natural," Mom tells me, the tone of her voice proud.

I shrug. I'm doing no more than she and Hell had done. My son settled, my thoughts return to Violet. "Do you mind taking him for me, Mom?"

"Oh, let me, please." Tulia's holding out her arms for him.

"You only want him now he's clean," Breezy laughs.

"True." Tulia's grin is unapologetic.

I'm happy to pass him over, knowing he'll be in safe hands. But I do issue a warning. "He's just been fed, so go easy." Then, having handed him off, I again catch the eyes of my mom.

"What?"

She walks over and hugs me. "Proud of you, son."

"Only doing what you taught me." Can't understand why everyone seems to be making such a big deal of me looking after the kid. I suddenly realise who's missing. "Where's Jeannie and Sindy? And Jayden?"

"Jeannie's gone back to her house, Sindy went with her. It was getting a bit crowded her." Makes sense. "Jayden's gone back with Pal to the clubhouse." She pauses and grins. "Those two don't like being apart." I know how they feel.

I returned to my old bedroom at exactly the right time.

Violet's sitting up, rubbing her eyes, and staring at the empty crib. Not in consternation, but with just a touch of motherly concern.

I put her at ease immediately. "Changed, fed and now being amused."

CHAPTER THIRTY-ONE

Violet

After being saved from being raped for the second time by Angel, after the commotion at the clubhouse, Mo and Hell's home seemed at first a hive of activity while the club girls and old ladies sorted themselves out, then an oasis of peace. Refreshments seemed the order of the day. Though I could feel the adrenaline that had kept me going for the past day disappearing, I'd tried to help. With her sharp eyes Mo had realised I was fading and pointed me to Demon's old room. I made no protest.

Having laid Theo down, I stretched out on the bed beside him. *I thought I'd lost him today.* It was at that point I broke down. Sobbing quietly with my hand stuffed into my mouth so I wouldn't disturb him, I relived the terrors in my mind. I suppose I must have been exhausted, a night with no sleep, and not much the night before, for two totally different reasons. Eventually, with tears still wet on my face, I must have gone to sleep.

Vaguely aware of someone lying behind me, I'd woken from a bad dream starring Angel threatening my son. I'd heard Demon's voice, but it had been his aroma inhaled with each breath which had done most to help me settle. I'd let myself relax into sleep once again, this time without dreaming.

I'd only just awoken and noticed Theo was missing, when Demon appeared, as though I'd summoned him.

"Changed, fed and now being amused." He eases my mind, knowing instinctively what I need. I wonder who sorted him, then put it to the back of my mind as Demon stalks toward me. His hand reaches out and lifts my chin, and his dark eyes flare as they look into mine. "Vi," he chokes, "I'm so fuckin' sorry. Angel should never have gotten to you. I didn't do enough to protect you."

He did. He saved me. He saved my son.

"Angel?"

"Won't be breathing much longer. That's if he's still alive now. He went against his family, Violet. Set up his father, wanted to become boss."

I shake my head, unable to talk about the details, some of which I already know, some I expect I'll learn. At present it's sufficient to know he's no longer coming after me.

"He told me this story, D. A story about my father." An unbelievable tale.

Demon comes over and sits beside me, taking my hand in his. "I know. Vi, I don't know what Angel said, but I can guess. I'm sure you don't want to credit it, but I'm afraid what he told you was true." He takes a deep breath. "Vittore Parma was the don for a rival Mafia faction. There was a power struggle, and Parma was involved in trying to take Lucio out. Instead, Lucio's son was tortured and killed. Angel witnessed it, well, he saw how his brother was returned. He vowed revenge."

"No, my father wouldn't..."

"The Silvestri came out on top. Vi, Don Vittore Parma disappeared and wasn't heard of again." He passes his hand over his face as though he's exhausted, and he must be, too.

But I need answers, so I press, "It's impossible..."

"Parma was a don, Vi. Just like Lucio. But once he stepped down, he lived a normal life, lived his cover and blended in. Your mother, she was also Italian."

"Mom is American as they come," I scoff.

"Blood, Vi, blood. Doesn't matter what language you speak. They were second-generation immigrants, brought up not to stand out. Your father made good use of that, changed his name, and built a life. Yes, he was an accountant. Maybe his eye for detail helped in both roles. But those trips he was taking? Those were so he could undertake his other duties. Until the wrong man was killed."

"How did Angel find out?"

"Lucio accepted his son had been caught in the war. He was upset, yes, but sensible enough to know it could easily have been someone on the other side who was killed. Were things different, it might have been Parma's son, your brother, who had been murdered instead. Part of why Parma kept his identity secret was to protect his kids. Angel, however, isn't his father. He wouldn't let it drop. As he rose in the organisation, he suddenly had the tools that he could use to satisfy his desire for revenge." He pauses again, shaking his head. "Technology's evolving all the time. It's becoming easier to find things out, delve into old records. Somehow, somewhere, he found the links between the names Parma and Palmer."

"If this is true," I ask, my brow creasing, "why didn't my father change his identity better? Go for a completely different name?"

Again, his head makes a negative gesture. "I don't know, Vi. The only thing that makes sense is that it was easier not to slip up. Someone asks his name? Parma and Palmer are similar. Same with Victor and Vittore, he'd always answered to Vic. His initials were the same. His ability to pass for an American... Hell, Vi, I look more Italian than your dad."

"You don't have Italian roots?" I ask suddenly, the question surprising me. *Would it bother me if he had?*

"No fuckin' idea," he replies. "But none that I know of. Who the fuck knows what mix we have in our DNA."

I need to process that what I thought were Angel's lies might be true. The man I'd looked up to, loved with every fibre of my being, had been a Mafia don? Responsible for killing people? Maybe involved in crime like the Silvestri? It's too much to take in.

"Vi." Once more, Demon gently raises my chin. "Your father protected you by making sure none of his dirt fell back on your family. He did what he did to keep you safe."

"It didn't work, did it? And Theo is the result." I bite my lip as I think what else Angelino had told me. "Angelino admitted Theo might not even be his son." My head falls into my hands as I process the implications of everything I'd heard while I was held captive. "I was unconscious, D. Raped. By two different men. I don't even know who's the father."

"The other man is dead. Angel went ballistic when he found out."

"And that's why he didn't want to pursue the DNA test."

"Do you want to know, Vi? Don't have to tell anyone else the answer, but do you want to know who fathered Theo?"

Do I? Would it bring me any peace? "He has a rapist and a murderer for his father either way. Knowing wouldn't help." My own father was a murderer, possibly just as bad as the Angel of Death. I suddenly sob at the thought of Theo's heritage, and what it might mean to him, what traits he might inherit.

I hadn't realised I'd voiced my fears aloud.

"Hey, Vi." Demon's hand curls around my neck, holding me firmly, dominantly. "Need to tell you something. Listen up, yeah? Hellfire isn't my father. He's my brother by blood. My true father was a rapist, and as black-hearted a man as ever lived. How do you think I've turned out?"

My eyes widen in shock. He's completely stunned me. *He's a product of rape? His dad isn't his true father?* Then as I realise I have to reassure him he's one of the most honourable men I've ever met, he places his fingers to my lips to stop me.

"And you. And Nathan. How did you turn out? You're the gentlest person I know. What's in our genes doesn't matter.

Theo? Don't matter who his father was, he'll be what we make him. And we'll do right by him, Vi. I promise you that."

I stare at him for a moment, trying to process the stunning revelation he's just told me. Then I'm back to worrying my lip. "Do you, do you think Nathan, is that why..."

Demon rears back. "You saying Nathan was a killer? That's why he joined up? As an outlet for any murderous tendencies? You're wrong as fuck if you think that. Nathan was the absolute best. He was protective, that's why he gave his life for his country. Adventurous, too, but a cold-hearted killer? Definitely not. Get that out of your head right now, darlin'."

"I wanted to kill too, D," I admit.

"I'm sure you did, and who could blame you? Angel was dead when he laid his hands on you."

"Not just Angel." When his eyes come to me, I carry on, "He wasn't going to risk another of his men getting to me this time. Vitalia, his wife, was heavily involved. She's a bitch."

I've shocked him. "His fuckin' wife?"

"She was my jailer."

"You want me to take her out?" Demon asks through gritted teeth as he processes this new information.

I don't know what to say. She's as evil as her husband. But here, in the cold light of day, I can't give him the words. After a moment he stops waiting for an answer. Then, slowly, nods. "Let's see how it plays out. Lucio might be cleaning his own house. I'll warn him about the snake he has in it."

There's a gentle knock at the door. It opens to reveal Mo. "Theo's out like a light. Thought you might want to put him down for the night."

There's nothing more that I want than to have my son and my man with me. "Can you stay, D?"

He might have responsibilities back at the club, but it's clear he's choosing me over anything else when he replies, "Not leaving you again, Vi. Not for a moment."

Mo smiles, as Demon stands and takes our son from her. She

closes the door as she goes out. Propping myself up on one elbow, I watch as the man I love carefully places Theo in his crib. As I gaze down on my son, I think on the words Demon spoke a little earlier. It really doesn't matter what his parentage is, it's all down to how we raise him. Demon might look up to Nathan, but he shouldn't compare and find himself lacking. Before I'd met him again, if I'd been asked who my ideal man was, it would have been someone like him. Strong, protective, a man who'd never willingly let me down. And, if he did through no fault of his own, like he'd done today, he'd move Heaven and Earth to save me.

Demon's standing, he seems transfixed at the sight of Theo asleep in his crib, his eyes soft, loving. He knows what it's like to be the result of a rape. He's not let it affect him, other than to admire the man who raised him. As Theo's dad, I know he'll be the same. I never need to have any doubts about him. If we ever have a family of our own, he won't treat his true child any differently.

I know he's wearing kid gloves around me; Angel had come so close to raping me today. But I need him. I need our wedding night that we never had, though we'd anticipated it the previous day. Seeing Demon standing there, such a magnificent specimen of a man, knowing he's mine, knowing how much I love him, I can't deny the effect he's having on me.

He catches me staring and tilts his head.

I lick my lips, then, feeling bold, rise up onto my knees. He's standing so close, he's within easy reach. My hands move toward his belt.

He has several different reactions. The bulge compressed by the denim starts to visibly grow, his hands catch mine. His dark eyes flare, showing his arousal, but he stays my movement. "Vi, I don't want..."

"You don't want me to touch you?"

"I fuckin' want that more than my next breath." His voice catches as I lick my lips again, and for a moment his eyes stare at my tongue. Angel might have overpowered me earlier, but now I feel the one in control. Demon shakes his head as though he can't focus on the words he's uttering. "I don't want to push you, Vi. Don't want... Oh, fuck."

His loss of concentration was caused when he loosened the grip of his hands and I'd pulled mine away and placed them on his belt. Now I'm undoing the buckle and freeing the leather. His indrawn breath shows his capitulation as I slide the button through the hole, then unbutton the next, and then the next. He sighs as I free him.

I didn't take the chance to examine him before. He's long, thick. Uncircumcised. His cock leans slightly to the left, but otherwise is totally straight. It's only my eyes on it, but it's growing as I stare, reaching up to his stomach. Idly I wonder whether he's gone commando as he was in a hurry to dress, or whether he always forgoes underwear. The button fly is obviously safer, no zip to catch his skin.

"Are you just going to look at it?" he growls, his control lost. "You can touch, you know."

Needing no further encouragement, I reach out my right hand, grasping it, relishing the feeling of touching hard steel encased in velvet. As I begin to move my hand upup-and and down, a drop of pearly fluid appears at the head.

Shuffling closer, I insert my free hand into his loosened pants. As I have difficulty grasping his heavy sac, he snarls and assists by pushing his jeans off his hips. Unable to help myself, I lean forward, licking that drop of pre-cum that's temptingly now within reach. I elicit another sharp intake of breath from him.

"Vi, fuck."

My mouth opens, and I draw him inside. His hand goes to the back of my head, tangling in my hair, holding me to him. I trust him, keeping my hand on the length of his shaft that's too much for me to take in, I lick around his frenulum, feeling his cock harden even more.

Then he starts bucking against me, as if out of control, but he's not forcing me to take too much.

I swallow, suck, lick. Each of my actions seem to drive him crazy when suddenly he hisses and draws away. "Fuck, Vi. I need to be inside you. Clothes, off. Now."

CHAPTER THIRTY-TWO

Demon

Jesus but her mouth is wicked. I was about ready to blow after just a few seconds. Having my woman back in my life, knowing she's here for good. Knowing Angel won't be able to take her again, I need to reclaim her as mine.

The memory of how I'd found her is locked in my head. He was so close, another second, he'd have invaded her. So fucking close to raping her today.

I hadn't returned to the bedroom to fuck her, that wasn't even on my mind. I was going to give her time to recover. To have therapy, fuck. This is the start of our life together, and if Angel had caused a hitch, well, I'd have waited until the time was right. But now she's made the first move, has taken my cock into her sweet, sweet mouth, and all bets are off.

I need to be quiet so we don't wake Theo, but damn, I'm going to love my woman hard. I don't give a damn that we're in my parents' house. I'm going to love her so damn hard she forgets another man's hands ever touched her; fuck it, make her forget her damn name.

She brought me to the edge so quickly, somehow her guileless exploration was more exciting than any practised hand and mouth I might have had on me before.

I can't take my eyes off her. I remove my tee as she strips off her top, then her bra, without embarrassment. Then, fuck me, she's wriggling out of her shorts and, with a wink, is pulling down her underwear. My mouth waters at the delicious sight in front of me, my eyes staring at her hand as she unwittingly flashes that wedding ring at me. It's the first I've had time to admire it. Pyro did a good job choosing it. And it marks her as mine.

Undoing my boots, I kick them off then shrug off my jeans. Starting at the end of the bed, I crawl toward her. Her body flushes at my approach, she's unable to hide how much I affect her. Firmly I take hold of her legs, and pull them apart, then up over my shoulders, opening her to me.

"Oh."

Yes. Oh. I lower my head, loving the way her back arches and she almost comes off the bed when I zoom in on my target and suck her clit into my mouth, tonguing it, nibbling it, then attacking her slit with my hand, fingers invading her, finding that spot.

"Jeez, D. I'm gonna..."

She must have already been aroused if I can bring her to this point so fast. My free hand reaches upwards, finding a nipple and pinching it. It's enough. Her thighs tighten around my ears, muffling the sounds, then she stills. Looking at her face, it's all scrunched up, and her fist is in her mouth to stop her screaming.

Suddenly her other hand comes down, pushing at my head. "Too much, it's too much."

I back off, gently kissing her mound, giving her a moment, before attempting an advance on her clit again.

"I can't, oh..." Quickly she discovers that she can. Fuck, I could play here all day, delighted to find she's multi-orgasmic.

"Demon, stop. I want you."

I've certainly got her ready enough. My face and hand are dripping. Reaching for my discarded tee, I wipe first my fingers, and then my mouth.

"Turn over, Vi. I want you on your knees."

I draw in a breath as she does, and that beautiful tat appears. 'Property of Demon'. My cock's jerking, but I take a moment to trace every letter. "You're fuckin' mine, Vi."

"Angel went crazy when he saw it."

I just bet he did. Then it occurs to me. "Did he hurt you, Vi?" Her silence tells me he did.

"He said he'd burn or cut it off."

"Did. He. Hurt. You?"

"He slapped me, yes." My cock starts deflating. "But erasing the tattoo? That scared me most of all, D. Even more than him raping me. That if you hadn't have found me, if he'd followed through with his plans, that I'd lose that connection to you."

I stare at her skin, noticing bruising that hadn't been there before. "You fought him?"

"Of course."

Yeah. Of course. "Vi..."

"Demon, can we talk later?" She wiggles her ass. "He's not here, you are. And, so am I. Yours, Demon. Always yours. Whatever he'd have done wouldn't have changed that."

My fingers again trace my name inked on her back. "I hate to think what I wanted got you hurt, Vi."

We might be having a conversation, but the words on her back do something to my head. Or rather, to my cock. *She's mine and everyone knows it.* Although it got her hurt, I'm glad Angel saw it. Saw that she could never be his.

"Fuck, Vi. I'm going in bare." I start rubbing my cock against the crack of her ass, then rubbing it in her own lubrication dripping from her sweet-smelling cunt.

"Demon..." she says in warning.

"I'm clean, and I'll pull out." The thought of rubbing my cum into her skin suddenly overwhelming. "Trust me."

"Fuck me!"

Jeez, I can't hold back. I try to be gentle, but I want to wipe the memory of his touch away. Careful to hold her away from any darkened patch on her fair skin, I push in, unable to stop until I reach her cervix.

She gasps. I pull out, her ass following me as though she doesn't want to lose the link between our bodies. "Demon, please. I need to feel you."

"You'll feel me alright," I lean over her and growl. "All day tomorrow, then we'll do this all over again. You'll feel me." My teeth find her neck, I bite gently as my cock slides back in, then suck, knowing I'm leaving yet another mark on her. By the time I'm finished no man will be in any doubt. *She's mine. Legally and in the eyes of my brothers. In every fucking way.*

Raising my upper body, I pull her back against my hips, knowing there's no way I can go deeper. She gives as much as she gets as she meets me, thrust for thrust, moving as much as she's able in the tight position I'm holding her in. I hold her around her stomach, my other hand on her breast. She starts shaking, quivering, holding her breath, then I feel her come, her muscles spasming around my cock. I can't hold off any longer, my balls are tightening and drawing up, I push her head to the bed and pull out.

Ribbons of cum cover her back, luckily avoiding, as I meant to, her still-healing tat.

I wait until I've squeezed out every drop, then my hands rub my cum into her skin. "Once this is healed, Vi..."

"I get the picture," she breathes out. "I'm yours, D. There was never anyone else."

And now, there never will be.

"Never anyone for me either, Vi. Though I had my head up my ass. I was waiting for someone, just didn't have the sense to know who it was."

My tee comes into service yet again as I wipe my cum off her back. When she's clean, she turns over. "Love you so much, Demon."

"Love you right back."

Our mouths meet. Our kiss is gentle, sweet. When I pull back, I notice she's closing her eyes. "Come, we need a shower..."

"No, I need to sleep."

"You're all sticky, Vi." I grin, knowing I'm responsible for that.

"And now I'll smell you all night. Want this, D."

When she says it like that, who am I to complain? I don't mind spending the next few hours with the odour of her on my skin. She doesn't need to say more to convince me. I lie down by her side, my body spooning hers.

She relaxes and I think she's sleeping when she speaks once again, "I don't care about me, D. But I need to know no one's coming for Theo. Maybe I'm more like my father than I thought, but I want to know Angel's dead."

"Hush. Go to sleep." Right now I don't think it's the time to tell her I do as well, or that I hope there's still something of him left as I want to be the one to dispatch him.

Theo wakes us nice and early. Vi tries to soothe him but the tooth that's trying to come through has literally got him all hot and bothered and even walking him around the living room doesn't seem to quiet him. Titsy and Bella emerge from one of the spare rooms rubbing bleary eyes. They might have thought me changing him and feeding him cute yesterday, but his antics this morning seems to have opened their eyes.

"Nope," Bella says, shaking her head firmly, pointing a finger Theo's way. "You can keep that. Not for me."

"Me neither." Titsy looks disgusted. "Hey, Prez. Any chance we can go back to the compound?"

Mo, also having been woken, tries to push past to get into the kitchen. She looks at the girls with critical eyes. "You causing trouble?"

Titsy holds up her hands. "Nah, Mo. Just want to get home."

Home. That's what the compound is to most of us. A bunch of misfits with nowhere else to go. As I watch my wife with a struggling Theo in her arms, I wonder whether it's appropriate to expect her to stay there. Now there's no danger, there's no reason we can't look for a house.

Is this really me? A man with a wife, and ready-made family, and who's now looking at home ownership? I place both my palms on the counter and lean forward, briefly closing my eyes. In the past few months it seems like I've become a stranger. A man who's found his father is his brother, his real father a rapist, then moved from VP to president. Who has responsibilities I didn't think I'd ever take on.

Mo catches my eye, and mouths something I translate as, *You okay?*

Suddenly I realise I am. So many things sent to try me, yet I've emerged unscathed the other side. I know my own background is what makes it so easy for me to accept Theo as my son. Maybe everything does happen for a reason. I wouldn't want to be anyone or anywhere else. I grin widely and nod at Mo, returning a *Sure am.*

I go over to my wife who's holding a now more settled Theo after a dose of some child painkiller. First, I kiss the top of his head, then I draw her into me and devour her mouth. When I pull away she's breathless and slightly dazed.

"Got to get to the compound."

"Yeah, you go do your stuff."

"Want company?" Hell emerges from his and Mo's room, already ready to roll.

"Sure." As we exit through the front door, I'm already in business mode. "We'll get everyone together for church. Send the prospects here to watch over the old ladies and club girls. Just until we're sure what's happening." I want to know Angel has taken his last breath and be assured we're facing no blowback from the surviving Silvestri before ceasing my vigilance.

Even early the compound is a hive of activity. Hammers are banging, drills are whirring, men whistling as they go about their work. The pile of stuff that's been dragged out seems to have been sorted. Scrap metal in one heap, the wood has disappeared. I stand looking at it for a moment.

"Hey, we moved the grills out of the furnace. Thought we could burn all the flammable shit in there."

I slap Pyro's back, noticing he's grinning broadly. Yeah, he'd like that. "Good idea." As he goes to move away, I pull him back. "Church in five," I tell him. "Spread the word." I'll never be able to make myself heard over the building work.

The kitchen at the back has luckily been untouched. Sparky, true to his word, has done his magic with the electrical and thank fuck the coffee machine is working. I take a cup and nod to Drummer.

The sounds start to fade as I go back into the clubroom. One by one the tools are turned off and or put down. Soon I have a group of nearly thirty men standing around me.

"Okay," I hop up onto the bar and get ready to start this impromptu church. "First time we've got together since, fuck, was it just the day before yesterday that all the shit went down?" It seems crazy, seems much longer. "I haven't had a chance to thank you all. Brothers from Tucson, Vegas and Utah included in that. I know you hadn't planned on staying…"

"Wouldn't have missed it."

"Wanted some excitement."

But the Utah group are quieter, and I have to remember they are returning home with one less than the number that came. "Let's take a minute to think on our brother Thumper." Men around me bow their heads and clasp their hands.

Then after a moment, Drummer starts, "Ride, Satan's Devils."

And is answered by, "Satan's Devils ride together."

"Thumper will be remembered. Never forgotten. He'll ride on, just not by our side." I turn to Snatcher. "You'll let me know if he has family…?"

Snatcher shakes his head. "He was a loner."

That's something I suppose. But he'll be missed by his brothers. It's a sombre moment, but time to move on. "Status report."

A man standing next to Drummer holds up his hand. I nod to Viper. "Checked out the building. Basically, it's sound. There's just one part of the wall I wasn't happy with, but we've put in an extra support beam so it should be fine. You have a few men handy at brickwork, they're moving along good now. Most of the rest is just window frames, new glass and then the cosmetic shit. Your old lady might want to get involved there, Demon."

She might indeed. I recall seeing the changes in Tucson, how the furniture was no longer mismatched and broken once they left it to the women to decorate.

"Jay already has some ideas," Pal shouts out.

"Okay, so men build and women furnish. Pyro, bikes?"

"We prioritised the bikes from the other chapters, Prez, so they can get home. Most of them just dropped so the scratches to the paintwork can be done anytime. Two were totalled, but they are both ours." He sends a glance of apology toward Mace and Ink.

I glance at them myself. "Order what you want and the club will pay for it."

Buzz wipes his hand over his face and cringes, but doesn't say a word.

I turn to the treasurer. "I'm gonna ask Lucio to cough up. His fuckin' son caused all this shit."

"What about my bike and Snatcher's?" Crash calls out.

"Already finished," Pyro replies fast. "Roadworthy as of this morning."

Bikes conversation over, Red changes topic, "What are you going to do with the men in the basement?"

Yesterday there was a moment I could have easily killed them with my bare hands. Killing when guns are firing and bombs exploding is one thing, taking a life execution-style is not my way. Pinching the bridge of my nose, I answer him, loudly so everyone can hear, "Told Lucio he can have them. They're soldiers. They've knowingly or otherwise disrespected their don. They're his problem, not ours."

"Prez!"

A sudden shout gets me turning. The gate has not yet been repaired so it hasn't stopped a man who's walking across the now-cleared parking lot with a purposeful stride, his hands held out at his sides. *Speak of the fucking devil. It's Lucio himself.* Close behind him is Roberto and one other man.

It's like the Red Sea parting as they walk in. A low growled murmur greets Lucio, and hands visibly rest on guns. Snatcher looks particularly uncomfortable, but Red places a warning hand on his shoulder.

"Don Lucio. I'd say welcome, but..." I wave my hand to show the damage that's been done.

He nods as he steps in front of me, Roberto and the other man standing either side, then Lucio turns around, facing the crews I'd been talking to. "I wish you to know the actions of my son were not authorised by *il famiglia* Silvestri. The damage that has been done was not of the family's doing, nor was it condoned. The relationship between us will continue as it was." He waves a man forward. "As a more concrete gesture of my apology, I'd like you to accept this." He breaks off, takes an envelope held out to him, then passes it to me. I pocket what I suspect is a check, without glancing at the contents. Lucio turns back to the assembled men. "My son has admitted that he was trying to expand our territory, dealing drugs where it was agreed we would not go. I am here today to confirm that the old agreements are still in place and you have my word they will continue. After today, our paths should not cross again."

"And the Angel of Death?" Drummer asks a second before I do.

A flicker of pain crosses the old man's eyes. "Is still breathing. As you requested." He turns to face me. "I have men ready to take the deceased. But there were more *soldati* you captured. You have them? Or have you dealt with them yourself?"

"They are alive and are your men, Don Lucio. You are welcome to take them. I don't care what happens after that, as long as there is no further retaliation."

When I'd been in his mansion he'd showed compassion for the men who'd failed so miserably to protect him. Now his face shows no such emotion as he follows Thunder down to the basement. Roberto and the unknown man go down too. Out of curiosity, I also tag along after them.

I may not have been able to shoot an unarmed man, but Lucio has no such repulsion. Roberto barks an order for them all to kneel. Six men, quivering, do so. One looks up with pleading eyes and shakes his head, tears flowing down his cheeks. The don approaches one man, then walks around to his back. The sound of the gun firing in the underground space is almost deafening. Two bullets to the back of his head.

When my ears have stopped ringing, Don Lucio addresses the rest of the men. "You have one chance and one chance only. If any one of you ever betrays the family again, there will be nowhere you can hide."

Thunder leans in, asking quietly, "An example, or was that the ringleader?"

Roberto overhears, and answers, a twisted smile on his face. "An example, chosen at random. Don Lucio won't even know his name."

Christ. It makes me feel cold. And glad I'm in an MC and not the Mafia. I stand aside as one by one, cowed men exit the basement, two bringing their dead companion. Even those not burdened by the body's weight move slowly. Unlike my men, these hadn't escaped unscathed.

"Our business is almost over," Lucio tells me. "I've brought what's left of Angel to you. My men will drop him outside."

I remember what Violet had told me. "Vitalia was part of it."

"Already gone." His tone is business-like. "She was killed in front of him."

I sigh with relief. "Then that's the end of it."

"Yes." He holds out his hand and I shake it. A strong grasp, neither of us back off. Then he continues up the stairs and starts making his way through the clubroom. Just before he exits the door, he turns back. "Take care of my grandson."

CHAPTER THIRTY-THREE

Demon

No, no, no and no. I freeze. Violet's not going to have this threat hanging over her head for the rest of her life. But I don't know what to do about it.

Drummer's there by my side as I suddenly realise I'm going to kill Lucio. Kill the whole fucking Pueblo branch of the Mafia. There is no way they are laying claim to my son. I make a move forward; the mother chapter president holds me back.

"There's more to this," he hisses. "I have a feeling in my gut and more times than not that feeling means I am right. Bring Angel in and see if he's up to talking."

I have no idea what Drummer is thinking, but I jerk my head toward Lizard and Rusty standing closest to the door, then wait to see what condition Angel is in.

Moments later it's plain to see Lucio hasn't left much for me. Certainly not someone capable of talking. Angel's jaw has been shattered. His chest is barely moving, the pupils in his eyes are dilated. A bullet now would do nothing but put him out of his misery, that's if he's capable of feeling any pain. A mercy killing.

I'm not feeling merciful. "Leave him to die." There's no point doctoring him just so I get the satisfaction of ending him.

My shoulders slump as I turn to Drummer, my hands open as

I shrug. Drummer presses his lips together, then looks around the room, finally spotting the man he was seeking and beckons him over.

"Cad. Your computers okay?"

Cad's face dark with anger shows that they're not.

It doesn't bother Drummer none. "Well, get on to Mouse. He'll look shit up for you."

"What shit, Drummer?"

Drummer takes him off, I just stare at the man at my feet, so far gone he's incapable of groaning, wondering whether I'm watching Theo's dad die. Knowing in that moment how Hell could have killed his, my father. And, from the club records I'd read, not without a fuckload of pain.

"What doesn't add up is this mystery man who supposedly raped Violet without Angel knowing," Drummer says, returning to my side once more.

I shrug. A *soldato* taking the opportunity of raping the unconscious woman he was supposed to be guarding.

"Why guard her at all? She was unconscious." Drummer's insistent.

"She could have woken up." *Does it really matter?*

Drummer gives me a scathing look. "They're drug dealers, Demon. They'd know what they were doing. They trade in women, I'd bet they'd know exactly how much to give for a woman of her size to keep her comatose for as long as they want. And handcuffs are just as good for making sure someone stays put. Angel wasn't stupid, but he was cunning."

We're already talking about him in the past tense. Looking down to the body at my feet I realise we'll be right before long.

"And the guard knew it was death if he'd admitted it. Look at all the lengths to which Angel had gone to get hold of his son. Going through the courts, bribing judges, coming over as an upright citizen. Wanting everything signed, sealed and delivered so there was no chance of Violet keeping her son."

"He wanted to hurt her. Destroy her. Because he couldn't destroy her father."

"Demon, you might be too close to this, but think it through. The man only became supposedly loose-mouthed when a DNA test was going to be performed. But when did Angel back off? When did he actually know?"

"What are you talking about, Drummer?"

He ignores me, turning instead to Cad. "Mouse get it for you?"

"Got into Vitalia's medical records. You were right. She had fertility tests. She wasn't the problem."

Drummer grins at me. "The problem was with Angel. Violet had to think she was pregnant by him for the mental torture to work. So yeah, he got another man to rape her." He closes his eyes, but I complete where he was going.

"Maybe more than one." At least she was unconscious and didn't know about it. "But he would have had to have drugged her again this time. But he didn't drug her yesterday." *Could Drummer be right?*

"Just because he was firing blanks didn't mean he wasn't going to have some fun." Drum might be the mother chapter president, but he's in danger of getting my fist in his face.

"He killed the *soldato* when he found out."

"Think man," Drummer snaps. "Lucio just killed a man in cold blood in front of you. This," he kicks the near corpse on the floor, "isn't called the Angel of Death for nothing. It wasn't because of what the man had done, but because he opened his mouth about it. Take some of his hair, Demon. Before you dispose of his body. Let's get a test done. I'd bet good money Theo isn't his son."

"But Lucio would never believe it."

"Then we challenge him. He'll be able to produce nothing to prove his case. Angel is not, and cannot be, Theo's father." Drummer drags his hand over his beard. "What's worse, Demon? Violet never knowing who fathered that kid, or having Lucio in the background waiting to lay claim to him?"

"Sometimes it's just something between a couple," I speak my fears out loud. "There's no physical reason to stop them becoming pregnant. It just happens." But there's enough doubt that Drummer's placed in my head. I think for a moment. It's actually a no-brainer. If the results go the wrong way, I don't need to admit it. On the other hand, if Theo was fathered by some unknown man, then Violet will be free of any future threat. "I need a Ziploc bag." Having made my decision, I waste no more time. A suitable container is found in the kitchen, and soon I have a bunch of Angel's hair contained. Man's so far gone, he didn't even flinch when I took it. I certainly wasn't gentle.

Having done that, I realise church hasn't yet officially ended. With a loud whistle, I get everyone's attention back. Well it takes a moment, men have wandered away, and more than one reappears from the kitchen with a steaming cup in their hands.

"Now, where were we before we were interrupted?" As I hoped, my light-hearted comment draws a few laughs.

"Thanking us, I think, Brother," shouts Beef, one of Drummer's men.

It's as good a place to start as any.

"Our thanks go without saying, Brothers. And of course, our offer to reciprocate any time needed is always on the table." My comment receives chin lifts, and a special grin from Drummer. He's probably remembering all the times we've gone to Tucson. "Now I think we're okay on our own."

"Be fuckin' glad to get back to Vegas, Demon." That's from Red. "It's quieter there."

"You sure you're out the other side now?"

"Yeah, Snatcher. You heard Lucio. That's the end of it." And hopefully for good, if the DNA tests confirm what Drummer suspects.

"You going to deal with... him?" Crash asks. "Need a hand?"

"Nah. It's all good." I eye the body that's inconveniently

taking up space in my clubhouse. "We'll get rid of him in the desert." *Yeah, we might know a few places to use.*

With the prospects guarding Hell and Mo's house, Pyro, Lizard and Skull volunteer to take on disposal duties. Might as well bury him now. He'll die soon in any event. And after what he put my woman through and was intending for her, if he knows he's being buried alive, so much the better. My view? He'll know nothing at all. He's stubbornly holding onto life by a thread.

Meeting over, Red and Drummer waste no time gathering up their men, and there's a round of goodbyes and back-slapping before ten bikes ride out, disappearing in a cloud of dust, heading away from the clubhouse. Hell offers to drive Viper back to the airport. Snatcher and his team hang back.

"You want to take Thumper home?" I ask the Utah prez, knowing what answer I'd have given, and already working out the logistics. He gives the response I expect. Calling Dan back to the compound, we load Thumper's bike, which ironically was one totally unscathed, and reverently lay his body down on the back seat.

Snatcher takes his position in front of the truck with Thor, Piston and Rascal behind. I give Dan stern instructions to obey every fucking law of the road; no one wants to get pulled over carrying a dead body riddled with bullets.

As a good prospect wanting his patch, Dan shrugs off my thanks and concerns as he prepares to set out on his eleven-hour journey to Utah.

"He'll be fine," Snatcher reassures me, as I walk to stand beside him. Reaching out, I clasp his forearm.

Looking down I take a deep breath, then raise my head. I have nothing to say that hasn't already been said. What more could I offer? Thanks seem inadequate to my group of brothers who came at a simple request, prepared to put their lives on the line, and who are going back one man less.

Clutching my forearm in the same way, Snatcher nods. "Been

Prez for a fuckin' long time, Brother. This life? It's what it is. Know that when we patch in. Accept the risks for the reward. Your kid back there, Dan? He wants the patch even knowing what's in store. We live and ride free, man. Hard at times, but Thumper knew the score. Every brother in my house put up his hand to come here, you know that? Thumper one of the first. We all knew we might not have made it home."

I don't take any umbrage that he's emphasising the difference in how long we've both worn the president's patch. It's a stupid man who doesn't learn from the knowledge and experience of others.

"You need us?" I offer. "Just shout."

"I'll hold you to that, Brother."

Then, with a simple jerk of his chin, he reaches forward and starts his engine. I step back as he twists the throttle, then pulls in the clutch and kicks up into first gear. With a circling wave over his head, he lets out the clutch and begins to move off.

I watch until bikes and truck have all disappeared and nothing remains but dust swirling in the air.

A week later and it all seems like it had been a bad dream. The clubhouse might smell of fresh paint and varnish, but it's better than it ever has been. Sindy, Jayden and Violet showed they had artistic flair and we now have tasteful, but hard-wearing couches, tables and chairs and a fucking great TV in the club-room, bigger than the last one we had. The fresh paint it had been in need of for years has brightened the place up, without the nicotine stains the whole room seemed lighter. The check we received from Lucio hadn't been sizeable, but enough to cover most of the shit. Ink went out one day, returning to say he'd bought an old jukebox at an auction, how or where I don't know.

Violet and Theo have moved back in, and all the club girls are back and doing what they're there for. Yeah, life's back to normal, well, better than before. While I'd thought having an old lady would be stifling, and not for me, Vi fills the role better than I could have dreamed. She's gone head-to-head with Jeannie a couple of times, but mostly they get along well. It's good to see Vi has backbone where it counts.

I do get concerned about making her live at the club. It was fine when she needed protection, but now? My memories of growing up in a family home come back to me. That's what Theo, and any future children we might have, need.

Thoughts of my childhood are what leads me to a real estate office one day. Hoping I'm doing the right thing, I put in an offer for the full asking price, surprising the woman sitting behind the desk when I state I'm going ahead without even requiring an inspection. Bit more than I wanted to pay, but hell, I have a feeling this is going to put such a big fucking smile on my woman's face it will be worth every additional dollar I paid.

While I was waiting for all the official stuff to go through, now that I was able to take the leash off Violet, I took her to visit to her mom. I think it was harder for me than my wife. At least Vi knew what to expect, but I found it hard to be faced with an all but catatonic woman when the person I remembered had been full of life and fun. We could do little more than check up on her care. Having satisfied myself that this institution was indeed one of the best, I left Violet with her mom, and visited the office where I made sure my bank details were handed across. Of course, the sale from Violet's old home would pay for care for a while, but I wanted to make sure Delly wouldn't be moved on if the funds ran out.

When I'd returned to Delly's room, she was staring, fixated, at the glistening ring on Violet's hand. I gave her a sharp look, but there was still no sign of recognition there. Was it just the sunlight catching the diamond and making it glint that was catching her attention, or did she realise somewhere in the depths of her poorly functioning brain, the significance? I like to think it's the latter.

A month after Angel was dispatched to meet Satan, we had church.

"We have the grand opening of the tattoo parlour lined up," Lizard informs us. "Interior deco was sorted fast. Probably 'cos we've had practice." *Yeah, if you could call repairing the clubhouse that.* But the next thing on the agenda had been getting our new venture open for business. "Vi's handling a lot of that shit, Prez. Doing one heck of a job. She understands business."

Vi's thriving. While she loves being a mom, she's also excited about working. Mo and Jayden have been babysitting to allow her free time, and both are more than happy to look after Theo. I've seen Vi come out of her shell more and more and am impressed as fuck how she's handled the publicity for the new shop, coming up with some great ideas, and being Liz's right-hand when he's been purchasing shit he needs. She'll officially become an apprentice when the shop opens, and has already produced some interesting sketches. One, Pyro's seriously considering getting inked on his arm.

Everyone's pleased, we're all certain the location and fresh, clean, modern-looking premises should bring in more trade.

"Vi's helped with some ads for the security business as well, Prez," Paladin states. "Got some more work coming in."

I try to keep the smile of pride off my face, but it's fucking difficult.

"Couple of lads have been hanging around," Thunder takes the opportunity to inform us. "Karl and Beaver."

"Potential prospects?"

"Could be, Prez."

That would be good news. Wills and Dan, in my view, are ready to patch in. "Cad, investigate their backgrounds, will you? And what fucking type of name is Beaver?"

Thunder shrugs. "Not sure if it's a surname or handle. But I'll get you full details, Cad."

"Any other business?" I wait, but all seem to be more than ready to hit the beer and get to the girls. "Before you go, want to extend an invitation." That's caught their interest. "Sunday. My place."

"You spoken to Vi?" Hell looks concerned.

"She'll be up for it."

"Son." It's unusual for him to refer to me as such at the table, so I raise my eyebrow, waiting. "Think you have a lot to learn about women."

Thunder's jaw drops. "You haven't told her?"

I can't see what the problem is. I think she's going to be delighted. "Only just got the paperwork."

"You've bought a house, and now are inviting us to a get-together, and she doesn't know anything about it?"

Well, yeah, that about sums it up. *But she'll love it, won't she?*

Now I'm subjected to the sight of my father cracking up. It's not long before the rest of them join in, and even my best imitation of Drummer's stare doesn't stop them.

CHAPTER THIRTY-FOUR

Violet

For more than a year and a half I've hated surprises. From learning my father had suddenly died to finding my mother deteriorating so fast, to getting pregnant, having Theo, then being scared of every envelope arriving about Angel's attempts to try to get custody, I haven't been able to plan or even think for myself. Everything has been a reaction. My marriage, well, I'd had no hand in that. While it had turned out to be the best thing that had ever happened to me, I would have preferred to make my own arrangements. I hadn't even been able to choose my own dress.

Demon knows this. Knows I hate having no control, especially in what Angel did to me. So why has he announced a surprise for me? And just where is he taking me today?

"I don't like surprises, D," I grumble again, as I settle Theo in his carseat.

"Trust me, okay?"

For a response I put my hands on my hips. "I could refuse to go anywhere unless you tell me what we're doing."

Demon's eyes flash. He stalks around to the passenger side of the truck, and puts his hands on my shoulders, then he leans down and kisses the top of my head.

"Trust me," he says again.

I might have been more able to stand my ground if his closeness hadn't had the normal effect it does on me. I've often wondered whether his scent, his touch, will ever stop making my toes curl.

"I was meant to be helping Lizard..."

"Lizard gave you the time off, didn't he?"

Another decision I hadn't made. "Yes, but..." I respond grumpily.

"We're wasting time. Come on. Theo's all set. Just need you to get inside."

When I capitulate, his helping hand on my ass as I climb into his overgrown truck gives me tingles inside. *This man is my everything.* With a smirk—he's won after all—he goes around to the driver's side. As he climbs in, I sigh. I should have known what I was getting into. I do trust him, with my life, that of my child. I've always known he was controlling. He'd never do anything to hurt me, it's just that at times, I can see us going head-to-head.

It's not long before I recognise the neighbourhood. As familiar roads pass, I have a sneaking suspicion I know exactly where we're going. I start to get a bad feeling inside.

"D..."

"Just wait, Vi."

"Please D, stop the truck. I don't want..."

But it's too late. He's turning into the driveway of my childhood home. The place I never thought or wanted to return to again. Who wants to see strangers roaming through rooms you remember having lived in all your life? New furniture in place of familiar items you grew up with? Changes made just to put a new stamp on a place.

"No, D. Take me home."

But he doesn't stop. Just drives straight up to the front door. He comes around to my side. *I'll refuse to get out.* As I think that thought, though, the front door opens. To my surprise, it's Vicky, standing there with the widest grin on her face.

Huh?

"Come on," Demon encourages.

What's Vicky doing here? I know the house has been sold; I received all the paperwork a few days ago, as well as the money deposited into my bank account. It was a weight off my mind, as I knew my mom's situation was sorted, at least for now. Vicky couldn't have bought it, she couldn't have afforded that much.

While I've been hesitating, Demon's reached into the back and has extracted Theo from his seat. Vicky, unable to contain herself, has run over.

"He's grown! Vi, he's grown so much. And is that a tooth? So many changes."

What mom can resist someone cooing over their kid. "He's six months now, Vicky. And yes, he has his first bottom front tooth and the other's trying to come through." The pride in my voice equates his accomplishment as if he'd earned a degree.

She responds in the same vein. "What a clever boy," she coos, taking Theo from Demon's arms. "What a good boy. You being good for your mama?"

It's great seeing Vicky. I'd forgotten how much I'd depended on her after Theo was born. Of course he has a wider support network now, but I do feel guilty I hadn't gotten in touch before. Truth is, even when I had my freedom back, memories of the past were painful.

"Why don't we get inside?" Vicky asks, as a drop of rain falls.

Because this is now someone else's house. Have they engaged her as a housekeeper? But as she kidnaps my child and takes him in through the door, what can I do but follow her? I stand, amazed in the entrance hall. I'd expected it to be empty, or furnished differently, but all the furniture I remember from my childhood is here.

"I made arrangements for it to be cleared."

Demon clears his throat. "I might have cancelled that," he says.

I can't understand. I look at Vicky, then around me. Then, sigh. I'd run with very little as I never expected to need much again. "Demon, if we're here to collect stuff..."

"Vi, we're not here to collect anything." He holds out a sheaf of paperwork he'd had in his back pocket. His eyes catch mine. All of a sudden, he seems uncertain, nervously fidgeting as he moves what he's holding from hand to hand. It's a strange look on my normally confident husband. "Vi..." Then he's voice trails off, and he shoves the papers into my hand.

I look down. It's a deed of ownership. For this house. "You bought it?"

"We bought it." He points to my name alongside his.

"Why on earth...?" I can't get my head around it.

Demon looks at Vicky who nods, something unspoken going between them. "Come, Vi." He takes my hand and I allow him to lead me through to the family room with the big windows looking out onto the garden. "See?" He points. "That tree? Remember the tree house Nathan and I used to play in? Yeah, not much left of it now, but we could rebuild it. Just think of Theo playing in it. Inviting his friends around. Maybe having a best friend like me."

For a second, I'm thrown back to those days. I must have been no more than three or four, standing at the bottom of the ladder pouting while Nathan and D had easily skimmed up. One of them would usually take pity on me and come back down to help me climb. My eyes glaze as I no longer see the rotting planks, but a proper platform, walls and even windows and a door, freshly varnished.

A laugh bubbles out. "I used to make you have a tea party with my dolls."

"Do you have to remind me of that?" Demon huffs. But a glance at his face shows he's smiling. "This yard, Vi, it's safe for kids. Theo could have a dog. The house is big enough for our family to grow."

I pull on his cut, turning him to face me. "Why, Demon? Why?"

"Because you loved this house, Vi. It killed you to walk away. I loved it, too, it brings back happy memories to me as well. When I was a kid it was my second home." He closes his eyes, then opens them again. "It's like Nathan's here, watching over us."

"You bought this as our home?" I can't get my head around it.

Again, he looks like he's having second thoughts. "We can sell it if that's what you want. We needed a home, Vi. And what better than the place that holds such good memories for us."

I shake my head. "It's all changed. My father wasn't who I thought he was. My mom too..."

"Nah, Vi. They were your mom and dad who loved you. You think Theo's ever going to look at me differently when he knows I'm the president of an outlaw MC?"

"No, because you'll be upfront about what you do."

His fingers touch under my chin. "Not everything, Vi. I'll never be able to share everything with you, and there will be things I may never want Theo to know."

He waits a moment for that to sink in. I'm not dense, and I know it's because who he is and what he does is the reason I'm free, and safe. I nod to show that I understand. There will be stuff that I never want to know, and won't, because I'm his old lady.

Then he changes tack. "How does this house make you feel, Vi? What does it do to you, in here?" He places his hand over my heart.

Now it's my turn to close my eyes. To stop thinking and to just feel. It's quiet, peaceful. Familiar sounds of the house settling. It feels like... home.

It comes over me in a rush. The immensity of what my man has done for me. Bought my childhood home to give me peace, make a safe place for my son to grow. Reunited me with my old friend.

"I don't deserve you, D."

Opening my eyes it's to see him smirk. "Probably the truest thing you've ever said, Vi. You could do so much better than me. But you're mine. You have my ring on your finger, my property patch on your back, and I'm never letting you go." He waves his hand around then says, as if I still need persuading, "We can make it ours. Change shit around..."

"Put a stripper pole in the bedroom," I drop in conversationally.

"Whatever you want... *What?*"

Oh, I wish I had a camera to take a picture of that particular expression on his face. Then I realise I shouldn't have taunted the bear when he suddenly yells out, "You okay with the kid, Vicky?"

He barely waits for her confirmation before picking me up, slinging me over his shoulder, and taking me up to the bedroom that had been mine since I was little more than Theo's age.

It appears he has one more surprise in store. I'd expected he'd throw me on the bed, tell me to strip, kiss me. He does the first, but then steps back, his eyes fixed on mine.

"Got something else for you babe."

My eyes flick to his crotch. "I can see that."

"In a moment. First, look at this."

He hands over a sheet of paper, I look at it. It's the results of a DNA test. I try to make sense of what I'm reading.

Paternity excluded. There were no genetic markers in the child's DNA profile which could be found in the sample of the possible biological father.

"The results are conclusive, Vi. I checked. There are no ifs or buts. Angel is not Theo's biological father. He has no links to the Silvestris."

"You did this?" I look up at him, a little angry, as he'd gone against my wishes. I'd been too scared of having Theo's parentage proven. Angel might be dead, but that didn't mean my son would be free of the family. There would always have been a threat.

"I had my suspicions, Vi. Took a hair sample from Angel, swabbed Theo's mouth. All completely painless. Got the results yesterday, seemed fitting to give them to you now." He pulls me to him, wrapping his arms around me, giving me security.

I need the comfort. On one hand I'm elated at having proof Theo was no relation to Angelino. On the other? It's confirmation that an unknown man had raped me. I'll never know who he was.

"You have me, Vi. And our son." Demon instinctively understands what's troubling me. "If you'd never met Angel? Likelihood is we wouldn't be here now. Same way, if Blackie hadn't raped Mo, I wouldn't be alive. Things happen for a reason. Sometimes the bad shit has to take place for the good to evolve."

He's right. Wasting time wishing things would be different is worthless. Everything I've been through, however painful, led me to him.

"I love you, D." I rest my head against his chest.

He'd been tense, and now I feel the stress seep out of him. His breath leaves him on a sigh. He waits, but only for one more moment before bending his lips to my ear and instructing, "Prove it." The rub of his hard cock against my pelvis leaves me in no doubt as to his meaning. I'm only too happy to oblige. I'm sure Vicky won't mind looking after Theo for a while.

We move in the next day. As the weekend starts, I begin to come to grips with the thought the house where I grew up is really going to be the home where Theo, and any other children Demon and I might have, is going to grow up. I realise Demon couldn't have done any better. While I've grown to like and respect his biker brothers, having a place of our own is far better than being full time at the compound. Vicky proves an amazing help, her suggestions on getting the place updated and fixed where needed are invaluable. I might have gotten a little pre-occupied with the changes I'm planning for Theo's room.

Sunday dawns and yet another surprise dropped on me. A barbeque with everyone from the club. I couldn't be angry, as I didn't have to do anything apart from get myself and Theo ready. Mo and Jeannie brought the sides, and the men brought a few animals' worth of meat. As everyone started to arrive, I have to admit, I'd decided some surprises weren't bad after all.

"You okay with this?" Mo asks as she flops down in a chair. "Living here?"

I nod. It hadn't taken long to get my head around it. Or for Demon to get a new bed bought and installed in the large bedroom we've decided to claim. One day, to be precise.

The backyard is large. Demon's standing with Theo in his arms, watching Mace and Pyro kick a ball. Hell had turned up in his truck, full of boxes inside. He, Bomber and Rusty are busy putting up a swing set and slide. I bit my tongue before I could say it would be a few years before Theo could use it. And I was glad I had. They'd even bought a baby seat to hang from the chains. *Theo is going to love it.*

Oh, and Cad's trying the slide out. I crease with laughter as he gets stuck halfway down and nearly breaks the thing trying to get out.

"Happy?" Demon steps up beside me. "Oh, yeah, Grandma." He passes Theo to Mo who's walked up and tapped him on the arm. Then he asks me again, "Are you happy, Vi? Did I do alright?"

I put up my hand, curl it around his head, and tell him, "You know you did. Everything you've done? Perfect."

"Perfect, eh? Things will be perfect when your man there appoints a fuckin' VP," Thunder grumbles as he walks past.

Demon just shoots him his finger.

"Hey, Prez. Give us a hand?"

Mace has started to pull down the rotten wood from the old tree house in order to replace it with new. As Demon turns to me with an eyebrow raised, I give him a little push. "Yeah, go play."

His amused glance makes me giggle. All of them are like little kids. I reckon that tree house will end up man-sized.

As I watch everyone milling around, relaxing and enjoying themselves, I use the moment of peace to reflect.

Not even two years back, when I was settled in a life far away, was this how I imagined my life would turn out. I could never have foreseen the turn of events that would lead me to this, here and now. Never thought I'd reconnect with the first love of my life. I might have been to hell, but I returned. Or, I smile softly and mentally correct, *a demon dragged me back out.*

Looking around at the members of the MC having fun, I could never have envisaged bringing my son up around men of this type. Now having an understanding of what's under their rough exterior, a strong commitment to family above everything, I know I need have no concerns.

I never expected to return to this house, but it's the best decision Demon has made.

Demon had it wrong all this time. Nathan wouldn't be upset that he and I had gotten together. He'd be happy for both of us.

As a gentle breeze blows, wafting aromas from the meat cooking on the grill, I imagine I hear echoes of children playing. Not Theo, but Nathan and Dave, and an annoying little girl trailing behind them, never leaving them alone.

Well, I grin, *D's got me for the rest of his life now.*

When I left everything behind to go nomad, I didn't expect to run into trouble before I stepped foot in the clubhouse I was aiming for.

I didn't expect to save a woman, not just once but multiple times.

I didn't expect to pit myself against the US Marshals or another MC.

I'd just extracted myself from one relationship, I didn't want another.

Sometimes what we get is what we never go looking for.

How this will work out, I've no idea. Would I survive on the outside, no longer being a member of an MC? Could I give up everything, even my identity to be with her? Or can I ask my brothers to step in and save us both?

Other Works by Manda Mellett

All books can be read as a standalone.

Blood Brothers – A series about sexy dominant sheikhs and their bodyguards

Stolen Lives (#1) Nijad and Cara

Close Protection (#2) Jon and Mia

Second Chances (#3) Kadar and Zoe

Identity Crisis (#4) Sean and Vanessa

Dark Horses (#5) Jasim and Janna

Hard Choices (#6) Aiza

Satan's Devils MC - Arizona Chapter

Turning Wheels (Blood Brothers #3.5, Satan's Devils #1) Wraith and Sophie

Drummer's Beat (#2) Drummer and Sam

Slick Running (#3) Slick and Ella

Targeting Dart (#4) Dart and Alex

Heart Broken (#5) Heart and Marc

Peg's Stand (#6) Peg and Darcy

Rock Bottom (#7) Rock and Becca

Joker's Fool (#8) Joker and Lady

Mouse Trapped (#9) Mouse and Mariana

Blade's Edge (#10) Blade and Tash

Satan's Devils MC (Colorado Chapter)

Paladin's Hell (#1) Paladin and Jayden

GLOSSARY

Motorcycle Club – An official motorcycle club in the U.S. is one which is sanctioned by the American Motorcyclist Association (AMA). The AMA has a set of rules its members must abide by. It is said that ninety-nine percent of motorcyclists in America belong to the AMA

Outlaw Motorcycle Club (MC) – The remaining one percent of motorcycling clubs are historically considered outlaws as they do not wish to be constrained by the rules of the AMA and have their own bylaws. There is no one formula followed by such clubs, but some not only reject the rulings of the AMA, but also that of society, forming tightly knit groups who fiercely protect their chosen ways of life. Outlaw MCs have a reputation for having a criminal element and supporting themselves by less than legal activities, dealing in drugs, gun running or prostitution. The one-percenter clubs are usually run under a strict hierarchy.

Brother – Typically members of the MC refer to themselves as brothers and regard the closely knit MC as their family.

Cage – The name bikers give to cars as they prefer riding their bikes.

Chapter – Some MCs have only one club based in one location. Other MCs have a number of clubs who follow the same bylaws and wear the same patch. Each club is known as a chapter and will normally carry the name of the area where they are based on their patch.

Church – Traditionally the name of the meeting where club business is discussed, either with all members present or with just those holding officer status.

Colours – When a member is wearing (or flying) his colours he will be wearing his cut proudly displaying his patch showing which club he is affiliated with.

Cut – The name given to the jacket or vest which has patches denoting the club that member belongs to.

Enforcer – The member who enforces the rules of the club.

Hang-around – This can apply to men wishing to join the club and who hang-around hoping to be become prospects. It is also used to women who are attracted by bikers and who are happy to make themselves available for sex at biker parties.

Mother Chapter – The founding chapter when a club has more than one chapter.

Nomad – In an outlaw MC a **nomad** is typically a member who's been given permission/instruction by the national president to enforce the laws of the club at other chapters.

Patch – The patch or patches on a cut will show the club that member belongs to and other information such as the particular chapter and any role that may be held in the club. There can be a number of other patches with various meanings, including a one-percenter patch. Prospects will not be allowed to wear the club patch until they have been patched-in, instead they will have patches which denote their probationary status.

Patched-in/Patching-in – The term used when a prospect completes his probationary status and becomes a full club member.

President (Prez) – The officer in charge of that particular club or chapter.

Prospect – Anyone wishing to join a club must serve time as a probationer. During this period they have to prove their loyalty to the club. A probationary period can last a year or more. At the end of this period, if they've proved themselves a prospect will be patched-in.

Old Lady – The term given to a woman who enters into a permanent relationship with a biker.

RICO – The Racketeer Influenced and Corrupt Organisations Act primarily deals with organised crime. Under this Act the officers of a club could be held responsible for activities they order members to do and a conviction carries a potential jail service of twenty years as well as a large fine and the seizure of assets.

Road Captain – The road captain is responsible for the safety of the club on a run. He will organise routes and normally ride at the end of the column.

Ronin – A biker who travels alone, sometimes wearing a patch denoting he's Ronin. Not affiliated to any club, but often bearing a token which will help ensure safe passage through territories of different clubs.

Secretary – MCs are run like businesses and this officer will perform the secretarial duties such as recording decisions at meetings.

Sergeant-at-Arms – The sergeant-at-arms is responsible for the safety of the club as a whole and for keeping order.

Sweet Butt – A woman who makes her sexual services available to any member at any time. She may well live on the club premises and be fully supported by the club.

Treasurer – The officer responsible for keeping an eye on the club's money.

Vice President (VP) – The vice president will support the president, stepping into his role in his absence. He may be responsible for making sure the club runs smoothly, overseeing prospects etc.

ACKNOWLEDGMENTS

When I started writing Paladin's Hell I knew Jayden and Pal would get together, but I didn't know what they'd find along the way. I knew nothing about Hellfire or Demon; they hadn't started talking at all. But once they did, wow.

What a history Hellfire has, a past which involves Demon down to the very fibre of his being. Hellfire has played the part of his father so admirably, Demon had no clue he wasn't his true son. It's Hellfire's amazing example that helps Demon cope with the circumstances surrounding his conception.

It had to have affected Demon. Had to make him examine himself and question what he carries within his blood. His own situation means he acts differently to other men might have done, stepping up to adopt Theo when other men might have stepped down.

The Colorado chapter is turning out to have a different feel to the Tucson one, and I hope that, like me, you're coming to love the members there.

The next book will also be from the Colorado chapter, but I'm being sneaky with this one. Until you read the book, you won't know who it's about. It will be called Devil's Due, and I'm hoping for a June release date.

In September I'm planning the (currently) final book in the Tucson chapter.

As always, I have to thank the team who are behind me, keeping me on track to produce the book you like to read.

Firstly my editor and great friend, Maggie Kern. This is the fifth book we've worked on together. I really appreciate her insights and help in getting a first draft through to the polished product. Now she's going one step further and formatting for me too. Just a comment that it was amazing to meet her in the flesh this year in Ohio.

My beta readers—what can I say about them that I haven't said before? I couldn't write without them. In particular, Tami whose knowledge of the area surrounding Pueblo is critical for the Colorado series books. Thank you for all your help, Tami. As for the others? I'm sure you already know how much I love and appreciate your input. You know who you are, but thank you again Danena, Colleen, Sheri, Terra, Zoe, Nicole, Alex and my husband Steve.

Yet another amazing cover courtesy of Lia Rees. I love the way she takes an image and works her magic on it.

It's the first time I've worked with Barbara J. Bailey for proofreading, but it won't be the last. Thank you for the help.

Last but not least, I'd like to thank Tracy Wood who's the best PA in the world. There doesn't seem to be anything she can't help with. My writing life is so much smoother with all her help.

As always, I've left the most important people to the end. So now please, every person who's taken a chance on this book, accept my heartfelt thanks. If you weren't buying my books, I wouldn't be able to write them.

You can help even more. If you liked this book, don't keep it to yourself. Tell a friend, hey, tell me. Every time a reader contacts me to express how much they enjoy any of my books, especially when they ask for more, it spurs me to continue writing. I appreciate every message you send or comment that you make.

Know what's even better? I don't care where. Just one or two words is helpful. Reviews help authors make sales, sales allow authors to pay editors, models and photographers, cover designers etc, and put food on the table.

To anyone asking the question, while the Tucson chapter may soon come to a close, there are still the other chapters.

One thing I can promise you, there'll be another Devil along very soon.

STAY IN TOUCH

Email: manda@mandamellet.com

Website: www.mandamellet.com

Sign up for my newsletter to hear about new releases in the Satan's Devils and Blood Brothers series.

ABOUT THE AUTHOR

Manda's life's always seemed a bit weird, starting with a childhood that even today she's still trying to make sense of, then losing her parents in the late teens. Going from the tragic to the bizarre, who else could be unlucky enough to have had two car accidents, neither her fault, one involving a nun, and another involving a police woman?

There isn't enough space to list everything that's happened to Manda, or what she's learned from it. But by using the rich fabric of her personal life, psychology degree, varied work experiences, and amazing characters she's met, Manda is able to populate her books with believable in-depth characters and enjoys pitting them against situations which challenge them. Her books are full of suspense, twists and turns and the unexpected.

Manda lives in the beautiful countryside of Essex in the UK, the area's claim to fame being the Wilkin's Jam Factory at nearby Tiptree. She can usually find jars of jam which remind her of home wherever she goes. As well as writing books and reading, Manda loves walking her dogs and keeping fit. She lives with her husband of over 30 years, who, along with her son, is her greatest fan and supporter.

Manda is thankful that one of the more unusual, and at the time unpleasant, turns her life took, now enables her to spend her time writing. Confirming, in her view, every cloud has a silver lining.

Photo by Carmel Jane Photography